# A DEATH IN TOKYO

# A DEATH IN TOKYO

## Guy Stanley

BANTAM BOOKS
TORONTO · NEW YORK · LONDON · SYDNEY · AUCKLAND

# A DEATH IN TOKYO

A BANTAM BOOK   0 553 17541 6

Originally published in Great Britain by Michael Joseph Ltd

PRINTING HISTORY
Michael Joseph edition published 1988
Bantam edition published 1989

This book is set in 10/11pt Baskerville
by Busby Typesetting, Exeter.

Bantam Books are published by Transworld Publishers Ltd.,
61-63 Uxbridge Road, Ealing, London W5 5SA, in Australia by
Transworld Publishers (Australia) Pty. Ltd., 15-23 Helles
Avenue, Moorebank, NSW 2170, and in New Zealand by Transworld
Publishers (N.Z.) Ltd., Cnr. Moselle and Waipareira Avenues,
Henderson, Auckland.

Printed and bound in Great Britain by
Cox & Wyman Ltd, Reading

*To my wife, Kayoko*

# PROLOGUE

At its lower reaches, the Tama is a broad river, almost a delta, with shallow entrails of water moving languidly towards oblivion in Tokyo Bay. By the late summer of 1982, before the heavy typhoon rains of September, the river had been drained by the demands of the farms along its course, consumed by the heat, and barely covered the gap between its banks which separate the capital's southern edge from the factories of Kawasaki City. In places it had split into streams, sometimes three or four disparate threads moving around grass and weed-covered mounds, shallow enough to allow seagulls to wade and pick suspiciously at the poisoned fish floating on their sides in the rivulets.

But the small carp that bobbed in the current were not alone in death on this August morning. A fisherman looking for his place near the Futako-Tamagawa Bridge came on a human body sprawled face down in the water. Specks of detergent scum were already attached to what must once have been an immaculate grey business suit.

# CHAPTER ONE

'Who is it?' Araki asked, flipping through a slim batch of photographs without looking at any one in particular.

'Nobody. Suppose we're lucky really. When we heard they'd found a body down by the Tamagawa we thought it was another kid. It would have been our sixth this year. The chief couldn't sit still till they'd brought it back. No, if it's who we think it is, it's a small-time crook called Tanimoto and he's got, or he had, a long record.'

The policeman wiped his brow with a wad of used tissues, content in the knowledge that the second murder of the year in Ota Ward would not overtax the energy of his men during the remaining debilitating weeks of the Tokyo summer. He was doubly pleased that the rash of killings that year, one by a policeman, in which the victims had been runaway teenage girls, had not spread to his precinct.

Araki, as on many Friday afternoons, was in the Meguro police station which incorporated sparse cells and a makeshift temporary mortuary. His magazine had gone to press the previous evening and was on the newsstands today with a gripping headline on the recent robbery and rape of a famous actress. The cover displayed a file photograph of the abused lady wearing a provocative string bikini. It would be a good issue, selling a hundred thousand copies, he estimated.

The reporter had known Inspector Nishii ten years earlier when he was a cub reporter on Japan's largest circulation daily newspaper and he had been assigned to attend weekly briefings by the policeman at the Metropolitan Police Headquarters. It was at informal chats after the meetings that the two men found they had a number of things in common, not the least important being the sharing of a common place of birth, a fishing village in Shimane Prefecture. For a while each week, they would revert to the dialect of their homeland, and once a month would meet in a red-lamp drinking-house in Shimbashi specialising in broiled seafood and a favoured type of succulent rice cakes from south-west Japan. As the sake flowed and they became unashamedly drunk, Araki would be party to information not normally available to other reporters. The material disclosed was not exactly confidential, nor was it used by Araki in a manner likely to harm the policeman's career, but it was not simply coincidence when the newspaperman arrived at the scene of a crime, or knew the name of the principal suspect long enough ahead of the tenacious competition to be able to file an earlier byline. This connection with Nishii became much more important to Araki after he had left his job on the newspaper four years before and the natural progression of his trade had taken him down to the cut-and-thrust of the popular weekly magazines.

The *Tokyo Weekly*, Araki's employer, catered to the limitless needs of Japan's literate population for trivia on a grand and regular basis, and competed with a hundred and fifty other titles which ranged, on a broad scale of quality and taste, from the esoterically intellectual, through sport to the perverted. The *Tokyo Weekly* trod the middle ground, its dual target readership being the bored apartment-bound housewife and the three million salaried workers aged between twenty-five and fifty, living and working in the Tokyo-Kawasaki-Yokohama conurbation. On a quality scale it would rank in the lower half. This week, as every week for the last fifteen years, it carried a mixture of crime stories, often with a sexual slant, in-depth analyses of the latest scandals perpetrated by actors, politicians and singers, as well as a cursory look at the week's economic and political news which would not tax the readers' faculties unnecessarily. Araki's function was to anticipate an item of interest or follow up a lead which had the basic ingredients of sex,

10

crime and overtones of scandal, and produce a three-page article that did not completely twist the truth but was not unduly constrained by such obstacles to circulation. He saw it as mental chewing-gum and enjoyed writing it. Or seemed to.

'How did he die?' asked Araki, not confident that his friend was the source of a story today.

Nishii sipped at a cup of bitter green tea and grimaced.

'I wish they'd change the tea more often. This tastes like something out of the Imperial moat. They haven't finished with him yet, but the back of his head is well beaten in. It could be a baseball bat.'

'A bat!'

Araki was instantly more interested. Murders were news; and violent batterings usually meant gangs. Double news.

'Can I see him?' asked Araki, with growing enthusiasm.

'Of course, I was going to show you anyway. There are two of your fellows down there already. They saw the crowds by the river and followed the ambulance back.'

Nishii led the way to the second basement of the old building whose maze of rooms and cells had once housed a detachment of secret police before and during the Second World War. Part of the underground section was a mortuary, and it looked it.

The visitors already in attendance were talking to a medical officer who was wearing a green rubbery apron over his white uniform and a surgical mask stained with sweat. In the centre of the room was a trestle table on which the victim's body lay, covered by a sheet. The two other reporters ignored the new arrivals even though the closing of the steel door sent round an echo like the thump of a temple bell. It was left to Araki to speak.

'A bit out of your line, isn't it, Suzuki?'

The thinner of the two looked up. He forced his pinched eyes open wide and nodded his head in recognition.

'Araki-san, how are you? We thought we might see you around. Koike here was just saying that this is where the fearsome sleuth Araki gets his inspiration.'

The man called Koike flushed with embarrassment and smiled at the floor. Suzuki continued.

'You're correct, of course, we're only observers, no real professional interest. I'm not sure there's much here for you either. It's not a woman after all. No, I don't think we'll publish anything about this incident.'

Too damned right you won't, thought Araki, as the police surgeon began loosening the sheet round the corpse. Suzuki worked for the *Shukan Kankyo*, worth nine on Araki's quality scale of ten. He had made his reputation only three years after he graduated from Waseda University, working under Kenji Okawa, the most successful of the Lockheed scandal muck-rakers.

Their team had demonstrated conclusively that the Prime Minister of the time was directly linked with the chain of pay-offs and bribes made by the American aircraft manufacturer through a Japanese multi-national trading company and an assortment of power-brokers, minor politicians and downright crooks. The Prime Minister and his Minister of Transportation resigned and were later indicted. The nationwide furore generated took away all attention from a sensational story that Araki had been researching for weeks and which came to a head with unfortunate timing, just as Suzuki's disclosures were bringing the government to its knees. Araki's exposure of bribery and the rigging of professional baseball games was dead.

The white sheet was drawn back as far as the hairline of its crotch to expose the naked torso of Akira Tanimoto. The mud had been carefully removed and the damaged tissue from the head wound was protected by gauze padding. They all stared silently at the body as if expecting it to acknowledge them first with a greeting. Suzuki grimaced and whispered something to his colleague. The pathologist stirred some thick purple fluid in a bowl, bored by the interruption to his work. Araki leaned forward tentatively, a mild feeling of nausea in his stomach. But it wasn't this that made the reporter terminate his note-taking abruptly and direct his attention to the corpse's face. His coverage of road accidents had removed any squeamishness. Like all discerning reporters, Araki had made a conscious effort during his ten-year career to develop his ability to memorise facts and detail, to refine the skill to commit an identity, a face or a trait to a memory bank he hoped would respond to a recall trigger at will. In Japan, with few divergences in physical size and colour of hair and skin of the people, it was a skill acquired with difficulty. If Tanimoto had died by drowning, the face might have been bloated and discoloured, or if the destructive force of the blow had been directed to the front of the head instead of the back, Araki might not have noticed the steeply angled eyebrows that even in death seemed to leave on the face a permanent look of surprise. The carefully trimmed moustache, so straight and thin it might have been painted on with a sumie brush, disturbed another corner of the reporter's memory, like a pebble falling from a great height on to a still lake. He had seen the victim before.

'Know him?' The policeman's enquiry was only for Araki.

'I don't think I've had the pleasure,' he lied. 'Did he have anything on him when you found him? Anything useful?'

'Only a season ticket for the subway and a book of matches. We checked the name on the ticket, and if this character is the same Akira Tanimoto as we have in our files we can put him in the Casebook Closed section. He has a record for drug peddling, bodily harm, aggravated debt collecting and we suspected him of a lot more. We'd like to know who got him, but we're not overcome with grief that they did.'

Araki found his friend's insensitivity irritating, but did not want to disclose any knowledge of the dead man until he was positive. He lapsed into thought.

Suzuki had been looking for a chance to depart without discourtesy and when Araki failed to pursue his interrogation he used the pause to express gratitude to Inspector Nishii and the attending doctor and excused himself on the grounds that he was already late for the appointment to which he had been going when he was diverted by the events by the river. He bowed firmly and graciously to Nishii but directed

13

a mere inflection of the head in the direction of Araki, as he and Koike moved towards the door. Without looking up, Araki merely grunted an acknowledgement: he was staring at the face on the mortician's table, trying without success to place the sallow, pale features of the dead man on to an animate human being who had crossed his path with enough impact for him to recollect the man's existence. Araki had met or seen the victim Tanimoto, perhaps only fleetingly, and for his own satisfaction he had to know where.

The policeman's blue shirt was wet from perspiration and the climb from the basement sent new cold trickles down from his armpits. He beckoned Araki to sit down with him at his desk. A small space separated the Inspector's desk from a long narrow table around which a dozen uniformed male and female clerks were working. There was something near admiration in Nishii's voice.

'One hard clout from behind with something hard, probably wooden, was enough. He didn't feel anything.'

He took a brown manila envelope from his desk and with care extracted a still moist book of matches and a ticket lodged in its holder. He held up the palms of his hands, an item of evidence balanced on each one, and raised and lowered them like imaginary scales.

'No coins, wallet, cigarettes, keys. Not even a handkerchief. They did a thorough job of stripping him.'

Araki took the ticket and matches and held them in gentle pincer grips.

'Why were these left?'

'He had two pockets on the inside of his jacket. We found these things in the small, lower one. I think you're supposed to keep your cigarettes or your lighter there. When they'd emptied the big pocket they may not have bothered to look in the same lining.'

Inspector Nishii was about to expound further when a young officer beckoned him from the adjoining table.

'Telephone from Headquarters, sir.'

'OK. I'll take it there.' He stood up, speaking to Araki

14

as he did so. 'Have a close look, but handle them with care. There are no prints, but they're the only evidence we have.'

The season-ticket holder was standard commuter equipment: a plastic sheath three inches square with a half-inch border made of leather or some synthetic material. To be opened, it had to be squeezed with some pressure at the rim, and this tightness had apparently protected the contents from the water. Looking through the plastic covering where remaining traces of condensation slightly blurred the letters, Araki saw that the ticket allowed travel on the Marunouchi underground line from Akasaka-mitsuke to Ikebukuro. As the owner's name was partly hidden by the border, Araki split the lip of the holder between the thumb and forefinger of his left hand and eased the ticket out with his right. The issuer of the ticket had written in faint but discernible script the kanji for Akira Tanimoto. The combination of the three Chinese characters used for the victim's name failed to stimulate the reporter's memory any further.

The impulse was silly, but not out of character. While his mind scanned the frontiers of his recent past for an image of the man with menacing eyebrows and fashionable moustache, Araki toyed with the empty ticket holder. When he was married he had kept shreds of paper tucked behind the ticket in his own pass holder and on these he wrote the telephone numbers of women he had met and wished to see again. Once he could reproduce the digits without assistance, he would destroy the evidence before it destroyed him. His index finger played automatically inside the dead man's ticket holder. Deep in thought, he did not immediately feel the resistance to his touch until he saw that he had dislodged a sliver of paper folded narrow enough to be hidden from view by the protective border.

Araki took a furtive glance to his side, certain that the extra seconds he had taken to verify the contents of the container and bring them to a new sanctuary in the fist of his right hand had been noticed. It was not so. Most of the clerks were speaking into their telephones and the others were deep in concentrated effort with their paperwork.

Inspector Nishii sat with his back to Araki, a telephone to his ear, while his right hand wafted the air as he tried to make a point to his distant listener. Araki made a show of holding the ticket and its holder up to the light and revolving them in his fingers before finally stacking them on the table. Still nobody seemed unduly interested. He then turned his attention to the matches, Tanimoto's only other apparent legacy.

He held the reddish, water-softened clip gently in front of his face while using his crowded right hand to fumble for a packet of cigarettes in the pocket of his loose summer shirt. He extracted the crumpled, almost empty packet of Hi-lites and with a dextrous flick of the fingers replaced them with the paper he had taken from the ticket holder. He looked again towards his friend Nishii, knowing that what he was doing was not a very friendly gesture, almost a betrayal of confidence in fact, but he justified the crime by convincing himself that if the paper contained anything which might materially help to solve the case he would inform Nishii, even at the cost of a rebuke.

The half-empty booklet of matches had been given away in a bar or restaurant. It was faded crimson in colour and had the name 'Camelia' written in phonetic katakana script diagonally across it. Araki wrote on his cigarette packet the still legible telephone number, recognising from the first three digits that 'Camelia's' location was in central Tokyo.

'Light, sir?'

Araki jumped instinctively.

One of the policemen proferred a cheap, throw-away lighter which responded at the second flick.

'Pardon? Yes, of course, thanks.'

Araki had left his cigarette unlit in his mouth as he studied the matches and was taken off guard by the courtesy. He drew deeply as Nishii returned, mumbling apologies.

'Sorry about that. There's always a lot to clear up at the end of the month.'

'Of course, I've kept you too long already. I'll be off.'

'No, I didn't mean that. Take your time. Have you found anything interesting?'

'Not really,' Araki said casually. 'There's nothing much to say, beyond the fact that there's been a killing; at least until you find out who did what and why. Anyway, I'd like to give you a call in a couple of days and get a progress report. With any luck, you may have found out that Tanimoto had been making dirty films and selling them to politicians' clubs, and that one of them had killed him because he was being blackmailed.'

Nishii chuckled. 'Don't talk to me about politicians. What we have to cover up for them already!' He shook his head in mock disapproval. 'Maybe better luck next Friday. And don't forget, we have to go back to that crab place in Nihonbashi. I hear they've got a couple of plump serving-girls just in from Tottori.'

Although the police station was not fitted with modern air-conditioning, the old bricks kept out the worst of the Tokyo summer humidity. The point was made clear when Araki walked from the building into a wall of debilitating heat. At four o'clock in the afternoon, the sun was a flaky blur in the sky, unable to penetrate the mix of haze and photo-chemical smog that would hang motionless over the capital until a seasonal thunderstorm or early typhoon brought temporary relief. It was ninety-two degrees and the pollutant count was two points from the Public Warning level.

Araki had sat in his 1975 Bluebird in the police station carpark and took a perfunctory look at the piece of evidence he had stolen. A single yellow sheet of memo pad had been folded with singular patience and was enscribed with lines of numbers, each one prefixed with a phonetic symbol. It meant nothing at first glance.

The Friday afternoon traffic on the Number Seven Loop was congested and moved forward in short irritable bursts. Windows were closed tight and engines were revving hard to generate cooling air as the vehicles came to frequent halts. The Bluebird had no mechanical air-conditioning. Araki used the time to delve again into the recesses of his memory in his search for the face of Akira Tanimoto among the thousands of black-haired and equally anonymous people with whom he had had some peripheral contact. He had no luck and even began to doubt having seen the man at all.

The ubiquitous boutiques, Western restaurants and other playpens of Tokyo's teenagers on the Meiji-Omote Sando crossroads were filled with the young and the trendy rich, three females for every man, milling aimlessly in the failing light. The crowds did not leave the main shopping precinct, as if prevented by some electronic barrier from the quiet, narrow backstreets where the residents of Harajuku lived. Araki's five-storey apartment building occupied a corner of two of these streets, leaving just enough space between the façade and the road to allow five cars to park. It was a plain grey shoebox of a building, a phenomenon of post-war Japanese housing, providing in this central location a town flat for the senior executive, a staging-post for the young married couples or a roost for the Ginza and Akasaka bargirls and the dispossessed divorcees. Like Araki.

He collected his mail from the box in the spartan lobby and, forsaking the elevators, ambled up the emergency stairs next to the porter's office to his apartment on the third floor. He was sweating even more than he might have expected and occasionally he shivered involuntarily.

The sliding door that gave on to his narrow terrace had been closed all day, and the unmolested air in the rooms was heavy with the resilient odour of cigarette smoke and night-time sweat. Unaired bedding littered the reed-mat room that doubled as bedroom and study; and dishes remained unwashed on the Western-style table in the other, slightly larger room. A kitchenette and bathroom completed the unit. Araki opened the terrace door and then jammed the front door open with a shoe. The flow of breeze this operation generated was light but refreshing.

He washed out a tumbler, half filled it with Nikka whisky from the bottle he had left by his mattress the previous night

18

and topped it up with ice from the freezer. The first long intake of liquid irritated his throat, confirming his fear that the tightness he had felt there all day was a symptom of a summer cold. Lighting a cigarette, he sat down at the table and opened his mail. The draught passing through the apartment turned unexpectedly cool and caused Araki to shake. It was six-thirty. The first letter was from the court representing the interest of his former wife and pointed out that he was two months behind in paying her alimony instalments.

'Avaricious bitch,' he muttered.

The other two letters described alleged indiscretions by well-known people, and the writers offered to disclose them for a fee. Screwing them into a communal ball and tossing them aside, Araki returned to a more important piece of writing.

There were ten horizontal numerical annotations, each one preceded by a single phonetic letter from the alphabet. The longest line of numbers contained ten figures. If the numbers represented money, thought Araki, that's five billion yen! His imagination could not envisage the small-time hustler Tanimoto involved in deals that moved enough money to buy out the *Tokyo Weekly* several times over. Small circles had been added after four of the lines of numbers, as if indicating some action completed or still pending, but there was nothing to indicate what event had caused the note to be written or why its bearer took such pains to conceal it. It was all quite meaningless but marginally better, Araki conjectured, than a shopping list. There were no telephone numbers or addresses, and this was disappointing. He resolved to request permission at the following day's planning meeting to pursue the story a step further, hoping in the meantime that Kondo in the Research Department might decode the riddle of the note as well as assist him in raking the past for a trace of Akira Tanimoto.

# CHAPTER TWO

The inconspicuous article on page eight of the morning paper added little to what Araki already knew. It said:

> Tokyo Metropolitan Police are investigating an apparent gangland slaying in Ota Ward. The body of Akira Tanimoto, 39, was found by a fisherman on the north bank of the Tama River at Futako-Tamagawa at 8.00 a.m., 28 August. The victim apparently died from a blow to the back of the head. He is known to be a minor racketeer with a record of violence and other criminal behaviour. So far, the police have no clues to the motive or the culprit but they are anxious to interview the driver of a green, or possibly blue, saloon car seen by another fisherman around 7.00 a.m., driving up the embankment on to the road near the Futako-Tamagawa Bridge.

Woken early by a feverish chill and an uneasy feeling in his stomach, and still clad in his knee-length summer pyjamas, Araki had skipped down the back stairs, taken the *Daily Yomiuri* from the Tanakas' letterbox and returned to his apartment. As usual on a weekend, he would check the important items in the newspaper and replace it before the retired couple stirred. When he reached the top of the stairway on his return trip, a glass-shattering scream echoed between steel and concrete, startling a pair of pigeons enjoying the sunrise from a telegraph pole, whose cactus-like appendages hung within touching distance of the balcony.

'Not again!' Araki's tone was more of exasperation than surprise; and he made for the flat adjacent to his own.

Yoko was crouched in the corner, her nightdress torn to her waist and her hair so dishevelled it seemed she had no face. A middle-aged man wearing only crumpled trousers and one sock was trying without success to disengage the attractive woman from her handbag. Yoko started to shriek again but stopped abruptly as her saviour in blue pyjamas seized her attacker in a firm bear hug from the rear.

'OK, OK, calm down.' At first, Araki's plea went unheeded and the three remained united, grunting and swaying and looking, in their varying degrees of modes of dress, like participants in some primitive tribal dance. Araki intensified his physical and verbal persuasion.

'There's a policeman in his box right round the corner,' he uttered, his own discomfort briefly forgotten. 'If he gets involved there'll be a hell of a scandal back at the office and you're in enough trouble as it is when you get home.'

This pithy summary of the alternatives struck a vein of comprehension in the mind of the confused and hungover businessman, and he relinquished his hold on the bag. Released from the arms that had held him immobile, he slumped disconsolately on the floor, covering his face and his shame with his hands. Yoko regained her poise and began soothing the man's violated pride while retrieving pieces of his clothing.

'You were superb, so gentle, it's never been so nice,' she purred.

Araki forced a smile, knowing the truth to be different. His passions and confidence inflamed by Yoko's force-fed whisky, the unfortunate man's body had not responded at the moment of truth, and he had passed out. But not before parting with fifty thousand yen; and this was the cause of the early morning tantrum as he tried to retrieve his money if not pride in his manhood. Araki watched the man dressing, with amused pity.

Yoko was one of Tokyo's hundred thousand 'water business' bargirls and she specialised in the middle-management group of clients. She no longer aspired to the plush Ginza

21

clubs that indulged entertainers and company presidents, and where a wealthy patron might be the prize. At her level, she catered to men from their late thirties to early fifties, whose work required them to entertain, not at home of course, three or four nights a week. She knew their habits, foibles and psychology to perfection and for a fee plus commission on drinks she satisfied their limitless hand-holding and knee squeezing needs, laughing at their jokes, giggling and deftly steering them closer and closer to drunken stupefaction, a state invariably reached between ten-thirty and eleven each evening.

For about an hour late every night, fascinating scenes, as ritualistic as any Kyoto festival, are played out in the streets of the capital. Girls and women of all ages and sizes, clad in bright evening gowns, elegant kimonos or more alluring attire, line up outside their respective establishments and bid farewell as their customers meander away towards the last trains. Others flag down taxis and help load their passive charges, ensuring that briefcases and umbrellas are in their owners' hands. The night is over for most people.

Like her colleagues, Yoko was not an overt prostitute, but once or twice a month she would take one of her clients, who had expressed an interest in more than just drinking, to a nearby 'love' hotel for a couple of hours. Occasionally, like last night, she met a regular customer, someone she knew and trusted who might be worth more than the normal twenty-five thousand yen, and they would go together to her apartment. The dangers were obvious: the adulterous Japanese male, unable to break the barrier of shame surrounding his lecherous intentions without numbing quantities of alcohol, became incapable of performing to a climactic finale and more often than not fell asleep. The following morning, overcome with remorse and resentment, he would demand reimbursement. Enter Araki, for the second time that year.

At thirty-one, Yoko maintained her good looks and slim figure by careful eating, and assured herself of enough energy by sleeping every day until noon. Twice a week she had ballet lessons followed by a sauna bath, and two cosmetic operations had trimmed the skin around her eyes and built up her stubby nose until it projected out from her face to a delicate point. She still kept the photograph of Natalie Wood she had shown to the surgeon when he asked what shape she wanted.

In the early stages of their relationship, and always after she had been rescued, Yoko would offer herself to a willing Araki. She had vented a degree of maternal feeling by nursing him through the shock of dismissal and later through the trauma of his divorce. Araki, in turn, soothed his neighbour through her post-abortion depressions (two of them) in long sessions over instant coffee and rice crackers. Over a period of three years, there evolved between them a mutual dependency which was as close to a state of love as might be definable between a man and a woman in Japan.

Just as his wife had done the previous morning, Yoko handed the hapless businessman his little black briefcase with shopping bag handles, and he departed without further comment. Araki scolded Yoko with mock admonition, saying that if she was not careful she would end up in one of his homicide stories. Yoko pouted and pulled her reluctant hero towards her by the lapels of his pyjamas.

'Don't leave me. I'll make some coffee and we can play a little.'

Araki managed a smile and pinched her ear affectionately.

'Another time, Yoko-chan,' he promised. 'I've got a heavy programme today, and I feel awful.'

The fact was, Araki wanted to vomit. Back in his apartment, he knelt on the cold tiles in the solitude of his bathroom and tried to induce himself to be sick into the toilet bowl. He heaved twice but nothing came. Abandoning the effort, he tried to rub some colour into his pallid face; but again his body seemed to have lost the will to respond. Perhaps it had given up. At five feet four Araki was slightly below the national average but the large squarish head, sloping gently away at the back, and the disproportionately long torso atop horseshoe legs qualified him as a typical male

23

of the Mongol strain. His hair was thinning at the front, and he let the rest grow long, falling in modish disarray over his ears and down to the collar. Although his nose was snubby, and greasy to the touch as the day progressed, his eyes were wide for a Japanese, and gave his face an attraction which was enhanced by the fact that he did not wear glasses. He was not overweight like the animal-fat eaters of the West, but his rice and pasta diet ensured that his intestines were longer than theirs by several feet and this was expressed in a well-rounded paunch like that of a pregnant woman. Cigarettes and alcohol in excess had left his complexion blotchy and aged him beyond his thirty-eight years.

Editor Kobayashi was not there when Araki arrived at the Shimbashi offices of the *Tokyo Weekly*. Kondo, the balding, mild-mannered custodian of the library and research department, agreed to examine the note from the dead man's ticket holder and give an opinion before Araki had to make his planning presentation to the editor. He was invaluable to the ten full-time reporters, not only as the source for information on half a thousand subjects he had collected in meticulous fashion over thirty-five years, but also for his knowledge of Japan's nebulous libel laws. He was also the profession's recognised expert at negotiating solatia, knowing the exact point and exact amount at which the lost face of the actress or the impinged reputation of the errant politician could be assuaged by a wad of ten-thousand yen notes.

Keiko, Araki's feline research assistant, tried to interest him in three days of assorted mail, but he went straight to the telephone. He lit the last cigarette from the packet on which he had recorded the number from the book of matches found in Tanimoto's coat and was soon in possession of the address of the Camelia coffee house in the college district near Ochanomizu Station.

It took a good five minutes before Inspector Nishii was free to talk, but when he was on the other end of the line he was as effusive and helpful as ever, testing Araki's personal shorthand system to the full. The police, Nishii had to admit, had lost traces of Tanimoto and while he had been

24

known as a strong-arm operator, he had not been arrested or questioned by them in the last three years. Tanimoto's life was, by design or destiny, calamitous and doomed. Araki could sense that Nishii was supplementing his description by reading from some sort of official record and from time to time heard the policeman cluck with disgust at the implications of a particular fact.

Araki would later embellish the victim's police record with the story of a disturbed childhood: a bright youth who forcibly defended his mother against a violent and alcoholic father, and at high school fought with fists and clubs those of his peers who openly mocked his troubled home. Tanimoto's mother was determined that her only son would go to university even though, after the sacrifice of a lifetime, she would only see him qualify for a four-year-course at a third-rate college, noted more for the right-wing extremism of the faculty and students rather than the pursuit of academic excellence. She did not live to see him give up his studies for the street life. Perhaps it was best.

Tanimoto quickly learned the skills of concentrated brutality in the university's martial arts club and practised what he learned by enforcing a military discipline on the male cheerleaders of the baseball team. This group, whose limited repertoire of wild, co-ordinated contortions, gesticulations and demented screams was honed to perfection by the masochistic submission of their bodies to the sting of the lash and the thump of the bamboo stave, shaved their heads and wore their black uniforms in sizes larger than required by their diminutive, muscular bodies. During the third year of the four-year course, he drifted into the Shinjuku sub-culture and inevitably into sniffing glue; and, being smarter than the average drop-out, he soon learned it was better on the body and pocket to sell the stuff rather than use it. It was during a periodic police sweep that Tanimoto was caught with his satchel full of thinners and plastic bags and earned his first entry on the record that Inspector Nishii now had in front of him. After spending a year in detention he made his way back to Shinjuku, where he worked as a barman and later a nightclub manager.

'We interviewed him several times over the years,' said Nishii, referring, Araki presumed, to the policeman's colleagues. 'He roughed up customers occasionally or stayed open too late, and we thought at one time he was running a stable of Thai and Taiwanese girls.'

'Didn't you pin anything specific on him?' asked Araki.

'Not for some time. Tanimoto's youth, and the fact that he stayed away from the gangs and drugs, were in his favour and more often than not he was let off with a caution.' The tone of the policeman's voice then changed abruptly from one of tolerant compassion to uncompromising severity.

'In July 1972 he led an assault on a rival drinking club, which he suspected of poaching his hostesses. He said he was only going to warn them off but there was a fight, knives were drawn, and the manager of the other club finished up slashed beyond recognition and one lung pierced. Tanimoto and a friend did four years in prison for attempted murder.'

'Anything since then?' asked Araki.

'Nothing. The record ends three and a half years ago when Tanimoto was released.' Inspector Nishii's voice trailed off, as if not wishing to stem the flow of words before the next fact came to hand. 'Let me see . . . it says here that his last registered address was in Funabashi, Chiba Prefecture.'

'That's a long way from either Akasaka-mitsuke or Ikebukuro,' offered Araki.

'Yes, I'm aware of that,' replied his friend with some irritation. 'When I find out where he's been working for the last three years or so, I might be able to tell you why he had a season ticket between those two stations. Otherwise, your guess is as good as mine; and if you do dig up anything useful, please let me know. But don't exert yourself. This case is definitely low priority. As far as I'm concerned, society in general is now a little better off without the likes of Akira Tanimoto.'

It was not hard to find the Camelia: Araki had roamed the streets of Ochanomizu as a student and recognised many landmarks among the pinball and mahjong parlours, book-shops, cheap curry and noodle joints and multi-storeyed coffee houses. It was squeezed between a shoe-shop and a tailor's on a narrow street with no sidewalks which ran parallel to the Sobu Line railway tracks between Ochanomizu and Kanda stations. The smoky glass window did not afford Araki a preview of the clientele, and his view through the sliding entrance door was obscured by a huge flower painted in blood-red and with the name 'Camelia' written above it in roman letters. Inside there were eight booths, each large enough to seat four people, separated only by the token privacy given by some artificial bamboo leaves stuck into the back-rests of the seats. The air was almost glacial, and Araki was shivering by the time he had eased himself between the low table and the imitation leather seat of the booth at the rear of the café, furthest away from the direct airflow of the cooler. Two university students were reading comics together, and these were the only other patrons he had passed on the way in. From his position, he could see no signs of life at other tables; no heads bobbing in conversation among the bamboo leaves and no tell-tale trails of cigarette smoke.

A plain, thin girl of about twenty seemed to be in charge and she brought a glass of water and a menu to the table. It was already half past one, and Araki ordered ham sandwiches to go with his iced coffee. When the waitress returned, he wasted no time coming to the point.

'Frightful news about Tanimoto, wasn't it?' The stage whisper echoed around the room; and suddenly the most important sound in the room was the low whirr of the air-conditioner. The students did not stir from their browsing and Araki was not in a position to see the instinctive jerk of the head and the expression that creased the face of a figure hidden away in the window booth.

'It certainly was,' she replied fidgeting with the utensils. 'The police were here all afternoon yesterday. We had no customers at all. My mother was furious.'

Araki was pleased to find such a talkative witness.

'Did you know him well?' he asked, taking a bite from a sandwich.

'No. He wasn't very chatty,' she said, and as an after-thought added, 'but always polite.'

So he had been a regular client, Araki thought, not just a passing collector of matches.

'About how often did he come in?' asked Araki, trying to sound casual.

The girl sucked in air and looked towards the ceiling. She concluded that she herself had served Tanimoto once, sometimes twice, a month but she shared the shop chores with two other girls and so he might have been in more often. Upon Araki's prompting, she confessed finding the victim attractive, particularly his stylish suits and, most memorable in a land where such expressions of individuality are discouraged, his moustache. She had also flirted with him unsuccessfully. Looking at her spotty, anaemic face and lip line distorted by an upper row of ugly, uneven teeth, it did not surprise Araki that Tanimoto, who had probably had his pick of the girls working in his clubs, rejected the advances of this undistinguished one.

'Was he always alone?' Araki continued.

'He was alone when he came in, but then . . .' The girl hesitated and her voice faltered, not because she was trying to remember, but because for the first time it occurred to her that her interrogator was more than the curious bystander she had thought. She fondled the edges of a drying cloth nervously.

'And then what?' Araki said, with persistence.

'Well, he was usually waiting for someone, at least, when I was here he was. As a matter of fact, the—'

The purr of the yellow telephone by the cash register was muted, but its effect was theatrically timely. The waitress took full advantage. She excused herself in mid-sentence, a contingency provided for in the Japanese language. Araki sipped unenthusiastically at the glass of coffee and watched the girl scurry away with false urgency.

She lifted the receiver, listened and nodded an acknowledgement. As he turned his attention to the last sandwich,

28

Araki almost missed the next rapid sequence of events.

The waitress covered the mouthpiece with her right hand and spoke to a figure Araki had not noticed at the window table. A slender girl in a calf-length black dress appeared and accepted the call. The long sleeves of her dress slipped down to her elbows and she clutched the instrument close to her mouth.

The waitress was coming back, and Araki could see she was agitated and intended to ignore him and take refuge in the kitchen. He reached out and tried to intercept her. It was then he saw the girl. She was looking towards his booth but instantly turned, gripping the telephone close to her face. Araki was left a view of hair as black as the dress it lay against, reaching down as far as the belt that hung loosely enough around her waist to outline the curve of her hips. The upper part of her body sporadically jolted forward as if she was emphasising a point. There was something incongruous in the sight of this slender woman, dressed as if for some formal occasion, apparently alone, and in a coffee house on a hot summer afternoon. Going to, or coming from, a wedding party, Araki surmised, but he was not in a position to see whether she was wearing a decorative flower or some costume jewellery. Most likely a funeral though. Nobody wears a long-sleeved black dress in this climate unless they are going to a funeral or . . . or they are in mourning. He could see a conclusion, one that tantalised him, but he needed the help of the waitress again. What had she said about Tanimoto meeting someone here? What was she about to say when the telephone rang?

He leaned further out of his booth to beckon when the thumping sound of a receiver being replaced with force drew his attention the other way. The faceless figure was now groping in her handbag. She took out some coins and dumped them indiscriminately by the cash register. Araki watched the rapidly evolving drama in fascination. Without looking back, the girl snapped her purse shut and moved towards the door. Araki's intuition told him to make contact, pursue this suggestion of a new story or even some passing connection with his original story. He knew there was nothing to lose by asking, and the niggling feeling of unprofessional work if he did not would always remain.

He slid briskly off the couch seat and directly into the path of the waitress. Seeing that the woman was preparing to leave, she had hurried from the rear of the coffee house to collect the money, picking up enough speed to make normal evasive action difficult when the legs and torso of her inquisitive customer impeded her progress. She applied pressure to the soles of her feet, but the momentum was too great and she fell bodily across Araki who slumped back into his seat with the waitress on top of him. Her hand clung to the nearest support it could find, which was Araki's throat. His left knee rose instinctively, cracking against the under-side of the table and upsetting the half-finished glass of iced coffee. He was more angry than hurt, and it seemed an hour by the time he had disentangled himself and was able to pursue his original intention.

But the place was empty and the automatic door had long since returned to its rut. In the street, where few people walked in the heat, there was no sign of the girl, and Araki was left with only the memory of the long black hair, swirling in troubled disarray.

'I'm sorry about the mess. Are you all right?' Araki scratched his sweaty scalp, more out of embarrassment than necessity. The noise had managed to distract the students and they stared at the perpetrator with contempt. The glass had rolled on to the couch and stayed intact, and the girl was dabbing up the mess it had left with a cloth. Her silence expressed her true feelings. Araki apologised again and ordered another iced coffee, asking to be served in the now vacant corner booth.

On the table, an empty water glass, a coffee cup, still half full, an ashtray and two barely smoked cigarettes, a light pink stain like a fingerprint on the amber filters, bore evidence to the recent presence. A neatly folded newspaper lay forgotten on the seat.

30

'Sorry to keep you waiting.' A nominal politeness had returned to the waitress's tone, reflecting perhaps her realisation that the excitement of the previous day, the mixture of fear, importance and pride she had felt when the detective questioned her, would never be repeated, unless by her own guile it could be prolonged just a little while more.

'Can I help you further?' she asked. 'Shall I get you a cloth? Your trousers must be wet.'

Araki was pleased the inter-personal balance had been restored in his favour and he disposed of the girl's supplications with a flap of his hand. His attention had already fallen on the newspaper, drawn by the article exposed to view where the pages had been opened and then creased to a quarter of normal size. He held up the sheets with one hand and let them unfold unaided. The page he was staring at was from the same national newspaper that he had read that morning, and the small rectangle, highlighted by the careful folding, contained the story of the killing of Akira Tanimoto. The waitress was clearing the table and wiping up a ring of moisture, generally finding any excuse not to leave. Araki caught her eye.

'Was that her?' he asked softly. 'Was that the girl Tanimoto used to meet when he came in here?' She pretended not to hear so he repeated his question, only this time more forcibly.

'It was his girlfriend, wasn't it?'

'Yes, it was,' she replied, her eyes reverting to the table.

'Was she here yesterday?'

'No.'

'Did you tell the police about her?'

'Yes. After we told them that Tanimoto came here from time to time, they asked if he came in with anybody or met anybody here. We told them the truth.' She was still too shy to question the identity of the unattractive man who had spent the last half-hour sneezing and snuffling into his handkerchief and talking and behaving like a policeman one moment and the next like a clown, but she made certain her voice conveyed her discomfort, and suspicion.

Araki had already read this non-verbal message and his need for more specific answers would necessitate some disclosures on his part. He had to keep his excitement hidden under an expression of dour severity. It was not easy. If he could locate the woman in black he would have the female interest to fertilise the seed of the story which was germinating in his mind. For a few thousand yen, probably not more than fifty he estimated, the grieving mistress might be persuaded to come out of mourning and help embellish his article with a little lurid detail about her sordid existence with the victim, and she would probably agree to a photograph, looking suitably sad and wearing mandatory sun glasses. Yes, it had all the makings of hot-selling copy, if only he could locate the girl in black. If he could not, then a credible piece of fiction would have to be created around her. No more obfuscation; Araki had caught the scent and now he wanted facts, and the timid creature in front of him, nervously squeezing a work cloth, was his source. He moved in for the kill.

'I'm a reporter with the *Tokyo Weekly*. You can see one of my articles, it's about gambling tours to Korea, in last week's. You've got it in your rack over there.'

The waitress looked over to where a collection of newspapers and popular magazines had been skewered on rods and hung between two supports.

Before she could absorb this confession, Araki continued. 'I'm writing a story on Tanimoto and want to fill in a few gaps.' He kept to himself the fact that the gaps were gorges, and the birth of the article, or its early demise, might depend on what she was able, or prepared, to disclose. 'I don't want you to tell me anything you didn't tell the police, and whatever you tell me will be confidential, just between the two of us. Of course, I'll give a small fee for your trouble.' He reached towards the back pocket of his trousers with an exaggerated flourish.

The girl's will, Araki had sensed, was on the brink of

surrender even before the possibility of payment arose, and when Araki took his wallet from the pocket it collapsed altogether. He had a new five-thousand yen note in his hand and was rubbing a corner of it between finger and thumb when the automatic door hummed again and another pair of students came in. The spell evaporated. Cursing the timing, Araki exchanged the note for a cigarette as the buck-toothed girl ushered the new arrivals to a seat. It was not even term-time. They were juku students like the others, cramming their way through the summer to master the trivial points of English grammar or Marxist economic theory which their university curriculum demanded. Five minutes later she was back, her guests settled for a long discussion on their university's summer programme behind glasses of ice-cold coffee. Her voice was hardly more than a whisper but she spoke before Araki could.

'Her name was Maki something or other. Sometimes he left messages for her. They just said "Maki".'

Araki interrupted. 'Did the voice today ask for Maki?'

'No, he just wanted the lady in black sitting alone.'

'How did he know where she was? Was she in here with someone earlier?'

'No, she came in alone.'

'Then he must have watched her come in,' mused Araki aloud.

'Pardon?'

'Nothing.'

In the next ten minutes the waitress gradually melted into her role; she stared dreamily at the ceiling and disclosed that the vanishing lady was a frequent visitor, four or five times a month she thought, and as she said earlier, on about half of these occasions she met Tanimoto. Like her companion, she was a rather reticent character and rarely exchanged more than pleasantries with the staff. The messages she, the waitress, passed on were always the same. 'Tell Maki-san to call the Bali urgently.' She had told the police about Tanimoto's occasional partner but they were not interested enough to pursue the point beyond a description, which was

33

simply that Maki was pretty in a childlike way and wore little make-up. The police did not know about the Bali, whatever that was.

'Have you any idea what the Bali is, or where it is?' Araki asked.

'No, the message was very short and always the same,' she replied.

'Do you think it was a bar or a club? Maki sounds to me like a hostess.'

The waitress sucked in air and twisted and lowered her head until her right ear almost touched the stiff collar of her blouse. Araki sensed there was something about the calls that remained within the boundary of her normally shallow memory and she was straining hard to find it. Araki prodded.

'Was it the voice? Did you recognise it? Was it the same as today's?'

She shook her head. 'No, I . . .' Her voice faded as her concentration deepened. 'It wasn't the voice . . .'

Araki leaned forward, his body language urging her, encouraging her. He stifled another urge to sneeze.

'It wasn't the voice,' she repeated over and over. 'No, it was music.' Her eyes popped open in delight. 'That's right, it was music. I remember now. I always had to listen hard to hear what the man was saying. There was some of that tropical music in the background.'

'Tropical music?' Araki interrupted.

'Yes, you know. It's always what they play on Japan Air Lines commercials for Hawaii and Guam and places like that.'

Araki tried to help. 'You mean the twangy guitar stuff. What's it called? They use an Hawaiian guitar, I think.'

'Yea, yea, that's it.' She smiled broadly, displaying in victory the dental disaster that was her upper gum. Araki rocked in his seat sharing the girl's enthusiasm. It had been a struggle but the result was a triumph for what Araki liked to call his prick-and-poke type of interviewing. He handed over the five thousand yen which the girl acknowledged with a low bow. Araki stood up to leave, waiting while she took his money for the drink. It was not hard to imagine the Bali as a bar or club where Tanimoto and his like enjoyed the company of hostesses, or trained the girls who worked for them. He wondered if Maki had heard his first conversation with the waitress. He assumed she did as he had made no effort to keep his voice low as he thought the place was empty apart from the two students who were of no consequence.

Had she reported his inquisitiveness to the person on the line? He was certain he had caught her looking towards him as she spoke into the telephone. When the waitress showed him to the door, he turned to her and lifted his index finger to his nose.

'I'm sorry, I didn't ask your name.'

'It's Abe. Abe Mihoko.'

'Mihoko-san, one more small favour. Would you sit in the seat over there for a minute?'

Once in the street, Araki pressed his face against the glass of the smoky black window. He could distinguish the shape of the fixtures in the corner booth that the woman called Maki had occupied. Then Mihoko the waitress sat down and stared at him with a toothy grin made more demonic by the discolouring effect of the glass. He repeated the experiment from a point across the street but could not see Mihoko's outline until he had walked to where he was only a few steps from the glass. He gave a wave of farewell but did not look to see if it was reciprocated.

The walk to Kanda Station gave him time to muse on the identity of the woman in mourning. Wife, mistress, lover, casual lay? For reference, he had only the long hair and a body shape from the back. Her buttocks had been high and curved and her legs were unusually straight, not the normal bowed variety so typical of the race. He wondered if she was Chinese, or even Eurasian. But it was the hair that excited him most and had revived bittersweet memories of his former wife.

He hadn't taken any particular interest in her during the

first two years at Keio, partly because their college courses had rarely coincided but more because fraternisation between the sexes at anything other than classmate level did not take place in that society. Until he sought adulthood with Kaoru, Araki reflected, the most significant source of information on sex were the explicit comic books he had swapped among his friends. Araki had no athletic ability or interest in any outdoor activity, even in the noisy cheerleaders, which immediately made him an outsider. Instead, he involved himself in the publication of the student monthly magazine, where his natural skills quickly became apparent, and by the end of his second year he was the editor. Using the limitless free time available to the Japanese university student, Araki also applied himself with ferocious energy to the study of English. Like all post-war students he had studied it compulsorily from the age of twelve but now compensated for the lack of conversational study by spending countless hours repeating sentence patterns, watching films in English and accosting white foreigners in the streets and parks to hear the real thing. He was soon chairman of his university's English debating society and led his team to the finals of the national tournament three years running.

It was at one of the debating society's meetings, when new members were introduced, that he first noticed Kaoru. Rather, he noticed her hair and the way it was swept back in pony-tail style exposing the full curve of her cheekbones. When she sat at her desk, she let the mane of hair rest across the front of her dress. Against other Asian women, and Araki's yardstick were now the Thais and Filipinos who competed with the locals in the floating world, she was not particularly beautiful, but amongst the Japanese she would be noticeable. Her skin was clear and pampered, and the eyes that later would scream with silent hate were broad and alive with youth and enthusiasm: as the daughter of a bank director she had the resources to lead a financially liberated lifestyle.

Kaoru's major was English and she became Araki's assistant, helping him to select topics for debate and organise teams, dates and venues with opposing universities. She did not mind his brusque manner and unrefined approach to social mores. In fact, she thrived on them and encouraged him to assert his provinciality, especially when in debate with the more élitist colleges. It was inevitable that the natural reserve of their race should begin to crack, if only from the temptations afforded by proximity.

A win in debate over a rival university would lead the team and their supporters to an evening of revelry over tankards of draught lager around an open hibachi on which skewers of tender chicken breasts and leeks sizzled amid swirls of charcoal smoke. As the group rocked from side to side in drunken bliss, hands clapping in time to the monotone beat of some plaintive village song, Kaoru's body, warmed from the drink and the bodies pressing against her, would offer no resistance to the young man who always seemed to be at her side at these times. She did not object when Araki's body was slow to disengage, even after the singing and clapping had ended. They participated in the range of childish games that typify the Japanese at play: adolescent antics as rigidly predictable as their behaviour in the home, the school and the office. There was the feigned indignation at being the object of a derogatory story or the butt of a joke, and the limp-wristed slapping and gentle pushing of the perpetrator by the victim of the offending story. Kaoru and Araki unconsciously sympathised with each other when they were the butt of the jokes and they never missed the chance to increase the pressure between their bodies. At one of the parties, when the seating order placed them together on a backless wooden bench, Araki gripped the edge and held his arms straight to support his aching spine. When Kaoru did the same, their hands touched, staying together but not daring to take the game to its next exploratory stage.

Kondo slurped at the bowl of steaming saporous noodles, holding it firmly on the counter with his left hand, and managing to ingest a good half-metre before the thread snapped.

'I've marked with a cross the photos you took yourself which were processed between April this year and last Friday when Tanimoto was found.'

Head bent forward to reach the bowl and legs that hung from a slender frame in a bow shape and barely touched the floor, Kondo looked from the back like a teenager just out of junior high school. But his hair was sparse and the business suit, which he wore even on a Sunday like this, was faded and shapeless. The skin of his face had long lost its olive sheen and was now the texture of scorched rice paper, darker in those places where it had pitted as he aged. He was over sixty, but no one knew by how much. He dabbed his chin with his knuckles and turned again to face Araki with his dark, murky eyes. His voice was precise but he had to stop frequently to clear his throat.

'I have not included those where the individual faces are too indistinct for recognition and I did my own survey to eliminate those that didn't show anyone vaguely like the man you described, but if you want me to fetch . . .'

'OK, OK. No, that's fine. I'm sure you're right.' Araki often interrupted the researcher, impatient at the way his passion for precision and accuracy led to what Araki considered a redundant use of words and therefore a waste of time. He always regretted his own short temper, although it never upset Kondo, as his respect for the dedicated old bookworm was enormous. This respect was mutual. Kondo was married, but his work was his child, indeed his life, first with a national newspaper and after retirement with the *Tokyo Weekly*. He never questioned the fall from grace that brought Araki to the magazine but soon recognised the dedication that he was prepared to apply, however trivial or lascivious the subject under review.

The photographs in the loose-leaf folder that Araki balanced between the counter edge and his knees were characteristically neatly arranged and impeccably documented with date, location, subject, author and, if it had been published, the date of publication. Araki's irritation was partly due to an intensifying discomfort which had not

38

been alleviated by the previous night's sleep. He took another long gulp of Kirin, but the pain unleashed when the cold beer washed past his inflamed tonsils caused him to gag.

The first half-dozen pictures were of no interest, but Araki stopped at one he had taken at night on a rainy June evening. It showed a couple 'caught' entering a motel, and Araki chuckled at the expression on the two faces as they stared into the flash. The man seemed to have a moustache, though it could have been a shadow, and he was shorter and stouter than Tanimoto. A few pictures later he paused at one he had taken during the summer Sumo tournament. He had forgotten about it as he had not been on a specific assignment, and he had to look hard at the figure Kondo had seen fit to circle with his black felt pen. The man was sitting in the second row behind and to the left of one of the impassive judges. The moustache was thick and prominent. Araki stared as if transfixed. Kondo sensed the thrill of discovery.

'Do you want it blown up?' he asked, mistaking Araki's close examination as a sign of positive recognition.

Araki muttered inaudibly and shook his head.

'It's not him. It's not Tanimoto.'

Disappointed that what he thought was the main candidate had been rejected, Kondo returned to his bowl of soggy noodles, while Araki continued flipping through the sheaf of photographs, stopping at most for five seconds, once for ten, at each one.

The veins in his neck bulged as the wiry owner of the noodle shop craned over the counter to glimpse the photographs. He was very bored and wiped the same glass over and over until a customer's order distracted him. There was not much trade on Sundays, but anything was better than staying in his two-room flat with the twin boys all day. The two *Tokyo Weekly* men were his only Sunday regulars, other clients being travellers dropping briefly out of the confines of Shimbashi station to eat before catching another train. He was starting to worry today about Araki's tetchiness and profuse sweating when he was suddenly startled by an outburst from the reporter.

'It's him. He's here, the bastard's right here!'

Kondo snatched the picture from his companion. It showed a partial cross-view of a room full of men. Here and there, individuals were standing gesticulating while those near them cowered and held their arms up defensively. Two in particular stood only a few feet from where the camera had captured them, and one of them was pointing a finger menacingly at the lens. The moustache alone was sufficient identification, but it was the eyebrows, in death prominent and ominous enough, which were now unmistakeable as they stretched defiantly in anger. Kondo took charge of the folder and read aloud the caption.

' "June 29, 1982. Shareholders' Meeting of Matsuhashi Corporation. Photograph by Makoto Araki. Not published. Reason: threat of legal action from persons unknown. All main subjects unidentified." '

Araki recalled the incident well and reproved himself for not placing Tanimoto in it before. He had been working on a study of the sokaiya, the quasi-gangsters who, after buying a single share in a public company, would approach the management and demand vast sums of money in return for which they would ensure that the annual shareholders' meeting would be completed smoothly and promptly with all motions proposed by the Board being accepted by over-whelming voices of approval from the floor. Long convinced that the gestures of impotence by the senior staff of the most powerful enterprises in Japan and their succumbing to what amounted to blackmail from the sokaiya were simply bogus posturings, Araki speculated that they actually hid connivance.

To prove his point, and expose it in the *Tokyo Weekly*, he had himself bought a share in Matsuhashi, a prime example of Japan's post-war economic power, and thereby the right to attend the stockholders' meeting and pose any questions to the Board should he wish. Matsuhashi had for some time been embroiled in a scandal over the hoarding of mulled

rice in anticipation of a national shortage, and they expected
an awkward confrontation from consumer organisations who
in turn had bought the right to address themselves to
the chairman. There were also rumours that several of the
company's overseas subsidiaries were in deep financial
trouble and that this fact would become apparent when
the consolidated accounts were announced at the 29 June
gathering.

Against all the rules, Araki had smuggled a Minox camera
into the crowded auditorium in Matsuhashi's modern headquarters in the Marunouchi business district. The chairman,
an elderly former bank president performing the duties of
his sinecure with the rigid discipline of a Kabuki actor, was
only six minutes into the presentation of the accounts when
the trouble began.

A small group of shareholders, probably no more than
six, raised their hands and voices in unison to attract
the speaker's attention and when their supplications were
ignored they began to shout. Araki thought he saw a
Matsuhashi official at the end of the platform raise an arm
to signal, but he could not be sure. In the event, no sign
seemed necessary, as from fifteen different points on the floor
crew-cut, sharply dressed men sprang to their feet, jeering
and waving at the original protestors and then applauding
the impassive chairman. It was the moment for others with
various gripes and complaints against Matsuhashi to stand
and shout and shake their fingers at the podium but their
protests too were drowned by the louder cries of support from
what Araki clearly construed were planted supporters
of the management. He found it repulsive to watch as two of
the hired hands converged on one of the more outspoken
protestors and forced him back into his seat, rotating
clenched fists menacingly in his face. Araki managed to take
two exposures with his miniature camera before he was
noticed by Tanimoto, who marked him for expulsion by
three of the sokaiya men who were closer. He was man-
handled out of the hall and escorted to the street where he
found that luckily the camera was still in his possession.

41

The article that Araki submitted was published in July and exposed vividly the degree of corporate collusion with sokaiya, but following a telephone call from a man claiming to represent Matsuhashi who suggested that *Tokyo Weekly* might have broken the law in bringing a camera into a shareholders' meeting it was decided that Araki's pictures, one of which was blurred and therefore discarded, should not be used to embellish the text.

The stuffiness Araki had been feeling all day momentarily disappeared, dispersed by his frenzied brain activity as he sought to evaluate the implications of his discovery. Kondo almost let a trace of emotion, even excitement, break the normal dispassionate tone of his voice, but he quickly regained his self-control.

'We must drink to this,' he said deliberately. 'Sake, please. Hot.'

The owner appreciated the order, his only other customers having left fifteen minutes earlier, and took pains to fill two ceramic pots and ensure they fitted into their slots in the electric heater without spillage.

'Leave the beer alone, Araki-kun, the sake's much better for your cold. Should I have him make you some tamagozake?' Kondo used the familiar honorific more as a father might to his son rather than a senior to his junior.

Araki was still holding the photograph which he had taken of the victim and dismissed the offer of the traditional sweat-inducing boiled egg and sake tonic with a throaty utterance and a wave of the wrist. He did not want to show that he was quite moved by the gesture and would have liked to accept. As the owner poured the steaming wine into the plain white thimble cups, he brought the conversation back to Tanimoto and murder.

'What does a sokaiya have to do to get himself killed? I thought they were careful to avoid messy gangster stuff,' he speculated.

Kondo was not to be drawn into anything that could not be substantiated. 'They usually do. Until I know where Tanimoto worked, and you should keep in touch with your friend Nishii on this point, and whether that crowd were major league racketeers or a bunch of lone wolves, it's impossible to say whether the killing had something to do with his work or his extra-curricular activities.'

'What about the list?' Araki asked hopefully. 'What did that tell you?'

'Ah yes, the list.'

As he watched Kondo extract the original, canary yellow paper carefully from his billfold, Araki already knew that it had not divulged any of its secrets.

'Do you think the numbers are amounts of yen?' Araki asked optimistically.

'No,' Kondo replied, unusually unequivocally. 'Big payments, or perhaps we should say pay-offs in this case, are almost always . . . no, I'll say always, rounded up to the nearest million, or at least to the nearest hundred thousand yen. But look at these carefully.' He held the list in the palm of his hands as if it were an egg shell and jabbed a bony finger at the figures.

'The first number has nine digits, seven of which are different. And even if it were money, it would be way above the sort of individual amounts the sokaiya could extort. Look, the shortest one has eight digits, beginning with number six. That would be more than sixty million yen if it were money.'

'It could be hidden in there somewhere.'

'I think there's a lot hidden in this list,' Kondo replied tersely.

'So you think it's a code?'

'It could be anything.'

Kondo drank the sake in one gulp and let Araki fill the minute bowl again. Araki should have known that the wily old man would not commit himself to a thesis without unimpeachable proof, but he was desperate for support and pressed on undaunted.

'What about the kana and the circles?' He ran his finger down the side of the paper tapping each of the single syllabic letters that preceded each line of numbers, and then performed the same operation on the other side of the list where small circles had been written with a felt pen next to four of the lines of numbers.

'I can only imagine that "to", "hi", "ka" and the rest are part of names or places, and the circles show that whoever used the list has done something and has made a mark to remind himself. I really can't say more than that until I've given the whole thing some closer analysis. Besides,' he said as an afterthought, 'there's no "ma" for Matsuhashi, which is a bit of a shame really.'

Kondo would not be drawn further. Araki was disappointed and not a little irritated. It would have fitted perfectly into the story he had yet to write. Was Tanimoto an enforcer for a group of sokaiya which included one of Japan's most prestigious trading houses among its clients, and had he been of high enough rank to be entrusted as a collector for the dubious payments they elicited? Had he been withholding all or some of the money, been found out and suffered the ultimate punishment? It was plausible. Barely.

Araki was becoming drowsy, swaying involuntarily on his high chair but recovering instinctively when his centre of gravity approached the critical falling point. The euphoria he felt at the discovery of the Tanimoto-Matsuhashi connection was wearing off and the alcohol was well on the way to nullifying whatever resistance his weakened body retained. On top of everything Kondo was now into a monologue, the point of which was not readily apparent.

'It's not easy to find the locations of companies or places of entertainment when only the name and not the activity undertaken is available . . .'

Elbow on the counter, head in hands, Araki felt drowsy. 'What? Oh, the girls. OK, but get on with it. I've got a deadline to meet in four days.'

Kondo let the sarcasm pass without comment. 'My initial enquiries show that there are at least eight candidates for that girl . . . what was her name? . . . Maki . . . Maki's place of employment. You can take your pick from two cabarets, a bar, a short-time hotel, two coffee shops, a hairdresser's and a Turkish bathhouse.'

'You said "at least",' interrupted Araki. 'There may be more?'

'Very likely,' Kondo replied. 'I've picked only those places from the telephone directory and my own trade guides that specifically have "Bali" in their names in the phonetic kana script. There could, and most certainly are, other places that use Chinese letters for the first two syllables "ba" and "ri" but then they wouldn't be recognisable as places of possible exotic pleasures. I'll have someone check them, though.'

Araki shook his head. 'I don't think that's necessary. We're not looking for a Chinese restaurant. Remember what the waitress said about the background music. That Hawaiian stuff. No, we're looking for a bar or a place using the island of Bali as its theme.'

'Bali's thousands of miles from Hawaii,' said Kondo.

'You know as well as I do,' said Araki reproachfully, 'that anything vaguely exotic or tropical means grass skirts and Hawaiian guitars. Mood is more important than accuracy.'

Kondo had to agree, and renewed his narrative undeterred. 'I contacted seven of the possibles by telephone. The eighth, for a reason which will be apparent later, I've left for you. The two cabarets employ about a hundred hostesses between them, mostly pros or housewives, and neither would admit to having a Maki or Makiko. In any case, like other clubs, they give their girls silly foreign names like Cindy or Sally. If a customer calls to book a particular girl for an evening he has to use the pseudonym. Your girl could be working there but you'd have to do some on-the-spot research and it might be hard to justify the expense to Kobayashi. We can almost certainly discount the hotel. That kind of place wouldn't dare employ young women for fear of attracting the attention of the vice people. It's all right to take a woman but you mustn't meet them there. The police are quite strict on the interpretation of . . .'

'I know what the law says. Please get to the point.' In

spite of the coolness of the room, Araki held his perspiring head firmly in his hands, elbows still planted on the counter, and feeling aggravated at Kondo's ramblings, which were keeping him away from the mattress and the sleep he craved. Kondo, for once, was sympathetic.

'Excuse me,' he apologised, and then continued, watching Araki closely and trying to stress a point between his spasms of attention. 'Forget the hairdresser's. They are closed for the summer holidays. Nobody could have contacted them yesterday. You can rule out the bar too. It's just a hole-in-the-wall run by an old actress. That leaves the coffee shops.'

'And the Turko,' added Araki.

'And the Turkish bath. But I'm coming to that.'

'Saving the juicy bits for last?' chuckled Araki, recovering his humour for a moment.

'One shop is run by the owner and his wife and sister. There's nothing there. The other admits to employing a Makiko, known to all as Maki.'

'You think we've found her?' asked Araki with sudden interest. Kondo was reading over the top of his glasses from a pocket diary.

'According to the brief details given, Maki is seventeen, has her hair cropped short and dyed brown and has never been seen wearing anything but jeans and T-shirts. Do you think that fits your missing mistress?'

In spite of his disappointment, Araki forced a sardonic grin in reply.

'Which brings me to the eighth and last of the candidates,' continued Kondo, 'the Turkish bath. Take a look at this.' He held out the notebook for Araki's perusal and held his felt pen over a particular annotation.

Araki read aloud. ' "The Bali, Turkish Bath and Sauna".' He handed the pad back to Kondo. 'Did you call?'

'No. Read on,' replied Kondo tersely.

' "The Bali, Turkish Bath and Sauna".' He looked up at Kondo, who was nodding with encouragement. ' "Four dash two North-Ikebukuro one-chome". So what?'

Kondo was exasperated, but he put Araki's unusually slow response down to the virus afflicting him.

'Look again. Can't you see it?' he asked soothingly.

Araki scrutinised the pad. 'No.' It was beginning to sound like a television guessing game.

'What was Tanimoto carrying when he was found?'

'Well, he had the Camelia matches and . . .'

'Oh, come on,' said Kondo, exasperation now evident in his voice, 'what about the season ticket?'

And it finally hit Araki too; he might have noticed it earlier had it not been for the drowsiness which dulled his mental process. He was excited, as he was at discovering the picture of Tanimoto, but a little dubious.

'It could easily be coincidence. Ikebukuro covers a lot of land.'

Kondo was quick to agree. 'Yes it does, but look at it like this: the dead man had a pass to take him on the Marunouchi line from Akasaka-mitsuke to Ikebukuro. A girl, who we now know was friendly with the victim, is believed to work or live at a place called the Bali, and we know there is such a place, in this case a Turkish bath, in Ikebukuro. It may be coincidence, but if you're going to investigate all eight possibilities with the same name, I strongly suggest you begin in Ikebukuro.'

Araki was ready to agree, but one point still disturbed him.

'The underground pass goes to Ikebukuro, but the bath-house is in North-Ikebukuro.'

Kondo was not to be deterred. 'That's not really important. Ikebukuro is on the Marunouchi line, but its exits are spread along the underground shopping arcade. Have you been to the Sunshine '60 building?' He didn't wait for a reply, assuming that Araki had indeed visited Japan's tallest skyscraper. 'Well, Sunshine '60 is actually nearer Ikebukuro Station than East-Ikebukuro Station, which is on the Yurakucho line. If you're going to pursue this case, and I'm not convinced it's a good idea, take in the Turko.'

\*　　\*　　\*

47

Dropping Kondo at the Kasumigasaki underground station, Araki drove through Uchisaiwaicho and up past the Diet building towards Aoyama and his home in Harajuku. It was almost three o'clock, and there were few people about in Tokyo's government office district. A group of gaudily-clad foreign tourists filed from their air-conditioned luxury coach into the clammy heat only long enough to be photographed in front of the country's beehive-shaped grey parliament buildings. Traffic was sparse, and Araki took only a driver's fleeting interest in the dark green Toyota saloon which had swung out behind him and appeared in his rear-view mirror as he passed the Supreme Court. It, too, seemed to be heading for Aoyama.

# CHAPTER THREE

It was only four-thirty in the afternoon, but the fever in the reporter's body was rising and his head was heavy and drowsy, begging desperately for sleep. The pills and whisky went to work, and soon after spreading his mattress he drifted into a semi-conscious state where real thought and mental awareness were replaced by hallucinations and jumbled and chaotic dreams. In his delirium, he saw himself presenting his embryonic story to the editorial committee of the *Tokyo Weekly*, but instead of Kobayashi, the chairman, he was speaking to the dead man, Tanimoto, who, naked to the waist and bleeding from the mouth, nose and ears, laughed dementedly at him. He was trying to be reasonable; he described the sokaiya and his suspicions surrounding Tanimoto's death, and the existence of a lover. But he was not getting through, and the mocking laughter of Tanimoto was joined by the screams and howls of other people who were materialising in the room. Kobayashi was there, and even his ex-wife Kaoru. And when tranquility infiltrated this nightmare he saw in silent mirage a figure running away from him in slow motion, long strands of hair trailing behind her which almost touched him. He reached out and made to follow her but his feet were transfixed to the road.

Araki's sweat-drenched body had responded to the tumblings of his mind and he lay at right angles to the mattress, his legs sprawled across the floor. It was late and dark and the loop-line trains had stopped. A cicada clicked urgently on the wall outside the window and somewhere nearby a taxi's automatic door slammed shut. Araki heard none of this; nor the faint metallic rasp of his door opening.

A figure moved on tip-toe towards him, and still he heard nothing. Hands closed on his throat but he felt nothing, not even as they unbuttoned his shirt at the neck and then unzipped his trousers, tugging them deftly from his unprotesting frame.

His body could offer only passive compliance to Yoko's tender insistence that he roll from the floor back on to the mattress. She covered him with a clean bath towel and then a sheet which she trapped at the edges between the bedding and the floor. Save for the deep undulations of his chest, Araki was now motionless and at peace. His neighbour dabbed some fresh sweat from his brow and kissed an unresponsive ear. She watched him for a minute and left.

There was no doubt that Araki felt better. Although he was under no obligation, particularly on a Monday, to arrive at his office at a specific time, unless of course a meeting was scheduled for an early hour, he had found himself conscious well before dawn. The air in the room was stuffy and the mattress damp, but the rest of the flat looked unusually orderly: his trousers were folded over the back of a chair and his soiled underwear, socks and shirt were rolled into a ball by the door. His temperature had fallen almost to normal and the weakness had gone from his legs, and he luxuriated in the security of a steaming hot bath. He had taken time to wash, scrub and shampoo his body on the tiles and when his bottom had settled on the floor of the tub and he had sunk low enough to let the soothing water cover all but his skull, he found his mind was clear enough to imagine the scenario that was bound to follow when he faced the editorial committee later that day.

There was a perceptible breeze in the street, hardly a wind, but enough to lower the air temperature to a more comfortable level. He had missed the rush hour, and the drive in to Shimbashi would take no more than fifteen minutes. The lack of real substance to his story perturbed him: Kobayashi, his irascible editor, did not mind speculation as long as some irrefutable facts, however insignificant, could

50

be injected amongst them. He had a victim (fact) whose rear cranium was brutally crushed (fact). Tanimoto was of unsavoury character (likely) and dubious profession (fair assumption) murdered by cohorts or rivals (pure speculation) with a mistress (assumption) who worked in a sleazy massage parlour (possible). He ran over the plot in his mind again. It might be enough.

It might have been, but when he arrived at the office with his well-rehearsed arguments a message awaited him to say that one of the outstanding issues had been resolved. It was already ten-thirty. Keiko, as usual, fussed around him, clipboard officiously cradled in her left arm and pencil poised in mid-air, ready to jab, erase or note as required. She was as efficient an assistant as he could have wanted, not the least of her attributes being her capacity to absorb Araki's outbursts of temper with supreme serenity. It annoyed Araki the way her large circular tinted glasses lay invariably imbedded in her thick, glossy hair, but he put this affectation down to her constant efforts to appear cool, aloof and liberated.

'You'd better look at this before you see the editor,' she said, handing him a scrappy piece of foolscap. 'Your friend Inspector Nishii telephoned about nine-thirty.' She cleared her throat disapprovingly, taking more effort than necessary to consult her wristwatch to inform him that the editorial committee would meet in twenty minutes, that is, at eleven o'clock.

He was late arriving at the meeting, but having finished his long talk with the policeman, mentally noting the indebtedness it created, Araki was elated when he confronted his editor with his findings. Kobayashi was of slight build and deceptively average in appearance; yet he could easily be taken as the archetypal middle-aged salaried man, complete with shiny dark blue suit and plain, almost general issue glasses that perched loosely on the low bridge of his nose and which required frequent adjustment. Daisuke Kobayashi was a survivor of thirty years in the popular magazine business. He was no fool. He was not annoyed at Araki's tardiness, having spent the last ten minutes being briefed by Kondo and sharing views with his adviser, Nobuo Taneda, and his senior photographer Kenichi Sonoda.

'I'm sorry I'm late, but there's been an important development,' Araki said, emphasising 'important'.

Kobayashi beckoned him with a flick of the wrist.

'Two hours ago,' Araki said, looking at his notebook and trying to make intelligible sentences from the hurried jottings he had made, 'a man walked into the Asakusa police station and made a confession in connection with the death of Akira Tanimoto.'

Kobayashi chuckled. 'It's obvious you got these facts from a policeman.'

Araki continued, 'On the night of 26 August, last Thursday, Toshio Kawazu, a one-time petty mobster but now an office messenger, was playing an all-night game of mahjong with some friends, including Tanimoto. Everyone was getting drunk on rough sake and about one in the morning he, Kawazu, accused Tanimoto of cheating. They started pushing and shoving and ended up in a serious fight. During the tussle Tanimoto fell against the edge of the table and knocked himself out. In fact, the sharp edge at the corner had cracked his skull and it was clear he was dead.'

Araki looked round for reaction; but there was none, so he continued.

'There was a general panic. All of the players that night had records and could not expect any sympathy from the police, so they hauled the body across Tokyo and dumped it in the Tama.'

Kondo was about to interject a question but Araki raised a hand.

'When they sobered up the next day there was a conference. No one wanted a full police investigation and it was decided that Kawazu should give himself up, plead manslaughter and serve some time. In other words, he looked for a deal.'

'What do the police think of that?' The speaker was Nobuo Taneda, retired from a major daily and now respected adviser to the *Tokyo Weekly*. Although he had no executive power, he sat at Kobayashi's right hand and exercised great authority and influence. His voice made his scepticism evident.

'They are not very surprised,' replied Araki, trying to sound nonchalant. 'Normally an organised gang would have punished Kawazu according to their own code and at the same time disposed of Tanimoto more conclusively. But in this case, neither the killer nor the victim had any gang affiliation, at least not that the police know of, and it seems the mixed bag of players on that night lost their heads and acted the way they did. Manslaughter was one thing, which may receive lenient treatment in some circumstances, but abandoning a corpse without excuse or reason would start an immediate murder investigation.'

'So the police are happy to keep it at manslaughter?' asked Taneda.

Araki replied, 'More than happy. They'll send Kawazu to the prosecutors straight away.'

'And so you've got a story for the magazine.' It was the editor. Until now he had sat back in his chair like a meditating Buddha. He had probably sat in on a thousand meetings like this, listening to the enthusiastic reporter explain why he should be given permission, and invariably money, to pursue a story to its conclusion. He leaned forward as Araki continued.

'I want you to allow me to build a story around the last few days of Tanimoto's life, climaxing with the game and the killing. I've already got a fairly good profile of Tanimoto's past. It's sad, but great copy. I'll check out his employers and do some background work on Kawazu. Nothing deep, you understand. I think I've found a girl-friend and I'll try to buy her story. That ought to sell a few more copies in Urawa. With Kondo-san's help I might even crack the list . . .' He realised too late that he had said too much. Even Keiko, who had been scribbling furiously, looked up.

'Ah, the list.' Kobayashi affected surprise and made a

show of lighting a cigarette. 'I was wondering when you'd get to that. I understand that you, or in a broader sense we,' he went on, 'are withholding an item of evidence which you took without the knowledge of your confidant, Inspector Nishii. Confession or no confession, that makes you a felon, and by association makes us liable too. Any comment?'

Araki threw up his arms in surrender. 'Kondo-san here will agree that there is nothing on that bit of paper to cause the police to rush out and interview anyone about Tanimoto's death, let alone arrest him.' He looked over at Kondo and was pleased to see he was nodding in conclusion. 'They've got their man,' he continued, 'so a scrap of paper won't make any difference, will it?'

The editor went into deliberation with Taneda and when their heads were almost touching their words were inaudible to the others above the burr of the air-conditioning unit which protruded through the wall above Kobayashi's head. Araki folded his arms and stretched his legs under the table. It was the usual scene. Kobayashi seemed most concerned about the legal implications of the removal of evidence unknown to the police and swung frequently between Kondo and Taneda as he sought a consensus.

Araki let his mind wander, and the strange dreams and subconscious wanderings of the previous evening drifted back. The hands he had felt, so tender and soft, had been almost real. He could not recall a face. It must have been Maki, the bereaved lover, because the fleeting encounter with her in the Camelia coffee shop had intruded into his delirium. He strained to remember. One thing though, he was sure he had been wearing his trousers when he had laid down that night.

'OK, you can go ahead.'

Araki looked up startled. Everyone was looking towards him, and Kobayashi was speaking again.

'You can proceed with normal expense allocation.' He examined a metal calendar clipped to the strap of his watch. 'Today's Monday. Have a draft ready for debate on Wednesday and let's see if we can get it out for Friday.' He would not admit it, but Kobayashi himself respected Araki's persistent and intuitive journalistic style and knew that he was more often than not two steps ahead of the opposition weeklies. He began stacking his papers in front of him, and it was Taneda who continued.

'How do you plan to put this story together?'

'For a start,' replied Araki, now full of confidence, 'I'll send Maeda to photograph Tanimoto's funeral tomorrow. That might give us some idea of his acquaintances. Kondo-san will pursue enquiries with his contacts at police headquarters and fill in some missing details on Tanimoto's life. What we want to know is whether there is any recent organised crime involvement. If there is, it would obviously enhance the quality of the article. I'll check into Kawazu's background and I'll see if I can find Tanimoto's girl in Ikebukuro.'

Kobayashi interrupted. 'Ah, Ikebukuro. All roads lead to Ikebukuro. The victim's season ticket and the mystery woman's presumed place of work.'

'I'm aware of that,' said Araki. He was anxious to terminate the meeting while he was ahead and his voice betrayed his impatience. 'We know that Tanimoto was a sokaiya and Kondo here,' he nodded towards his colleague, 'will look into the business of his employer, the New Japan Socio-Economic Research Centre. They have an office in Akasaka.'

'So he had a season ticket from his place of work to his girlfriend's.' It was Taneda again.

'To where we think she works.' Now Kondo spoke in defence. 'I've narrowed down the likely places called Bali and the most likely is a massage parlour in Ikebukuro. Apart from the entertainment sites the whole area is a mass of cheap rooming-houses and flats and it wouldn't be surprising to find someone like Tanimoto living there.'

'Fine, that's settled,' said Kobayashi, pocketing his ballpen. 'Just show extreme caution please, Araki.' The editor's voice softened with a paternalistic admonition, as it always did when he ended an interview with his reporters but he emphasised 'extreme'. Talk of violent death, of sokaiya and gangs disturbed him and he only tolerated reference to them in his magazine's stories out of deference to his readers, to whom the sordid underworld of secret corporate extortion and feudally styled crime syndicates were unknown and, as such, of immense interest.

'Be careful,' he repeated, 'and I'd like you to take someone with you. Keiko-san.' Leaving her note-taking, Keiko slid from her chair.

Araki's head, which had been bowed in respect for his superior's wise guidance, suddenly snapped upwards. He made a face, a pained look which stretched the muscles around his mouth. He had made it to the end of the inter-rogation without conceding a major point. Until now. Please don't let it be Junichi Kato; but he's the only candidate. It wasn't that Kato was a difficult person, or even unlikeable, but he regarded the company of the promising second-year cub reporter as a liability. Twice he had been assigned to Araki's team and had acquitted himself without disgrace, doing the legwork, making anonymous telephone calls, keeping watch on subjects, often all-night vigils in the rain, and drafting articles which Araki would re-write completely. His enthusiasm was infectious and Kato was a popular young man, but to Araki, the loner, he was still a nuisance. He had to protest.

'You know what happened last time I took Kato with me. The story about the socialist dietman with the love-nest in Shinanomachi. That bargirl hit him with a bottle, knocked him out. I don't think he's been the same since.'

Kobayashi raised his hands, palms towards Araki. 'It's not Kato,' he said.

Keiko appeared with a shy-looking foreigner of about twenty-five with sharp features and thin straight lips. His hair was naturally curled and had no parting. It was also light yellow, almost pure blond in colour.

'This is Chris Bingham,' Kobayashi said, his pronunciation of the name excruciatingly Japanese. The young man attempted a bow, but to no one in particular. He was tall and lean and had not learned to join his feet and bow from the hip. Although his action was disjointed and loose, the effort was appreciated by those around the table. Some reciprocated with an inclination of the head and shoulders.

'Bingham-san is English,' Kobayashi continued, beckoning the foreigner to an empty chair. 'London, ne?' The editor was trying so hard he was almost shouting, but his pronunciation of the city was not at first recognised by the Englishman.

Keiko seized the moment to say proudly in halting, but intelligible English, 'Are you from London, Bingham-san?'

'Hai, Hai,' he replied, smiling. Everyone relaxed; editor Kobayashi beamed and proceeded in Japanese.

'Bingham-san will be with us for three months,' he said. 'He's already been in Japan for nine months as part of a one-year study and work assignment, part of a prize for being young journalist of the year or something. He's been on secondment from, . . .' – again he agonised with the pronunciation of the British daily newspaper and drew his notes closer to his glasses – 'and has worked with the *Kanto Shimbun*, our adviser's former paper. Through his intervention, Bingham has come to us to do some research on the magazine side of the industry.'

Stoically, Taneda acknowledged his role as go-between with a sharp nod.

'I've assigned him to you,' Kobayashi insisted to the reluctant Araki, 'because you're reputed to be the English expert. Take him with you, explain what we do and let him help you with the articles you'll be writing over the next few months. The central plan is that he is to produce.'

Araki watched the young Briton nervously fingering the lapel of his creased, short-sleeved safari jacket as he tried to pick up the sense of the editor's speech. Sensing his unease at being the object of everyone's attention, he leaned across the table with an outstretched hand and said, 'Hello, Chris. Welcome to the *Tokyo Weekly*.'

'What's your background?' Araki asked as they took coffee at his desk after the meeting. It was several years since he had had to sustain a conversation in English and he found himself resorting to textbook pattern idioms.

Chris made a space among a covering of press cuttings for his paper cup. 'I took a degree in modern languages at Bristol University and went into journalism. It was that or teaching.'

'What won you the year in Japan?'

Chris wafted a cloud of smoke which had drifted across the table. 'I wrote an essay on the Western world's favourite economic theme,' he said smiling at the thought. 'The Japanese attitude to foreign imports and the bureaucratic barriers set up to keep them out. The economic counsellor at the Japanese Embassy was one of the judges.'

Araki smirked. 'I'm surprised you won.'

'The others were far more critical. He was the most sympathetic.'

They both laughed.

Araki said, 'Have you followed up any of your theories at source?'

'I tried,' Chris sighed, 'but I ran into a few barriers myself. Taneda's newspaper kept giving me projects which meant days in temples in Kyoto or watching endless tea ceremonies. I interviewed a lot of businessmen and politicians but God knows what my reports looked like in Japanese. From what non-aligned friends tell me, I'm the greatest supporter of the Japanese economic miracle since Herman Kahn. I don't think the translations were a true reflection of my intention. But what can I do?' He threw up his hands in a gesture of surrender. 'Towards the end of my stay I was giving English lessons. It was much more rewarding.'

'And how's your Japanese?' Araki was probing, looking for Chris's supply of initiative, assessing how much use he would be. He seemed to have evolved the right level of scepticism about the Japanese way of doing things. He liked that. 'Can you hold a conversation?'

Chris shrugged. 'Obviously I can't analyse the influence of Kakuei Tanaka on the government's policies but I can find my way around. My language background helps. Do you think it's enough for this job?'

Araki leaned back on his chair. 'I'm sure it will be,' he said, 'as long as you remember that about half of what the Japanese say is honorific. Whoever's on top by reason of job, age or a man talking to a woman, dominates the conversation. The other party just nods.'

'Seniority didn't seem to bother *you* back there,' Chris said.

Araki shuffled some papers and lit another Hi-lite. 'I spent too long abroad, almost a year in all.'

Chris was puzzled. 'What's that got to do with self-assertion?' he asked. As soon as he had finished he realised he had known the answer almost since he had been given the series of innocuous assignments with the conclusions presented to him by subtle innuendo in advance of his research. The method, the approach was so subliminal he had found himself acquiescing in the pursuit of a line of enquiry which would lead to the result agreed by the initiators.

'It may be hard for you to comprehend, Chris,' Araki was saying, 'but in Japan when somebody says something you have to believe him. You know he's a liar but you don't challenge him, not because you fear the libel law, that's a non-starter. If it turns out he's wrong he'll take the responsibility: a salary cut, a suspension or the ultimate, suicide. And always there'll be a deep, demeaning apology. Everybody accepts this procedure, as long as the apology is deemed sincere. When I studied in London and in the States I couldn't get away with regurgitating what my teachers had said or simply apologising for Japan's ambivalent role in world affairs. People kept asking me why. Why can the ex-prime minister, an obvious bribe-taker and fixer, be allowed to run the country? Why don't Japanese mix socially? Why do Japanese smile when they drop your cut-glass vase? At the beginning, I used to reply that we Japanese were different, unique. That's what we are taught in school. But I was pressed to explain and it made me look at who I

59

was, and who the Japanese were. In time I started to ask "why" myself and it became a habit. It made me assert myself, regardless of the seniority of the person I was talking to.'

'Doesn't it cause offence?' Chris asked.

Araki slapped his folder shut.

'Often,' he said.

It was still light when they parked illegally beside a telegraph pole in a narrow, unlit street. The car radio had reported that a tropical storm, spawned at the weekend in the South China Sea, was veering north-east and might land on Japan if it kept the same course. Already the temperature was lower than normal for late summer and was a bearable and pleasant seventy-five degrees.

The area known loosely as Ikebukuro sprawls around the remote northern curve of the Yamanote Loop, the circle railway line that passes by Araki's apartment six kilometres away on its western track, then runs due south before curling suddenly when it reaches the Bay, and from whose track all commuting distances are measured and land values appraised. Inside the Loop, in Tokyo's inner city, property prices are the highest in the world.

In front of the east exit of Ikebukuro Station where two underground lines, the Loop and a group of suburban lines converge like the centre of a spider's web, is a plaza with fountains and stone benches, and behind this an entertainment district catering to every taste: cinemas, showing three new Western films for only six hundred yen; yakuza and all-night soft-porn films in abundance; six-seat bars run by ageing actresses and cabarets employing two hundred hostesses; touch-touch pink bars, dangerous clip joints and yakitori stalls under railway bridges; raucous beer halls and secluded, discreet private guest houses, quiet coffee shops, gaudy strip clubs and a cluster of love-hotels for quick liaisons. Ikebukuro lacks the class and youth attraction of Roppongi, or even Shinjuku and Shibuya on the Loop's western edge, and it competes with Ueno as a terminal for runaway youths and a doss for tramps. It's also an area where the country's organised gangs prosper under the watch of an otherwise strict police force.

The station's north-exit entertainment district was not where Araki had played in the past in Ikebukuro. It seemed more squalid than the parts around the east and west exits which had thrived around a clutch of huge department stores. Its buildings were older, crammed with tiny offices and shops.

They walked away from the railway tracks down the main street, which was split into blocks by even narrower passageways, past dingy cabarets with neon-lit boards spilling into the road, a small savings bank, a rusty shack housing a tatami maker, two or three weather-beaten ferro-concrete buildings, their basements hosting bars, their other floors loan sharks and mahjong parlours. It was in one of these narrow lanes, five blocks from the station, that they found the Bali. A neon sign, lit by white and mauve bulbs and mounted on a stand, stood by a doorway with two artificial palm trees which stood incongruously in their pots on either side, attempting without much success to create a tropical atmosphere. A small unlit plaque, inlaid into the wall, declared that a refreshing massage was available for seven thousand yen and requested the visitor to make his way to the reception on the second floor.

'Araki-san,' Chris said, laying a firm hand on Araki's elbow. 'I'll wait for you here.'

'It's OK, it shouldn't be more than forty thousand yen for the two of us. Look.' Araki drew a bulging buff envelope from his jacket pocket and waved it triumphantly in Chris's face. 'I picked up a hundred in advance. We may as well enjoy the job.'

'Look, Araki-san, what I want to say is this.' Trying not to offend the man in whose care he found himself, the young Englishman said nervously, 'I might be meeting someone afterwards.'

Araki looked at his companion, enjoying his discomfort.

'You're living with someone, aren't you?' he said.

61

'Not exactly living,' Chris answered, embarrassed. 'I've an idea. Why don't I go round the corner and telephone the Bali and ask for Maki. That'll only cost us ten yen. If she works there we can go in and talk in the reception.'

Araki shook his head, his patience wearing thin: Chris's limited knowledge of Japanese would fail him after the first exchange and his ignorance of the system was appalling. Above all, he was being kept away from some pleasant on-the-spot investigation, and although the street was deserted he felt self-conscious arguing in front of a massage parlour. He tried not to sound irritated.

'Look,' he said, in the voice of a kindergarten teacher, 'the girls in these places never use their real names. If you telephone for an appointment with someone in particular, a girl who has looked after you before, you have to use their business name.' He lowered his voice and looked over his shoulder. 'The people on the desk won't even acknowledge the existence of a girl by her real name in case the caller happened to be a husband who's wondering why his wife's able to buy Gucci handbags and Hanae Mori dresses from her part-time waitress's wages.'

Chris seemed enthralled, but the look of pained apprehension returned and made it appear as if some invisible hands were tugging at his cheeks.

Araki raised his palms towards Chris. 'OK,' he said glancing in both directions before pointing towards a window which jutted out slightly from the natural line of buildings. 'There's a coffee shop over there next to the magazine shop. Sit in that bay window and make yourself useful by watching for any action. Camera loaded?'

Chris nodded, and weighed the machine in his hand for assurance.

'Catch a couple of pictures of clients going in, not coming out. I don't want their faces exposed and I don't want to have to blank them out. Got it?'

Chris nodded again, and his 'yes' was sharp and unequivocal.

Araki continued. 'I won't be more than forty-five minutes,

and then we'll go down to the Roman for a few drinks. Do you remember where it was? I showed you the building on the way through Shinjuku.'

Chris raised his hand. 'No problem. You just behave in there,' he said, as he crossed the road smiling.

Araki looked for an exit, a stairway or a passage into the entrance, but there was nothing in the gaudy hallway except the elevator. Reaching the second floor, his eyes struggling to adjust to the dark, Araki walked into a huge potted palm tree, rattling its solid base. The reception was suitably dark, surreptitiously sombre, lit only by a pattern of yellow and blue bulbs grouped in the shape of pineapples and hung in clusters from the ceiling. The walls were dotted with assorted shells, including a shiny giant clam, and miniature Polynesian catamarans made from straw or reed. The decorations were as artificial as the atmosphere. And the music – they probably only had one tape, but it was enough to complete the phoney South Sea image. It was the same wailing, electrified Hawaiian guitar music that the waitress in the Camelia had heard in the background when the telephone call had come for Maki. The reporter felt close to Tanimoto's girl. A short thin-faced, bored-looking man in a faded dinner jacket stood behind the corner reception desk and took Araki's seven-thousand yen basic fee.

'Do you have an appointment?' he asked, without looking up.

'No, anyone will do.' Araki wanted to ask for Maki, but caution told him that if Maki had been involved with a man whose death was being investigated by the police it would immediately arouse suspicion, even from the dullard behind the desk. On a rainy evening, he thought, there won't be too many girls on duty, and he might just get lucky.

'Thank you. Please wait over there.' The man beckoned towards a row of cubicles. Araki could see the knees of a man sitting in one of the booths, but strands of tiny seashells hanging half-way to the floor obscured the face. Cigarette smoke oozing between the shells shrouded him in more privacy.

Araki had finished his own cigarette and was thumbing disinterestedly through a pornographic magazine when a woman, wrapped in a crimson knee-length bathrobe, brushed open the curtain, and without looking at him said 'dozo' and beckoned with a hand. He followed her obediently, noticing as he did that all the cubicles were now empty, and was taken to a room on the ground floor, or possibly the basement, by way of a stairway at the end of a corridor. She locked the door and led him to an alcove, separated from the washing area by a thin plastic curtain. The woman was in her early thirties with an attractive, experienced face, but she affected a natural shyness, commenting demurely on the weather, on the impending typhoon, all the while undoing the buttons of his shirt and the belt of his trousers. It was all very formal. Very Japanese.

'What name do you have?' he asked in a voice he would normally use to a woman cutting his hair rather than one removing his underpants.

'It's Shima,' she replied, taking his watch and placing it on the pile of clothes she had carefully folded and stacked on a tray well away from the water. He caught a northern rasp in her voice. Her hair curved around and under her sharp, angular cheekbones and her lips were full and moist.

'Have you been in Tokyo long?' Araki asked, accepting a cigarette.

'About two years.'

'Hokkaido?'

'Akita.'

The couch on which he was sitting naked was in a dimly lit alcove raised above a tiled washing area, whose only outstanding fixture was a bulbous steam cabinet in one corner. The woman was holding a cheap, disposable lighter and stood so close her skin almost touched his; and with her free hand she tapped his elbow, encouraging him to lean forward to reach the lighter. Araki flinched as the fuel combusted in the semi-darkness of the chamber and he adjusted his position to meet it. She urged him closer and chose the instant the flame and the cigarette met to tug

64

imperceptibly at the knot of the cord holding the crimson bathrobe tightly to her.

It opened slowly of its own volition, tracing the curve of her breasts, and exposing a widening triangle of pale skin before falling from her body, dislodged by a shrug of the shoulders. The loose top of the towelling now at her feet had flattened her chest but, once unchecked, her breasts were small, but firm and prominent. Araki wondered if they were real, but opted to postpone the pleasure of touching them until the game had run its course. From where he sat, his eyes were nearly level with the top of her sheer bikini briefs and he stared with silent joy as she waited long enough for him to enjoy the taut, smooth skin and dark triangle showing through the fabric at her crotch. The absence of fatty flab around her panty line excited him.

He drew deeply on the cigarette, stubbing it out only half-smoked; he knew what she was going to ask now and also knew that she need not have bothered. He could not remember the last time he had had sex: perhaps it was with his willing neighbour Yoko six months ago after a bout of drunken horseplay in her flat; but more likely he had relieved himself in the privacy of his own bathroom after watching the late porn shows on TV. But now, as he looked at the lithe body of the young woman, he felt a forgotten heaviness in his scrotum and an intense self-satisfaction at the involuntary swelling of his organ. Shima smiled for the first time, genuinely relieved that Araki was behaving like an ideal customer, docile and, more important than most of the men realised, sober. She respected him for not being drunk, obnoxious and generally uncooperative, like her usual patrons.

'Would you like my special service?' Shima asked, kneeling beside him, a breast against him. 'Or would you just have the steam bath?'

Araki chuckled aloud. 'Yes I would,' he said, wondering what she would do if he asked for the latter. 'How much?'

'Twenty thousand yen please,' she replied, with protracted formality, like a salesgirl in a department store.

'That's a lot,' he said, commenting rather than complaining and leaving the woman in the same position, her hands resting between her knees, as he went to his wallet. He handed her three clean, folded bills, knowing exactly what the magazine's money would buy: and what it wouldn't. He was sure, for instance, he would not be clamped into the steam tub squatting forlornly and cosmetically in the corner. That was there simply to justify the Bali's licence to operate a Turkish bath. Araki smiled again, suspecting that the box was just that: a shell with no working parts inside. The only other items of furniture were more functional: an assortment of ladles, soap dishes, two stools and some pink basins, all made of plastic and arranged so as to be easily reached from the edge of a deep, sunken double bath, covered, like the rest of the washing room, in tiles of cloudy turquoise with occasional palm trees painted among them to remind the guest of the theme. A rippled air-mattress had been inflated and stood upright against the back wall.

Shima flicked a hidden switch and the room was invaded with light orchestral love music while the white light faded out completely to be replaced with an infra-red glow made misty by the steam rising from the water, which wasn't unbearably hot. Even so, Shima knelt down by the bath and stirred with a ladle to release the cooler levels below while her client squatted patiently on a low stool watching the changes and undulations of the near-naked woman's body an arm's length away. He wanted to touch her, and be touched, but he felt inhibited, most likely because he was fully sober.

Shima sensed his anticipation and anxiety and began scooping out ladlefuls of hot water which she poured over him, admonishing as she did so with mock petulance when he protested about the severity of the dousing. Then she soaked a sponge with liquid soap and rubbed it over his body until the frothy lather it produced had cleansed away the sweat of the day and covered him from the neck down. The split seat of the stool allowed her to clean beneath him, which she did with coquettish relish from the rear. Her breasts brushed his back as she leaned against him, close enough for her nipples to reach his skin and graze little furrows through the coat of foam. Enveloping his genitals in a soft, spongy cocoon she squeezed lightly, adjusting the pressure to his breathing. She released and fondled again, while her little finger probed his anus, until his penis responded and swelled hard against his abdomen. Araki's eyes were closed and his breathing reduced to a series of short, irregular gasps. He pressed his midriff forward.

'Don't stop,' he somehow stammered. 'Just like that. Please don't stop.'

And when he thought she might obey him and prolong the delicious agony, Shima giggled and woke him from his coma of pleasure by pouring a cascade of water over him. He shook his head to divert the streams running into his eyes and steeled himself for a fresh assault. It came, but this time it was more gentle, and she brushed away the surviving islands of foam with her hand before inviting him into the bath. Moving behind him, she laid a hand on his shoulder and drew him backwards until he came to rest on the sloping end, his head on the hard rubber rim. He felt the tenseness leave his neck as the hot, soothing, clean water lapped against it. The tub was deep but it was American in length, and Araki enjoyed the new thrill of being immersed to his neck but having his legs outstretched instead of doubled up to his chin.

'Please relax there for a few moments,' she whispered, patting his cheek. 'I'll be ready soon.'

The water relaxed his body and shrivelled his erection in no time to the size of a walnut. While he watched the girl busy herself cleaning and stacking the few utensils she had used and hosing away any traces of soap into the drain, he luxuriated in the womb-like buoyancy of the bath.

His thoughts returned to Maki, the real reason he was here. For all he knew, she was in the next room providing the same service to another man. But he was not convinced: there was something about the poise she had shown under stress in the Camelia coffee shop, and a quality and taste about her clothes and dress sense not normally associated with a massage parlour girl. Kondo would have laughed to hear this. He would have commented, rightly, that Araki had had no time to make such a judgement and he, Kondo, would be delighted to name ten leading actresses and singers, possessing the same poise and class that Araki admired so much, who had started on their roads to fame by bringing relief to tired male bodies in pleasure dens like the Bali. But Araki valued his own intuition in this case. Kondo was invaluable when he took an overview or drew up a list of alternatives, but he failed miserably when he was asked to choose one of his own options. He lacked the street experience; he could not see the lying and deceit that hid behind the façades of respectability that the reporters faced every day; he was too willing to accept the polite vagaries and face-saving posturing for which the Japanese language has been shaped and manipulated, and this caused him to miss the real meaning, the real intention of the speaker.

He was about to pursue his mental questioning of Kondo's conclusion about Maki, and regret his own haste in accepting it in the first instance, when he was again aware of Shima. As he watched, helpless and exposed, she ran her thumbs down over her nipples and stomach and into the elastic top of her panties, which peeled away without resistance. Taking Araki's hand for support, she stepped naked into the bath.

Chris looked nervously at his watch for the fourth time. He had been in the coffee shop over thirty minutes and was toying with his second cup of coffee, where a last piece of ice was moments from extinction. From his window he had a clear, though sharply angled, view of the doorway of the massage parlour, but it was still only eight o'clock and there were two hours of drinking time left before the girls faced their rush-hour and would have to speed up the turnover.

He could not afford to be selective with his targets and snapped the profile of a middle-aged man ducking furtively

68

into the doorway a few minutes after Araki. He followed it with a rearview shot of two Japanese accompanied by a tall, balding Westerner; no doubt, Chris smiled to himself, the fate of a lucrative export contract was about to be sealed in Japan's favour through the attentions of a nubile oriental girl. So far, none of his subjects had noticed the flash, a testimony both to Chris's dextrous use of the camera and to the latest technology which had developed a powerful concentrated bolt of light, hardly distinguishable from a struck match. He thought how easy and less dangerous it would be to concoct a picture using the magazine's staff as 'customers' of the Turkish bath, but Araki would not permit his stories to be embellished with anything other than authentic photographs. To Chris, these were curious scruples: he had been told that Araki had the reputation of a piranha for pursuing and holding a victim until the facts were exposed to full public examination.

Chris took another sip from his glass and then peered into the alley again. Darkness had fallen quickly and the only illumination came from the neon signs, the Bali's being the brightest. They were so spaced that the territory covered by their shafts of light overlapped, and when his eyes had become adjusted to the murkiness Chris found he could see as far past the Bali as the corner of the street. He had not noticed before but the road curved slightly and the coffee shop was positioned on the bend. It levelled out past the Turkish bath before disappearing without end into the night. Chris looked the other way but the curve was against him and he could barely see more than a few yards in that direction.

The young reporter already had two photographs, which might suffice, and as he saw no immediate prospect of another he decided to follow Araki's parting guidance and move on to their designated meeting place in Shinjuku. He moved to look away, but as his curve of vision swung from the street back into the coffee shop a new image disturbed its path and caused Chris to peer again into the darkness.

Past the Bali, a group of people were materialising like

apparitions through a wall. He pressed his nose to the pane and strained to see. As the images sharpened, what at first seemed like a tight knot of people was in fact two men of vastly different physique. The nerves in Chris's cheeks twitched as an involuntary spasm of fear overcame him.

The shorter of the two men was of average build and wore a beige lightweight suit, the jacket of which was square and padded at the shoulders, over a dark blue, possibly black, open-necked shirt. He had an old-fashioned crew-cut and completed the stereotype of a minor hoodlum with a pair of square sunglasses, a sight not uncommon in this part of Tokyo. It was not the sight of this almost comical figure that caused Chris's face to tighten with anxiety but the grotesque, menacing creature striding purposefully alongside him towards the café where Chris was taking refuge. He wore a suit, but would have been more in character in a Sumo wrestler's yukata. At the very least, the wrap-around kimono would have let the man's grossly bloated arms and legs swing and move more freely and the swollen undulating paunch of flesh at his middle hang loose inside the gentler binding of the obi. Forced by his massive bulk, he walked with body stooped forward, arms arching from his shoulders and his square, neckless close-cropped head bobbing in and out of his torso like a giant turtle. A casual observer, seeing this two hundred and fifty pound bulk in the half-light of a humid Tokyo evening, could not have been criticised if he were to assume that he had seen a gorilla stomping the streets.

Chris was relieved when he saw the strangers slowing their pace. They were not looking to take coffee with him. But his sense of deliverance was short-lived. A shadowy figure appeared in a doorway and spoke with emphatic gestures to the two men. After a brief exchange, the three disappeared into the entrance of the Bali.

Araki propped himself up, his back against the tiled wall, legs dangling over the edge and wearing only his underpants. He drew long, deep relaxed drags on a cigarette and watched Shima, dressed again in the purple bathrobe, as she busied

70

herself by tidying up the bottles of scented water, oils and creams and the other tools of her profession. She took time off to offer her client a cold drink from the small fitted refrigerator which he accepted eagerly with a nod of thanks and watched as she knelt again on the floor near his feet. He was almost ready to talk – but not quite.

She had not stayed long in the bath with him. She let him caress her breasts and thighs and probe her intimate places until he reached the point where his passion became urgent and she had to rebuff him politely, teasing and entwining her fingers in his and pushing him gently away.

'Just relax again. I won't be a second,' she had coaxed.

Naked, her skin glistening wet, Shima laid out the air-filled mattress, and splashed it with warm water and liquid, fragrant soap, and beckoned Araki to leave the bath and lie face down on the slippery bed. He rested his head on the bolstered end of the mattress, gripping the edges firmly as the slightest movement caused his body to slither across the ripples towards the tiles. He felt drowsy, and perfectly calm in his vulnerability as Shima worked her skills, slowly whipping the scented soap into a rich lather on Araki's back and buttocks and lingering, as she had done earlier, to press, squeeze and coax his sex parts into life until she had restored his erection and embedded it in the comforting folds of the foamy air-bed. Then she was on top of his back, moving her body effortlessly, rhythmically, back and forwards over the lubricating film of soap they shared.

Like a human wash towel, Shima's body followed the contours of Araki's body, prising open his legs so that her breasts could roll between his thighs and then down the inside, followed closely by a tongue that licked clean the furrows left by her nipples and by teeth that nibbled and teased the soft flesh in their path. Araki chewed a plastic corner while wanting desperately to turn over and see, touch and enjoy the torturing ecstasy he was feeling. But Shima had already spread his legs even further apart, and before he could turn she had slid feet first under him, supporting herself on her elbows and rubbing her midriff against his with a casual stirring motion, all the time complimenting him with exaggerated sincerity on the size and firmness of his erection. She scooped a mound of bubbles and massaged them between his buttocks, pressing and probing until a forefinger eased itself into his back passage. Araki squirmed: he wanted it to end quickly. He grimaced and grunted and pressed his swollen genitals down against the slippery body beneath him.

The rest didn't take long. Shima, the expert, was in full control. In the previous half-hour she had brought him close to climax twice, and when it was obvious he could hold his erection she wanted the real one on her own terms – on the couch, clean and dry and near the protectives. She wriggled from beneath him and stepped again into the brimming tub, entreating him to join her. They stayed only long enough for the suds to dissolve: it would not take more than a few minutes to fill it again for the next customer. The massage girl mopped the dampness from their bodies and laid out her client on the couch like a corpse before rubbing a sweet-smelling oil on his chest and then sucking his nipples. Araki did not notice the pause in the downward trajectory of her lips and wet tongue, nor the hand that reached for the strategically placed condom lodging in the mouth which barely paused before reaching its goal below. With great deftness, Shima inflated the sheath over his hardness. He came only seconds after she had turned him over and inserted him into her. He had gripped her shoulders, thrust wildly and didn't even give her time to affect the sounds of orgasmic delight she had come to perfect over the years.

Sexually expended, and a little guilty for having paid to have his physical need squeezed and burst like a malignant boil, Araki turned to the woman laying out his clothes, seeing her now not as the source of his relief but as the map that would lead him to Maki. She was his antagonist, standing between him and a story that would enhance his hard-won reputation as the ace investigative reporter on the *Tokyo Weekly*. She looked older with the light dimmed; the spotlight illuminated the chamber's almost clinical austerity. Her manner was distracted and disinterested, even as she chatted about inconsequential things and handed him his clothing.

Araki took an envelope from his trouser pocket. He had folded it over itself until it was the size of the name-card he had sealed inside.

'Would you give this to Maki-san please?' he said, optimistically holding out the buff-coloured wedge of paper and looking for some sign from the girl's reaction that she had recognised the name. She was kneeling on the floor by a box of assorted bottles and packets, her left hand holding up the right-hand sleeve of her robe away from the damp patches that remained on the tiles, and was replacing a slim bottle into the lacquer container.

Araki saw a split second of hesitation, perhaps an interrupted blink in an otherwise delicate and exquisitely executed movement, and when she looked directly at him he saw, or thought he saw, a passing flash of fear cross her face.

'Excuse me?' she said, barely audible.

Araki saw no reason to play cat and mouse in a whorehouse.

'When I came here, I asked for Maki,' he lied, 'but the man told me she doesn't work on Mondays.'

Shima stayed silent and expressionless, not drawn to the bait. Araki realised he was still holding the envelope out in front of him and felt slightly foolish. He placed it on the couch within her reach and pressed on.

'I know she works here,' he said, tugging up his trousers. 'Please tell her that a friend of Tanimoto-san has something from him for her and ask her to call me.' He motioned towards the envelope. 'My home number's inside.' And remembering his Wednesday deadline he added. 'She ought to try and get me there anytime between midnight tonight and noon tomorrow.'

The girl absorbed the words and still staring at the floor said slowly and deliberately: 'I think you've made a mistake. There's no one here by the name of Maki.' And as if to compensate for her rudeness she said, 'But there is a Miki. Perhaps you mean her.' With that, she stood up and shuffled Araki's shoes noisily in the doorway, a not very subtle hint that his time was up.

'Look, Shima-san,' he said, in a less aggressive tone as he picked up the envelope that neither of them wanted and followed her to the door. 'I know it's difficult for you to talk openly. I can't tell you who I am or why I have to talk to Maki, but I can tell you that I'm not from the vice squad and I'm not a private detective. I have no interest in getting you into trouble or ever coming here again, but I have something for Maki from someone she knew well and is now dead.'

Araki was surprised at the gentle intensity of his own words and the conviction they held as they flowed from him. He reminded himself that he still had no concrete evidence to link Tanimoto with Maki or Maki with the Bali, and conjecture, inspired or not, had to be used sparingly in the final story. He needed a breakthrough quickly: the girl had to take the envelope.

'What I have to say, and what I have to give to Maki will not hurt her in any way. In fact, there's financial reward for her,' and in an inspired moment he added, 'and for you too.' He drew two ten-thousand yen notes from his billfold and held them out with the envelope.

'All I ask is that you give this envelope to Maki as soon as you can.'

Shima stared at the floor. Then, palm upwards, a hand came cautiously from the sleeve of her robe turning as it emerged. But the hand that had reached out suddenly now withdrew as if it had been bitten by a snake.

A noise, a shuffling of feet, grew louder in the corridor outside the room and they both reacted. The fear that Araki had suspected earlier was now visible in the woman's eyes and frozen features. A man's voice could be heard, speaking in hushed tones, very near their door. It was joined by a woman's, emitting high-pitched giggles. Shima breathed out and smiled nervously as a door closed nearby and the sound of voices melted behind it. As if on cue, a red light over the door chose that moment to flash.

'Thank you for coming here,' she said, bowing lightly, her poise and self-control restored, 'but I'm afraid my next client is here.' She brushed past him to open the door. As she did so, she took the envelope and money without further comment and ushered him outside.

# CHAPTER FOUR

A welcome breeze, a deceptive, frisky forerunner to the winds of the typhoon now gathering strength to the southeast of Okinawa, was causing flimsier signs to sway and creak on their rusty hinges. Araki breathed the refreshing air deeply and allowed himself a few sharp stretches of his arms and a wide head roll, which left him revived and invigorated. He hoped he had found the right place, but he wouldn't object if his search took him somewhere similar. He felt good, knowing that the weakness in his knees was not entirely the after-effects of his fast disappearing summer cold, and looked forward to Mama Yoshida's draught Sapporo at the Roman. But his euphoria evaporated, and this time the weakness was in the pit of his stomach. Chris was not sitting by the window in the coffee shop opposite.

Araki shook his head in disbelief. 'Please, not again' he pleaded into the night. He remembered finding his last assistant lying among some bags of garbage in a dead-end alley. Inexperienced and impetuous, he had tried only eight months earlier to interview a woman involved in an affair with a prominent politician, and having no idea how to phrase the pertinent questions he was rewarded with a bottle blow to the cranium. There was a slim chance that Araki would find Chris paying his bill at the counter, but he knew he wouldn't. The waiter said yes, he had noticed a foreigner with a camera sitting over there and yes, he did leave in a hurry. That's the last time a clown or a gaijin is foisted on me, thought Araki, as he too left in a rush.

He never should have driven his car. It was almost the last

day of August, the unofficial end to the summer holidays, when, however hot the weather, the swimming pools close down and the Japanese population dutifully return on time from their three-day summer breaks and prepare themselves mentally to begin the final assault on the economic targets they have been set for the year. Snarled in a lurching snake of traffic in Meiji-dori on the final approach to Shinjuku, Araki assumed that many of the passengers were having a last fling. It took him a full forty minutes to drive the three kilometres from the Bali to the speck of road he chose to park on in front of the Koma theatre. The Roman was one of half a dozen dim snackbars sharing a basement in the narrow shaft of a building, purpose-built for restaurants of all sizes, and whose clientele was made up of regulars. All three tables were occupied and the two resident hostesses flitted from one to another, staying just long enough to giggle at the wit of the red-faced salarymen and help them along the road to oblivion by pouring generous helpings of whisky from the bottles the men kept for their personal use, paying only for the soda, snacks and service.

Araki's friend of many years, Abe, sat at the counter with Mama Yoshida, a fat old ex-geisha whose make-up could be removed with an oar. The only other guest of the house was a stranger to Araki and he sat at the end of the bar fondling a glass of whisky with both hands while staring at the array of bottles along the wall behind the counter.

'Araki-san!' screamed Mama, 'come and sit over here. We were just talking about you.'

Araki greeted the hostesses and Abe, and hoisted himself on to the backless stool beside the extrovert Mama Yoshida. He ran his hand playfully under the fold of her kimono and squeezed her generous thighs, causing her to cackle with delight.

'How's business, Mama?' he asked, forcing a smile, in spite of the apprehension he felt about Chris's safety.

'Twenty years ago,' she quipped with mock indignation as she removed his hand, 'twenty years ago you'd have had to finish what you started. Now, what can I get you? Your bottle?' She made her way awkwardly to the other side of the counter.

'No, I'll start with beer. By the way,' he asked, addressing his question to the room in general, 'has a thin, blond foreigner been here looking for me? I hope you didn't refuse to let him in.'

Mama sucked in air and inclined her head down and to the left. 'No, I've not seen him tonight. What about you Shoji-san?'

The bartender shook his head and continued his search for Araki's personal bottle of Suntory. He found it and put with it an ice-bucket and a bottle of soda water next to the large glass of beer Mama poured for Araki.

The beer was instant relaxation as it ran down a parched throat. Araki blinked and licked away a moustache of froth before finishing the glass in a single gulp.

His thirst satiated, and enjoying the lull in the conversation as Mama Yoshida prepared his whisky and soda with exaggerated care, Araki's thoughts and the trepidation he felt for the safety of his young charge returned. His anger had turned to real concern and his mind to the many scenarios that could have caused Chris to disobey his instructions. He looked at his watch. It was well after ten.

At best, he hoped Chris had taken his pictures and then become browned off with waiting and, having forgotten that they had agreed to meet here at the Roman, had gone straight home to his flat in Mita. But the world Araki and his colleagues observed was outside the fortified and sterilised environs in which the protected populace lived: where the housewife saw a pinball parlour, a massage house or an all-night gay bar, Araki saw an underworld struggle for territorial supremacy with police pay-offs and protectionism; when the childish pranks of the drunken salarymen had ended and the hostess clubs were closed Araki found the pimps and their stables of women, the blackmail and the drugs; when the politician appeared on television displaying an impassive façade of immense propriety, Araki already had a file on his corrupt manipulations of Japan's fragile democratic processes, his pay-offs and his mistresses; and when the president of Mitsu-this or Sumi-that pontificated with unbearable sincerity on the policy of social responsibility being pursued by his company, Araki saw the cartels, the rebates and the unprincipled, opportunistic strategies of a market dominated by greed. And the violence.

There was no doubt that among the economically rich nations, Japan stood out as the safest in the world to live: the streets were free of muggers and rapists and bank robbers were rare; children ride the trains late at night in no danger from the ubiquitous drunks. Araki had often tried to comprehend this unusual phenomenon of an almost crime-free society and tried now to rationalise away the fear he felt for Chris. Apart from the obvious passivity of the people, the high degree of civil obedience probably had much to do with the fact that it was very hard to get away with a crime here. The whereabouts of every citizen was always carefully recorded and monitored by the local ward administrative offices and in the omnipresent police-boxes scattered strategically around residential and entertainment areas. On top of this, the Japanese aversion to strangers makes it impossible for the wrong-doer or the runaway to melt into the environment, even in bustling Shinjuku or Roppongi. In spite of the physical similarity of the people. Araki stifled a chuckle, contemplating that any one face on the 'wanted' posters outside police-boxes could easily fit most of his friends, and a good half of the Japanese population.

But was this abhorrence of violence a real reflection of the Japanese character, or was it a superhuman effort by the generation of the eighties to suppress their natural expressions of release? Since he had fallen from the stage-managed world of political reporting to what was called 'social' coverage, Araki had subconsciously and inevitably come to believe the latter thesis. He had worked on stories where a normal, staid salaryman, unable any longer to bear the futility of polite, self-effacing complaint against a noisy neighbour or the inhuman and wretched tolerance towards an ignorant and bullying boss would, in a moment of mental

79

aberration, seize a kitchen knife and bury it into the chest of the first person to meet him when his self-control finally cracked.

It also happened on a mass scale. During a token morning work-to-rule by members of the National Union of Railway Workers only the previous March, commuter trains, which have to run three minutes apart to prevent an unimaginable congestion of humanity, were arriving at stations of the high density Chuo Line ten minutes apart. At one station, the sight of a train stopped defiantly fifty metres from the platform caused a unified explosion of anger among the normally tolerant commuters. The railway staff were jostled and harassed, the station master's office stoned and wrecked and when they had vented their displeasure the frustrated travellers spilled on to the tracks, where they risked their lives to complete the journey by foot. The threshold of tolerance, the moment when the cork pops to release the bottled, pent-up emotions that parents, teachers and employers have worked tirelessly to force the Japanese to keep suppressed, is a long way beyond that of the average Latin or even the American.

'But when we cross that threshold, go over the precipice, we become irrational, unable to temper the response to the required degree of gravity of the situation.'

Araki had the undivided attention of Mama Yoshida and the bartender, neither of whom were used to hearing a discourse on behavioural psychology in their bar, but Abe was deep in conversation with the younger of the hostesses who was taking a break from her table duties to sit at the counter.

Mellowed with whisky and encouraged by the docile nods of agreement from his captive audience, Araki intended to launch into part two of his monologue, having strayed from his initial theme, which was his growing fear for the safety of his colleague, Chris. The table parties were breaking up; one group was pooling their funds and the other was already meandering unsteadily towards the door. Araki did not have to check his watch to tell it was eleven o'clock, time for the evening rush hour. One of the men, his head flopping around like a puppet's, was gesticulating, with the deliberate insistence of the drunk, to convince his friends he was capable of negotiating the doorway and the steps beyond without help. As it was, his faltering hand came to rest on the doorknob at the very moment someone chose to turn it more forcefully from the other side. His body now irretrievably off-balance, the unfortunate man, a look of astonishment fixed on his face, tumbled outside, narrowly missing Chris who saw the danger and stepped nimbly aside.

He had the wide-eyed look of a hunted man, and as Araki steered him towards a vacant table it was obvious Chris had been moving in a hurry through the muggy streets. His skin shone from the sweat and his hair was plastered down as if he had been through a shower. Araki tried not to look or act relieved.

'Give him a beer, Shoji-san, and make me a refill please.' Then he turned to Chris.

'Are you all right?' Araki asked with feeling, his English hurried and poorly accented. Chris was sucking at the froth and then gulped audibly as his lips reached the beer, slowing down only to look in Araki's direction and nod in reply. 'Then where the hell have you been for the last three hours?' he asked, his voice now suddenly deep and harsh in his throat.

Chris settled back in his seat and put the nearly empty glass in front of him. Mama Yoshida and one of her girls gathered round, begging for a translation.

'Well, I took a couple of pictures of people who went after you into the er . . . er . . .'

'Turkish bath,' said Araki, barely hiding his disdain for Chris's modesty.

'Er, yes, quite. But as it was still early for these places, and don't forget it's still only Monday, I decided to pack it in and make my way here. In fact, I'd already asked for the bill, when I . . .'

'Chris, my friend,' interrupted Araki, 'you sound more like Kondo every day.'

'Excuse me?'

'Nothing, carry on.'

'Well, two men came along. They looked like your real gangster type. Crew-cuts and pinstripes and all. One of them was really weird. I don't think he was deformed, probably a thyroid problem, but he was built like that Sumo wrestler Kitanoumi and looked like Godzilla. I don't know why, but I thought they were coming for me. Just when I was about to look for the back entrance a man came out of the Bali and spoke to them, and then they all went inside.'

Chris saw the incredulous look on Araki's face, and anticipating a question, waved his hand. 'I was going to follow them in and somehow alert you.'

'Thank the gods you didn't,' Araki interrupted. 'Sorry. Carry on.'

'Well, I stayed in the coffee shop for about ten minutes and then hung around on a corner. I was really confused, I didn't know what to do. They could have been regular customers for all I knew, and I couldn't have talked my way in with my Japanese. Anyway, I was still debating the options when the two men came out. I suppose I reacted automatically. I walked up to the door, looking as casually as I could at the sign and trying to look like an inquisitive gaijin. They took a quick look at me and carried on chatting in the doorway. They were grinning and saying something like "hayaku, hayaku".'

'Quickly,' Araki translated.

'Right, I got that and I thought I heard your name.'

Araki's face was creased with scepticism. He ran his fingers through his thinning hair, looked into his drink and said: 'So what did you do?'

'What could I do?' replied Chris, throwing up his arms. 'I followed them.'

Araki looked at the young reporter with resignation, recalling the aftermath of his predecessor's individual quest for honours and the smell of ether that accompanied the repairs, but beckoned him to continue.

'They went to a private parking lot near the station and

got into their car. The big man was driving, and he had a hard time getting through the gate. I had lined up my camera to get them as they went by. Honestly, I hadn't planned to follow them, but an empty taxi had to slow down to let their car out. The guy wouldn't take me at first, I think he wanted a drunk out to the suburbs, but when I told him to follow the dark green Toyota, he said . . .'

Araki placed a hand on his colleague's arm, firmly enough to make him pause. 'What did you say?'

'I said that the taxi driver wouldn't take me because . . .'

'No, no, what did you say about the car?'

'I told him to follow the green Toyota,' Chris said, puzzled.

'That's what I thought you said. Quickly, what happened next?'

'The traffic was pretty bad, especially around Mejiro, and the cab stopped so close to the Toyota so often that I was sure they'd notice me. Anyway, they kept going down Meiji-dori towards Shinjuku, and I hoped they would stop there so that I could get out myself and come to the Roman. Unfortunately, they stayed on Meiji. With me behind them.'

'Did you get the number of the car?' asked Araki.

Chris was exasperated. Nothing he said seemed to satisfy his boss's appetite for more facts. What did he want? The colour of their eyes and the names of their favourite baseball teams?

'I'm sorry, but I never really got a clear view straight behind their car, and when I did get close the lights played tricks and . . .'

'And what?'

'I'm not a bloody detective,' he said trying to control his temper. 'Anyway, I'm not very good at numbers, but maybe something will show up in the photographs.'

'What photographs?' asked Araki, almost choking as Chris's words caught him with his glass tipped well into his mouth.

'Well, as I had my long lens on anyway, I thought I might snap a few when I could. I was almost level with their car

83

a couple of times at traffic lights and squeezed off three or four shots. I don't know what they're like because I had to take my glasses off to take the pictures.'

Araki slammed his empty glass on to the table, causing Chris to wince. 'You're crazy. You know, absolutely mad. The last time one of my assistants tried to photograph from a distance of three metres he nearly had a Nikon rammed down his throat.'

Araki listened as Chris mumbled on about golden opportunities and risks worth taking, but his own thoughts were on the two occupants of the green Toyota. Green Toyota. The description of the car interested him, the colour stimulating his memory, but there was something unusual about the behaviour of the pair in it that disturbed him. Even if the underworld managed the Bali, it was most strange for two of their enforcers to be so overt as to appear at its door during business hours. It would certainly frighten away any potential customers. And customers they were not. According to Chris, the employee in the tuxedo clearly knew them when they appeared at the Bali and he had led them inside. What for? Something to do with Araki? No, it did not seem possible. No one outside the editorial group of the magazine, and Inspector Nishii of course, knew that he was working on the Tanimoto story, and even if he had been noticed at the Camelia, or reported by the dim waitress to the next investigator to come along with a thick billfold, no one would have known he was to be in the Bali on this Monday night. Unless he was expected. Unless someone feared he might probe further, tempted by a potentially salacious story. But if he had been picked up at the Bali, for reasons he could not fathom, why was he being followed? The two men were at the door of the Bali even before he had started to question the girl about Maki! And the massage girl herself had no chance at all to send out signals or warnings. The man on the reception desk had his description and was waiting for him.

'Wait a second,' he said, his thought returning to the car. 'What colour did you say it was?'

'What?'

'The car. The car you followed.'

Chris shrugged his shoulders, 'Green, dark green.'

'Mama!' Araki's sudden outburst jolted the lone drinker who had been dozing at the counter.

'Mama, have you got Saturday's *Yomiuri*?'

'No, I don't take it.'

'Do you have any Saturday paper?' he asked impatiently.

'Wait a moment, I'll look.' Mama Yoshida slid awkwardly from the stool and shuffled off to her back room, returning within minutes with a small heap of ruffled newspapers. 'I've found an *Asahi*, a *Fuji* and the racing paper. Any use?'

'Let me have a look at the *Asahi*.'

Araki sorted through the pile of papers, discarding the financial and advertising supplements until he found the main body which held the ordinary news of the day. He found what he was looking for on page four, and nodded while he read, confirming what he had suspected. He pushed the page in front of Chris, forgetting his colleague could read nothing, and resumed the conversation in hushed tones.

'Just what I thought. The *Asahi* quotes the same police statement as the *Yomiuri*. Can you understand what I'm getting at?'

Chris frowned: he clearly could not see what Araki had. 'Wakaranai,' he said.

Araki leaned across the table and tapped the paper with his forefinger.

'Read the last line of the police comment,' he ordered and then he remembered who he was with. 'Sorry Chris,' he said. 'It says: "So far, the police have no clues to the motive or the culprit but they are anxious to interview the driver of a green, or possibly blue, saloon car seen—" Now do you get it?'

Chris did, but he shook his head in apprehension.

'It must be coincidence,' he said, with obvious scepticism.

'It probably is, but I want you to note three recorded sightings of a green saloon. Where the body was found; two

85

days later behind me near the Diet; and now you actually followed one. Anyway, where were you? Oh yes, you'd taken photos from your cab window. Get them printed and blown up as soon as you can. Carry on, I can hardly wait to hear where your grand tour of Tokyo ended.'

Chris took a moment to collect his thoughts and proceeded. 'We stayed on the main road, what's it called?' He tapped his brow.

'Meiji. Meiji-dori,' Araki prompted.

'Right, Meiji. We stayed on Meiji and, as I said, we went through Shinjuku. The traffic was lighter once we'd passed Isetan department store and it looked as though we were making straight for Shibuya; but just past Yoyogi they turned off the main road.'

'They what?' Araki's voice rose with surprise. 'Where exactly past Yoyogi?'

Abe, three seats down, saw a chance to practise his English and hollered confidently, and loudly enough, to distract the speakers. 'Are you American?'

Araki turned on him, dismissing Abe's flippancy with a swipe of his arm. 'What were you saying, Chris?' he said.

'Let's see. We crossed three or four sets of lights after going under the expressway and they turned just before we reached the next main intersection. Is something the matter?' He saw Araki's expression change.

'Which way did they turn?' Araki demanded.

'It was right, they turned right.'

'When they turned right,' Araki hissed, each word etched with urgency, 'did you notice a school on the left?'

Chris rubbed his wrist against his chin. 'I seem to remember that there was a two- or three-storey building on the left. There were no lights on, so it wasn't an apartment block. Yes, I suppose it could have been a school. Why do you ask?'

'It was a school,' replied Araki. 'Sendagaya Primary. Did you follow them down the side road?'

'No, it looked as though they had reached their destination so I stopped the taxi on the corner and just watched.' Chris,

86

in his innocence, was beginning to sense his colleague's unease. 'They went down the road about two hundred yards and stopped. I had the driver drop me at Harajuku Station and I came straight here on the train.' His voice trailed off to a whisper.

'You know where they went, don't you?' Chris said.

Araki drank the contents of his glass in one swallow and stubbed out a freshly lit cigarette. He motioned Chris to finish too. His voice was controlled when he began but broke up by the end.

'Yes I do. They went to my apartment. Let's go.'

He drove carefully and deliberately, wary of police patrols with their summary powers to confiscate his driving licence for the slightest trace of alcohol in his blood. It was after one o'clock before he woke the janitor, a fragile retired man who would not have been much use if the intruders were still there, to make up a trio with which to face whatever fate had in store. Araki knew he had been set up, but by whom? He was now sure he had been followed as early as Sunday morning when the only car near him on the quiet avenues in the Diet had been a green saloon. Or even before. Had they picked him up sooner? At the Camelia? He cursed his inattention. As far as he could tell, there was no possible reason why he should be marked, but he also knew that the two characters spotted by Chris had used the time he had been a captive client in the Bali to violate his apartment. He hoped they had left. They had.

Chris gaped, while the old porter clasped his face in despair. Araki looked at the mess with resignation, then with increasing anger as his vision came more sharply into focus on the scene of utter desolation and waste, like the aftermath of an earthquake he had once covered for an article.

Rectangular pieces of tatami mat which had covered the floor of his living-room and study had been torn from their concrete beds, slashed and scattered round the apartment. The desk and bookcase had been emptied and their contents thrown into the holes left by the tatami; a sharp instrument

87

had been used to rip open his mattress and quilt, and bits of orange foam filling and snowy down spilled out like the guts of a disembowelled chicken. Strewn among the debris were the reporter's underwear, cuff links, spare wallet, scarves, gloves and other accessories he kept in the drawer of a fitted cupboard in his sleeping area.

An emergency fund of fifty thousand yen in five old notes had been unearthed from its hideaway at the bottom of a small tea-chest where Araki kept his winter clothes and somewhat curiously, Araki thought, left in a neat bundle on the floor. To reach the money Araki tiptoed across the kitchen floor where globs of corn oil, milk and soya sauce had been emptied with sugar, rice, coffee, green tea and the contents of his refrigerator. He kept his shoes on and motioned Chris to do likewise. The examination had been thorough. If they had been looking for something it must have been small, for every possible hiding-place had been searched: they had even torn open his record sleeves, scattering the contents like discarded frisbees.

Araki picked up a lacquer rice bowl, filled it with whisky from his mercifully unbroken collection of bottles, and drank deeply.

'I've made a big mistake, Chris,' he said. 'I've missed something. Some fact, some incident between the morgue and the Bali stared me in the face and I missed it, and this is the result.'

Chris was quietly suffering his own brand of remorse, which was much more painful to take after the high he had felt from his success with the photographs. He buried his chin in his chest.

'It's completely my fault,' he stammered, almost in tears. 'I should have known where you lived and called the police. I can't find words to say how . . .'

'Shut up, Chris, you're starting to sound like a Japanese. We can fairly assume,' Araki continued diffidently, 'that this bust-up is not an ordinary burglary and has got something to do with my story about Tanimoto's death.'

He moved around the room, clearing the debris aside

with his feet and laying strips of reed mat back into their place.

'What gets me is why nobody heard what was going on. Didn't anyone report any unusual noise? Did you see any odd-looking strangers come in?' He addressed the porter, who shook his head and hissed in response. The old fool was probably drunk, Araki assumed, or watching television, or both, and his enthusiasm for overseeing the comings and goings in this apartment block had long since waned; and he was so used to fielding complaints about noise from Araki's flat that he no longer took them seriously. Araki was raising his voice again, and lights he couldn't see were popping on like coloured tiles on a mosaic all over the building.

'Oughtn't I to call the police?' asked the old man with trepidation.

'No,' said Araki, pushing him firmly towards the open door. 'Nothing seems to be missing. Probably some mistake. Calm the neighbours down and get to bed. Many thanks for your help.'

Relieved, the porter shuffled off down the landing bowing in atonement towards the source of the voice on the fifth floor which requested in polite tones a greater degree of silence.

'Araki-san, look at this.' Chris was holding his hand against the side of a triple-tiered music centre. 'The power switch is lit up. The machine's still on. It's warm.' Chris hoped his discovery would restore him in some measure to Araki's affection and confidence.

'That's how they covered the noise,' said Araki with grudging admiration for the intruders. 'I wonder if they knew that Yoko wouldn't be home yet and the old man on the other side is away in the country on a prolonged obon.'

He lifted the record, an old noisy collection of Rolling Stones hits he had not played for years, and spun it between his forefingers.

'They even knew what to play,' he mused. 'Hey, where's the phone?'

Chris's head pivoted and he scanned the room without knowing where to look.

Araki ran his hands over the desk where the telephone and his pens and notepads should have been. It was already well past two, and he had left a message that he could be contacted any time after midnight. Araki slapped his thigh in anger. Had the unlikely happened? Had Maki existed, and was she working as a massage girl at the Bali, and had she been dialling his number without success, anxious to get her hands on a few thousand yen in exchange for the sordid details of her life with Tanimoto? Impatient to go home to sleep, had she decided the whole thing was a hoax and given up? Where was the damned phone? He dropped the record on to the turntable and knelt down to rummage through a heap of books and papers swept on to the floor out of anger, frustration or perhaps sheer pleasure by persons unknown. Unknown, at least until Chris's pictures were developed.

The telephone was on the floor where it had fallen, its impact cushioned by a heap of mats, and was covered by bits of bedding and other debris. It was still connected to the wall socket. Relieved, he pressed the receiver to his ear and tapped repeatedly at the cradle. It clicked instantly and went into a constant purr. He quickly hung up and held the telephone for a moment before replacing it on the desktop. He then wanted to be alone, to be rid of the Englishman and to dispel the growing feeling of fear and excitement until tomorrow.

'Get your photos printed early tomorrow and bring them round here. I have to stay here all morning in case Maki calls,' he said. 'See what Kondo's got for me and ask him to come with you if he can. You'd better be off, we've a lot to do tomorrow.'

# CHAPTER FIVE

In his semi-comatose state, Araki confused the chime of his doorbell with the hoped-for ring of the telephone. He rolled over, his right hand groping for the leg of the desk and then feeling its way up until it found the phone. His fingers juggled the receiver until it held firm.

The ringing had stopped, to be replaced by the persistent rapping of a fist against metal. Araki shook his head, replaced the instrument and scratched a greasy, itchy scalp. His brain was slow to react to the entreaty from outside, and he slumped back confused. Sprawled on a makeshift futon of reed mats, torn bedding and mattresses he looked as if he had been dropped from a great height on to matchwood furniture.

He had worked on late into the night, almost until the pigeons had begun squawking on the telegraph lines outside, scribbling an outline, blowing it up into a rough first draft which would be his submission to the editor. He created contingencies in places to cover a scenario with Maki, the female interest, and another without her. Finally, as he lay on his pathetic bed, he planned another series of probes into the death of Akira Tanimoto for the week ahead.

The sounds were falling into place; the raps on the door were now interspersed with a voice imploring him to open it. They had a sense of urgency, as if the speaker expected Araki to be in danger or somehow indisposed. It was Chris, standing mouth agape in some fearful expectancy, with Kondo and their feline assistant, Keiko.

Keiko grimaced at the sight of a greasy, unshaven, unwashed Araki standing in the doorway, one hand acting as a prop, and wearing nothing but his dirty, wrinkled underpants which hung like a shrivelled jock-strap beneath a fold of belly flab.

'We've come to help you clean up a bit.' It was Keiko who broke the silence. 'Why don't you take a shower while we get on with it.'

Two of the general office girls materialised bearing mops, rags and buckets and, led by Keiko, began establishing priority tasks. By the time Araki had washed, shaved and dressed, the cleaning operation was well under way. The mess on the kitchen floor had gone and the freshly scrubbed vinyl tiles were almost dry; the cracked or broken containers were discarded in black plastic garbage bags and the shelves stacked again with bottles and jars that had not been broken. The team were about to start on the living- and sleeping-rooms.

'Listen to me for a second please,' Araki commanded, feeling revived and invigorated, and wanting to lose no more time – it was ten-thirty and he wondered whether he had slept through a telephone call. 'I'm going to the coffee shop for some breakfast with Kondo-san and Chris here. Keiko-chan, stay here and organise the clean-up please, and keep alert for a phone call. I think I've traced Tanimoto's girl and she may call me.'

Kondo lifted his head, but, not surprisingly, received no acknowledgement or thanks for having deduced her whereabouts by a process of elimination.

'If the voice is female,' Araki continued, 'just ask if it's Maki-san. If it is, ask her to wait and haul your lovely bottom at Olympic speed to the coffee shop. Turn right outside the block and it's right there on the corner of Meiji-dori. Got it?'

Keiko nodded and adjusted her sunglasses until they almost disappeared into her hair.

In the coffee house Araki quickly brushed aside the photographs of the Bali's clients. They were only of cosmetic value and would suffice. No, he wanted to see the pictures Chris had taken impetuously and at some risk from the back

92

of his pursuing taxi. He wanted to see his aggressors, to heap unspoken hatred on those who had violated his privacy and to commit their faces to his memory bank. It was clear that the evocative noises Araki was emitting between bites of toast and boiled egg were expressions of admiration at the clarity of the four exposures laid out on the table.

'He's a big bastard,' he mumbled.

They stared at one picture in particular. It showed a clear profile of a man so large that he was hunched in the driving seat, head and shoulders compressed and the bulk of his body obscuring all but a fragment of the wheel. Kondo anticipated Araki's question.

'I haven't been able to identify him yet – I only saw the picture myself an hour ago, but the way Chris describes him, I would bet a year's salary he has some sort of record.'

The other three pictures showed the rear and side from a widening distance because, as Chris apologetically explained, he feared discovery after taking the first one almost alongside the mark and fell back. Araki spread the photographs on the table, nodding his head in approval and grimacing from the strength of the thick, oily coffee. They were remarkably clear given the circumstances of the surreptitious chase and the inherent danger.

'That's a Corona, isn't it?' Araki said speculatively.

'No, it's a Mark Two, eighteen hundred, probably last year's model,' Kondo corrected. 'Unfortunately, the number plate is obscured and Chris was unable to observe it clearly during the journey.'

Araki looked at his watch: it was five past eleven. He beckoned the waitress to bring more coffee before offering his next theory.

'The police said someone saw a green car driving away from the place they found Tanimoto's body. I'm certain in my mind that it was the same car.'

He knew he was being provocative, and without moving his head he flicked his eyes to capture the reaction of his colleagues. Kondo was shaking his head.

'I think you'll find the report said "green or blue". And

there really isn't any evidence to connect the break-in at your flat with your Tanimoto story.'

Araki knew his wiser colleague was trying to help but he saw his own success was a tribute to his sharp perception and unusually accurate intuition and he took Kondo's dangled bait harshly and thumped the table for emphasis when he spoke.

'There has to be. These two characters came out of the Bali knowing I'd be stuck in the bloody bath for half an hour and very likely to move on to the nearest bar. They knew they had enough time to wreak a little havoc in my flat.'

Kondo interrupted. 'But they couldn't have known where you lived.'

'They could,' retorted Araki. 'And they did,' he grinned ruefully. 'It was the coffee shop. I had to tell the waitress where I worked. I even showed her one of my articles in the magazine. With the help of five thousand yen it impressed her enough to talk about the dead man and the woman he used to come in with.' He scoffed, himself the object of his derision. 'And she was sitting in a booth, a half-dozen paces away!'

Chris heard mention of the Camelia and comprehended the context from Araki's gestures and tone and said in English:

'You think Maki or her friends called or came back to find out who the inquisitive stranger was?'

'I'm certain.'

'They must have worked quickly,' the Englishman said. 'They knew where you worked but they'd have to talk to someone at the magazine to get your home address.'

'They wouldn't have to,' said the journalist. 'I left my name-card by the cash register when I paid.'

Chris groaned, while Araki translated for Kondo.

'Like the one you gave to the girl in the massage parlour,' the older man said.

Araki could only nod.

It was now Kondo's turn to pause in contemplation. Araki's watch read eleven thirty-five: he looked towards the door, begging it to open. Chris, his high forehead furrowed as he tried to follow the Japanese, used the silence of his colleagues to think aloud.

'If what you suppose is correct, Maki's had your home address and telephone number for two days. If she hasn't called you so far, why should she do so now?'

'Because I've asked her to,' Araki retorted.

Chris continued to provide the logic. 'But if her first contact with you has led to your flat being turned over, what will the next one do?'

'It hardly looks as if there'll be a next time.'

Chris went on undeterred. 'Your activities at the Bali,' he said, unable to hide a trace of distaste, 'gave those two men the chance to wreck your flat while you were otherwise occupied. I would say that they were trying to give you a message, to scare you off.'

'No they weren't,' replied Araki with certainty. 'They could have done that much more convincingly in the bath-house.' He chuckled as he recalled his vulnerability on the mattress and then shivered to imagine what they could have done to him. 'No, I think they were looking for something, and the only thing I have to connect me to Tanimoto is the list. And I don't even have that. You have it, don't you Kondo-san?'

'Have what?' Kondo asked perplexed.

'Gomen-nasai,' Araki said. 'Do you have the Tanimoto list with you?'

Kondo produced from his wallet the unintelligible list of letters and numbers Araki had found hidden in Tanimoto's season ticket. He held the brittle paper at arm's length, shaking his head and studying the annotations with an intensity which showed that the solution still eluded him.

'I presume you haven't cracked it yet,' said Araki, munching on a piece of toast and checking his watch.

'No, I haven't, but can I fill you in with some details of Tanimoto's employers?'

'Please,' replied Araki.

'The New Japan Socio-Economic Research Institute is the

umbrella organisation for a group of ten sokaiya.' Kondo cleared his throat, a request for attention. 'They operate out of offices in the Nagano Number Ten Building near the TBS studio in Akasaka: and the president is one Teruaki Ogawa. Their income for tax purposes is, like most of the other sokaiya, ostensibly from the sale of subscriptions to a monthly newsletter which gives a rather puerile overview of economic and financial matters, and if Matsuhashi is anything to go by, they probably have some very influential clients amongst their subscribers. The whole thing is, of course, a cover for their normal role as enforcers of the peace at shareholders' meetings in return for substantial fees.'

Kondo lowered his papers, giving Araki the chance to translate for Chris. He waited and then said, 'And as your own research showed, any company that refused the protection of the sokaiya would find that the skeletons they had carefully hidden in the corporate cupboard were suddenly liable to fall out.'

'Blackmail,' interjected Araki.

'Blackmail in all but name,' replied Kondo, 'but few, if any, of our industrial giants would prefer disclosure of even minor travesties if, for a relatively small sum, they could guarantee temporary respite as well as receive some un-official support with troublesome shareholders.'

Chris had listened patiently, concerned about the time but bemused by the conversation and his ignorance of the topic.

'What are the police doing while this is going on under their noses?' he asked.

'The police,' replied Araki condescendingly, 'the police cannot act unless there's a complaint, and so far there haven't been any from the corporations, big or small. The poor old shareholder occasionally submits a private complaint when one of the sokaiya comes on a bit heavy, but otherwise this is a dark facet of Japanese-style management that goes unrecorded and unpunished.'

His watch showed that it was only ten minutes from twelve o'clock. Ten minutes had evaporated amid conversation and pauses to think and drink, and there was still no sign of the messenger, Keiko.

Kondo shuffled his papers until he found one in particular.

'I've updated some of the statistics you used in your earlier article on the sokaiya and thrown in some of my own comments.' He looked to Araki for a sign to continue. The latter nodded. 'There are about seven thousand individuals operating as sokaiya, some alone and some, like Tanimoto, under the control of a legitimate organisation. In 1981 they shared more than a hundred and seven billion yen in income.'

Kondo spoke precisely, confident of the accuracy of his records. 'We are certain that at least half of the fourteen hundred companies listed on the Tokyo Stock Exchange pay fees to the sokaiya for their help in speeding the passage of stockholders' meetings in June and December. Individual payments range from twenty thousand to twenty million yen. There doesn't seem to be any trend away from the sokaiya,' Kondo speculated. 'Our corporations have so many grey areas of business that there's always something worth paying to be kept quiet. The Commercial Code will be revised in October with the specific objective of curbing the sokaiya.'

Araki was distracted and stared out of the window, but Chris was mesmerised.

'Are they connected with the crime syndicates?' he asked, in simple Japanese.

'Who? The sokaiya or the companies?' In his effort to stay with the language, Chris missed Kondo's attempt at wit.

'The sokaiya,' he said innocently.

'By the nature of their business,' Araki explained, 'they must have some connections, but if they are in fact controlled by the big gangs they take very great pains to conceal it. If it was proved that the sokaiya shared the same bed with self-confessed underworld names, then the police would be obliged to act. No, no one has got around to trying to unravel the puzzle, which is what the sokaiya and their kind are, without running into a wall of silence that makes the Mafia code of *omertà* sound like the La Scala Opera Company in full cry.'

97

Chris saw the logic and pursued the argument. 'But I think we've found a connection. We know that Tanimoto was a sokaiya and two of his gangster friends wrecked Araki-san's flat because he was getting close.'

'Rubbish!' said Kondo, with uncharacteristic ferocity. He could not express himself in English, but understood it perfectly. He spoke to Araki in Japanese. 'If he's going to use that kind of logic he won't make it as a reporter, not in Japan anyway, even with the *Tokyo Weekly*. Let me remind you that all we have is a man who may or may not have been a fulltime sokaiya; who may or may not have been the lover of a woman who may, but probably does not, work in a turko from where two men emerged who may or may not be mobsters and who may or may not have broken into your flat. That's what we've got, and,' he looked at his watch, 'if this is correct, that's about as much as we're going to have.'

It was ten past twelve.

'She's here. It's Keiko!'

Araki's assistant was walk-running towards the café, trying to hold her hair in place, but Araki was out of the door before she reached it.

'It's her. It's Maki,' said Keiko, breathing rapidly and gesturing unnecessarily towards the apartment block.

Swishes of furry grey cloud twisted urgently across the clear sky, and even the noxious smog seemed to have sensed the fury of the winds massing two thousand miles to the south and made its escape. Araki ran with nervous anticipation, gratified at the success of his strategy so far, and forsook the waiting elevator to take the stairs three at a time to the third floor. Miki-chan, the younger and more emotional of the office clerks, was smiling contentedly at the cleanliness she had bestowed on the kitchen, but to Araki's horror the diligent Noriko was standing by the telephone, her hand still clutching the instrument she had just replaced on its cradle.

'What are you doing? You're crazy. You've hung up on her!'

Noriko was trying to speak but was silenced by the

vehemence directed at her. She stepped instinctively aside as Araki grabbed the telephone, expecting by some technical wizardry a reconnection with the reluctant masseuse. He turned on Noriko.

'OK, tell me what happened,' he said, now more composed.

'Well, I was holding the phone while Keiko went for you. The woman on the other end was getting more and more irritable. I tried to soothe her but she decided to hang up.'

'Oh my God,' Araki thumped his forehead with his fist.

At that moment, the three others who had followed him home entered, and stood in the doorway staring quizzically at Araki.

'That was quick,' said Kondo.

Araki glanced at him. 'She hung up. She fucking well hung up.'

Noriko tried to intervene. 'That's not quite right, she—'

Araki pounced. 'She what? She had a wrong number? Her ten yen ran out?'

Araki paced around the tiny, crowded room. His voice rose and he degenerated to sarcasm. 'Don't tell me. She was trying to get the Imperial Palace.'

'If you let me finish,' said Noriko calmly, 'she was trying to get you. When you weren't here she became a little impatient. She said that she didn't know whether or not she'd still be in but she left her number and hung up.'

'She left her number?' said Araki incredulously. 'Why didn't you say so?'

The voice was deeper than he had expected; it was firm, confident, controlled, unlike the vacuous intonation that Japanese women are forced by custom to affect when speaking into the telephone. There was evident irritation in the tone and an urgent curiosity which Araki hoped he could manipulate in the bargaining to come. But what most surprised and disconcerted him was the fact that Maki dispensed with the usual verbal pleasantries and honorific sparring which allow the speakers to establish the superior and inferior roles. After all, he had made the initiative and he had the money, and this woman, from the lowest strata of the floating world, should be grateful for whatever he had to offer. But the level of language Maki chose was curt and unadorned, with none of the feminine self-effacement that was to be expected.

'I hear you have something for me.'

'Yes, I do. I'm glad you got my message and I hope I didn't embarrass you.'

'As a matter of fact, you did,' she replied tartly, 'but it doesn't seem to bother you reporters very much. Now, what is it you have?'

'Tanimoto-san left a note with me,' said Araki, carefully bypassing the fact that he had taken the piece of paper from the man's corpse, 'and since you were his girl I think you should have it. And if you'd like to earn some money out of all this, and there's no reason why you shouldn't, I'm happy to pay you for the answers to some simple questions about the victim. You know, what kind of man he was, his hobbies and the sort of things you and he did together.'

There was a silence on the line, and he thought he had played the money card too early. He cursed himself. Then the voice returned.

'How do you know I was his girl?'

'You had to be. You were at the Camelia, the scene of many meetings with Tanimoto, you were dressed in respectful black and had the newspapers open at his story. You then got one of your regular calls from a place called the Bali, and it was only a matter of finding the right Bali, which wasn't difficult. You've proved you had a close relationship with the dead man by calling me now. Please, let's dispense with the obvious and get together to talk about you and him.'

Araki was conscious of his own abruptness, and he regretted it, but when the woman called Maki answered her voice was mellower and disarmingly sensuous.

'Yes, I did know Tanimoto well.' She paused again. 'But I don't recall him ever mentioning you.'

'Well, to be frank, I didn't know him well, but I would like to write about him in the *Tokyo Weekly*.' He was not prepared for the sarcasm in her reply or the harsh reality of her evaluation.

'Oh yes, I forgot, you're a reporter. Hardly the intellectual magazine though.'

Araki was now even more confused: not only was this bereaved girlfriend of an inconsequential street bum balking at his offer of money but she had the audacity to make a vague judgement of his job. What irked him most was the fact that he considered Japanese women to be the most predatory and avaricious in Asia, and Maki's job as a bathhouse whore placed her at the top of the local scale of greed. Yet she did not take the bait. Had Tanimoto really meant something to her? Was she a sensitive person underneath?

'Araki-san,' she continued, aware of his unease, 'you obviously know what Tanimoto was. It was in all the newspapers. As far as I'm concerned, it's all over; only I know the kind of person he really was and I don't want any further involvement. If you can't send me whatever it was you took from him then let's leave it at that.'

'I could do that,' he admitted, 'but it wouldn't help me to know him better and it wouldn't help you either. I can be very generous.'

'So what do you propose?'

Araki felt close to victory. 'Meet me this afternoon, and we can wrap everything up nicely.'

He sensed the distant apprehension in the silence that followed. He nestled the receiver between his chin and shoulder and struggled to extract his cigarettes and matches from different pockets.

'That's impossible.' She gave no explanation why.

'It has to be today: I have to write my article by tomorrow. Can't you make an effort?'

Again, the maddening pause. It suddenly occurred to Araki that she might not be alone and whoever she was with was telling her what to say. But she had not covered the telephone because he heard a bell ring in the background.

'Hello, are you there?' he called.

'I'm sorry I'll have to go. There's someone at the door.'

'OK, will you meet me tonight?'

'All right, but not for long,' and then she explained, 'I work the late shift at the Bali on Tuesdays.'

'There's a small coffee shop on the second floor of the Pantheon building in Shibuya. You can't miss it. There's only one and it's at the entrance to the shopping arcade. Do you know it?'

'I know the building. It's got three or four cinemas.'

Araki could hear the bell again. This time in short sharp insistent bursts. 'Right, I'll see you there at six.'

'OK. How will I know you?'

'There are only six or seven tables. Wear your hair like you did at the Camelia, and I'll know you. I'll be carrying a camera anyway. See you later.'

# CHAPTER SIX

They drove east at rooftop height on the elevated Expressway Number Seven, and crossed the choppy Sumida River within sight of Ryogoku-bashi before dropping down to sea level into Koto Ward. Chris sat motionless in the passenger seat, clutching his camera in his lap. His eyes were open but saw nothing. Araki needed little sleep, forcing his heart to pump hard into the night on a stimulant mixture of black coffee and cigarettes, but his aides invariably succumbed when he was on a tight deadline. It had taken Araki some minutes to realise that Chris could doze with his eyes open, like a Japanese, having assumed that the nodding motion he made with his head was a sign of agreement with Araki's ceaseless chatter. What had given him away this time was a question from Araki as to whether Chris knew what an Edokko was. Araki had been glancing down at the spread of blue- and dull orange-tiled rooftops, and said that if Chris was a native downtown Tokyoite he would probably have been born out there.

The heights of the buildings had declined since they picked up the expressway at Gaien, skirting Chiyoda Ward, with its lush greenery of the Imperial gardens and the modern office towers of prosperous Marunouchi.

'See that one over there, with the black, smoky glass windows?' he had said, not knowing at the time that the nod from Chris was not a reply. 'That's the headquarters of Matsuhashi Corporation, where I first saw Tanimoto.'

They drove under railway tracks running west from Tokyo Station and into the old Low City at Nihonbashi, the legacy of its merchant past retained by the small print works, single-product family-run trading companies and local finance houses. The fresh wind carried traces of rain and there were already some umbrellas among the pedestrians.

The evocative Sumida River was another frontier. The functional urbanscape of merchant Nihonbashi gave way to rows of wooden dwellings with their colourful roofs. Some of the houses were recent, and the wood was as dark as teak, but most of them were ageing and a faded brown in colour.

The detached and more opulent houses had cantilevered roofs which turned upwards at the edges, a touch of traditional taste in an otherwise nondescript landscape. Among the houses were the factories, the vulnerable sub-contractors, supplying parts to the giants. The drab sprawl was dissected by roads and a web of lanes and barely passable alleys which divided row upon row of orderly houses and shops. Here and there, a cluster of wooden buildings had been demolished to make way for a mansion block giving cheap and semi-western style accommodation or office space for the small wholesalers. The only open ground they had seen from the elevated road since swinging around the Imperial Palace six kilometres ago were school playgrounds, factory yards, bursts of tree-top indicating the precincts of a shrine or temple and now, as they crossed the rivers and canals, which spread like a delta on Tokyo's eastern flank, the dusty tracts of bottom land by the banks, given over to baseball, soccer pitches and driving schools.

Traffic was crawling into town from the direction of Narita Airport, but going north, the Number Seven, an over-burdened artery into the metropolis, was only moderately busy, allowing Araki to hold his speed at thirty without tailgating. The clouds had stopped running and were congealing into a murky mass which merged with the land, engulfing buildings and rapidly reducing visibility. In places, the cloud cover was pierced by funnels of sunlight which picked out patches of land like a spotlight. The threatening sky reminded Araki to switch on the radio. It was five past two and he listened inattentively to the political news before the weather report was read.

'The Meteorological Agency reports that Typhoon Ten may reach the Kyushu region on Thursday or early Friday if it maintains its current course and speed and has warned shipping in the area and the residents of Okinawa to prepare for a powerful storm.' The male voice droned on. 'At six o'clock this morning, the typhoon was located three hundred and fifty kilometres south-east of Minamidaito Island, about three hundred kilometres east of Okinawa Prefecture. Winds of ninety-five kilometres an hour are blowing at the centre and at fifty or more within a radius of four hundred kilometres on the northern side and two hundred and fifty kilometres on the southern. To repeat, Typhoon Ten is moving north-west at fifteen kilometres an hour and appears to be heading for Kyushu. Because of its slow speed it may not reach the main islands until late Thursday or Friday.'

Araki switched off the radio and, steadying the wheel with his forearms, he tugged the metal ring off a tin of Coca-Cola. Drinking deeply on what was now lukewarm liquid, he pondered the arrival of Typhoon Ten. He remembered a typhoon, it was also the tenth of the season, but could not recall whether it was in 1968 or 1969. It was not particularly powerful in terms of wind strength, but when it came ashore at Naruto in Shikoku it behaved unusually, not veering to dissipate itself in the Pacific or continuing along the west-north-west path of most typhoons, finally to destroy itself on the Asian mainland. What it actually did was to stop dead and whirl around until its energy was entirely spent over the Japanese archipelago. It did this for fifteen days. It had happened in August, and the population saw their Obon festival and summer holiday either washed out by continuous rain or generally spoilt by overcast skies and high winds.

'It's too early for typhoons,' Araki was saying. 'They usually arrive in September.'

Chris stared ahead, nodding.

The old two-storey wooden building they sought overlooked a drainage canal which had lately been covered with paving stones and fitted with children's slides and sandpits.

It stood roof-to-roof and back-to-back with the homes of other working people. A stack of full black plastic garbage bags encroached on the narrow road, some of them blown over and ripped. There was a faint smell of effluent, probably seeping from the canal. At the side of the building was a metal stairway which gave private access to the rooms on the upper floor. Because of the sticky heat the swings and slides were, like the street itself, deserted, except for two police officers.

Araki made a mental note to thank his friend Inspector Nishii for the tip-off that had again helped him stay ahead of the competition, but he knew he would not make it to the front door. The older of the two, his grey summer uniform rumpled and darkly stained below the armpits, placed himself in the way. He looked suspiciously at Chris.

'Can I be of use?' he said.

'I'd like to speak to the householder,' Araki replied perfunctorily, trying to look over the policeman's shoulder. 'I'm a reporter. If I could just ring . . .'

An arm, brown, muscular and hairless, sprung up like a railway crossing gate. 'I'm afraid our instructions are not to let anyone except family have access to these premises while police investigations are proceeding.'

A textbook reply, thought Araki, backing off and peering through the half-shuttered windows. He wanted to invoke Nishii's name but this would betray their understanding. He joined Chris who had stayed by the canal and was photographing the house under the disapproving stare of the second policeman.

'Have you got your foreigner's card?' he asked, smiling as if he was asking the time.

'No, I haven't,' Chris replied, lining up the house again in his viewfinder.

'Chris,' Araki said, pretending to indicate the required angle of the shot, 'you're an outsider here, a gaijin.'

Chris tried to protest but Araki persisted. 'I'll join you, before you leave, at the ward office and we can burn your bloody card in front of the Prime Minister. But now, I'm investigating a killing as part of my job. I don't want to be arrested with a bloody gaijin carrying the human rights banner. Please carry your card from now on. Come on, walk easy.'

As they passed a neighbouring house, the front door opened and a middle-aged housewife wearing a frilly white smock and clutching a string shopping-bag edged sheepishly into the street. Araki kept pace with her until they were out of hearing range of the police guards, then quickened his step until he was shuffling alongside. Without stopping, she acknowledged his introduction and accepted the apology which it contained with a stooping nod. Chris gave them privacy by keeping a discreet distance behind.

'Terrible business, wasn't it?' said Araki, shaking his head with her in an expression of concern. He continued. 'There must have been a racket, when was it, last Thursday night. Did it wake you up?'

'I can't say it did,' she replied. 'As I told the nice gentleman from the police station, the one without the uniform, we are so used to noise from Mr Kawazu and his friends, especially since Mrs Kawazu left, that we can sleep through most of it.'

Araki tried to conceal his surprise. 'You mean Mrs Kawazu doesn't live there?'

'No, she moved down to Osaka about two weeks ago.'

'Did she leave him?'

They were nearing the corner, where the shops were filled with housewives on their daily errands. Araki waited patiently while his companion ran her hand over a basketball-sized water melon, kneading the sides firmly with her knuckles. When she was ready to answer, her tone had become evasive.

'This is a very quiet neighbourhood. We are not used to seeing men swaggering down the street in their summer underwear. They'd go round to the public bath and then back to the Kawazus' house for some more gambling.'

'Is that why his wife left him?' asked Araki.

The woman shook her head, still preferring to study

107

unconvincingly the array of fresh vegetables which spilled out of the shopfront to the street.

'No, it wasn't. Their son has been trying to get into university since he graduated from high school last March. He's quite a bright boy, but his parents couldn't afford to send him to a crammer in Tokyo. Anyway, his mother said they'd found one in Osaka with close connections to one of the local universities so she's gone down there with the son to live with relatives.'

The woman was nervous; she fidgeted in her purse without finding the right money. Araki sensed they were near the end of their conversation but wanted to clarify one more point.

'The police said that after a fight at the house on Thursday night Mr Kawazu and his friends took Mr Tanimoto off to the Tama river and left him there. In a quiet neighbourhood like this, the noise of a vehicle must have been heard by someone.'

The woman stuffed a bunch of long-stemmed leeks into her shopping bag, hesitated, and then sucked in breath.

'We've all become so used to the comings and goings and the commotion at the Kawazus' that we don't notice any particular visitor, and we sleep through the noise as if it wasn't bothering us,' she said with a shrug of resignation.

Araki's voice showed his frustration. 'Didn't you see any of the other men who were supposed to have been in the mahjong game on Thursday night? Anyone different from the usual run-of-the-mill callers? No cars?'

Her brow creased and her mouth opened wide, the muscles around it taut and prominent. She touched her teeth lightly with a clenched fist.

'I'm really sorry I can't help you any further,' she sighed. 'I've told the police everything I know. And that's only that I can't remember seeing anything special on Thursday.' Her voice faltered, and the last syllables came out separate and distant, unmasking the doubts that had invaded her thoughts in the middle of the sentence.

'Of course there was the van,' she added.

'What van?' asked Araki with firm politeness.

'How silly of me to forget. It was only when you mentioned cars just then,' she said, frowning even more deeply as she sought the answer. 'It was about four o'clock in the afternoon; my daughter was up from Shizuoka, and we had just stepped out of the house to go to the shops when this man in one of those vans stopped and asked me if I knew where the Kawazus lived. So I told him.'

Araki was confused. 'And you didn't tell the police this?' he asked.

'It was just one of those everyday things. And besides, I was very concerned about my daughter: she's pregnant and not having an easy time. It was the name on the side of the van that struck me. Nozaki. Nozaki Transport. That's what it said.'

Fascinated by the woman's power of memory, a forte he considered his own, he asked her politely how on earth she could remember such insignificant detail.

'That's easy,' she replied cheerfully, 'it's the same name as mine. I'm Mrs Nozaki. Isn't that a coincidence?'

Araki rubbed a circle on the windscreen. Chris was thinking aloud.

'I can't follow the sequence of events. If Tanimoto was killed on Thursday night surely someone must have seen or heard something at the Kawazus' house. It must have been one hell of a brawl. Do you think the Nozaki truck was used to remove the body in the middle of the night? That Friday morning? Why did it arrive at four in the previous afternoon?'

They were back on the expressway and stop-starting in heavy traffic moving towards central Tokyo. The radiator was overheating, and Araki hoped that the rain, which had begun to fall in large, irregular drops, would cool the raging motor until he reached the Ginza turn-off, where he hoped for a less congested run to Shibuya. He let the windscreen wiper trace its arc twice and then stopped it. It was already after five o'clock and the encounter with the female interest in his story was less than an hour away. They had come to a halt near the City Air Terminal. Araki put the Bluebird into neutral and gunned the engine. He watched the needle slither away from the red zone and let Chris unscramble his thoughts alone.

'Now that I think about it,' Chris said, trying to answer his own question, 'the driver could have been in the mahjong game, in which case he could have kept the firm's van for his own use. He couldn't have known he'd have to carry the body of Tanimoto away.'

'If you recall,' said Araki patiently, 'the only vehicle seen on an otherwise normal Friday morning was a car, a green car, and it was actually driving across the fields away from the river towards the road. Cars usually park down there on weekends to watch the sports but not at eight o'clock on a Friday morning.'

'So there might be at least two vehicles involved,' Chris said.

Araki nodded over the steering wheel. 'Right. A van outside the scene of the killing and a green saloon where the body was found.'

His calculation had been correct. The traffic split in his favour at Edogawabashi, and as the temperature gauge stabilised in the centre of the dial, Araki relaxed enough to pursue his own train of thought.

'I have tied Tanimoto through his girlfriend Maki, or whatever her real name is, to a bunch of thugs who seem to operate from a massage parlour in Ikebukuro. My intuition tells me, and the only fact I can call on is the colour of car you followed and the one seen at the river, that the very same thugs were also known to the self-confessed killer Kawazu and were probably at his house on Thursday night. The whole mess stinks of conspiracy, not of accidental death.'

Chris's reply was drowned by a concentrated, high-pitched scream as they sped down the underpass below the west side of Ginza and he had to repeat it when they surfaced. 'If that's what you think you should tell the police, or at least get Taneda's opinion.'

The reference to the magazine's adviser, its token establishment spokesman and apologist, made Araki cringe. There was uncharacteristic venom in his voice when he spoke.

'I'm writing a story for a lot of bored housewives and frustrated office workers. I don't give a noodle who killed Tanimoto or why. That's for the police to decide. My article is there for entertainment, to shock, titillate and surprise. Sure, I object when someone takes offence and busts my property but when that story goes to press on Thursday night that's the end of it. I end all my sentences with "maybe", "perhaps" and "I think" and that covers my bum adequately.'

'But you said it might be a conspiracy to murder,' said Chris persistently.

'Listen carefully,' said Araki, pausing as he negotiated the Takagi-cho interchange. 'We are nothing more than reporters; we are not the police or the moral conscience of Japan, so treat the principals in this story as the street riff-raff that they are and thank the spirits that their lives are sordid enough for us to make a living from.'

They parked in a side street behind Shibuya Station at a few minutes before six. The rain had abated, but the gun-metal grey clouds, drifting ghostlike overhead, were heavy and threatened more downpours.

'By the way,' Araki shouted towards the retreating figure of his companion, 'give Keiko a call when you get home and have her look in the telephone books for Nozaki Transport. Speak slowly, her English is shaky. See you.'

There was no door to the coffee shop, only a gap in a row of boutiques and bric-à-brac shops in a broad arcade where knots of office girls dallied on their way home. She was twenty minutes late arriving, and the long black hair he had asked her to wear the way she had at the Camelia was tussled and windblown. Standing in the doorway and patting her hair into place with the poise of a model, the lover of the strong-arm man who had once threatened Araki

111

surveyed the customers in search of the face that in turn sought hers. She wore a beltless knee-length dress, the pastel pink colour of a yae-cherry blossom, which followed the contours of her trim, almost boyish, frame. A light mauve kerchief was knotted at the side of her neck, the points hanging forward over the slight mounds rippling the upper part of her dress. Her skin was light, almost Caucasian, and the nose high-ridged and finely pointed, almost touching the groove at the peak of her sloping upper lip. Her front teeth protruded delicately, almost imperceptibly, shaping her small heart-shaped mouth into a permanent faint pout.

Araki had positioned himself in a corner seat, hidden partially by the heads of a couple at the table in front, to give him the advantage of an extra moment to appraise his prey, to gauge her apparent strength and plot a strategy. Araki saw the hostility in her taut, unhappy expression. He raised his arm limply, but she was already heading towards him.

She sat down opposite him, smoothing her dress demurely and reciprocating Araki's greeting in barely audible words.

'Has it started raining?' he then asked tentatively.

'Maki Takegawa,' she answered, ignoring the pleasantry, 'and you're Araki-san. You'll understand that I hardly find this meeting a particularly welcome one and would be grateful if you would reach the reason for wanting to see me as soon as possible and let me return to work. I am busy in the evenings as you know.'

He perceived the same depth of voice, the same disdain for language protocol she had conveyed on the telephone, but amid the confidence and sarcasm he detected Maki's desire to learn what he knew, to be tempted by an offer and to benefit from the encounter. He shook a cigarette to the edge of its packet and offered it across the table. Closing her ringless fingers together she fluttered her hand like a geisha's fan in front of her mouth. Araki took the cigarette himself, feeling awkward in the presence of such serenity and feeling his own composure, which he was struggling to maintain in this first encounter, threatened by a persistent snuffle, a reminder of the fever that had recently abated. He relieved the irritation by emptying his nose into a paper napkin from the dispenser on the table, knowing that he had fallen even further in the low esteem he knew Maki had of him. A waitress forced suspension of their preamble when she placed two small glasses of iced water between them.

'Coffee? Tea?' he snuffled.

'Tea please. Iced.' Maki spoke to the waitress as if it had been she who had asked the question, and then looked to Araki to continue the dialogue.

'I'll have the same. It was good of you to see me,' he said on cue. 'Thank you for coming in such awful weather.'

'What exactly did you want to see me for, apart from returning some of Tanimoto-san's property to me?'

'I'm doing a story for this week's edition of the *Tokyo Weekly*.' She showed no expression when he mentioned the name of the magazine she had derided on the telephone earlier in the day. 'I know that Tanimoto worked for a group of sokaiya and that one of their clients was Matsuhashi. You've heard of them, of course?'

Reference to one of Japan's most prestigious companies, a name as evocative to all Japanese as that of Sony, Honda or Mitsubishi, again elicited a contemptuous silence.

'I've pieced together a picture of the man, his work and his killer and would like you to give me some insight into his character and his relationship with you. You can say whatever you want to and cover up anything you have to. I only want some frills and I'm willing to pay for them.'

'And what about the note you talked about?'

Maki's indifference was starting to annoy him. She should have asked about the money he was offering.

'It's a list of letters and numbers.' He reached into his shirt pocket and held out a copy of the piece of paper he had taken from the dead man's ticket holder.

'Is this the original?' she asked, rubbing the crisp paper between her fingers.

Araki shrugged contemptuously. 'Are you joking?' He didn't wait for a reply. 'I took some copies and spread them around the office in case you arrived here tonight with some of your friends.'

'What are you talking about? Friends.'

'Come off it Maki-san! Somebody else wants that scrap of paper and wrecked my flat last night looking for it. Somebody who found out about me because of my interest in you at the Camelia coffee shop and who knew you well enough to order you out of it.' He leaned forward until he could smell her lily-scented cologne above his own stale sweat and the acrid odour of the cigarette-stub dying in the ashtray. 'Just tell me enough for my story and I won't implicate you when I hand over the list to the police. Just tell me it was your pimp who phoned you and he was just being protective and wanted to scare me off.'

If Araki had miscalculated in his crude attempt to provoke it could not have been more apparent than in Maki's reaction. Or lack of it. She remained impassive, her posture of composed serenity intact as she poured a few drops of milk into her glass of tea. Just as she had on the telephone, Maki showed signs of independence and spontaneity, so uncharacteristic of Japanese women, taking control of the confrontation as she proffered the porcelain containers in Araki's direction.

'Both?'

'Just some milk. Thank you.'

She waited until the drops had spread in slow motion cloudlets around the glass and then said, 'You've been very clear. You guessed right. My employer was calling me at the Camelia. He wanted me back to do an unexpected booking.' She forced a wry laugh. 'There I was, in mourning and wanting to throw myself under a train and I have to go and let some man . . .' Her voice trailed off to a whisper. 'How did you find me?'

The interrogative in the sentence left her lips apart in the pout Araki had noticed earlier, the glossed pink lipstick matching the colour of her dress, and making a mesmerising border for her barely perceptible teeth. For an instant the reporter lost his concentration, recovering it in time to react

114

to a repeat of the question. He recounted his brief sight of the book of matches taken from Tanimoto's corpse and his discovery of the list inside the underground season ticket. He reminded her of the newspaper, opened at the page containing the Tanimoto story, she had left on the seat as she hurried from the Camelia. A few selected questions to the waitress and the conclusion was there to be taken. It was only a matter of finding the right Bali.

'Your timing was lucky,' she said. 'I hadn't been to the Camelia for weeks, and nobody ever called me there.' Araki knew she was lying. The waitress had said she had passed on several calls from the Bali to Maki. He said nothing: she seemed to want to continue talking in a more relaxed, almost melancholy way.

'Yes, I was what you'd call Tanimoto's girl and I suppose it would help if I unburdened myself of some of it.'

Araki tapped another cigarette against the table top and signalled his intention not to speak by clamping it between his teeth and rolling a book of matches cartwheel fashion, and then toying with a match he had taken from it. Maki took the cue.

'I'll help you with your story, if only to stop you inventing things and bothering me any more, but in return I want you to tell me what you know about Tanimoto-san's death. If you've been as thorough about that as you were in tracking me down, I'm sure you know more than the papers have said.'

'Not a lot,' he replied, accepting the condition and breaking up a sheaf of new notes he had taken from his shirt pocket.

'I'll give you fifty thousand for your story,' he said, counting aloud from one to five as he stacked the notes in front of him. He withheld two more ten-thousand yen notes. 'And this is if you let me take a photograph of you.'

She took a sip of tea before replying.

'I suppose you want one of me in that black dress, perhaps some dark glasses as well, for effect.'

'Not necessarily,' Araki said, absorbing the sarcasm. 'I'd like to take one of you in the street.'

Maki pondered for a second. 'All right, but from the back. I don't want my face shown clearly.'

Araki nodded his assent. It was not an unusual request from the sort of people he dealt with, people who might be answerable to violent masters. Maki would also have to consider her regular clients who might be intimidated away from her charms when they discovered the company she was keeping.

'And you'll use only my initials.' It was a command rather than a request.

'Of course, it's normal practice.' Araki scrawled the letters MT after the reminder heading 'Name' in his notepad.

'Given name only please. Ne?'

He scowled, crossed out the T and resisted the urge to ask her if she would prefer a pseudonym. He looked across at her, trying to be subtle but unable to apply the adjectives he would normally use in describing the women of the floating world. She wasn't cheap or bawdy like his neighbour Yoko, and she wasn't from the paddy fields like the girls who served in the regional restaurants he went to with his policeman friend Nishii. The expensive simplicity of the dress, the confident voice and precise, correct grammar, the poised trim figure and the netsuke smoothness of her skin reminded him of his former wife in the days before they were married and in the all too brief honeymoon months afterwards.

He ran his hand across his greasy scalp. He too had walked to the meeting, his body tugged and pulled by the clammy squalls, his clothes and hair blown this way and that by the playful gusts of wind that were the prelude to the typhoon, and yet Maki sat before him, her skin dry, her dress unblemished and snug. She had patted and teased her hair into shape and draped its length over a shoulder. It was as though she had emerged from a beauty parlour next door while he had walked straight from a sauna fully clothed. A young woman bundled into the coffee shop, obviously late, and was still shaking her umbrella as she hurried past their table to join her date. A few droplets of rain stained Araki's notepaper, others fell on his writing hand and shirt; Maki was untouched. it was as it should be.

'Where should I start?' she asked, enjoying his discomfort.

Araki sucked at the moisture on his wrist with exaggerated gusto and wanted to think that the faintest of smiles he thought he saw was from genuine amusement and not disdain.

'Let's begin,' he answered, flipping back through the pad to his checklist, 'with your first meeting with Tanimoto.'

Slowly, deliberately, almost as if she had rehearsed it, the woman with the saddened eyes began to unfold the story of a twenty-five-year-old hostess in an exclusive Ginza lounge club where rich and lecherous company presidents and balding politicians would sign a 150,000-yen bill to cover a few hours in her company over drinks. She had been scouted while working as a waitress in an after-hours bar for the lower corporate strata by the retired Kabuki actor who owned the Ginza club and had risen in status and popularity to the point where she could command a hefty reservation fee from customers who preferred her or who did not want to take pot-luck with the other girls. Not that the others were disappointing. They were all former models or actresses in their mid-twenties and earned up to a million yen a month from commissions alone, more than most of their clients, but then these were spending their company's or the government's money and not their own. The old female impersonator retained a finely tuned perception of femininity and he knew that Maki would become the choice pick of his girls once he had taught her refinement and the art of playful deception.

In August last year, just before Obon, she was called to entertain a party of four men. The leader, older and less well groomed than the others, had called for his regular hostess, but she had returned to her native town for the return-of-the-spirits festival and instead Maki had officiated. It was obvious the men were not salaried workers: the younger ones wore lightweight American suits in clear, patternless tones and their hair was brushed back and longer

117

than normally proper in business. They also paid in cash and did not ask for a receipt. The one called Tanimoto returned to the club the following week without his senior. In early September he came again, alone, and asked for Maki. It may have simply been the youthfulness of the man – after all, she only knew of middle-aged men and their habits – that attracted her to him. He was young, courteous and readily supplied with cash, which he liked her to see when he paid. Inevitably, he had asked her out 'to a pretty Italian restaurant in Roppongi' Maki said with a smile, and almost as inevitably, at a luxury hotel overlooking Lake Ashi in Hakone, they had become lovers.

There was a pause in the narrative as she savoured the memory. It was long enough for Araki to catch up with his note-taking and slip in a question.

'Didn't you know what job he was doing? Where he was getting all his money from?'

Maki drained the last of her tea before continuing. At first she thought he was the playboy son of some company owner or other. They saw lots of them at the club, but he was a little too old and didn't have that certain behaviour that always goes with spoilt children.

'I had never heard then of those people who go around blackmailing big firms without getting punished and so I believed him when he said he was an importer of cars.'

They spent a lot of time together in that first blissful winter and spring and were not inclined to meet each other's friends. At least that was until the passion had spent itself, their physical needs satiated, and she was introduced into his coterie of pals. They were a lot like him: they had money, which they spent freely, a penchant for dark suits with charcoal grey pinstripes and enjoyed each other's company, and none seemed to have a regular girl except Tanimoto. They let her sit in on their card or mahjong games, some-times as dealer if the game was hanafuda.

Did she suspect they might be racketeers?

'Of course, they had some of the mannerisms.' She smiled at the thought. An older man sometimes sat in on the games

118

and they used to raise their level of language a few grades when they talked to him. But on the whole she found them too self-disciplined, almost too educated. 'They talked of corporations and profits. Most of the time I didn't know what they were talking about. They swapped stories about top men in business and giggled like schoolgirls if it was dirty. About that time I read in one of the magazines, yours I think, about those extortionists who operate quite openly and apparently above the law. You know the . . .'

'Sokaiya,' Araki assisted.

Maki paused in her narrative, placing her elbows on the table and holding her hands clasped in front of her mouth, a forefinger stroking the ripples of her lips as she tried to assemble the jumble of memories into chronological order. Araki found himself staring at the finely sculptured features of the woman he had worked hard to trace, and at the pout, which attracted him most. He found it easy to imagine what had caused the violent Tanimoto to display tender feelings, perhaps for the first time in his life. Certainly the last.

Then she resumed, having established the sequence of events. Her affair with Tanimoto started to fade in early June, when the first downpours of the annual rainy season were spreading north from Kyushu, and their meetings alone were rarer and rarer. He had been spending one or two nights a week in her apartment, but by the end of June the bell never rang and the gambling sessions evaporated. There were no more romantic dinners in foreign restaurants and no more love-making in top-class hotels in and around Tokyo. She couldn't understand what had caused the change. All relationships peak, some continue in a different form, and some just die, but the change in Tanimoto's character was so abrupt that she had become frightened. He had insisted on meeting in strange and out-of-the-way places, and then only for a few hours. Instead of the hotel, their needs were satisfied in cheap motels by the Chuo and Tomei expressways and their impromptu chats took place at the Camelia. Once he had asked her to meet him urgently in Shimoda, two hundred kilometres away from the capital.

'Why Shimoda?'

'He was there on business,' she smiled to herself. 'I thought he might be saying he wanted to start over again. An inn overlooking the bay. Do you understand? As it was, I met him near the port and was on the next train back to Tokyo.'

'What did he want you in Shimoda for?'

'I brought some messages back to Tokyo for him. He couldn't trust the post by then. Or anyone but me.'

From the end of July until that day in mid-August when his lifeless body had been found, Maki met the victim only once – at the Camelia. That just about tallied with the recollection of the waitress, Araki recalled. He was very agitated, perhaps even frightened, states of mind she had not noticed in him before, and he warned her not to see any of the people he had introduced her to, saying that he himself would be going out of circulation for a while but would contact her when he could. He did not, and the next she heard of him was his death notice in the press.

'Coincidence, ne? Him dying so soon after going into seclusion.' As an afterthought Araki added. 'He certainly wasn't in hiding when he was killed. He was gambling the night away with his friends.'

Maki ignored the implication that she was lying.

'I think that's all I can tell you,' she said, verifying the time on her watch for longer than was necessary. Araki finished scribbling moments later. He had written from left to right, preferring it to the vertical script used by his colleagues, especially at awkward times when the pad was difficult to hold securely. The five pages of notes were orderly and legible but in a personal brand of shorthand which he had developed in his college debating days and which was unintelligible to others. He tapped the pad with his ballpen, the story already written in his mind.

'I think that's excellent,' he said, scanning the pages at random. 'If there is anything else, perhaps I can call you at the Bali.'

'No, not there,' she jumped in harshly, taking the pen

120

from him and writing down a number, leaving Araki to attach her name to it.

Again the exchange district eluded him: he would have to practise more with his assistant Keiko. He made to leave, pocketing his pen and reversing the pages of the notebook until the green covers appeared.

'I'll take your picture outside the flowershop. At least the bridge will keep the rain off. You may have to hold your skirt down though.'

'I think you've forgotten something,' Maki said, ignoring the humour. 'You were going to tell me about Tanimoto's murderer.'

Araki had genuinely forgotten and apologised for it, even adding an instinctive jolt forward of the head. There were no words in response, only a plea radiating from the dark, moist, sullen eyes across the table. He would tell her what he knew.

'As it said in the papers, there was a fight at a gambling session, and a man called Kawazu admits brawling with your friend who, in a fairly violent struggle, was knocked unconscious against the edge of a hard, low table. Kawazu panicked and drove all the way across Tokyo in a friend's car and dumped Tanimoto into the river. Hard to say whether he was dead or alive before he entered the water, all rather academic really.' He found himself apologising again for his insensitivity. 'The other three involved claim to have been rendered temporarily irresponsible by the shock and the drink but came the morning light they realised the trouble they were in and persuaded Kawazu to confess, saying they would stand by him in court, blaming Tanimoto for starting the fight in the first place. They'll get slapped on the wrist for it and Kawazu will get a light sentence for manslaughter if it's shown Tanimoto died as a result of the accidental fall and not deliberate drowning. The police want to clear it up without a lot of fuss, but personally I think . . .' his voice faltered, the sentence petering out uncompleted. He did not wish to divulge much of his own personal sentiments in case they should compromise him.

'You were saying?'

'I was going to say that I think the whole thing smells,' he replied cautiously, deciding he had all the information he needed to help fill his rice-bowl. In any event, it would be almost impossible to persuade the review committee to carry the story into another edition when he had already inserted it as an extra in the existing project list. But he wanted to know clearly why Maki had given up a highly paid hostess job to go down the scale to be a massage girl; he needed to confront her about two thugs who were seen coming out of the place where she worked; and he would like to force out of her what exactly was said to her on the telephone at the Camelia coffee shop. And deep inside, that part of him which held the power to override rational decision, to blot out unpleasant experience, activated itself and sent out the message to every vital organ that he simply wanted to see this woman again.

Outside, the rain had eased, giving way to the brisk fresh wind which blew Maki's hair across her face and protected her identity as she feigned interest in a display of flowers, now sensibly removed from the pavement to the interior of the shop Araki had chosen for the photographs. She declined his offer of a lift and opted for the direct train to Ikebukuro. Her body moved easily up the station stairway, the mane of smooth hair held aloft by the swirling wind, beckoning him to follow.

He did not need the wipers, although the newscaster on his car radio was reporting that Typhoon Ten was lashing Okinawa, 1,500 miles to the south, with torrential rain and 100 kilometre-an-hour winds. In Shikoku and the southern prefectures of the main islands, they were gearing up for the onslaught, securing their fishing-boats and coastal freighters and gathering family members behind storm windows. He felt relaxed about the article, in spite of his concern over the assault on his property and the uncharacteristic poise and intelligence of the female interest.

At each traffic light on the short trip to his flat, he glanced at the scribbled notes. They had reached the end of the

122

interrogation session and Araki had indicated this by drawing a line across the page. It was then she reminded him that he had agreed to tell her all he knew about Tanimoto's death. Was it his memory or had she really said 'Tanimoto's murderer'? He had made no more notes but was certain she had said the latter.

The other curious feature was the list, the bait he had used to entice the reluctant witness into meeting him. She had not raised the subject beyond asking whether it was the original. Perhaps it was a meaningless jumble of figures only. He reached into his pocket for the copied version he had shown her and when he couldn't find it there he checked his wallet and trousers. Nothing. He slumped back in the driving seat, feeling truly outwitted. She had somehow held on to the list he had let her study. He hadn't even noticed.

# CHAPTER SEVEN

The smoke drifted no higher than the top of the partitions which barely fenced off enough space for the conference table and its eight chairs and gave token privacy to the editorial committee. Each member perused in silence a photocopied example of the handwritten draft.

In the general office it was a typically chaotic day before printing: more telephones were ringing than there were people available to answer, and the moshi-moshis were curt, reduced almost to rude hisses. Although the flimsy walls muted the worst of the hubbub, the irascible voice of sub-editor Ono could be heard berating a clerk for her inability to find a missing manuscript.

Editor Kobayashi sat at the head of the table, brow furrowed in concentration, too experienced to be distracted, occasionally dabbing away the sweat with a handkerchief and wafting the torpid air to no great effect. Taneda, as usual, was scribbling furiously into the margins, his hawkish, distinguished face devoid of expression. Kondo had his familiar pile of reference material and pages of jottings. Maeda, a competent and imaginative photographer, his long unkempt hair dangling into his eyes as he leaned forward, sat between Kobayashi and Araki, ready to describe the history behind the stack of photos he had assembled and to advise which were most suitable for reproduction in the week's edition. Chris's chair was vacant: he was somewhere supervising the printing of the pictures Araki had taken the previous evening of the victim's erstwhile lover, and clearing up some oddments of research. The team was completed by Keiko, the self-assured girl-Friday, who busied herself tabulating the individual characters in the draft and computing the printing space they would require.

Since Araki had last seen her only two days earlier she had had her hair straightened, cut square front and back and tinted a light shade of copper. He liked the new image, the uncluttered view of her unblemished neck it revealed. He only wished she would condemn those sunglasses to the bridge of her nose or to her handbag and not the crown of her head.

Stifling a yawn, Araki stubbed out a cigarette and toyed with another while his colleagues went over his work with the critical eyes of their separate disciplines. He had worked late into the night and through most of the early daylight hours on the first draft of his article and a clean revision. The result pleased him: six pages of neat script, each character in its personal box without touching the edges, and no messy alterations.

The story flowed smoothly from the discovery of Tanimoto's body, the circumstances of his death and the confession of Toshio Kawazu. He had written a protracted sentence on the game of mahjong, out of which the brawl ensued, and made conspicuous mention of the illegality of this activity if money changed hands. He asked his readers to reflect on the character of the victim and to imagine a game of tiles being played solely for the fun of it. He protested against Taneda's suggestion to change the tense to a less definitive one in the passage alluding to the confessed killer's connections with criminal elements but Kobayashi agreed with his senior adviser, acknowledging Araki's point that Tanimoto had a police record, and everyone amended their drafts. The section on Tanimoto's troubled youth and history of violence went unchanged and all agreed to the inclusion of the photograph taken in June of him gesturing menacingly at the unseen figure of Araki.

There was another clash of opinion. Taneda spoke softly, but his tone was uncompromising and precise.

'I would like you to remove the name of the company from the photo's caption and from the part where you describe the New Japan Economic Research Institute as being' – he ran his finger down the page until he found the offending sentence – ' "sokaiya to the most prominent commercial and industrial enterprises such as Matsuhashi Corporation".' He looked up at Araki for his reply.

'To show him selling muscle at the annual general meeting of Matsuhashi would add some weight to my contention that Tanimoto was not just a street punk but a guy who through his own perseverance finished up working for one of the élite sokaiya groups, thriving like the rest on protecting firms like Matsuhashi from their shareholders' right to know what lies behind the figures.' Araki looked for support towards Kondo, who nodded. He continued, 'The picture was suppressed when I did my first article on the sokaiya in June because of outside pressure, threatening telephone calls in fact. I agreed then, but it won't do any harm to publish it now.'

'Matsuhashi is immaterial to the context of your story,' Taneda said adamantly. 'It would invite critical comments which we do not need.'

It was now up to Kobayashi to adjudicate. He re-read the script, tapping it with his pencil, and consulted with Kondo.

'We leave Matsuhashi out in both cases.' The decision carried its own finality: to object would have been insolent.

Chris's firm, lone rap on the door rattled the adjoining partitions and broke the brief silence. He entered sheepishly, his short-sleeved shirt, white except for the yellow, sweat discolouration at the armpits, hung easily around the bony frame. He passed an envelope to Araki before taking a seat.

The envelope contained the photographs taken the day before outside the flower shop in Shibuya. They were passed around, stopping longer in front of Maeda, who, as the expert studied them with a technical eye, and agreed on one which had Maki almost in profile, only a hand restraining some unruly strands of hair. The wind had been gusting from behind, forcing the pliant, unresisting pink fabric of her dress against her body, and the camera had captured, unintentionally Araki pointed out, the outline of her legs and buttocks. Maki's legs were straight and carried a short, trim torso. Araki was probably not the only man at the table to make mental comparisons with Keiko, whose slightly arched legs and long body were more typical of the race.

'What's the latest on the typhoon?' Kobayashi asked the room. 'Is it going to mess up our distribution and is it going to keep our readers indoors all weekend instead of out shopping around the newsstands?'

'It's moving slowly.' It was Keiko who responded and then added reassuringly, 'We won't get the eye. According to the seven o'clock news it's moving north-east towards Shikoku and weakening, but it's broad and has a long tail. We're in for some heavy rain from tomorrow night.'

The editor shrugged and returned to his papers, a signal for the review panel to continue its scrutiny of Araki's article. The text on Maki was received sympathetically, even Kondo nodding approvingly to himself.

The narrative carried the relationship from its happy start in Ginza to its tragic end. The male reader would like the macho images: the violence, the forbidden gambling and snippets from the underworld of extortion, drugs and sex for sale. The morbid sentimentality of the Japanese female would thrill to the inevitable tragedy of the man and woman, bringing to life the fantasies of a dozen daily television 'home dramas'. But there was a tone among the words, a nuance so hidden as to be opaque. There was understanding and compassion towards a woman whose way of life would normally receive Araki's contempt. Flowery, complex constructions using multi-stroke kanji, which sent Keiko to the dictionary to check, replaced the writer's normal, harsh, simple descriptions of carnality with a sympathetic account of one woman's attempt to bring feeling and something near to love to a short, doomed affair.

Kobayashi broke the silence. 'It's not as punchy as you usually make it. After all, this is the leading paragraph. The bit that matters. You let the massage girl off lightly.'

'I thought about it a lot,' Araki replied, less than convincingly. 'I set out to find the female interest, the sex

127

angle, but I had to remember that I needed to know more about Tanimoto and his connections, even more so when I became the object of their violence.' He raised his hand to postpone any objections to this supposition. 'We'll come to that in a moment. I'm convinced the raid on my apartment wasn't a coincidence. No,' he continued, 'I was looking at Maki to lead me into a deeper investigation, not just to give me the lurid bits about her love life.'

The editor pondered. 'I accept your reasoning and unless there are any objections I'll let it stand. As a matter of fact, I find your approach quite refreshing.'

There are those who knew Araki from before who would swear that his misogyny could be dated from the moment he announced that his wife had left him and taken their child with her. Until then, his writing had reflected the influences of his stays in the egalitarian environments of London and New York and he had received some critical acclaim for his work on the equality of opportunity. Then there was the bitter divorce, the public disclosure of his wife's affair and the influence of his wife's powerful banker father on the board of Araki's newspaper which forced his resignation.

From then on, his social conscience was effectively erased and the cutting edge of his enthusiasm blunted. Worst of all, the people he had written about as mere incidentals to the serious investigative journalism he had pioneered were now the objects of his interest and the subject of his scorn. Politicians, actors, top company directors, women of the floating world and the tattooed posturers of the underworld became the target of his antagonism, the vehicle for his revenge.

An office girl brought in a tray of green tea. The motion of the door stirred the stagnant smoke for a brief, refreshing instant, and brushed aside papers and photographs as she placed the steaming cups with practised indifference in a neat line down the table. Editor Kobayashi passed his cup from one hand to the other until it had cooled enough to hold in one. He would have preferred a cold mugi-cha.

When he was happy, he said: 'If there are no objections

to the last part I'd like to talk briefly about these yakuza you claim are after you.' He pointed a stubby finger at Araki.

The table was silent. There were no critical comments on the vivid account Araki had written of the night when tempers flared after a long session of high-stake mahjong fuelled by several bottles of Suntory Gold, and how Akira Tanimoto fell heavily on to the knee-high game table, its sharp metal corners penetrating the base of his skull, rupturing the spinal cord. Death was moments away. Araki had used his most outrageous superlatives to evoke the drink-induced panic that ensued: the confused brooding on the limited options, the flight across the capital until the expressway ran out and the search for a stretch of river bank far enough away from the road to leave the body and flee undetected. And later, sober, frightened, and not without remorse, the calculated decision to throw Kawazu on the mercy of the court.

But Taneda was puzzled. He was looking at the document, cupping his sallow cheeks as he spoke. 'I know it's not pertinent to the context or purpose of the article, but I find the whole incident too pat, too perfectly explicable, every loose end tied up. Why were there no other people in the apartment who saw or heard the fight? Why go all the way to the Tama river, fifteen or sixteen kilometres away at least, to dump the body when the Ara and the Edo or even a paddy field in Chiba were only a ten-minute drive away? Ne?' He looked around for support.

'I share your doubts, Taneda-san,' Araki said with an audible sigh, 'and I take your point about the open-and-shut nature of the matter. The wife, as it happens, has gone to live in Osaka because the son had got into a university there.' He waved his arm to suppress the expected question. 'I know most kids go off to college and live in dormitories on their own, but it's also not uncommon for the parents to live apart in these difficult years while the mother lives close by the school.' He held up the original police statement. 'At the moment there's no real proof that this incident was anything more than an accident, but if the victim had been a more valuable member of society I think the police might have been less hasty in reaching their conclusion.'

'Are you still claiming that the break-in at your flat is connected with your own probing?' Kobayashi asked sceptically.

'It has to be. Take a look at these.' Araki passed across the photographs Chris had taken hurriedly from the back of the taxi while following the two men who entered and left the Bali on the way to Araki's flat. Kobayashi brought them close to his nose.

'The passenger's just a blur. You've got a profile of the driver: not enough for identification though.'

Araki's exasperation showed. 'Quite. But what a profile! The head's almost pushing through the roof.' He leaned backwards and spoke through a swirl of smoke. 'Tell everyone what you've discovered, Kondo-san.'

Shuffling his papers until he had them in the order he wanted, the meticulous old man wore a rare smile of satisfaction.

'As you can see, the pictures are not complete enough to extract a positive identification, and if those two characters were both of normal size it would have been impossible. But the driver isn't what you'd call normal. Look at him. He can hardly fit in the car. Anyway, with Bingham-san's description and photograph I was able to build up an accurate picture of the big one and, assuming some sort of criminal activity, these extraordinary characteristics should stand out in police computer records.' Kondo was rambling again so Araki took it on himself to summarise what happened next.

'So you went up to Police Headquarters where your classmate Toyama is still in charge of records, and after you assured him as usual you would not bring any shame and dishonour on the metropolitan police by injudicious disclosure of your source he tapped a few buttons, scanned some fiches and produced a batch of candidates. And' – he looked at Kondo, passing on the credit – 'and you found him.'

Araki held a precarious balance on the back legs of his chair, but the others leaned forward in anticipation. Even Taneda looked mildly excited, straining to hear Kondo's next delivery above the din permeating from the main office.

'His name's Masao Ezaki and he's the only son of a former professional wrestler of the western variety, with a thyroid problem he seems to have handed down.' Kondo sought the undivided attention of his audience. He caught the expectation in their eyes and held it unnecessarily.

'Ezaki's thirty-eight, slightly retarded mentally and prone to violent outbursts. His condition has kept him out of long-term jail but he has spent time in Fuchu and other places for up to a year at a time on four occasions. The point is' – Kondo adjusted his glasses yet again – 'the main point is Ezaki is no ordinary chimpira, your average club doorman. Since he was seventeen he's been attached in one way or another with the Yanagida-gumi.'

Knowing nods acknowledged the drama of the disclosure and there were audible ejections of breath at the mention of the syndicate. Then a silence of trepidation. They all knew that the story was now written on a treadmill of egg shells. Araki had written an exposé of gang activities as long ago as the spring of 1980, when the police knew of the existence of over 2,800 organised gangs with 131,400 men, and a few women, on their payroll.

The largest gang, the Hosokawa-gumi, ran a tight, nationwide network that would do justice to a trading company, with branches, affiliates and dependent sub-gangs represented in 450 cities in thirty-eight prefectures. 16,000 people pledged allegiance to the Hosokawa-gumi and were paid for it. The police made token clampdowns, usually when territorial disputes generated violence and the public demanded some action, but otherwise the syndicates concentrated their energy on loan sharking, bar and nightclub management, prostitution and protection, content to collect the omnipresent droppings of the prosperous, insecure society around them.

Some gangs realised the changing nature of Japan, and the way it was reaching maturity as a consumer as opposed to a productive, industrial society. The Nippon Yamato-Kai, with 102 chapters in fourteen prefectures, were behind a string of money shops, legitimate fronts charging eighty to a hundred per cent interest on loans to impatient consumers, using money passed down from the major regional banks through local credit banks and co-operatives until the respectability and anonymity of its origin was diluted to the satisfaction of each level.

Other syndicates, the Osaka-based Mine-gumi and Umeda-yoshi-kai, in particular, mastered the strict immigration controls to rotate a stable of girls from Thailand and the Philippines on six-month visas to work in their networks of 'pink' clubs, massage parlours and brothels. But the product of the eighties, the safety prop of the busy, the bored and self-indulgent, was the stimulant pill. The gangs struggled amongst themselves for the growing market increasing inter-gang violence and the use of the handgun, often a toy replica converted to fire a low calibre bullet, in replacement to the traditional short sword.

Although Japan's organised crime syndicates are amply documented, they are nothing more than an irritating appendage, a minor part, a bureaucratic footnote to Japan's orderly, statistic-dominated society. The inner workings are deliberately confused and the television portrayal unchallenged. Like the faithful company salaryman, Japan's latter-day samurai, the recognised gang member, plays out a role which involves codes of loyalty and submission to a stratified hierarchy reminiscent of the feudal bonds that bound the warrior to his lord. The oversized pointed shoes, the suits with padded shoulders covering muscular frames scarred with garish dragon and flower tattoos, the jaunty, confident strut in the street and the quaint structured language with its arrogant, rasping drawl: these superficial qualities identified the professional rogue to the public, the secure, protected man and woman in the street, who treated him with a degree of sympathy as long

132

as his violent outbursts were directed at his peers.

Bloody gangland feuds, which were growing as the territorially based syndicates moved tentatively across prefectural frontiers in search of new business, would increase the circulation of the *Tokyo Weekly* as long as it could describe the events in the same dispassionate language it would use for a corporate takeover or merger. To social outcasts like Ezaki, affiliation to a recognised underworld syndicate was as important to him as belonging to one of the thirteen giant City banks or the top five trading companies was for the average commuter.

What was Tanimoto's affiliation, Araki wondered, as he searched his memory for a slot labelled 'Yanagida'. Where were his loyalties? Who would he cut off the tip of his finger for?

'Weren't they the ones who appeared at that Sumo wrestler's wedding in February? Or was it March?' the Editor asked.

'No it wasn't, with respect,' Kondo replied, with a flutter of his wrist. 'That was the Yanagisawa Group. The Yanagida are much smaller, not even in the top ten.' He found a new page of notes. 'They're based in Kanagawa Prefecture, Yokohama to be precise, so it's not surprising their operational net takes in Tokyo and Kawasaki as well as the urban centres in six other prefectures. The police estimate 1,400 active members are on the payroll. Old man Yanagida's past his peak and thought to be confined to the family estate in Kohoku Ward. His son Ichiro and another, probably the child of one of his mistresses, are vying for control of the clan. The struggle could split it. Strongarm protection used to be their speciality. You may recall that it was a Yanagida-gumi man who was arrested for beating up a poison victim protesting outside the Tokyo headquarters of the chemical company later indicted for dumping mercury into Yokaichi Bay.'

Araki was almost uncontrollably pleased with Kondo's findings but hid his feelings behind a posture of scepticism. 'Is it possible that you're wrong about Ezaki?'

133

'Unlikely. We also made a tentative identification of Ezaki's companion. If it's who we think it is, he's also a Yanagida man.'

Araki said, 'Does Yanagida manage the massage parlour, the Bali?'

'I can't be certain. It's incorporated with restricted, nominal shareholdings. It could ultimately be owned by anyone.'

Araki pressed on, anxious to establish the business connection between the two heavies and the Bali. He turned to Chris and said in English, 'Wouldn't you say that they went in and out with more poise than the usual furtive client?'

Chris crooked his head and hissed. He had picked up the habit.

'Come on, Chris, you were there. You followed them to my place. Surely they weren't in there long enough for a rub-down.'

It was the Editor, Kobayashi, who came to Chris's rescue after Araki had translated the exchange.

'Let's accept,' he said, 'the two were not customers.' He looked at Araki. 'Unlike yourself, of course. Let's assume that they were in fact part of the establishment. That means, does it not, that Maki is involved with the Yanagida-gumi, whether as a simple employee of the Bali or at some higher level?'

'Yes it does,' Araki conceded, with a hint of disappointment in his voice.

'And are you suggesting also,' Kobayashi continued, 'that Tanimoto, and by definition his employers' – he consulted his notes – 'the New Japan Economic Research Institute, are also connected to this underworld organisation?'

Before Araki could reply, Kondo was flapping his right hand loosely, a centimetre from the tip of his nose. 'We mustn't assume,' he broke in, 'and it would be dangerous to imply as much in print, that such a relationship exists. Ogawa's firm is as respectable as it is possible for a sokaiya to be.' Araki accepted the qualification and then said, 'You

134

told me yesterday I think it was, when we were waiting for a call from Maki, that the rules are changing.'

'That's correct,' Kondo confirmed. 'From 1 October this year it is illegal for business enterprises to pay money to the sokaiya, and it's also stipulated that only persons holding more than a thousand shares in a company are allowed to participate in its shareholders' meetings.'

'They'll survive,' Araki interposed.

Kondo was poised to continue the discussion, and Taneda had raised his hand to show his willingness to contribute, but the Editor saw no reason to debate an issue irrelevant to the article. His conclusion was completely in character.

'Thank you everyone,' he said, fitting his papers into a transparent cover. 'I'm satisfied with the article and the photographs.' He nodded towards Araki. 'Congratulations for a fine effort. Please proceed with the redrafting as usual. Next item please.'

'The season ticket Tanimoto was carrying was from Akasaka-mitsuke, near his sokaiya employers' office, to Ikebukuro, where Maki and her gangster friends are based. Are you convinced?' Araki asked, as he dodged the rain with Kondo from doorway to doorway on the way to lunch.

'Coincidence,' Kondo said thoughtfully. 'Can I ask you something? I've known you about seven years and I've never seen you eat anything for lunch except tanuki-soba.'

Araki drew hard on the delicate, brittle threads, guiding them delicately with his chopsticks.

'And the list. Did I tell you Maki took my copy of the list, the one her lover had been so careful to hide?'

Kondo looked up reflectively, leaving a dribble of curry sauce to escape to his chin line.

'I think he died for that list,' Araki added casually.

Revised texts were stamped with the Editor's seal and passed out for typesetting as soon as they were approved. The Tanimoto story had been in the middle of a heap, making way for a more difficult and important article on the possibility of changes in the cabinet and the influence of former leader Tanaka, which had required greater scrutiny.

'It's a very good story, very thorough.'

But Kondo's mollifying words elicited no immediate response from Araki who was standing by the window and staring into the evening drizzle. There was a long queue at the taxi-rank outside Shimbashi Station. The drivers enjoyed the rain and cruised greedily around the plaza, taunting the stoical citizens before they attached themselves to the yellow and green snake of private and company taxis at the approved stop. From the third floor, the bobbing umbrellas looked like a gathering of molehills, until a sudden gust turned one inside out, the owner drenched as he wrestled for control.

'Have you made any progress on the list?' Araki asked. 'Not that it matters very much now.' It was obvious the answer would be negative.

'I've examined the notations for signs of repetition, pattern and consistency, groupings of numbers which might show whether an amount of money was hidden in the code or some tangible element. I'm afraid that's something only the intended reader of the figures can tell us. The real key seems to be the katakana letter in front of each of the twenty-two rows. It must be the first syllable of a person's or a place's name. Some point of contact between the bearer of the list and the recipient of some action.'

'How long will it take you to crack it?'

Kondo expected his embarrassed silence was reply enough. When it was not, and Araki looked at him with tired, puffed eyes, he folded the faded yellow paper along its original creases and offered it to the reporter. He spoke compassionately.

'The story's over for us, except maybe for a paragraph or two when the manslaughter case goes to court. You must have understood the Editor's line today; and you will know the normal procedures. For the police, the case is all but closed save for some bargaining between the prosecution and the unfortunate killer. I think you have every reason to take your suspicions to them but you may find yourself under the lamp for stealing evidence and not reporting a serious crime at your home. I cannot see what this course would achieve and strongly advise you to concentrate attention on next week's stories.'

Araki waved the list. 'Doesn't it matter to anyone that a man was killed, probably murdered for this miserable scrap?'

When he reached the door he turned. 'I'll talk to you about it again tomorrow.'

It was Friday morning, usually a relaxed day. The magazine was on the newsstands and the writers and their staff took time to file claims for expenses, watch the sales figures come in, keep a watchful eye on the reception their favourite articles attained and browse through a heap of competitor journals. It was also the time for planning, for presenting a new idea or reviving one shelved earlier, for preparing a campaign. Kobayashi had met three project teams and heard their thoughts in this preliminary stage. It was almost midday; he wanted to leave soon for his regular Friday lunch with some journalist friends. There was a certain testiness in his voice when he called Keiko on the inter-office telephone.

'Where's Araki-san? He knew we had a meeting this morning.'

'I'm extremely sorry, Editor-san. I've tried his apartment and some of his friends, but he's not at home and nobody's heard from him or seen him.'

'Was he in the office yesterday? Has Chris seen him?' The replies were both negative.

It was a rule without exception: whenever a reporter was out of the office, his general whereabouts or plan must be left on record in the office and if he was unable through unforeseen development to be at a scheduled meeting he should by some means make the office aware

137

of his inability to attend. Keiko was distraught, and it showed in her voice which uncharacteristically rose in pitch.

'He told Kondo-san on Wednesday that he would discuss the Tanimoto story with him on Thursday but there was no contact. He simply seems to have disappeared.'

# CHAPTER EIGHT

Araki had woken early on Thursday, an active day in prospect. He breakfasted on green tea and cigarettes and left his sparsely furnished flat at eight-fifteen.

A soft, almost warm curtain of rain was falling from the grey blanket sky, broken only by an occasional squall of wind. At Gaien Station commuters waited for their underground train in disciplined lines three abreast at the designated spots where the doors would open. Since Araki kept irregular hours, his profession demanding it, he had almost forgotten what it was like to be a commuter. His flimsy anorak over a light blue summer sports coat, open-necked shirt and slacks whose crease had just been flattened by the rain, were out of place among the sombre business suits, neatly greased hair and briefcases with shopping bag handles. A touch of colour came from the rubber rain boots most of the men wore and which they would change in their offices for more appropriate footwear. Standing in formation, trousers tucked into and bunching over the tops of their boots, they looked like troupes of Russian dancers. Order, not that any was needed, was maintained by station attendants who bellowed warnings and advice through overhead loudspeakers on the dangers of standing too near the edge of the platform, the perils and social menace of smoking, the destination of the next train and so on.

Araki's train was absurdly crowded. The overhead fans gave little relief from the steam of evaporating rain which clouded spectacles and mixed freely with the sweat and traces of garlic and alcohol released through the pores. Eight of the ten people sitting on Araki's side of the train were asleep, while the conductor, successor to his station colleague, added an exhortation to the honoured guests not to forget their umbrellas and asked them to be patient while the train spent an extra forty seconds at the stop in order to fall in line with the schedule.

Nothing has changed, Araki thought, elbow to elbow with the crowd leaving through the central exit at Akasaka-mitsuke. There were no better educated people in the world than the Japanese but if education was the spark that ignited the flame of inquisitive questioning of government, and the laws and guidelines by which they were ruled and the values on which their lives were based, in Japan it had produced a literate but completely passive and submissive society.

The Minoda Number Ten Building was a grey, functional structure, its basement housing a cluster of five-stool bars and a Chinese restaurant, a flower shop and a unisex hairdresser at ground level. The New Japan Economic Research Institute occupied part of one side of the fourth floor, big enough, as Araki could see through the half-open door, to hold a dozen or so people in open plan and others he could not see behind a section of the office partitioned off to make some private rooms. Outside one of these Araki could see two men engaged in a mild argument, with a third standing impassively behind them.

The one in the centre, the dominant participant in the quarrel, was surely Teruaki Ogawa, Tanimoto's employer and president of the Institute. He was tall for a Japanese, his hair had been styled and his suit was tailored and did not shine with age like that of the agitated, bespectacled man he was trying to calm with words and pats on the forearm.

A girl clerk noticed Araki and hurried towards him, bowing as she came. She obstructed his view but not before he had taken in the three faces with a trained and experienced eye. Ogawa and his man were trying, or so it seemed, to bundle the other into one of the offices but he was resisting physically and with his high weak voice. He turned towards Araki, for a second at most, but long enough for the reporter to glimpse

140

a flash of crimson from the button-sized company badge in the man's lapel.

'Can I help you?' the plain clerk asked agreeably.

'I don't have an appointment,' Araki said, trying to look over her shoulder, 'but I'd like to have a few words with Mr Ogawa. I'm from the *Tokyo Weekly*. The magazine.'

The girl accepted the request and asked him to wait. He had estimated the chance of meeting Ogawa as slight, if not nil, and was surprised to be shown to a room, more of a large cubicle, and again asked to wait. The main open office area was separated from Araki's room by a floor-to-roof partition, half of which was frosted glass, and which prevented the reporter from seeing the rapid departure of the smooth-suited protagonist of the conversation he had witnessed but not heard a few minutes earlier. He had begun to sketch on his notepad a face, a suit and a badge when Teruaki Ogawa made his entrance accompanied by his broad-shouldered aide.

'I'm Ogawa.'

There was an exchange of name-cards and perfunctory bows, all in silence. Ogawa had poise and confidence and keen eyes behind smooth lids. He waited cross-legged in the host's chair making no effort to pursue the normal pleasantries. Araki sensed that the man in front of him knew who he was although the article that mentioned Ogawa and his profession would not be on sale until the next day. The silent bodyguard, whose name was Kaneda, took from his jacket a small, yellow pad and prepared to take notes.

'It's good of you to see me without an appointment. I suppose you're tired of the press and all the questions.' Araki was unable to stop his voice trailing, his gaze attracted and fixed to the yellow notepaper. His throat was dry, but there was no sign of the polite cup of tea or soft drink.

'Frankly speaking,' Ogawa said, in soft mellow tones, 'what with the police enquiries and the reporters, it's been very upsetting for all of us. I suppose your magazine will be writing on the incident soon.'

'Yes, as a matter of fact we will. There's an article on

Mr Tanimoto in our magazine coming out tomorrow. I thought I'd like to come along and express my regrets at your employee's death and ask you a few questions, if I may.'

Ogawa allowed himself to look perplexed. 'You mean there's more to come?' he asked.

Araki cleared his throat. 'We like to get a story out while it's still fresh and then a few weeks later tie up some loose ends when new information appears.'

The aide was scribbling into his pad. Into the yellow pad.

Ogawa interlaced his long fingers, and his face returned to an icy expression of distaste. He anticipated the first question.

'Tanimoto worked hard for me, was very loyal, but in the end it seems he played too hard. It was sad to hear of the accident but not particularly surprising.'

'Did he leave any family that you know of?'

'He was orphaned in his teens. He may have a sister in Okinawa. It wasn't his character to talk about relatives.'

'Did he ever marry?'

'No. He lived on his own somewhere in . . .' Ogawa looked at Kaneda who responded without lifting his eyes from the notepad.

'Nakano.' His voice was thick, with a trace of Kansai slur.

Then Araki said, 'The police said the only thing the victim had on him when they found him was a season ticket for the underground. It's odd Kawazu and his friends should have stripped poor old Tanimoto before they dumped him. Panic does strange things, I suppose.' He was wasting time while baiting the trap, looking all the time for an exchange between the two men, some flick of a wrist, an upraised eyebrow, a wink or some secret signal that would tell the other to be on guard. There was nothing, until Ogawa pushed his sleeve up and glanced at his watch. It was a gesture of impatience intended for the reporter.

'The strange thing is,' Araki continued, ignoring the message, 'the pass was for travel from here to Ikebukuro.

142

Would you happen to know why he would want to commute there? Did you have a branch office perhaps?'

A trace of exasperation was beginning to crack Ogawa's placid face. 'What my employees do outside office hours is of no concern to me,' he pronounced firmly. 'He probably had a girlfriend there whom he lived with. We have no representation in Tokyo other than this office. As I said before, I didn't care what his pastimes were as long as they didn't affect his work.'

'If I could ask one more question,' Araki said diplomatically, 'what exactly did Tanimoto do here?'

Ogawa leaned back in his chair, his hands together as if in prayer, and stared at the ceiling. It was clear to both men that the dialogue had developed into a process of mutual evaluation, a game of words in which the winner was the one who learned the most while disclosing the least. The sokaiya chief's eyes saw nothing as they stared blankly through the window behind Araki's head. His lips pursed before he spoke.

'He was one of my senior subscription salesmen. We produce a monthly newsletter designed mainly for the top one hundred companies on the first section of the Tokyo Stock Exchange but open to any subscriber.'

'I've heard of it.' Araki spoke without sarcasm, preferring to continue the game on existing premises of grudging politeness. What Ogawa had meant was that Tanimoto was the person who would confront a senior official of, say, the country's largest electronic calculator company, Y, with the facts, as obtained by bribery, or gentle coercion, from a drunken section chief, that the company planned to cut back drastically their procurement of components from forty-two sub-contractors who depended on Y to buy ninety per cent of their combined production. Y was currently experiencing a drastic fall in the export of its principal lines and was on the point of redeploying a large part of its workforce in anticipation of the development of a new range of video and other equipment. By forcing the economic substructure to take the brunt of the periodic business downturns, pushing

143

production line workers into menial tasks in the service sector or even back to the agricultural villages of their birth, company Y could survive without demoralising lay-offs and help perpetuate the myth of harmony and lifetime employment so admired outside Japan. In Y's case, the cutbacks were top secret, pending negotiations with the sub-contractors and agreement on compensation, and any early disclosure could cause severe disruption in the supply chain. Y would agree to 'subscribe' to Ogawa's magazine and provide substantial contributions for further economic research into problems in their particular industry. It was the price for silence.

'If I can be of further assistance,' Ogawa continued blandly, 'please let me know.'

The irritation in Ogawa's voice was not missed on Araki, but there were other implicit signals that the meeting was over. Kaneda, the mute witness, had closed his notebook and put away his ballpen. He folded Araki's name-card across its middle and sharpened the crease between his thumb and forefinger with growing ferocity and pressure. It remained only to discern the level at which future relations between the reporter and the businessman would be conducted. If at all.

'There are in fact a few points about Tanimoto's private life I'd like to clarify. Would you mind if I interviewed some of your staff?'

'I don't think,' Ogawa said definitely, 'anything more need be added to this unfortunate incident. The reputation of my company has been damaged enough by an event in which it had no involvement. I cannot, therefore, agree to your request and would be most disturbed if you were to do so without my knowledge. And now, if you'll excuse me, I have another appointment.'

A helpful bunch, Araki thought, as he sifted through the undercurrents of the conversation and mulled over the thinly veiled threat while waiting for the lift. In the foyer, a line of red public telephones reminded him of his obligation to call his office and report his whereabouts. He fumbled in

144

his pockets and snapped his fingers. He was impatient to get home and follow through a notion that had tantalised him since he had watched the three men arguing. He had to hurry, while the memory stayed fresh. With no tobacconist or other immediately available source of change, he promised himself to call from the apartment.

The damaged furniture had been removed, new tatami laid and his books and magazines stacked against the wall. The matting gave off a pleasant, earthy smell of freshly cut reeds. Araki boiled a kettle of water and poured it over a tub of instant curry-flavoured noodles and found an over-ripe tomato and a small bottle of Kirin in the fridge that had somehow survived the swiping hand of the intruder while less fortunate contents had perished on the kitchen floor. He rubbed the tomato across his chest before eating it.

After measuring fifteen paces from the front door and repositioning his study table on the spot he drew a circle, a fraction larger than a shirt button, on a plain piece of paper which he then taped to the door a metre and a half or so up from the floor. The search for a red pen was fruitless but while he was rummaging through the desk drawers he found the round black enamel bowl containing the soft cake of crimson ink used to produce his personal seal. Even better, he thought, even closer to the real thing. He dipped the wooden, oval chop into the ink until the waxy compound formed a cap. The stick was smaller in diameter than the circle he had drawn but after he had pressed, dabbed and twisted it over the paper the red blob filled the space and was thick enough to obscure all but a faint impression of the two personalised characters for Araki in the seal. Araki stared at the spot as he sucked noisily on the noodles, satisfied at the distance, the size and the colour.

His books were arranged haphazardly at the best of times, and tidiness rather than order was the priority when the office staff cleaned up the mess. But the book he sought was large enough to stand out by its bulk alone and with 2,520 pages, a tome eight centimetres thick, the *Tokyo Stock Exchange*

*Company Directory* was not easily mislaid. Companies were segregated first by industrial sector, be it manufacturing, commercial, financial or service, and then in the order of the phonetic scripts. The big names, the Mitsubishis, the Sumitomos and the Mitsuis, had a whole page dedicated to each of them, listing five years of business results up to 31 March, 1982, alongside balance sheet footings, principal product lines, main subsidiaries, overseas representation and the six or seven largest shareholders. They were proud of their pedigrees, their market shares and their roles in the individual industrial groupings of which they were part. The Sumitomo logo, reproduced in colour at the top of any page where a Sumitomo company was represented, appeared in the commercial section above Sumitomo Corporation, Japan's fourth largest general trading firm, as Sumitomo Bank and Sumitomo Trust and Banking in the chapter on financial institutions and as Sumitomo Metal Industries in the iron and steel section. Likewise, the three diamonds of the Mitsubishi Group was represented in virtually all of the categories in the directory.

It was forty minutes, still a half-hour away from noon, before he found what he was sure he was looking for. He had flipped through the pages: there was nothing under textiles or heavy industries to divert him but he paused in the finance section, his senses excited. He tore a page from its bindings, hung it on the door next to his sketch and retreated to his base fifteen paces away. His excitement evaporated. The logo was indeed mostly red, but the colour was broken by two distinct wavy blue lines across the centre of the disk. He tried to believe that the man he had seen in the sokaiya's office had worn a similar decoration, but from whatever angle he viewed it the curved lines split the disk cleanly and dominated the whole thing. He would certainly have recalled these features. Pity, he mused, since it belonged to one of the City banks.

Another bank, a local bank he had never heard of from the Hokuriku region, drew his attention and caused him to mutilate the directory again and scrutinise its logo from the

146

middle of his flat. But like another he found in the heavy industry section, the shades of red in both badges faded into a pale pink before he had retired half a dozen paces. He dropped the bulky tome in frustration, his mind looking for a short cut through the maze. Who would have the gall, the courage, the desperation, the confidence to appear at the office of their blackmailers and run the risk, however slight, of exposure to the danger of recognition? He realised he may have been wasting his time in examining the thirteen City banks, the six trust banks and the three long-term credit institutions as their activities were too carefully guided by the Ministry of Finance and their scope of business too narrow and defined to be open to speculative coercion by the Sokaiya. He should have looked to the Sogo Shosha, the general trading companies, Japans real secret weapon in the trade war, when he began his quest. If there were warts on the nose of Japan's hard earned image of respectability, the infestation would be isolated in the boardrooms of the middlemen and the countless captive companies they controlled.

Araki paid scant heed to the plain three lines, the 'three' in Mitsui, the roman letters C and I for C.Itoh, or the distinctive diamonds of Mitsubishi Corportation, even though their carmine flashes urged closer inspection. Knowing his quest was over, he tore the page describing the sixth largest of the monster conglomerates and tacked it to his door.

It was almost inevitable, Araki would ponder later, that a seemingly unrelated sequence of events should divulge a name which would be common to all. Although detectives of broad and long experience have always said that coincidental discovery is the key to four-fifths of crime solution, his own perception of destiny was mightily strained as he sat at his table and studied the tiny logo reproduction stuck on his front door.

The room seemed close and stuffy, in spite of the open window, and it wasn't until he had stripped down to his loose-fitting summer underwear that the flow of sweat ceased.

He stubbed out a half-finished cigarette so that his left hand was free to hold the directory and the index finger on his right available to flatten the torn page against the door, allowing his eyes to examine from close range what they had only seen from a distance.

Engraved into the disk, and split into two parts like an arrow's flight cut through the shaft and turned upside down, was the profile of a tree, its three branches hanging like eyebrows from the trunk to give the illusion of a healthy pine. Joining the two parts was a pair of concave parallel lines, a hump linking the stems of each half of the pine tree. If it was meant to represent a bridge it was like those that spanned the country's streams and canals two and three hundred years ago, some of which remained.

He looked again at the picture stuck to his door, admiring the photographer's skill at reproducing every contour of the original badge without blurring the image. He wondered whether the bridge had crossed a tumbling mountain brook or dry gulley in a forest of pine trees near the founder's birthplace, or symbolically represented his profession as a cutter of lumber or carpenter at a time when the tree was the country's most valuable and ubiquitous asset. Whatever its origin, Araki was ninety-five per cent certain, even from a distance, that the harried salaryman he had seen three hours ealier in the office of a known corporate extortionist was an employee of Matsuhashi Corporation; Pine Bridge the first two characters read literally – one of the most powerful business concerns in the land.

He took the reference book again and selected another from the pile. Specks of rain were being blown through the crack in the terrace door on a cool, sharp breeze, and Araki sat within their reach on the new tatami, notebook open, eyes searching the room for some elusive inspiration. It was not the fact that an offical of a respected company should confer with the likes of Ogawa that puzzled the reporter: he had already proved that a relationship existed when he identified Tanimoto at the shareholders' meeting of Matsuhashi. What did astonish him was the blatant nature of the liaison, the sheer disregard for an act which at best merited censure and at worst violated the laws of the Commercial Code. The dubious transfer of money, and any other surreptitious transactions, were usually done in circumstances of extreme discretion, yet here was a man who, in a moment of confusion or carelessness, had allowed himself to be witnessed, giving away, through his lapel badge, the identity of his employer in a place totally detrimental to the reputation and image of that company.

It was no wonder, Araki mused, that Ogawa had seemed to be trying to hide the salaryman away when he saw Araki standing in the doorway. The appearance of Matsuhashi in two separate situations in which the other protagonist, in both cases, was a group of corporate extortionists was inexplicable in any other terms but coincidence. He rushed to paper, keen to set down the delicate multi-coloured bubbles before they burst, the overdue telephone call to his magazine now far from his mind.

He wrote it like any other story: brief, uncomplicated statistics within undemanding sentences suitably embellished with superlatives. His eyes swung inquisitively between the items he had underlined in the directory and in a guide in English to industrial groups.

Matsuhashi Corporation had not been among the massive industrial-financial conglomerates that had encouraged, armed and provisioned the imperial war effort and were dismembered by the occupation forces. Under its founder Kambei Yagi, a low-class samurai who sprang from the revolution which overthrew the Tokugawa shogun and reinstated the imperial line in 1868, Matsuhashi prospered as supplier of lumber, textiles and sundry goods to the military. Energetic producers of timber and family weavers of cloth in the Kansai were organised into co-operatives which, when they became dependent upon Matsuhashi for their continued prosperity, were absorbed into a group that now carried goods to Japan's conquests on the Asian mainland in ships owned by Yagi's descendants. By the end of the Great War the symbol of the pine bridge

149

on a sheer crimson backcloth flew over a hundred ware-houses in Japan's industrial heartland and at the masthead of a score of coasters and deepwater freighters. Although six bloodline descendants of Kambei Yagi were detained briefly by the American occupation forces in 1945, the wrath of the conqueror fell most heavily on the giant zaibatsu which, with the military, were judged responsible for the excessses of the war and broken up, their central holding companies made illegal and those leaders found guilty of being instigators or leaders of the military-industrial conspiracy imprisoned.

The dissolution of the great zaibatsu favoured those trading companies like Matsuhashi that remained. They emerged with a large degree of corporate identity intact and, blessed with benevolent treatment instead of the retribution expected, they were able to fill the gap vacated by the fallen giants. In Matsuhashi's case, the post-war prosperity of the surviving company, now run by senior managers under Daisuke Mizuno, was assured by the utter destruction, caused by the blanket fire-bombing, of Japan's wood-built cities and the urgent need thus created to reconstruct vast tracts of urban devastation. The timber cutters, the merchants and the carpenters came together again, reviving the spirit of Matsuhashi in the Kansai and the Kanto to build simple wooden dwellings, back to back, to meet insatiable demand. The Korean War gave an incalculable economic boost to Japan, which gave massive logistical support and tacit impetus to the allied cause. Matsuhashi rode the boom, branching defiantly and aggressively into concrete and pre-fabricated structures as the demand pattern changed from the traditional to the functional requirements of an emerging modern state.

During the second half of the fifties the assets and debts of thirty-three enterprises with strong pre-war ties to the Yagi family business were formally absorbed under the name of Matsuhashi Limited. They were mostly secondary dealers in textiles, machinery, timber, construction equipment and fuels and they were to form the nucleus of the burgeoning trading conglomerate. Manufacturers not affiliated with the resurgent pre-war zaibatsu houses sought strength from unity with companies of similar or greater resources and ambition, and it was the sale of vast tracts of what had become prime industrial and residential land in and around Nagoya that enabled the heirs of Kambei Yagi to buy substantial interests in a steelworks, a chemical complex on Tokyo Bay and a maker of primitive transistor and other basic electronic components, supplying them with imported raw materials and exporting their production. Like their major trading company competitors, Matsuhashi took on the role of the quasi-bank, borrowing from recognised financial institutions, and financing the production of a wide variety of manufacturers themselves, buying the end products for domestic and overseas sale.

It asked little in return for the vast turnover generated; Araki noted that Matsuhashi, while ranked seventh among the top ten trading companies which handle half of Japan's total imports and exports, earned only two billion yen, before paying tax, in the 1981-82 business year on sales of 4,550 billion yen. Whilst the sales figure would not have disgraced itself as the gross national product of most of the countries it dealt with, Matsuhashi's profits were negligible.

He also found among the figures confirmation of a suspicion getting stronger in his mind that all was not well at the corporation. The two billion yen they claimed as profit had only been generated by the sale of fixed assets, including its old head-office building in Osaka, where it retained its corporate registration although business was now conducted from Tokyo. The sale realised twelve billion yen, all of which was used to provide more than ten and a half billion yen's worth of bad debt provisions made necessary in liquidating eleven affiliates, nine of them in real estate, and to cover severe losses incurred on trading in stocks and shares.

The reporter jotted a summary of the figures into his notebook, and related the shareholders' complaints, so effectively silenced by Tanimoto and his sokaiya at the annual general meeting in June, to the abysmal and dubious trading results of the company. Where they had paid a five-yen dividend per share in the previous year, Matsuhashi could only offer a token one-yen to those entrusting their savings to it this time. It was more surprising because Matsuhashi was the only one of the big ten to have to pad out its results with extraordinary profits from the sale of assets and the only one to reduce its dividend.

It seemed that the president of the Kansai bank which had supported and financed Matsuhashi's post-Korean War expansion and was itself swollen by merger and takeover, perceived a threat to the unaffiliated enterprise from the reunification of the splintered zaibatsu companies, now separately constituted and independently managed. With holding companies illegal, these companies, running across the complete financial-industrial world, had restored their inter-dependence by holding each other's shares so that the former steel-maker of the pre-war zaibatsu was now owned in its majority by its reborn zaibatsu colleagues. In 1971, the astute banker, seeing the resurgence of the old zaibatsu groups as an overwhelming economic force, had secretly contacted his major non-affiliated customers such as Matsuhashi Trading Company and suggested that they all reach a formal understanding in order to compete on equal terms with the already mutually aligned conglomerates. Seventeen firms, with their phalanxes of subsidiaries, connected companies, captive subcontractors and tied relationships answered the call. For a decade, the bank, The South-West Bank of Japan, was the undisputed leader, the catalyst, in the great adventure, but by the mid-seventies the strength of the Matsuhashi Trading Company was drawing a swarm of local and foreign bankers to its finance division, their briefcases full of open-ended lines of credit, and to the simple, evocative image of the pine tree and the bridge which the presidents of the seventeen chose when they let it be known in business circles, the 'zaikai', that they wished to be identified as members of the Matsuhashi Group. Of the eighteen primary enterprises whose presidents met every second and fourth Monday at the Matsukai, the Pine Committee, the highest policy making level of the Group, four bore the kanji for Matsuhashi in their corporate names and these Matsuhashi Real Estate, Matsuhashi Construction, Matsuhashi Pulp and Paper and Matsuhashi Steamship were either leaders, or competed for the top position, in their field, carrying on into the future the original business interests of the founder. The strength of each member of the combine emanated from the stocks which each held in his brother company, and merited its reputation from an identity with the group and its confidence from knowing that its survival during hard times was in the hands of friendly, vested interests and not the whims and frivolity of the common shareholder or a cold, dispassionate bank. Yes, Araki thought, as he drew together the threads, he had first-hand knowledge of how private investors are kept at bay.

But at the end of his research there was only one evaluation, one assessment, common to the journals and newspapers he scanned: Matsuhashi Corporation produced the worst results from among those ten trading companies on which the future of Japan Incorporated was measured and on whose performances investment decisions around the world were made. Little wonder the shareholders had tried to voice their concern at the annual general meeting last June, only to be silenced by Tanimoto and his hired thugs.

Araki was more confused than before: were there two stories? The death of Tanimoto in a petty sqabble? The declining fortunes of Matsuhashi Corporation and the prospect of a major financial collapse? Or did something connect the two, an event, a person . . . or a scrap of paper? Uncharacteristically he tidied up, or at least stacked his reference material, hoping to check with Kondo into the diffusion of yellow notepads.

# CHAPTER NINE

The rain had eased a little as Araki drove north through the
endless urban sprawl on the route he had taken on the night
of the visit with Chris to the Bali. Was it a need for
vengeance, a desire for reprisal, that took him back to the
alleys of Ikebukuro, a search for the grotesque thug Ezaki
and his wiry but no doubt equally destructive crony? Or did
he hope to glimpse the woman who had baffled him the day
before with the display of emotions and responses ranging
from those of a grieving lover to the scheming of a calculating
thief.

He still needed the continuous wiper, whose defective
motion etched parallel arcs of vision through the haze. The
sky was a leaden, bulging ceiling, threatening to crack and
unleash the full power of Typhoon Ten. Driving through
Shinjuku, where a scattering of neon lights were already lit
against the premature darkness, he suddenly slapped the
wheel, remembering he had not called the office to tell them
where he was and to apologise to Kondo for not meeting
him as promised. He would do so from Ikebukuro, although
it was already three o'clock. Impulse, curiosity and a degree
of free time at the end of the publishing week were leading
him there and though he had no idea what he was going
to do or look for, he was certain that the death of Tanimoto
had somehow broken a connection between the house of
pleasure and the shady, influential sokaiya group run by the
silky smooth Ogawa. And lurking behind the whole
unpleasant picture was the recurring image of Matsuhashi
Corporation.

One point bothered him more than the rest. Where had

the two wreckers, the bull-necked Ezaki and his fellow Yanagida-gumi gangster, come from before they entered the Bali? Chris had seen them turning the corner to his left as he watched from the coffee shop opposite. Then Araki knew where to look. If he walked round the block, away from the Bali, he would re-appear in front of the massage parlour on the same route as the two thugs. Probably nothing, he told himself, but it was the only excuse he could use to justify his being out on the edge of Typhoon Ten.

The street was deserted except for a newspaper-boy who found shelter by hugging the unbroken row of buildings between deliveries. The entrance to the Bali was awash with rainwater. Araki walked quickly by, glancing only long enough to note that their business day had begun fifteen minutes ago at three o'clock. He held his umbrella tight to his head, but his torso and legs were swept by chilling, sodden squalls. He intended to inspect the area by walking east round the block where the Turkish bath occupied part of a nondescript grey building on its southern perimeter. There were no other bathhouses in the alley, only the row of coffee shops opposite and the four- or five-storey utility buildings, housing mahjong parlours, restaurants, cheap snackbars and small businesses. A cook looked forlornly through the window of his cheap eatery, assessing the business prospects for the evening. Lodged in between these intrusions of ugly ferro-concrete were the wooden dwellings of grocers, fishmongers and liquor stores which had temporarily escaped the hand of the developer.

Walking briskly, he ignored the shops, the life-blood of the pleasure houses of the district, but backed into the tiled foyers of the buildings which might hold a rack of mailboxes or some other clue which might reveal a familiar identity. There was nothing to hold his attention, except for the common loan sharks who reeked of the yakuza, and the road ran abruptly into another of slightly greater width.

As he looked for traffic before crossing the space, he saw the car coming towards him, its driver enjoying the deserted road to move at speed, forcing a knee-high jet of water t

155

doorway level on each side. Subconsciously, Araki had been expecting something and had even thought of reactions and responses to the physical threats which he knew existed around the story he had just completed and the investigation he insisted on pursuing. But when it happened, when the attack on his person seemed inevitable, he froze, staring at the car careering towards him, seeing only the grille, like the mouth of a giant predator about to strike, and the headlights on full beam which blinded him as they approached.

The driver was a victim of his own complacence, unaware that the combination of artificial light and premature darkness had broadened his scope of vision but obliterated objects at close range. When Araki materialised in his sight, only four car-lengths away, he braked hard, but had the presence of mind to pump the pedal and avoid a skid. The car responded to the sudden turn of the wheel and veered around the immobile reporter. Araki watched it go. Soaked from rain and sweat, his heart pumping uncontrollably and angry at his own paranoia, he resumed his journey, now north on the eastern side of the block.

The smell of roasting chicken with a distinct flavour of soya sauce was brought by the wind – some distance too, because he checked the tenants of two low, office blocks before he found the yakitori restaurant on the ground floor of a third. The thin kebabs of skin, breast and liver, sizzling over a bed of smouldering bright charcoal, were for the only other customers, a young couple engrossed in themselves and pouring beer for one another in the customary way. Early in the day, Araki thought, shaking the rain from his umbrella at the entrance.

'You're a little optimistic, aren't you?' Araki asked, taking up one of the stools at the counter in front of the owner. The thick-featured man with a handband round his forehead was stacking another selection of skewered chicken meat on to the substantial heap he had already prepared.

'The heavy rain's not due until late tonight,' he replied, without looking up, selecting Araki's order which he placed nimbly on the grill. 'I should get some office trade about half past five, six-ish. Typhoons do this to people.' He jerked his head towards the couple. 'It's like a holiday. They leave work early and have a few drinks and a snack before the heavy rains arrive.'

Araki sipped from a cup of hot sake, his attention drawn to the gap in the sliding door and the restricted view of the street outside. Passers-by were few, and none took any interest in his refuge.

'Have you seen a big man around here?' he asked, trying to appear disinterested. 'I think he's called Ezaki. Looks like a retired Sumo wrestler.'

The owner wiped the sweat off his head with his forearm, pondering the question innocently, and drew breath through his teeth with a loud slurp.

'Don't recall anyone of that description. I get students mostly ,' he said, again gesturing, this time with a thumb to the couple at the end of the counter, 'and later on the salary-men crowd. They like a few skewers before they catch the last train out of Ikebukuro. No, can't say I recall any wrestler.'

Warmed by the sake, Araki resumed his frustrating promenade, hunching his shoulders against a new, persistent downpour that found a way around his inadequate umbrella. When the crack came, Araki was in the centre of the street, almost to the next corner of the block, having stepped out to avoid a gathering lake of rainwater which was already reaching towards its twin on the opposite side of the slight cantilever. It was a sharp, echo-free report. What a pistol shot might sound like, if Araki had ever heard a real one, and realistic enough to propel him through the deepening puddle into another refuge, this time a gap between two low buildings, wide enough for some half-empty plastic garbage bins and the now sprawling figure of Araki who fell heavily amongst them. Instinctively, he felt his body, searching for a wound.

'Are you all right?' asked the stooping figure of an old lady in a transparent ankle-length plastic raincoat. 'Are you ill?' she continued, meaning drunk, but in understanding,

157

polite if slightly reproving language, and then went on her way when she saw he was not.

Araki grunted, and when he rose awkwardly he slipped on a patch of spilt watermelon skin and decaying chinese cabbage leaves. He felt stupid, and wondered what he was doing there. Brushing off a clutch of black sticky melon seeds from a bare arm he retrieved his umbrella from between the bins and when he opened it with a flourish, four of the prongs holding the taut material in a protective cover tore away from the cloth, leaving a quarter of the webbing free to slide down the unfettered skeleton. Rain dripped playfully through this open window. Araki threw away the mangled contraption, resigning himself to his own stupidity and an aimless wander in intolerable conditions. Then he remembered the shot, or whatever it was, and looked back cautiously down the street. His paranoia returned, and with it the chilling sensation of fear.

He blinked through the rain, now running unimpeded down his face, shaking his head and squinting at the emptiness beyond. Whoever or whatever had been there had moved smartly into any one of half a dozen gaps. Araki breathed hard, pressing himself against a wall, oblivious to the wetness, and waited two, perhaps three minutes. When it seemed that it had been his imagination at work again after all, he stepped away from his sanctuary and saw the figure of a man leave a doorway. It was barely within the range of visibility, but Araki strained hard to see some gesture of hostility, or some feature to commit to memory. The man looked towards Araki, pointing the object he held. For an instant, the reporter thought the whoosh when the automatic umbrella opened was a muffled pistol shot and he grimaced in anticipation of the impact.

The bedraggled reporter felt ridiculous, impotent and angry at his fear. He was finished with the exercise and determined to give only passing inspection to the premises on the last half a block left before his car. In fact there was little to attract him; and he paused only once in the doorway of an office building which, according to the rows of nameplates housed a discount travel agency, a brace of personal loan financiers, a pair of import-export firms and the rest were identified only be personal names. The north side of the block gave on to a main road with a narrow sidewalk cluttered with telegraph poles and bus-stops. The traffic was light, but the faster moving cars heading for Nerima sprayed the inside lane and sometimes the unwary walker with water. He passed the forecourt of a garage with a car showroom and a parking lot under the same management. The parking space looked deep enough to back on to the Bali's building in the alley parallel to his main thoroughfare and Araki wondered whether any of the berths were reserved for use by the bathhouse's clients. He quickened his pace, noting only a chemist, a half-completed ferro-concrete structure and a small post-office.

Although the rain had eased, Araki was thankful to round the corner into the final section of the block where his car waited, looking forward to a warm bath and few hours drinking at the Shinjuku Roman. The road had no sidewalks and although one way going south it was wide enough to overtake; and like his own, a number of cars were using the spare room to park illegally. Araki looked casually into a rice shop and a dim and empty coffee house. He stopped at a real estate agent's window and studied the rents being asked for two-room apartments like his and saw that his own in fashionable Harajuku commanded twenty thousand yen more a month than seedy Ikebukuro.

Had the old, grey, weathered building been less imposing, he would not have bothered stopping, but, almost at the corner of the block, it stood out incongruously among the wooden shops and cheaply built concrete boxes that were the product of post-war Japanese rapid reconstruction. Araki construed that it had probably been the site of a local military headquarters in the thirties when this part of Tokyo was still paddy fields and hamlets. Now it added a measure of decaying dignity to an area that had become a major commuter railway terminal within metropolitan Tokyo.

For a city where space is used to the optimum the

building had a generous lobby area in which soft-drink and cigarette vending machines had been installed. The only decoration was an information board screwed to the main wall. There was no elevator, only a narrow staircase at each side of the lobby.

Araki bought a can of orange juice from the machine, and when he pulled off the flap a spurt of liquid under pressure hit him below his left eye. He wiped it off with his arm and lit a dry, welcome cigarette while he perused the list of occupants. To his surprise there were many, and although there were only three floors the number of tenants on each suggested that the building was deep at the sides. He counted at least two more loan sharks masquerading under the name of consumer finance companies; there was a complex of doctors on the second floor, representing various specialities and trading under the name of Ikeda Medical Centre, but in general the building was home to the small business sector, the sub-stratum of Japanese economic life that exemplified the people's application to competition, diligence and sacrifice more than the Mitsubishis, Sonys or the Matsuhashis could ever do. Maido Pearl Wholesalers, Ogiwara General Merchants, Sato Consultants: the same names, just different people, could be found in the cold country of Hokkaido and the hot-spring lands from Tokyo to Kyushu. He read on: Gekkei Trading, Mita Eyeglasses, Nozaki Transport . . . Nozaki, Nozaki Transport.

Araki stared at the sign board. What had the old lady said? A small truck had stopped and asked for directions to the Kawazu home the day Tanimoto was murdered there. She only remembered because it had her own name written on the side. Nozaki. He knew that Keiko had checked in the Tokyo Metropolitan Telephone Directory and had found four of that name advertising transport services. She had called them all, but none admitted to a job in Koto Ward on Thursday, the twenty-seventh of August. On a hunch, she surveyed the directories for Funabashi and Ichikawa, near to Koto Ward but falling in Chiba Prefecture. There were only two Nozakis, branches, in fact, of the same

160

transport firms and carrying only oils and chemicals. He wanted to confirm the name with her, but unusually for a building of this size, there was no battery of red and yellow public telephones.

The offices were arranged on three sides of a dimly lit windowless configuration of corridors, their names stencilled in black on frosted glass. There was no one in the corridors of the third floor, and the only sounds came from a telephone and a radio in separate offices. A raised voice penetrated the walls and caused Araki to look instinctively towards the sound and study each doorway. Nozaki Transport's office was at the end of a long corridor, and a light was burning behind the glass door.

On his way up the stairs Araki had rehearsed a monologue during which he would ask for a quotation to move his belongings from a fictitious apartment in Ekoda to a new location in Tokorozawa, both in Nozaki's presumed catchment area. Depending on the gullibility of the person in charge he would expand the enquiries. He was within half a dozen steps of the entrance when the light inside was extinguished.

Araki was momentarily surprised, frozen to immobility, but he recovered quickly and retreated to a turn in the corridor. The door opened violently, swinging back on its hinges as the figure of a man emerging backwards appeared. Araki leaned out for a clearer view and was horrified to see patches of moisture on the floor which, had the objects of his pursuit any suspicions, would have led to him. As it was, the curious exit was due to the fact that two men were carrying between them a metal trunk, not very large but obviously heavy, and their attention was concentrated on this endeavour. They lowered the container carefully to the floor while the second man, dressed like a manager in suit and tie despite the stifling heat, locked the office. The other wore a green sweat-stained T-shirt and floppy light slacks over his stocky worker's frame.

Araki could have stopped the two men then and there, made his inquiry casually and departed, but he felt

161

something tantalisingly suspicious about an office closing so early in the afternoon, notwithstanding the proximity of Typhoon Ten. He darted self-consciously down the corridor and the stairs, hearing his own footsteps thudding on the bare stone. Outside, he looked both ways and saw that his car was parked about twenty metres away on the corner of the block. He walked as inconspicuously as possible, ignoring the rain which seemed to hang suspended in the air, and concealed himself in a doorway. He did not have long to wait. The two men appeared, almost doubled up under the weight of their burden, and walked past the reporter to the rear of an off-white 1000cc Honda utility van, unblemished apart from the Chinese characters for Nozaki Unyu Kabushiki Kaisha in black print on the nearside door. They loaded the trunk into the van and drove off. Araki had no hesitation in following them, his senses excited by the thrill of a new, though probably irrelevant, discovery and the possiblity of further revelations ahead. He could barely see the tail lights of the Honda ahead, and in his concentration failed to notice that the fuel gauge needle in his own car was in the red zone and that each sudden motion caused an orange corner light to flicker in warning.

The two vehicles took a circuitous eastward route, following vaguely the tracks of the Yamanote Loop Line as they zigzagged before arching southward towards central Tokyo. The traffic was moderately heavy, moving cautiously over windblown and slippery roads, enabling Araki to keep the white van in his view without being detected. It stopped for the first time near the main intersection outside Nishi Nippori Station. Araki was taken by surprise when it suddenly swung left off Shinobazu Avenue and he had to cut inside abruptly, making a metropolitan bus bellow in protest, before following the van as far as the station and then into a narrow road.

He pulled over at once when he saw that his prey had come to a halt at a dangerously close distance ahead. The two men did not seem perturbed and without glancing in Araki's direction they opened the rear door and pulled the metal trunk to the edge. The well-dressed man used a key, opened the container and took out what to Araki looked like a small white lunch box of the type carried by primary school children on excursions. The driver returned to his place behind the wheel while the other man carried the box carefully under his arm into a basement coffee shop. Araki scribbled the name of the place in his notebook and an idea of the location. He had to hurry, for the man was inside for less than a minute. Whether he was simply huddled against the rain Araki could not tell, but he seemed to be clutching something tightly under his jacket. He locked the back door of the van and joined his henchman.

More deliveries followed, and each time Araki was more concerned about being detected. The stops were usually in the cluster of neon-lit shops and restaurants around the stations. Two were near Ueno Station, to a pachinko pinball parlour and a hairdresser's; three just off Showa Avenue between Okachimachi and Kyobashi, two of them to intimate-looking bars and another coffee house. In Yurakucho it was a mahjong parlour, he thought, above a Chinese restaurant. Each time the procedure was the same: the apparent leader, his suit looking more and more creased as the journey progressed, would deliver a solid, identical white box and appear to receive an envelope or small package in return. The other man waited in the van, studying the map he had spread over the wheel.

As the pattern evolved, Araki began to anticipate a drop as the driver of the small van slowed to find his way and found he had time to identify the spot with greater accuracy from the signs suspended from the traffic lights hung across the main intersections. By the time the target was reached Araki had looked for, and usually found, the narrow blue plaque and had jotted down the block and site number. His first complete address was Taito One-chome, 7-14, near the Izumicho crossroads, which would take him back if necessary to the Bar Azami. Of all the drop sites he had five complete addresses, two approximate and two where he could only rely on his memory. At the later stops, and depending on

163

how near he dared to approach, he compiled a choppy description of the two men. The driver was a short paunchy, scruffy man with a wispy, lazy growth of beard, and perfectly suited to his job. The other, the obvious leader, retained a distinguished appearance in spite of the humidity and its effect on body and clothes. The wind failed to tussle the full head of hair brushed back with no parting. The sharp, angular features of his face creased as his glance darted from side to side when delivering the white boxes. More than once Araki thought he had been detected in the man's sudden piercing search.

The van was now in the outside lane on Hibiya Avenue, indicating through the darkness its intention of turning right at Uchisaiwai-cho to aim, the reporter thought, for the lively districts around Toranomon or Roppongi. It was then, while he was waiting in a parallel lane to turn with the Honda, he noticed the fuel gauge. The needle was well into the red warning zone and the triangle of light in one corner, controlled by the liquid level in the tank, was no longer flashing intermittently. It was bright orange and constant. Araki tapped the dashboard hopefully – and hopelessly. He decided to give up the pursuit, but since the other vehicle was moving in the general direction of his apartment, two kilometres away, with his local petrol station between, he would stay with it a little longer, perhaps one more delivery.

The Nozaki Transport van swung left at the Diet Building, whose eerie presence was accentuated by the billows of mist draping its bee-hive cap, and continued to the web of narrow clustered streets around the main Roppongi crossing. Araki knew Roppongi well and in ten years had seen the inside of most of the discos and pubs that made it the focal point for up-market society and the young, and confidently left his car away from the quarry in a familiar side-street before running back to the road he had seen the white van enter.

The soft, blustery drizzle was not deterring the fun-seekers; a couple giggled as they huddled close under an embattled solitary umbrella, and youths and girls in groups of three and four trotted from door to door in their search for an early start to the evening's revelries. Araki could have been waiting for his date in the entrance to a complex of bars and restaurants but his attention was on the Honda and a change in the routine practised so far. He leaned out, pleased for the diversion and thinking the chase had run its course.

The van had drawn up as close as it could to the back wall of a restaurant and the driver was squeezing across the gear shift and after much deep breathing managed to depress the door handle and ease himself into the road. He had not been out of the van since they had left Ikebukuro. The man in charge was already at the rear doors, now he was reaching into the trunk containing the boxes. Araki leaned further out, watching with renewed concentration. Words were traded, with the driver robustly protesting. He seemed to want a break and must have convinced his colleague because the two men and one of their precious boxes disappeared into a doorway festooned with neon signs. Whether a refreshment break or the last stop, Araki could not tell, but the white Honda stood unattended, like an old friend in need of company, or more accurately a quick inspection.

He left his refuge and approached cautiously, one eye always on the neon-lit doorway on the other side of the van. He tried to look relaxed behaving like the owner as he turned the handle and eased the hatch-back door up on its hinges. The clasp on the trunk was stiff and did not respond to his first, light tug. He took a firm grip, poised to try again. Then he froze.

Through the front windscreen he saw a man emerge from the doorway. Araki was petrified to inaction, his extremities unable to react to the urgent warning signal and the orders for prompt withdrawal which were surging through his nervous system. The man raised a hand, looked over the van and walked briskly past the stooping reporter towards a group of salarymen friends beyond. Araki breathed deeply, relieved and calmer, even though he could feel the bumping of his heart against his shirt. Pushing the trunk with the palm of his left hand, he again raised the clasp on the lock, this time with firm but controlled pressure, and jerked it until it opened with a snap. It must have held a dozen of the familiar white boxes in its foam rubber-lined interior but only three remained, each with a green cross stamped on its lid identifying it as a common family medicine pack. It was not the impulse of a normally honest man spitefully seeking some reward, however petty, for a tedious, wasted evening. It was a deliberate, unhurried action, and in seconds Araki had one of the boxes under his arm and was off in a running walk back to his car.

Only when locked safely inside his ageing Bluebird, with the victims of his crime two streets away, was Araki able to rationalise his actions and measure the consequences. He had the presence of mind to close both the trunk and the rear door and hoped it would allow some leeway before the discovery of the missing box was made. He hurried to finish the scene, tearing the adhesive strip from around the rim of the box and forcing the lid. It was indeed a routine medical supply box, the type every family is urged to keep as part of their earthquake escape kits, or such as a company might keep in their medicine cabinet. It was divided into two trays, the upper carrying bandages, tape, a pair of small scissors, a thermometer and other pieces of basic equipment. The lower layer held more specific medicines, bottles of mild antibiotic pills, water purifiers, pain-killers and other tablets and antiseptic creams.

It all looked very innocent, and from Araki's throat came a chortle of self-derision at the absurdity of the situation. What had he expected to find in the box? Gold coins? Newly printed banknotes? Uncut diamonds? By stretching speculation and expectation to the point of seeing a grand conspiracy at every turn in the road, in every office and coffee house, he had played the role of private detective to the full, including car chases, bribery, deception and hiding in doorways. And at the end of his little adventure he had committed a criminal offence – his second if he included taking the list from the dead man's possessions. He had stolen again, and now felt uncharacteristic remorse. When they reached the end of the delivery contract, he thought,

166

the Nozaki Transport workers would find they were a box short and would probably have to make another trip all the way to Ikebukuro to get one. They would not be pleased, but it would not occur to them that someone had bothered to rob them of an item worth five thousand yen, the cost of a bottle of whisky, at most. But then they might recall seeing an old Bluebird more than once during their deliveries and perhaps it was worth reporting this fact to the police. Again a spasm of guilt passed through him but it wasn't enough to make him contemplate returning to the white van and possibly confounding the felony by being caught trying to return the box. He found a paper shopping bag among the litter on the back seat of his car and emptied the contents of the medicine box into it, wrapping the bundle tightly and stuffing it under the passenger seat. He leaned across and slid the incriminating container out of the offside door and into the gutter behind a telegraph pole.

The traffic at the intersection was congested with taxis and cars that had double-parked to drop their passengers as near to the Roppongi action as they could to avoid the rain. The area was flooded with light in which the shredded rain seemed suspended. Doubled-up figures scurried around the glistening, multi-coloured cars, whose reflections lay like psychedelic carpets in the puddles. Araki could not cut across the lanes to turn right and take the shortest way home past the Self-Defence Force Base. Instead, he let the stream take him towards the Takagicho crossroads a minute's drive away. He still had to urge his way into the traffic, acknowledging the trouble he was causing with a nod and a wave, and it was when he scanned reflexively left and right before executing a final manoeuvre to bring him into the dry but darker passage beneath the expressway that he glimpsed another green saloon.

The image was blurred by the condensation on the inside of the window and streaks of water on the outside but the other car also appeared to be having problems. It had been parked at the kerb and in its haste to leave had forced a taxi driver to brake hard. The driver's face was not visible, and

167

there were soon six cars between them. Araki tried to rationalise away the fear that had returned to loosen his bowels and quicken his heartbeat. Since Chris had identified the car carrying the yakuza who vandalised his apartment as a green Toyota, he had been unusually alert to the colour and the model, although he had to make a conscious effort not to stare at cars that drew up near him. There was no reason for this one, or the others, to be the one that Chris had followed the night his apartment was wrecked or that had been spotted at the scene of Tanimoto's discovery. It had to be a different one – yet the car somewhere behind did, he thought on reflection, have the long low body of a Toyota Mark II and its stretched toothy grille.

The traffic thinned and Araki steered into the far right-hand lane which ran under the expressway. There was an abrupt silence as the thud of incessant rain on his car's roof ceased. Two cars followed him down the wall-less tunel, past the chipped pillars, but neither tried to close the gap as they passed through two sets of lights. Araki adjusted his mirror, straining to identify the invisible shapes behind glaring headlights. The lights at the Azabu turn-off changed to red when Araki's Bluebird arrived as the first in line on the single-file road. The car behind had extinguished its headlamps as local practice required and was coasting towards the reporter. Araki watched, his eyes locked on to the dark, olive form materialising out of the darkness. With the familiar Toyota badge studded to its centre, the broad silver grille stopped a bare half-metre from the Bluebird's rear bumper. Again, the apprehension followed by rationalisation. Every fifth car in Japan is a Toyota and probably ten per cent of those are green. Araki felt the tightness return to his stomach, but he still could not distinguish the shape or number of the car's occupants. The pedsestrian sign was flashing but there was no one at the crossing to heed its warning

Gripping the handbrake, the reporter depressed the clutch and engaged first gear. He pressed the accelerator until the car groaned under the strain and glared again into the rearview mirror. A spasm of utter terror shook his body, loosening the muscles around his bladder. He released his grip on the brake and the wheel and twisted the mirror until it captured the windscreen behind him. In the bright red reflection of the brake lights, Araki saw the hideous bloated features of the giant Ezaki, a full set of twisted and deformed teeth grinning in recognition straight back at him. Next to Ezaki, also simpering in the silent glow, sat the rough, unshaven man who fifteen minutes earlier had been at the wheel of the Nozaki Transport van, and in the rear were two more human silhouettes. Like images seen by a dying man, the events of the past seven days passed fleetingly through Araki's mind and merged like the coloured tiles of a mosaic: the body of a man of criminal credentials; a Nozaki van like the one he followed, at the supposed scene of the killing; the ransacking of his apartment by the men now behind him; the parasitical Ogawa and his professional blackmailers; the recurring presence of Matsuhashi Corporation; and lastly the cool intelligence and self-assurance of the dead man's woman, Maki.

The Bluebird's tyres slithered and finally bit into the wet tarmac. The green Toyota followed with equal determination and speed but with more control. The big man behind the wheel was an expert. The light at the Takagi-cho intersection had changed to green in fortunate sequence, and Araki twisted his aching vehicle in a U-turn round the central pillar. He had three choices: to go back towards Roppongi the way he had come, to bear left and filter into the probably crowded Gaien road and make for home, or take the ramp on to the overhead expressway. He chose the last option, needing the uninterrupted progress to give him time to assess the situation, to avoid having to stop. He thrust a thousand yen at the toll-booth attendant, not waiting for his change. He saw a chance of blending and disappearing into the traffic which was well spaced and travelling smoothly at around sixty kilometres an hour.

He moved into the fast lane with ease, checking the mirror as intently as driving conditions permitted. The rain, which was now settled into an incessant vertical torrent, and the darkness were in his favour but his driving experience in such conditions was not. The cross-city section was congested, the tail-lights stretched as far as he could see in an unbroken red line, so he branched right off on to the Haneda Airport-Yokohama loop. The treacherous conditions were forcing other vehicles to show more discipline than usual but one car was reacting differently. Araki had already reached the Oi Racetrack when he saw in the mirror a set of headlights veering and weaving impatiently in and out among the traffic some distance behind. He squinted as he tried to hold the meandering beams in view. The tightening returned: he badly wanted to urinate. The car trying to make ground on him was suddenly illuminated in the lights of a heavy lorry. It was green.

Araki left the expressway at the Haneda exit and followed the feeder road to the airport roundabout where he turned and headed his car back along the Dai-ichi Keihin. He was determined to beg protection from the first police box or station on his route. He had not seen his pursuers, although they must have passed going the other way, until he heard the frenzied screech of tyre against greasy road. He was horrified to see in his mirror the green Toyota dispensing with the formality of the roundabout to career on two wheels across the central dividing studs and appear only fifty metres behind him.

He was surprised at his own composure; he no longer wanted to apologise to Ezaki, to beg forgiveness for intruding into matters that did not concern him. Anger was replacing fear, and he wanted only to subject his pursuers, his enemies, to the same danger he was facing, even if he had to hurt them, even kill them. His driving improved as his confidence grew. He pushed the car hard, thrusting the gear stick in and out like the bolt of a rifle. With the road leading comfortably towards the safety of Shinagawa, Araki changed lanes frequently in the sparse traffic, using his brakes as little as possible. He drove through red lights brazenly, glancing often at the pursuing car, whose headlights seemed to be transfixed to the Bluebird as the two cars followed a similar erratic course. Araki was luckier at red lights than Ezaki, who was twice stymied by crossing vehicles and forced to give up ground.

Araki's plan for deliverance from his unknown fate was to reach a main railway terminal. He could not remember whether it would be Oimachi or Shinagawa first but he glimpsed flashes of railway track between the buildings. They were running parallel to the road and must reach a station soon. There was always a police box at the main junctions and after abandoning his car wherever he could he would unravel his story to the law. He pressed on, happier than before and confident of outrunning his pursuers over the final stretch.

The traffic light in front was set at red, and a heavy lorry was following a bus across the intersection. Cursing loudly Araki braked abruptly, and when the tail-lights of the lorry had passed he jerked the gear stick down into second and stepped down hard on the accelerator. The engine responded with a deep, vibrating roar, propelling the Bluebird onwards. And then, just as abruptly, it coughed, lurched and died. Araki slapped the wheel, a cry of helplessness sticking in his throat. He steered the lifeless hulk to the kerb, twisting the ignition key desperately as he went. The stalled engine exploded into life once, jerking its load forward, before dying and leaving nothing but the rasping of the healthy but ineffectual electrical contact.

The event was so sudden and unexpected that Ezaki, who had closed to within two car lengths, had to swerve to avoid a shattering collision with Araki's car in front and actually overtook it. When he braked, the car slid precipitously until he brought it under control at the kerbside. Araki was trapped, the way ahead, the road to Shinagawa and safety blocked by Ezaki and his cohorts, now visible through the downpour, leaving the car.

In an almost mindless state of panic, he left the stranded Bluebird and raced across the road into a side street, checking behind him once to see four silhouettes framed where the illumination of the main road met the darkness of the lane. He ran on past shuttered shops, his unexercised body labouring painfully on heavy feet. Behind him, Ezaki and the other driver trailed their more slender friends who were gaining on the reporter with ease. Araki shouted but the cry for help seemed like a whisper compared to the pounding of heavy rain on wooden roofs. His voice carried nowhere, and the wooden row of dwellings remained dark, with only slivers of light visible through warped rain shutters. This suggestion of life expressed in the intimacy of families forced together to see out the storm, offered no refuge, and it was only a matter of seconds before he would be overtaken.

The computer in his mind had assessed the dangers but could not forecast the outcome, so it was transmitting messages of disbelief, urging Araki to awake from the nightmare and try to sleep again. Araki shook his head, as if to revive himself, but it only seemed to make the taunts of his pursuers louder. And so he lumbered on, turning aimlessly into an even narrower lane, almost crying as his body failed to respond to his will to escape. He rounded another corner of the maze that forms the low-lying Shinagawa docklands, and his hopes rose as the mocking cries of his tormentors were lost beyond the houses he had rounded. If he stopped at any of the doors he would be caught and dragged away before he could attract the attention of those indoors.

He ran on, past the impenetrable façades of houses shuttered against the storm. He paused for breath at the entrance to a shrine, holding on to one of the round, red pillars of the torii for support. The squat, wooden, structure housing the deities was small, typical of a thousand such local festivity centres in the metropolis, and the plot of land on which it stood was equally typically a children's playground with a slide, sandpit and swings and a ring of trees, its branches swinging drunkenly in the wind, around the edge. Araki ambled first left and then right but the darkness was deceptive and concealed only the recessed parking bays of the corner houses. The street ended at the shrine.

Instinctively, he turned the way he had come, but the high pitched cry 'Over there, he's over there' caused him to stop. The only escape route was now over a two-metre wall separating the shrine precinct from the buildings beyond.

Araki dashed across the ground, which after three days of intermittent and now constant rain was a lake of ankle-deep mud, and threw his weight at the barrier. His body was heavy and unresponsive, his hands clawed and reached for the top edge. He found a grip for a foot in a groove and was able to haul his torso on to the rim. His legs swung free, and he needed only to heave himself over the top. Stranded, his arms aching, he stretched upwards but could not complete the final push up.

A hand held him firmly by the belt, another by a trouser leg. He looked down at a face streaked with strands of soaking hair. Falling backwards into a terrible void, he heard himself scream. As he fell into the mud he lashed out with heavy feet at the figure trying to secure a hold on any of his thrashing limbs. His matted, soaking hair was stuck over his eyes but he managed to keep his assailant at bay until a second, coming up behind the reporter, delivered an off-balance kick which thudded against his jaw, killing his strength to resist.

His head slumped face down in the slimy earth; the fight leaving his legs. He managed to roll over, spitting out blood and a tooth and sucking in loose gravel as he struggled for breath. Opening his eyes, he tried to cry out but the burning, searing pain in his jaw froze his mouth. Looking up helplessly, he saw that the men he knew as Ezaki, the deformed thug, and the driver of the Nozaki Transport van which had lured him finally into a trap, had reached the shrine and were standing over him. Ezaki was carrying a baseball bat, so small against his arm it looked little more than a policeman's truncheon, and was issuing orders.

'Out of the way, out of the way,' he commanded, brushing his three companions out of range. 'Let me finish it quickly.'

Araki saw the bat raised above him. Instinctively, he

moved to his left, his right arm across his face, as the bat waved above him. His clothes were soaked and heavy and his entire body was the same deep brown colour as the muddy morass in which he lay.

Ezaki's feral bloodshot eyes leaped around, trying to coordinate the moving slippery target with the trajectory of the weapon he held aloft. He brought it down, aiming low, but in the unlit darkness of the shrine the damaging force at the tip of the bat missed Araki's kneecap and buried itself in the ground.

Ezaki cursed, his voice an urgent raspy snarl. He bawled at the others. 'Hold the bastard down. Bakayaro!'

One of the attackers fell on top of Araki, smothering his face, stifling the scream which tried to force its way through the pain, and pinioned his shoulders down like a wrestler. The bat fell again, and this time struck against a fleshy thigh. Infuriated, Ezaki kicked at the squirming torso until its protests ceased and then lashed at it in uncontrolled frenzy with the bat, breaking ribs and then, in triumph, hearing above the continuous drumming of the rain on rooftops and the howl of frightened dogs, an unmistakable crack as a joint in an elbow shattered. Araki's back arched in agony.

The man who had delivered the boxes now stood outside the arc of the flaying bat. When Ezaki paused to select the next piece of Araki's anatomy, he moved forward taking a firm grip on his vicious crony's arm.

'That's enough,' he bellowed. 'They don't want him dead.'

Ezaki reeled on the man, his eyes red with rage, his face blotched with mud and rain. He shook away the other's hand and returned to Araki, who rolled on the ground. The reporter's senses were in disarray, his last conscious sensations were the drip of blood inside a broken head, and the hideous smell of the bloody, sweaty, earthy compound in which he seemed to be drowning. Another blow struck, but it no longer mattered.

# CHAPTER TEN

*Friday*

It was not yet eight-thirty and the air-conditioning had not switched itself on, leaving the atmosphere in the long open-plan office still stale and close from the day before. The typhoon winds had blown the rain away before it, but the imperial gardens and stables were barely visible through the heavy, hanging atomised mist they left behind.

When the deputy manager of the Small Financial Institution Section of the Domestic Finance Department, Kazunori Ninomiya arrived, Kikuo Ikeuchi, his superior, was already sitting at the end of his table, his head bowed over a cluster of papers. A handful of employees were also early to work, scattered almost out of view down to the office. At the far end of the huge complex, beyond the rows of desks and filing cabinets the informal meeting areas of soft chairs and sofas surrounded by tall potted plants, Ninomiya could see the General Manager of the Domestic Finance Department, Sosuke Hatano, who was leaning back in his chair browsing through the *Economic Daily*.

Ninomiya was a bespectacled, frail man in his mid-thirties, with thin lips in a pale narrow, bony face. His hair was thick on top but shaved close to his skull well above his ears. After a ten-year career in the major products divisions and a period in General Affairs he had been promoted to the yen finance department and finally given a title, that of kakaricho, deputy manager of the section charged with arrranging borrowings from hundreds of small savings and loan banks and other minor financial institutions and introducing them to the mass of medium-sized manufacturers who would borrow to produce goods which Matsuhashi had contracted to buy. Ninomiya's section would also lend directly to the more important, long-standing customers, taking their promissory notes or more tangible liens as security. He hoped in a few years to move to the prestigious City and Regional Bank Section where he could negotiate with the financial giants of the business world and foreign banks with branches in Tokyo. With the red badge of Matsuhashi on his lapel, he would be welcomed and entertained by his counterparts in the fast-moving forces of Japan Incorporated instead of the struggling fringe. But before he could settle into the routine of the day, Ikeuchi had noticed him and beckoned him over.

'Ohayo Gozaimasu,' Ninomiya said, bowing.

'Ohayo,' Ikeuchi replied perfunctorily. 'Did you hear the news this morning? On NHK?'

Ninomiya understood and nodded. 'Hai.'

'Strange, isn't it? A man writes a story, no different from the thousands of tales produced by the weeklies, but he ends up fighting for his life in hospital after getting into a brawl.'

Ninomiya looked uncomfortable and could only mutter, 'So desu ne?'

Ikeuchi tapped a cigarette from its packet. 'Is everything under control from your point of view?'

'I think so,' Ninomiya answered nervously. 'I warned them that we were worried there might be problems.'

'Good,' Ikeuchi said, amid a cloud of smoke. 'Where did you call from?' He saw the hesitation in his subordinate.

At that moment, Ninomiya knew that he had overplayed his mandate; he had made a serious mistake. He said: 'I thought it more appropriate to speak to them directly. I went to see them yesterday morning.'

Around the desk people were saying 'Good morning' to each other with varying degrees of deference. The manager of the section, Ikeuchi, heard nothing. He just stared at his junior manager, the sharp furrows on his high forehead and the wordless expression of horror on his face conveyed the full extent of his disapproval and the sheer force of the suppressed anger inside him.

The persistent late summer humidity was heightened in discomfort and intensity, and the sliding door's wooden frame had swollen causing it to resist the old woman's finger-tip pressure and balk against the sides of its rut. A black lacquered tray balanced on the palm of her left hand tilted as she applied more strength with the other until the screen of fine white paper slid into the wall. Nudging each slipper off and leaving them neatly side by side in the corridor, she backed stooping into the compact tatami room, decorated only with a fading scroll showing a snow-capped Mount Fuji and a simple flower arrangement in the rear tokonoma recess.

Four men sat in shirtsleeves on cushions around a low table, their legs hanging comfortably in the sunken well and their backs resting against spring supports. To the left of each man was another, smaller table holding their drinks, saucers of savoury rice crackers, strands of chewy dried squid and their smoking utensils.

The slender, red-cheeked lady, her piled hair dyed solid black and cut so uniformly straight around her head that it almost reached the narrow openings of her eyes, fell deftly to her knees beside Hatano. The line of her olive-green kimono was unruffled.

'Domo, Bucho-san,' she intoned, her head tilting slightly as she placed the bottle of Chivas Regal and mineral water on the table alongside a bucket of ice. 'You're all very welcome. But we haven't seen you for weeks,' she admonished with childish petulance.

'Ah, Pico-chan,' he said with mock humility, 'how can I play with you when I have to spend all my waking hours watching these lazy youngsters.' They all laughed knowingly.

Hatano liked the simplicity of the old woman's guesthouse, its plain façade near the Tsukiji fish market hiding a private retreat for the most senior of Matsuhashi

177

group officials. The briefest of signs outside, the wooden panelled door and slattered windows gave no hint of the exclusivity of the premises. Kimuraya was Hatano's safe house, a place for discussing intimate matters with his peers or juniors. Business guests were taken to the Ginza and Akasaka clubs where mood and conviviality were bought for small fortunes in luxurious surroundings. They would never see the inside of Mama Kumura's house.

Hatano's companions knew that the evening entailed far more than the game of mahjong for which the room had been readied. He gestured towards the others.

'That's Ikeuchi, my finance manager and his deputy Ninomiya. This is Aida,' he said motioning to the overweight, sweaty man in his early fifties. 'General Affairs.'

Aida was almost the same age as Hatani, but his career had gone no further than a functionary in the vast department which controlled personnel, public relations and general administrative matters of the company. He had worked for Hatano a decade earlier and even now enjoyed his confidence and favours in return for continued loyalty and service. While Hatano bantered with the hostess, the other three shuffled the tiles and separated the scoring counters into equal shares worth 26,000 points.

The door slid open again and a younger woman entered carrying a tray of bottles. Her cheekbones were high and prominent and her nose was elevated and pointed. The stiff collar of her pink, patterned kimono emphasised her long smooth neck and firm jaw.

'And this is our new girl, Teri,' the Mama said.

Hatano guffawed in appreciation, beckoning the newcomer to sit beside him. She placed the tray on the red mat floor and knelt alongside the general manager, her head bowed towards her lap. Mama was pleased.

'Teri-chan will look after you tonight. Please favour her, Bucho-san, she's only been with us since the spring, but scold her if she's slow or cheeky.'

The young girl joined in another round of giggles and

178

busied herself pouring Scotch for the Bucho and Suntory Gold for Ikeuchi and Aida. Ninomiya received a foamy glass of beer, fidgeting nervously as the girl's sleeve brushed across his bare arm.

Hatano suddenly became serious. Lowering his voice, he spoke to the Mama. 'Are we alone tonight?'

'Apart from the sensei, you are the only guests,' she replied, reciprocating the change of tone. Hatano felt relieved. The clever old professor, retained by the corporation after his retirement to lend a degree of academic responsibility to the economic research department, spent at least three nights a week at the Kimuraya, entertaining his former colleagues from Tokyo University and impressing them with tales of life at the pinnacle of big business. The young woman made to leave with her mistress, but Hatano, recovering his playful mood, bade her stay and sit beside him.

'Come and bring me some luck,' he laughed, patting the kimono which covered her knees. 'These young things are out to depose me as mahjong champion of the finance department.'

It was certainly a fact that the general manager was the most skilful player in the department, perhaps all Matsuhashi. He was an insuperable technician, with a poker player's awareness of probabilities and an exceptional ability to bluff. He was also a very bad loser. They were only playing for small stakes, but Ikeuchi knew that his senior considered mahjong a rite of manhood and the payment of a 70,000-yen loss without change of expression, even though it was a quarter of an opponent's salary, a sign of arrival. They drank a cheery toast with a clash of glasses and when the madam of the guesthouse had left the game got underway.

Ikeuchi drew the first turn as oya and led off with a useless north-wind tile. Although Hatano joked and flirted with the girl Teri, Ikeuchi knew that the cunning old devil was watching every discard and every selection. After two rounds of the first set, Hatano picked up a white dragon and five

179

rounds later a red one. The others drew air audibly at each revealing move, though probably only Ikeuchi noticed that the general manager had no bamboo discards, and the six of that particualr set was the bonus tile. Ikeuchi, as oya, was going for the simplest of wins, no ones or nines in his hand, no winds or dragons, in order to prolong the advantage of the dealer's double-point reward if he won. The other two had now realised the threat and were throwing away safe tiles while trying to collect a winning hand, but when Aida picked up an unwanted bamboo six he was forced to place it casually among the thirteen in front of him and discard a safe one. Two more rounds of play later it was Ninomiya who was made to retire when the tile he drew would probably give the game to his general manager.

Unluckily for him, but to the relief of all except Hatano, the ball eight he threw away gave the game to Ikeuchi, who picked up a miserly 2,500 points from his subordinate and prepared for one round as oya. Hatano scowled half in jest, collapsed his tiles and dispersed a potential 12,000-point hand among his other discards. He flattened the tiles left by the loser Ninomiya and by Aida and, as he expected, they had both retained one of the bamboo nines which would have given him the round. Instead, he shrugged and turned his attention to the girl while his juniors shuffled and constructed four new walls.

'Turn the cooler off. Let's enjoy the breeze while it lasts. And let's have some food before this game gets serious,' he said.

Paper, glass and wire-mesh partitions were drawn aside and a cool damp airflow replaced the dry icy atmosphere created by the refrigeration unit.

'What can I serve you?' Teri asked, resuming her position on the floor and displaying a grey fold of heavy paper overwritten in thick flowing script.

The next round was half over before the four had agreed on a single dish which would quell their hunger but would not distract them from the game. Teri scribbled the order on to the back of the menu. As she manoeuvered to stand,

Hatano's stubby, hairless hand toyed with the rim of her kimono at the knee and made pleasurable contact with the skin beneath before it disappeared.

There were no big winners in the first full set of play. Aida did manage a mangan on the strength of a set of bonus colours but he was so far behind at that stage that the 8,000 points barely dented the deficit he had accumulated over the rounds and it was Ninomiya, to his own surprise, who had his nose in front at the first score marking. Concentration in the second set was distracted by bowls of chirashi-zushi and side dishes of pickles and soup served by Teri. The players struggled to hold the bowls in one hand and juggle the chopsticks and tiles that passed through their grasp in rapid succession. The game slowed further when one of the players was caught teasing a sliver of raw fish into his mouth or when he paused to make a difficult choice. Between moves, and the chivying banter, Hatano gave covert signals that he had not gathered his juniors simply for a pleasant game of mahjong but the signs were missed on all but Ikeuchi.

Aida's failure to progress in the company could be traced to his inability to distinguish between after-office drinking with his colleagues and the carefree drunkenness this entailed and the entertaining he was required to do for Matsuhashi with customers. He would lose control of himself too often in both situations. Even now, he had not noticed how little the general manager was drinking (the Chivas Regal had only been opened twice) or the absence of joking and noisy comments that usually accompanied their mahjong bouts. Already reddened from whisky, he was addressing Hatano in loose and familiar terms. Ninomiya was hardly comfortable in the presence of his manager Ikeuchi, much less so with Hatano, and he fidgeted nervously on the cushion, occasionally brushing at imagined or real mosquitoes or slapping them against his jaw.

By the middle of the third round of the second set, with Hatano as oya, the general manager had retained the dealership for four consecutive games.

Flipping a discard forward with the tip of a finger he said, 'I don't want any of the events written about in the press this week to influence the fund-raising targets we have established and which are vital to the successful outcome of the countermeasures that have been agreed as a matter of policy.'

Ikeuchi noted that this general manager was delivering his statement in the monotone, nodding manner of a formal speech, staring at some spot on the green cloth of the table.

'At the same time,' Hatano continued in the same dull voice, 'we must exercise caution in furthering the relationships which are necessary in the pursuit of these goals.'

They played another round, Ninomiya picking up a bonus south wind to attempt a late rally with little else.

'Have the other parties been made aware of our concern?' Hatano said, his voice resuming a more normal pitch and directed towards Ikeuchi. Ikeuchi struggled to find words, counting chips.

'Ninomiya assures me our wholesalers have been advised of our concern,' he said, trying to emulate his superior's grave tone while regretting his own lack of concentration on his unwanted tiles. 'They hope that this minor incident will not impede the smooth availability of resources.'

'It won't,' Hatano grunted, his voice swamped by the crashing, shuffling and piling as new walls were erected, 'as long as there can never be a connection made or implied between us and our wholsalers and retailers.'

Ikeuchi took a long, cold swallow of diluted whisky, his hands toying with a new stack of tiles, his mind on the conversation with Ninomiya at the start of the working day. He could not possibly report to Hatano the fact that his junior manager had lost his senses in some moment of confusion and had visited the wholsalers in broad daylight, oblivious to the stupid, unnecessary risks his lapse had exposed them all to. Had the equally misguided reporter from the smutty, trashy magazine seen him there? Had enough been done by all parties to remove the threat which would result from such a possibility?

The breeze was sharp and fresh, and Ikeuchi shivered at his own thoughts as a gust swept the pall of cigarette smoke away and lifted ash and paper napkins from the side-tables. He drank deeply again, knowing that the message, more accurately the warning, had ended and woebetide any man at the table who ignored it. He glanced sideways at Aida who was mildly intoxicated and rocked gently against the backrest, reacting only languidly and indecisively when his turn came to poach a discard or choose a new tile every twenty seconds or so.

Ikeuchi had never fully understood Aida's role in the operation, conceived and orchestrated, he had always assumed, from above, but he himself had devised a cashflow that satisfied the needs of all parties for total discretion. With Hatano's agreement Ninomiya had been taken into confidence on a restricted knowledge basis and was doing a lot of legwork. The implications of Hatano's comments tonight must have passed over him. Would his unimaginative, hard-working, dedicated junior manager ever question the purpose for the endless payments between minor savings banks in the Tokyo-Kawasaki-Yokohama region and the suitcases of 10,000-yen notes delivered to silent counterparts in isolated coffee houses and shopping centres?

His musings were interrupted by Hatano who had decided it was time to relax. He summoned the serving girl to his side with a couple of claps and as he took control of the third and final set, he arrogantly attempted to explain for her benefit what he thought was the meaning behind his opponents' discards, summarily dismissing those he considered reckless or obvious. Ninomiya was a constant target for the mockery and tried to laugh it off with nervous, embarrassed giggles. The girl Teri shuffled on her knees to fill the glasses of the other players but quickly returned to devote her fawning attention on the general manager, lighting his cigarettes and topping up his glass of whisky and water with unnecessary frequency.

183

Hatano held the dealer's place for a further three rounds, collecting two strong wins from riichi declarations and luck with the concealed bonus tiles, and was 20,000 points above his starting base when Ninomiya led off the final round. After three hours at the table, the players were feeling the effects of a long day at work and a long week of fourteen-hour days. Apart from Hatano, who was flushed, noisy and playful, the others read their companions' minds and were playing for cheap, quick wins or low-scoring sacrificed losses.

Ninomiya seemed to win the first round of play by pure chance. He found a set of east winds among his opening hand of fourteen and it was only a matter of time before he had picked up enough discards and new titles to win with minimum value after only five or six circuits of the table. Ikeuchi yawned and shuffled the tiles indifferently as Ninomiya tossed a black, 100-point bar into his corner to remind all that it was to be another round of play with the advantage as oya to him.

The junior manager was astonished to find in his opening hand a pair of each of the three dragon suits and he swallowed instinctively when his first take from the walls was a smooth white tile which completed his first hidden dragon bonus set. It was too early for his opponents to discern from his discards what he was planning or what his hand contained and when Aida played a conventional game and threw down an unwanted, solitary red chun it was normal and unsurprising for Ninomiya to claim the red dragon. He rattled the set of three against the rim, impressing on the others that he had enough to win the round, however cheaply. What the others did not hear was Ninomiya's thumping heart nor sense his controlled excitement nor imagine that the self-effacing fellow needed only three tiles, including one of the remaining green dragons in the pack, to complete a rare daisangen and collect more than 40,000 points, which would wipe out all the others if he should pick up the winning tiles himself or bring the whole burden down on one of them if they should be careless enough to discard it. He had only achieved this yakuman once and that was more than fifteen years ago when he was a student and no money had changed hands.

The next six rounds of play were agonising for Ninomiya as he watched his general manager fondle the girl while keeping all the tiles his turn provided and discarding winds and ones and nines. The other two concentrated intensely, looking for a cheap win and quick release from the game. Ninomiya had now collected a pair of bamboo nines for the head and a 2-3-4 run of balls to complete the highest hand save for the elusive green dragon. He hoped the others assumed he was trying to win at all costs with the dragon pon. A clear-headed player, and from the florid faces around him only Ikeuchi qualified, would be suspicious. He had, in fact, picked up a green dragon and sensing something abnormal in the mix of discards was holding it in reserve to throw away in the later stages or keep as a spoiler if his fears were confirmed.

Still Hatano made no move to recognise the absence of green dragon tiles among the jagged rows of throwaways. He kept yet another tile and to everyone's surprise laid the discard on its side and so declared he needed only one more to win, foregoing the right to change his hand from now on. 'Yoshi!' he shouted, more to impress his fawning female companion than intimidate his opponents. 'Riichi.' He threw a 1,000-point counter into the centre.

Aida's concentration returned when he sensed a high-point threat and he joined Ikeuchi in perceiving a dragon play, obviously from Ninomiya, and with Hatano's declaration and accompanying show of confidence he opted to give up and try to throw away safe tiles. Ikeuchi was already playing defensively and although he had a potential winning hand it was not worth enough to risk giving the game away with a careless discard to one of the others. Ninomiya was trying desperately to conceal his excitement and anxiety. It now looked impossible for anyone to discard either of the two remaining green dragons if they were no longer in the quickly shrinking walls, although Hatano would have to do so if he picked one of the sixteen or so eligible uncovered tiles still left in the game.

The director had committed himself to one tile – the winner, and in the next two rounds, as the final wall fell away, he tossed unwanted tiles on to the table without an apprehensive glance towards his opponents. Ninomiya, in contrast, agonised over each unwanted tile he picked up. He was a cowardly player, preferring to drop out early unless the win was ninety per cent assured, and at this stage the pinzu ball eight he rubbed against his fingertips would normally be taken into his hand and a harmless tile discarded.

For the first time, his hesitation caught Hatano's eye and he saw a marked change of expression on his director's face. He invoked the universal deities and placed the eight ball sheepishly before him. At that moment, the man who controlled all their careers knew that he had been horribly distracted. Ninomiya had a set of red dragons displayed; only one other dragon had been rejected, by Hatano, early in the round; none of the four greens had been discarded and he himself had none in his hand. So that was it. The normally timorous creature next to him must have a hand. A big one. Otherwise, it would have been the action of an idiot to throw away an eight ball at this stage of the game. Hatano was waiting for a four or a seven ball to win.

He pushed the girl's hand off his arm and picked up a tile from the wall, rubbing its unseen face with his thumb. He felt a single straight horizontal indent. Safe, he thought, and placed the bamboo-one on the table without pausing to look. Only two more circuits of the table. Ikeuchi and Aida discarded tiles which had already been seen and ignored by the two contenders.

Ninomiya had never mastered the touch recognition technique for all thirty-four variations in the three suits, the winds and dragons, and flipped the next tile off the top of the stack with a twist of the wrist. It was a perfectly safe manzu two. Hatano had already rejected one and could not now win with it. Even before Ninomiya had slapped the

unwanted harmless tile with a clack against the others
Hatano's thumb was describing the contours of a complex
tile. He found nothing round to fit his need for the four or
seven ball, nothing consistently straight from the bamboo
suit and nothing as obvious as the clear number sequence
of the manzu suit. He hoped desperately for the simple
strokes of the four winds, but the sensitive fingertips moulded
into the sloping roof and then into its twisting compact
interior. He tossed the killing cube towards Ninomiya and
it fell, green face up, among the tiles the beaming junior
manager was already overturning for display to an envious
and relieved Ikeuchi and Aida. Ninomiya assembled the nine
dragons.

'Yakuman!'

# CHAPTER ELEVEN

No pain, no feeling, no sensory needs. Only whiteness. The middle stage was not disagreeable, and Araki hoped his relatives would choose a name-in-death of sufficient character to take him to an even better afterworld. He heard himself speak, a simple greeting and then an inquiry, but the angel or priestess dressed in white did not turn towards him. He tried again but the words choked in his throat as a surge of pain racked his cranium. The figure in the starched white uniform turned, startled, and rushed towards his bed.

'Don't try to speak, Araki-san,' she implored, cupping his face gently in her hands. 'You are going to get well, but you mustn't try to move or talk. Your jaw is fractured.' She picked up the telephone and dialled once. 'Moshi, moshi. This is Room 18. Please tell Doctor Oi that Araki-san has regained consciousness.'

When he came to the conclusion that he was not dead, he let his eyes scan and try to interpret the surroundings as temporal phenomena. He was alone, save for the nurse, in the pea-green room which was bare but for a wall clock and a stand on either side of his bed. Focusing downwards, he saw the tubes, curling between his lips. At the limit of his lateral vision he could see someone sitting on the other side of the open door. He wore a dark blue uniform. An intense-looking doctor arrived in under three minutes and immediately began poking and kneading Araki's flesh.

'Don't try to move and don't try to talk,' he intoned. 'If you can feel,' he continued, pressing a finger lightly into

188

Araki's neck, 'lift a finger on your right hand. If it hurts clench your fist.'

Araki raised an index finger.

'Good,' said the doctor, unbuttoning Araki's pyjamas and pressing selected places. Araki's finger went up and down but when the doctor depressed the skin on the left of his rib cage he made a fist and closed his eyes as a spasm of pain convulsed him.

The doctor was thin to the point of frailty, but his eyes were clear and seemed to penetrate the spots of flesh under examination. He sensed the barrage of questions unable to escape the prone shape in the bed.

'You've been very lucky, Araki-san. You have a hairline fracture of the jaw, some lacerations of the lower gum, a dislocated left elbow, severe abrasions to your right knee and shin and contusions all round your lower rib-cage.'

'That's lucky?' Araki wanted to ask.

'There was no internal bleeding of any consequence and when you vomited on the ground you were fortunate enough to expel it rather than choke on it.'

Araki pointed towards the clock. The doctor understood.

'You came in thirty-six hours ago,' the doctor said casually. 'We've fed you intravenously but we might be able to get some liquids and semi-solids through your mouth if you can swallow without too much pain.'

Araki lifted his arm again and pointed to the figure sitting outside who was now peering in.

'Ah yes,' said the doctor with embarrassment, 'the policeman. I think you'll find you're under arrest.'

'Arrest!' Araki wanted to shout. 'I'm the victim. I was almost killed. They can't arrest me. What have I done?'

Doctor Oi allowed no visitors until his patient knew the full extent of his injuries and the remedies being applied. Vitamin-rich liquids were fed to him through a tube. The brace was loose enough to let him swallow, first painfully and then with a gurgling smooth rhythm. The doctor found no humour in Araki's request made by wafting two fingers close to his mouth, to stick a cigarette into the tube.

189

Communication at first was limited to questions from the doctor which needed only a yes or no in reply, one raised finger for the former and two for the negative.

At breakfast the next day, the nurse brought him a writing-pad and a pencil. From his prostrate position he could only guess at the direction of the pencil, but like his feeding technqiue he improved by trial and error. It was another day before the doctor considered his patient strong enough to receive visitors and it was a police inspector, younger than Araki, looking fit and muscular in a tight-fitting grey summer suit, and a uniformed officer who were given priority.

They sat down close by Araki's bed and the plain-clothed inspector put two plastic bags on the bedside table.

'I'm Inspector Miyagi and this is Officer Noguchi,' he said, a trace of embarrassment in his voice. Perhaps he thinks he's talking to a corpse, Araki thought. 'Inspector Nishii sends his regards and wishes you well. He speaks highly of you and has acquainted me with the circumstances of your meeting with him at the morgue. I presume you were following up the story you began in your magazine when you met with this accident.'

Araki lifted a finger and the uniformed officer made a note. Remembering what the doctor had said, he beckoned the inspector to wait and scribbled on to his pad, *Am I under arrest?*

'Not exactly,' the inspector replied politely. 'Are the contents of these bags yours?' he asked, holding up the two plastic bags, the bulkier one containing bandages, tiny bottles and spatulas and a pair of fingernail scissors. The smaller bag held a collection of white and multi-coloured pills.

Araki hesitated, recognising the contents of the medical box he had taken from the Nozaki van and stashed thought-lessly under a seat in his car. He sensed the danger of a precipitous reply. He lifted two fingers and reached for the pad. He wrote laboriously, the two policemen leaning over to read, and he tried to guess what the interrogators knew, thinking desperately how to say enough to satisfy them without admitting his own criminal indiscretions more than necessary or disclosing the complete web of contacts he had built. He wanted the violent element removed but saw a chain of questions which would not be answered by the arrest of Ezaki and his thugs.

*I found the place where Tanimoto's girlfriend works.*

Inspector Miyagi was nodding as he read, but it was clear from his face that the police investigation had not discovered the Bali from their visit to the Camelia coffee shop or perhaps even found and interviewed Maki Takegawa. *Recognised a pair of underworld characters*, he wrote, bending the truth and hoping they wouldn't press the point. *Followed them to Roppongi. I took one of the medical packs they were distributing. Instinct. Frustration. I knew I had wasted my time.*

The inspector waited impassively, in the manner of all policemen.

Araki turned the page. *They must have seen me leave. Followed me in another car until I ran out of petrol somewhere down in Shinagawa. The last thing I remember was lying in the mud and rain being beaten up.*

Before Araki's pencil had stopped, the policeman asked: 'Were they the same men you believe wrecked your apartment?'

Araki hesitated, deciding in his mind that his colleagues at the magazine must have disclosed what they knew when it seemed he might actually have been murdered. He lifted a finger sheepishly.

Then Miyagi held up the plastic bags: 'You said these are not yours, but they were in your car.' His tone was still polite but becoming subtly firmer. 'You're saying you didn't buy them?'

Araki tried to shake his head but it was held immobile, leaving only his eyes and a flapping right hand to convey his reply. He lunged for the pencil, anxious to disown the innocent-looking little packets, but could only sweep it off the bed. The silent uniformed officer retrieved it.

Araki wrote in agitated script, describing how he had

191

given up the chase in Roppongi and after finding nothing more sinister in the white box than an assortment of first-aid articles threw the empty box away keeping the goods as a measure of compensation.

'How much do you think they are worth?' the inspector asked, indicating the bags.

*Five, six thousand yen*, Araki wrote.

'Wrong,' Miyagi said, harshly. 'The ten red and green pills are common brand-name painkillers.' He took one out and held it up to the light. 'But each of them has been loaded with point zero three of a gram of amphetamine, worth, on the street, about ten thousand yen. I have to advise you, Araki-san, that you have been found in possession of 100,000 yens worth of stimulant drugs.'

At last it came. Irresistibly, desperately, from the confines of his throat, a croaking, monotone attempt to express the emotion, conviction and sincerity his writing on the pad could not. His mind articulated the argument but only the groan emerged. A nurse waiting near the door rushed in, followed by Doctor Oi who mopped Araki's brow and urged the interrogators to depart.

The police were allowed back late the next day. Although he was sitting higher in the bed, Araki's cheeks were sunken and his skin sallow and pale. His hair was greasy and matted and tipped in grey like his sparse, spiky four-day growth of beard. He had practised several variations on some guttural sounds and by altering the tone and pitch was able to convey a positive or negative attitude and even emit the sounds of words which did not depend excessively on the lips for their construction. He was also able to swallow well-cooked vegetables and some soggy rice mixed with shredded fish.

Inspector Miyagi held a typed transcript of the previous day's interrogation.

'You came across the two dubious characters about four-thirty in the afternoon last Thursday,' he said, finding an underlined part of the text. 'You claim to have taken the white medical box from their van in Roppongi at about seven-thirty. I need hardly say that it would take no more than an hour, even in the most congested conditions, to drive from Ikebukuro to Roppongi. Do you recall stopping anywhere in between?' he added, allowing Araki to remember without embarrassment.

Araki remembered his notebook and wondered whether the policeman had found and read it and was now teasing him to corroborate what was in it.

An appropriate compromise now, he thought, would save face and leave room to make more useful disclosures without incriminating himself.

*The car they were driving*, he wrote, *stopped a few times on the way to Roppongi. I didn't know what they were up to. It was raining fairly steadily – I stayed in my car and waited for them to finish their business.*

'What was this business?' the inspector asked.

'Saaa,' Araki hissed.

'Did they distribute some of the white boxes?'

'Dark. Too dark,' the patient croaked.

Inspector Miyagi leaned over the bed. 'Do you remember exactly where any of the stops were?'

*I might remember*, he wrote. *I'll try and trace the route on a map and when I'm up again I'll drive around. Don't forget it was a miserable night and it was pitch black.*

'Yes it was,' Miyagi said sceptically, 'but I'm sure your experience and professional training will be enough to supply us with enough useful guidance as we pursue our enquiries. Meanwhile, and until I see you again,' he said, gesturing towards the other policeman, who closed his book, 'please make your best effort, without tiring yourself unduly, to write down an account of the events of last Thursday. Do not sign it: it will not be used in any way as evidence against you, but your cooperation would be held in high esteem. Is that acceptable?'

The innuendo, the implied threat if cooperation was withheld, were perfectly acceptable.

\* \* \*

193

When editor Kobayashi had made his first visit to the hospital around noon on Friday, four days earlier, after the police had cleaned up the contents of a battered, filthy wallet with Araki's name-card in it, his journalist was still unconscious though not critically injured. Now Araki was propped up, reading a weekly magazine, with no tubes or drips in sight. He had been bathed and shaved and the warmth of the water and the stimulation from gentle hands had cleansed and enlivened his skin. Kobayashi smiled, relieved, his annoyance at the whole avoidable incident temporarily under control. Araki reciprocated his greetings without recourse to the pen and added an apology for the trouble he had caused.

Kobayashi waved it away. 'Don't worry about it. We've put you in an inset on the cover of today's edition.' He read Araki's change of expression. 'That's right. You've been here a week already. It's Friday today. The mag's on the street.'

He pulled a copy from his briefcase and handed it proudly to Araki. It was unruffled, sharp at the edges and still thin and unsoiled. Later it would swell and crease as it was read and passed around.

'The doctor tells me,' he went on, 'you'll need at least another week here and then a month of recuperation at home. If it's not a strain, I will ask you to do some editing and rewriting, nothing excessive, when you get home. In the meantime you can live a clean, uncomplicated life under medical supervision.'

Araki raised his arm and then reached for the pen and paper.

*I've got the makings of a scoop*, he wrote. *I can link Tanimoto to the Yanagida-gumi and I can prove they are involved in stimulant drug distribution and the motive for the killing is probably tied up with this trade.* He had constructed the character for 'police' and was on the point of explaining his talks with assistant inspector Miyagi when editor Kobayashi lifted the ballpoint with restrained force from his fingers.

The veteran newsman spoke with the concern of a schoolteacher, his voice carefully modulated, his speech deliberate and controlled.

'The Tanimoto story is dead, like the man himself. And he wasn't deliberately killed. I have also been speaking to the police, much of the time spent on defending your reputation and eventually agreeing to act as guarantor for your future behaviour. I will now tell you the outcome of the talks and where we all stand.' He paused, half expecting his stubborn employee to continue the protest.

'The mystery of the Tanimoto death has been closed up, as you well know. The police are satisfied that Toshio Kawazu killed him accidently during a brawl and dumped the body when he and the others present panicked. The case is over. With your cooperation, the police will pursue an investigation into the attack on you and the sale of stimulant drugs by organised crime.'

Remembering the police officer still on duty outside the room, Kobayashi lowered his voice and leaned forward. 'The police accept that you are not a pedlar, and that you acted impulsively in stealing the box. You deeply regret your actions and will attempt to atone for your misdemeanour by disclosing everything you know and have so far concealed. In return for information, you will be absolved of any complicity in the matter.' He stood and brought his hands together in a gesture of finality, of a mutually satisfactory outcome reached. 'Have you been asked for a statement yet?'

'Hai,' Araki croaked and reached for the pad. He wrote: *Aren't the police interested in the possibility that the Yanagida drug-pushers are connected through Tanimoto to Ogawa's sokaiya? It seems to me this is the sort of diversification the sokaiyas are exploring when their blackmail of big business gets harder after 1 October when the law's due to change.*

Kobayashi waited patiently, reading awkwardly from the notebook as Araki completed his laborious task.

'Listen carefully,' he hissed, his face so close to Araki the latter grimaced. 'Write whatever you like in the statement, but remember you're writing for the police and not for a housing estate in Kichijoji. Tell them exactly what happened and what you know – not what you imagine.' He leaned back and said, 'And when you've finished that you can give some reflection to your career on the magazine. First, you're lucky to be alive. Secondly, you are guilty of severe breaches of discipline and magazine regulations by going off alone, like a private eye on a divorce case, without even advising the office where you were or what you were doing. Apart from the loss of trust of your senior colleagues, you will probably suffer a ten per cent salary cut for three months. When you are reinstated and fully fit you will be ordered to confine your stories to those assigned by the editorial committee. And when your statement is done, a letter of apology to the police, the ambulance service and the president of the magazine would not be inappropriate.'

Araki reached for the pad. *I appreciate your understanding*, he wrote, but unlike the modulation in a voice, or the implications of a deep bow, his words failed to convey any feeling of regret or even apology or sincerity.

He had been mulling a new story-line in his mind in the days since his editor had admonished him and when Keiko came to his room with the first batch of manuscripts for him to read he was feeling happier than he had been for a long time. Since he had met Tanimoto's woman Maki Takegawa, in fact. With the aid of a crutch he had made some tentative hops around the room, the pain in his ribs making him flinch. His speech was also improving. Like a ventriloquist he learned to speak from the throat without moving his lips. Keiko also brought some flowers and a card signed by the magazine's staff.

'Ogenki?' she asked.

'Never better,' he managed. He tried to speak again but could only gurgle. He wrote instead: *Get into bed and find out how genki.*

He almost choked with amusement at seeing her shock and then pretended embarrassment. She slapped the bed playfully.

'Always the same with you. Sex and sake.'

He had always teased her, not just for the sunglasses in the hair, but for her skinny model's figure and giggly television talent manner. Her voice could be petulant, nasal and very erotic.

Kondo and Chris arrived as Keiko was leaving. The ageing newspaperman was genuinely pleased to see his colleague not only alive but not permanently damaged. The first thing Chris did was to apologise in halting Japanese for not being with him on that awful Thursday. Araki's wave of the hand absolved him of blame, and he thanked them for the stack of new magazine issues, including their own.

'Did you bring the other things?' he asked in English.

Chris dipped into his briefcase again to retrieve a flask-sized bottle of Suntory whisky and two packs of Hi-lite.

'What are you going to work on now?' Kondo asked.

'I've been thinking about the life of your average salaryman. His work, family, sex life and whatever else motivates him.' He neglected to tell his colleagues he had already chosen his subject for study, if he could find him. 'I'll work on it from home.'

'And the stimulant drugs angle?' Chris asked, almost hoping for a more interesting assignment.

'That's finished,' Araki replied. 'The police have taken over the investigation and Kobayashi thinks the subject of drugs has been overdone by the media.'

They were all disappointed but the *Tokyo Weekly*, and their competitors, had saturated the reading public with lurid accounts of the growth of stimulant drug use in the last years of the 1970s and the levels it had reached by 1982. Kondo had compiled the statistics and a full exposé had gone out in January of that year.

It tried to prove that the traditional activities of the yakuza, the massage and pachinko parlours and usurous money-lending, had reached saturation point and vices with wider appeal had to be created and exploited. Japanese studying abroad, and even hard-pressed businessmen probably learned the benefit, if not the pleasures, of the

197

coloured pills, bringing back a supply which, when exhausted, left a handy and potentially lucrative gap for the
underworld to fill. Soon the habit-forming stimulants made
from the colourless liquid chemical called amphetamine and
sold as benzedrine, dexedrine and methidine made up half
of the yakuza's multi-million yen income. The gangs looked
to offer the student, the housewife, the entertainer, as well
as their fellow criminals, a powerful stimulant which would
increase alertness and physical stamina and, particularly
for the house-bound salaryman's wife, something to
help overcome depression as well as aid their slim-
ming programme.

Together with most organised gang members, perhaps
half a million people had become involved in the sale and
use of the drug, imported in powder, liquid- or pill-form
from South-East Asia, Taiwan and South Korea. Drugs
bought abroad for three to five thousand yen per gram
reached the streets at three hundred to five hundred
thousand a gram, and it was estimated that three tons of
the stuff entered the country in 1982 to satisfy a potential
client base of several millions. Marijuana, cocaine and heroin
had yet to find a foothold outside the drop-out and the
entertainment business.

The Mine-gumi of Osaka perfected the 'jonokin' system,
whereby each level of seniority among its three thousand
members paid a proportion of the profits from drug sales
to the next strata above. They sold the pills or phials of liquid
to their friends, younger colleagues, mistresses and then
directly to the public, carrying their sales pitch down to the
junior and the high schools, offering the first few fixes free
and then charging for the goods as the target became a
regular customer.

When an addict went berserk on the streets of Tokyo in
1981 stabbing six people, killing four of them, the government became concerned and was jolted into enacting the
Stimulant Drug Law to combat a social disease it insisted
could only exist in the decadent, undisciplined West. 28,000
people were arrested under it for illegal use, possession or

distribution, a figure three times greater than the previous year. Half of those arrested were gangsters, and eighteen kilos of stimulant, a fraction of the amount in circulation, was confiscated, most of it at eighteen ports around the archipelago. And now, a journalist from the *Tokyo Weekly* had been so incautious as to witness a transaction and it had almost cost him his life.

'What happened to my notebook?' Araki asked hopefully. 'Did anyone find it?'

Chris hissed like a Japanese and tapped his forehead with the heel of his hand. 'Completely forgot,' he said, producing the slim pad from his jacket pocket and handing it to Araki.

It was torn and dirty. The spiral rings at the top were distorted, a few strands hanging uselessly into space, and the thin cardboard covers were matted and stained and the pages stuck together in clusters. Letters he had scrawled in ink had ballooned out of recognition.

'It probably fell out of the car with me,' Araki opined, fingering the papers as if they were part of some ancient manuscript. He separated the brittle pages carefully but urgently, searching for the jottings he had made during the pursuit. He found them spread over three pages. They had been written in pencil and were legible, within the confines of Araki's less than precise script.

'Do me a favour,' he asked, handing Kondo the notepad. 'Tidy up these addresses and try to plot them on a street map for me. I'd better give the police something to work on.'

The unpredictable September breeze seemed to follow his moves, lifting a fine spray from the ornamental fountain and casting it over whichever bench he moved to. By the fourth day of his vigil he had determined which of the seats in the paved plaza gave him the broadest view of the imperious glass-fronted entrance of the Matsuhashi Corporation. By the second day of his convalescence, he was bored by the enforced inactivity and his mind roamed freely among the events of the last few weeks.

The shadow of this close encounter with death haunted

him by day and disturbed his sleep at night. He determined to try to exclude Maki and the list she took from his mind, and leave the yakuza Ezaki and his violent friends to the attention of the police. But his thoughts had returned to the man from the respectable trading company whose head-quarters he now stood before. Should he try to identify the man who had jeopardised his company's reputation by visiting a sokaiya, the extortionists whose employee had been killed in a violent struggle? He had nothing better to do, and nothing to lose.

The brick walls around an adjacent underground entrance made his position less conspicuous, as did the constant flow of people and vehicles behind him along the outer moat road which separated him from the leafy imperial palace compound. When his buttocks ached from prolonged immobility he walked around the plaza or dropped into the mall of the Shin-Marunouchi Building for a glass of iced coffee. At eleven-thirty, when the first waves of lunchtime diners were disgorging from their office block only to be sucked down the subways towards their favourite sub-terranean eateries, he would stand beside a young gingko tree, its leaves mottled by air pollutants, its growth restrained by a thick bed of concrete. At first the bubbling mass of uniformly black hair confused him when it disintegrated into clusters outside the doors and he found himself unable to apply his attention to more than a handful of the men. He felt frustrated and disillusioned.

It rained heavily on the fifth day, an excuse he used to stay in his apartment and work on the growing stack of manuscripts delivered by Keiko, who, disturbed at never finding him home, had stamped a neat row of 'urgent' across the front sheets before stuffing them into his mailbox. In retribution, he re-wrote an article by the magazine's most promising reporter on the influence of the disgraced former prime minister Tanaka over his protégé, the incumbent Nakasone, when his brief was only to edit. When the article appeared in print, he found it had been restored virtually completely to its former version.

His neighbour Yoko, sleeping late as usual after the late nights in her new bar, reported being woken by the telephone ringing every half-hour in his silent flat. He guessed the real source, but only called Kondo. His colleague was evasive, hinting only that Araki's less than strenuous recuperation was not finding favour at senior levels, and saying, in an almost inaudible whisper, that he had made a discovery and had to speak to Araki urgently.

Undeterred, Araki started his final week of rest outside the imposing office block in Marunouchi, watching the dark suits come and go and searching for his elusive salaryman. Chris joined him when he could to share the vigil. After continuous days on this exercise he was becoming adept at eliminating the obvious non-candidates and pursuing with his eyes those who measured up to the features on the thin, hawkish face he had seen being hustled out of the office of the sokaiya Teruaki Ogawa. Sometimes he would follow a man, trying to look casual as he peered self-consciously for the blood-red of the Matsuhashi lapel badge and the shiny pressed trousers.

With only three days left, he found his man. Or rather the man found him. Araki was sitting with his back to the pavement, looking across the concourse and trying to keep watch and read a newspaper during the mid-morning lull when a man bumped into his bench, his attention apparently distracted by a voice behind him.

'Ninomiya-san!'

The man regained his composure, apologised into space and turned round, unaware that the dishevelled figure on the bench had been looking for him for two weeks.

'Ninomiya-san, you've forgotten this folder.' The man, a fleet chauffeur in a dark grey suit, was holding a bound folder in his right hand and waited beside a black Nissan President whose front door bore the bridge-and-pine logo of the company. Araki was barely two metres from the handover between the driver and the man called Ninomiya and heard the brief conversation.

'Ah, domo,' Ninomiya said, retrieving the dossier. He

turned away and then remembered. 'Are you our driver tonight,' he asked.

'Hai so desu,' the driver rasped. 'Komban, dochira deshyo ka?'

Ninomiya paused for thought and then said: 'We're going to the Sana-ei Club in Aoyama. Please be at the garage at six.'

Araki was again angry at himself. Perhaps it was the niggling spasms of pain in his jaw which diverted his concentration, but he found it ludicrous that he had not considered the possibility that his prey would leave the building through the basement garage or indeed the direct exit below ground to the shopping mall and the trains. As it would now appear, Ninomiya had access to a chauffeur-driven car and had chosen today to be dropped in front of his headquarters instead of waiting in the congestion of traffic to negotiate the corner and then descend to the subterranean garage complex which stretched for three kilometres below Marunouchi. Araki watched him walk through the security checkpoint, seeing him fumble for his identity pass, almost dropping the folder. He seemed an uncoordinated man, nervous and defensive. And vulnerable, Araki thought.

The Sana-ei Club was in the basement of a modern block on the main Aoyama road near the university of the same name. Potted plants and floral displays from the ground-floor florist spread across the forecourt, almost to the pavement's edge. The Sana-ei was listed on the board above ground and when the polished sedan arrived at six-twenty, Araki had already explored the basement complex of shops and bars and classified the Sana-ei, from its padded mock-leather door and briefest of nameplates, as an expensive members' club patronised probably by the banking and the general trading sectors, like the Matsuhashi staff about to arrive.

There was an older, more composed man with Ninomiya and the way he left Ninomiya to talk to the driver left Araki, who was watching from across the road, in no doubt which

202

one was the senior. After the initial recognition and the important next contact at the club, the man called Ninomiya became as predictable and regular as the cherry-blossom, arriving at the Matsuhashi headquarters just before eight-thirty, and more often than not leaving the building within an hour by chauffered car.

On one occasion, Araki impetuously ordered a taxi to follow the sedan and although they ran against the incoming rush-hour traffic flow he had little change from a 3,000-yen note by the time his quarry had stopped at Iriya Station in Taito Ward, emerged from the booking-hall and returned to where his car was parked in front of the local savings and loan bank in a busy road. Leaving the taxi, Araki watched Ninomiya enter the building and emerge within twenty minutes carrying the widest of the executive-style range of briefcase. He looked taller, his body was erect and judging by the angle of his shoulders, the case was much heavier on the way into the bank than on the way out. Fate did not provide a passing empty taxi this time, and he could only watch, his curiosity intensified, as his subject disappeared.

He tried to return to a normal working timetable at the Shimbashi office of *Tokyo Weekly* and had to switch his private surveillance to the evenings. He started at a slow pace, confining himself to the office and sending Chris out on research missions, but when he reported that he was working on a major study into the habits of the average salaryman, Japan's latterday samurai, he was free to leave early and resume his watch at the gates of the Matsuhashi nerve-centre. Only Kobayashi showed curiosity, bordering on suspicion.

'What is your method? Are you observing, interviewing, spying, or what?'

Araki had a story ready. 'Three of my contacts, all from élite backgrounds – one Tokyo, two from Waseda – are now working in insurance and banking at junior managerial levels and have agreed to be studied, anonymously of course, over some months and to answer all kinds of intimate questions.'

It would be easy for Araki to create a credible imaginary lifestyle for those people and so he continued to lie.

'They've agreed to talk off the record,' he said, 'and let me watch them out of work time. As you'll agree, this can only be done after normal office hours.'

One afternoon, Araki took Chris Bingham with him.

'His evening routine is very predictable,' he explained in English as they stood in the narrowing shadow of the Matsuhashi building. 'If he hasn't left in a company car by six or six-fifteen he'll appear through those main doors over there around seven-fifteen with two or three colleagues. He rarely goes straight home. You watch.'

They sat on a bench and watched the last of the office girls disappear giggling and chattering in all directions. Then the first pairs of salarymen made a surreptitious exit ahead of a more general withdrawal.

'You didn't tell Kobayashi you were studying someone from Matsuhashi,' Chris said, in his politest tone. Araki heard the inference. 'The Editor won't like it.'

'His name's Ninomiya,' Araki said undeterred. 'I first saw him in the office of the sokaiya Teruaki Ogawa. I checked on the company badge he wears in his lapel and spent most of my sick-leave sitting here looking for him. I picked him out about two weeks ago and I've looked for him every night since.' He tried to rationalise his obsession. 'But it could have been anyone. He's got typical habits which I can wed to the interviews I'm planning to hold with people I know.'

Chris was still not convinced. 'It could be said you are continuing your Tanimoto enquiries.'

'I know it could,' the reporter intoned, his annoyance evident. 'You're sounding more like a Japanese every day, Chris.'

Chris's brow furrowed as he composed another probing question. 'Are you suggesting that this company is a part of your drug conspiracy?'

Araki reddened but his embarrassment was spared by events. 'There he is now,' Araki motioned. 'He's going out to play again.'

Ninomiya looked relaxed as he carried his jacket over his shoulders and chatted with two men of similar age and, presumably, rank. As they had done before, they walked under the railway tracks to Kyobashi, intending to spend a couple of hours in a basement bar called the Flora. Araki and Chris followed them in and ordered mizuwaris from high swivel-back stools at the bar on the shorter side of an L-shaped room.

'Is it all right for me to be here?' Chris asked, conscious of the inquisitive glances of the other drinkers.

Araki grasped his young charge's shoulder. 'You're with me, Chris-chan,' he said. 'You're a curiosity, not a threat.'

Along the back of the room was a line of booths, separated by ceiling-high cushioned headboards and in the corner a stack of karaoke equipment. A portable microphone with a long coil awaited the performer. It was a little too early to pass the mike; the patrons were still sober enough to be inhibited. Meanwhile, the background music from unseen speakers was the modern warbling kind of enka Araki detested. The jovial ruddy barman in evening jacket was probably married to the slender distinguished Mama-san who glided, with barely a crease in her deep mauve kimono, to greet each guest on arrival, most of whom she knew by name anyway. When not doing this, she moved from table to table exchanging chit-chat and sharing a joke.

Araki ordered more whisky and asked the barman to serve them round the corner in the main part of the drinking club. From his new perch, he could swivel to talk to Chris, watch out of one eye the shirtsleeved and relaxed figure of Ninomiya in a booth with two friends and a hostess.

There were three young hostesses in the bar in matching flower-patterned short skirts. They fetched bottles and snacks from the bar and encouraged their customers to drink more and to sing. They accepted drinks, but only from the customers' personal bottles. There were no signs of colourful concoctions or other deceptions and Araki classified the place as a cheery, noisy but intimate bar catering to regular

205

middle-level managers on limited fixed pocket money from their wives. It was more than likely that the girls might earn some commission from drinks sold to casual visitors or the late-night wealthier clientele, but the early evening mood was definitely designed for the salaryman. Even the heart-shaped medallions around the necks of the bottles of medium-quality whisky arrayed in rows on the shelves behind the counter bore the customer's company name alongside his own.

They were all there: several Sumitomo companies, the banks, trading conglomerates with local headquarters in Nihonbashi, and some small regional banks with Tokyo branches in the less prestigious real estate south of Tokyo Station. Chris found a Matsuhashi Corporation bottle, but its owner was called Maruyama.

A burst of laughter rose above the music and general noise and even the barman looked momentarily towards the table where Ninomiya sat with his colleagues and the young hostess. They were all convulsed, and Ninomiya himself was shaking with uncontrollable abandon at some funny anecdote. His eyes narrowed and his face reddened around his sharp cheekbones. One of the others flapped a limp hand at their fawning hostess, and she skipped off to fetch the microphone and a pair of floppy songbooks. With his perception of rhythm and tone dulled by alcohol and the sound of his voice enhanced by the echo effect of the speakers, wherever they were, Ninomiya may have felt pleased with his impassioned rendition of 'Feelings' in what, to Araki's trained ear, was a form of pidgin English which belied the singer's decade of formal education in his country's second language.

The girl beside him, gently restraining his free roving hand, had a narrow, flat mournful face, so agreeable in its woodblock classicism to middle-aged Japanese men. She listened patiently to the end, holding open the songbook to which her guest referred only fleetingly. When he had finished, she led the enthusiastic applause and persuaded him to take the stage around the karaoke equipment and bless the clientele at large with his music. He seemed to know the machine well, pressing and twirling the dials and knobs until he found the right beat to accompany a melancholy Japanese ballad of early post-war origin.

The girl moved on to another group of salarymen to retrieve the moist, cold face towels with which they had rubbed away the toil of the day.

'Pleasant place,' Araki said, asking the barman for his bill. The man beamed and gave a jerky bow of appreciation.

'As you can see we have very fine guests,' he said. 'Would you like a receipt?'

On the way out, where the top step broadened into a landing to meet the door, Araki stopped to scan a simple schedule of tariffs aimed no doubt at the casual visitor, and the piece of paper hanging from it. He summarised it aloud for Chris who didn't seem anxious to leave.

'They are looking for part-time hostesses. Two nights a week, it says.'

'So what?' Chris said.

'I don't know,' Araki replied, shrugging his shoulders. 'They must be doing well.'

Chris held the door open but had to wait when Araki stood, his head on one side, with a cynical smile creasing his face.

'How do you rate him?' Araki asked as they walked towards Tokyo station. 'Typical salaryman?'

Chris inclined his head. 'He looked so mild and self-conscious in the street, but in there he was singing his heart out and touching up the girls.'

'Just like you do,' Araki said with a grin as they crossed the road.

'Steady on,' Chris said, putting his arm across his chest. 'I'm British. What's "gentleman" in Japanese?'

'Shinshi.'

'I'm a bloody shinshi. Remember? Which is more than I can say for your friend in there.'

Araki raised his outstretched palms defensively. 'OK, OK, but don't be too hard on him. He's typical of millions.

207

He spent the day under strain, controlling his sentiments, suppressing his natural aggression, refraining from speaking out, intimidated into passivity, pressurised into conformity and forced to perform. When night comes and he's alone with his peers, what's the outcome? Total relaxation with some acceptable drunkenness and boorish behaviour.'

'I know the feeling,' said Chris, his blond curly hair reflecting in the street lights behind Tokyo Station.

Araki side-stepped a group of red-faced salarymen meandering towards the station, their arms entwined in mutual support. One of them broke loose, accidentally jostling Chris in his lurch towards the kerb and splashing the young journalist's shoes as he vomited violently at the foot of a thin roadside tree.

'Gomen, gomen,' one of the drunk's coherent friends shouted, moments before breaking into laughter when he saw the foreigner.

'Normal?' asked Chris.

Araki steered the other way. 'Normal,' he said. 'Unlike the others,' Araki continued as he saw Chris off through the ticket barrier. 'You may have noticed his hands were busier than his friends'. And I'm not talking about holding the microphone and twirling the dials.'

'He's only playing,' Chris suggested defensively. 'You said so yourself. Probably doesn't get much from his wife.'

'I'm sure he doesn't,' Araki responded quickly. 'She's plain, mousey, thin and as typical a housewife as he is a salaryman. She takes the two children to school and shops with the same servile smile on her face.'

Chris was about to walk away on the other side of the barrier but stopped. 'How do you know all this?'

'I followed him home last Friday and hung around his company apartment block all Sunday morning. See you tomorrow.'

Eleven-thirty was still early by Yoko's standards and so Araki was surprised to see a line of light below his neighbour's door and hear the sound from a television somewhere behind it. Araki rapped on metal and eased his way inside. He saw Yoko through the open bathroom door, standing in her underwear and leaning over the sink, her nose almost touching the cabinet mirror as she dabbed off her make-up. She saw his image in the glass and smiled.

'It's only me,' he said quietly. 'I'd like to ask you a favour.'

He stood on the terrace, a tumbler of iced whisky in his hand, staring past the trees towards the distant tracks as if mesmerised by the flashing of lights from late trains snaking between the buildings. Through the late coolness of the evening, in the rare moments when the distant drone of traffic and the hissing of insects ceased, he could hear the muffled rasp of the platform announcements at Harajuku Station.

He thought of Maki Takegawa. She wouldn't work every day, he assumed hopefully, and he had been calling her at home between ten and midnight for the last four days and sporadically during the afternoons. He had tried to talk to her ever since he had responded to Kondo's repeated request for an urgent meeting and had been shocked and saddened by what his conscientious researcher had had to say when he finally confronted him the previous Saturday, before Araki was dressed.

Kondo had spread a street map of Tokyo over Araki's worktable, folding the ends over the edges like a cloth. He produced some notepaper and the yellow page taken by the reporter from the dead man's ticket holder. Araki had rubbed his eyes and yawned.

'I wish you'd throw that away,' he said, handing Kondo a mug of coffee and pointing at the incriminating note. 'I'd rather the evidence of my crime was erased.'

'I will,' Kondo replied without conviction as he hunched himself over the map and chewed the top of a red ballpen. Then he looked up and said: 'Do you still have your copy?'

Araki cast a hand in the direction of his clothes. 'Of course I do.' Then he remembered. 'No, I don't. She took it.'

'She?' Kondo said, now preoccupied and poised over the map with the red pen.

'Maki Takegawa. Tanimoto's woman. I let her have a look at my copy and somehow she managed to hang on to it. It's time I called her again.'

Kondo looked up disapprovingly. 'The Tanimoto story's as dead as he is and as dead as your career will be if you pursue it much further.'

Araki raised the palms of his hands towards the older man. 'OK. Whatever I do now is personal.' Then he held up the crumpled list between his forefingers. 'What about you? Why have you brought this up again if you're so concerned about my future?'

Kondo was not to be daunted.

'I'd like to think,' he said calmly, 'that this is my last contribution to your obsession. I did think about not telling you but I've spent so much time trying to make something out of the numbers it would be a waste not to tell you what I've found.'

Araki made to speak but Kondo would not be stopped from adding a rebuke and then finishing with some advice he managed to work into his reply.

'You won't admit it, I'm sure, but you're not looking for the petty creeps who shove cigarette butts down kimono sleeves or peep on couples in Yoyogi Park. You've finally taken on your real yakuza, like Ezaki, who probably deeply regrets not fracturing your skull or breaking your back.'

'He came close,' Araki interjected, rubbing his jaw.

'I'll tell you what I've found,' Kondo continued, 'but I want you to share the facts with the police. You're then clear of any guilt and can enjoy whatever protection they feel appropriate.'

Araki proffered an open palm, like a Sumo wrestler ceding the advantage. Kondo accepted it and continued. He had not intended to start with the map but Araki's attention was on the five complete red circles and the three dotted ones Kondo had painstakingly drawn on the street guide.

'Do you see anything familiar?' Kondo asked.

Araki ran a finger between the circles. He felt tense and excited. 'They're the places where they dropped the boxes with the drugs, aren't they?'

'Right,' Kondo paused to assemble his thoughts. 'I plotted the locations of the addresses you put into your notebook as you followed the Nozaki van around.'

Araki raised a hand to interrupt. 'I can't say they're 100 per cent accurate. I didn't start taking notes until we'd stopped three or four times and when I did try to get the bearings I may have taken the nearest visible address plate. I reckon I pinpointed three of the drop sites.'

'Fine,' Kondo said, placatingly. 'Just let me finish. First the list.' He held up the yellow page again. 'If you recall, we had already decided that the eight or nine numbers in each of the ten lines could not realistically all be amounts of yen.'

'Unless we're talking of big money,' Araki said, pointing to one of the lines. 'That one would be, er . . .' – he nodded imaginary divisions in the digits – 'five billion, one hundred and fourteen million, three hundred and twenty thousand. I suppose you're right,' he conceded. 'That's a lot of money, even for big business or politics.'

'And don't forget there are nine more lines like that one,' Kondo added, 'but I think there is some money among the numbers. Look.'

Araki leaned forward.

'All the lines end with at least three zeros, some of them four and these three have five. So let's believe that we're talking about thousands of yen, more like monthly salary figures.'

'And what about the other numbers?' Araki asked, his impatience rising.

Kondo refused to be diverted. 'Now we come to the map,' he said, running his fingers across the creases. 'I spent far too much time on the money angle, and it wasn't until I heard about your adventure with the delivery boys that I started to think a bit more about what Tanimoto's job with the sokaiya was or might have been. He was clearly an odd-job man, helping with a strong arm here and there, mixing with known hoodlums, possibly acting as a liaison agent and then, as my supposition goes, as a collector, a messenger. Or a distributor. Are you with me?'

'Loosely,' Araki replied sceptically. 'But carry on.'

'If he did have some delivery or collection role then it would be logical for him to carry an address book or – and this is where speculation almost got the better of me – if his business was shady, even illegal, it would be even more logical of him to keep his destinations separate, hidden, most likely in shorthand, even in code.'

'The list was certainly hidden,' Araki said, remembering the way the note had been creased by the plastic season ticket into the contours of the holder. 'What makes you think there are addresses in it?'

'Look at the first numbers in each line. See anything unusual?' Araki gave only a casual glance. 'I've wasted hours looking at those numbers. One night I dreamt about them.' He pushed the list aside. 'To me, they're just lines of meaningless cipher.'

'What's the highest number?' Kondo asked, basking in the possession of superior knowledge. 'Only the first numbers in each line.'

Araki's finger hovered over each number as it moved down the list. 'Five.' He looked up at Kondo, who was smiling, willing him to see the significance. Araki didn't. 'So what?'

Kondo clucked, expecting much more from a man of renowned intuition. Perhaps, he thought, the blows to his head had damaged his reasoning. He transferred his colleague's attention to the map and to the bold numbers in brackets which seemed to dominate the centre of dozens of equal-sized portions of the guide. He withdrew to a corner with his coffee. It wasn't long before Araki's muscles loosened and he began to nod gently.

'Naruhodo, naruhodo,' he said, thumping the table. 'Congratulations, although it does look obvious now.' Kondo was pleased with the praise.

'All the main "chome" divisions are outlined like this,' he said, tapping a bracketed figure at random, 'and if you look closely, you can see that each block in the chome is also given. When I finally started thinking about addresses it occurred to me that the chome can be given at the beginning of the sequence of the normal three numbers in a Tokyo address. And if you look quickly across the map you won't find many chomes above five. Try it.'

Araki did; and it was some seconds before he found a six, and next to it a seven, both buried in the central area of Koto Ward.

'So I convinced myself,' Kondo went on, 'that the first few digits of each line in the list were addresses. All the first numbers are five or under. In fact there's only one five and two fours.'

Araki drew a chair up to the table and sat down, excited, waiting for the next revelation. When Kondo aligned the Tanimoto list alongside the scrambled jottings he had made during the fateful pursuit of the Nozaki van he knew what it would be. His colleague had been professional and thorough. Luck played no part.

'Look at the third line in Tanimoto's list,' Kondo commanded, waiting until Araki had stabbed the spot lightly with a pencil. 'You've got the katakana symbol "to", followed by a two, a seven and a thirteen. Ignore the other numbers for the moment.'

Araki was now totally absorbed. He cupped his chin, rubbing a free finger over his morning stubble.

'Now look at your notes,' Kondo continued, tapping an entry on the other page. 'This one.'

Araki read it aloud. 'Torigoe two dash seven dash thirteen. Unbelievable.'

'Is it?' Kondo asked. 'Then what was your next full address?'

Araki studied his barely legible notes. 'Higashi-Kanda one, eight, six.'

'And what's the fourth entry on Tanimoto's list?'

213

Araki's voice evaporated as he read past the 'Hi' and reached the six. Then he threw the pencil into the air, enveloped Kondo in a bear hug and carried him to the kitchen where he poured two generous portions of whisky into tumblers. Kondo scratched his scalp, embarrassed as much at the praise as the time of day and drank deeply from the glass.

'Why don't you get dressed and we'll go and have some breakfast?' he said, examining the recesses of the kitchen cupboards but finding nothing other than a few tins of soup and a single pot noodle. While Araki shaved and dressed, Kondo joined him in the bathroom and filled in the gaps.

'The rest of the numbers must be money, probably the amount to be collected for the stimulant drugs being delivered in those white boxes. The Torigoe drop was the biggest. Two, five and four zeros. 250,000 yen. The five places where you were able to get the district, the chome and the sub-division all appear in the Tanimoto list. I've marked the approximate location of each of them in red on the map, which of course does not show the final number in the address sequence. It doesn't matter, of course, because the police will have enough to take them straight to the door. Sorry, did you say something?'

Araki stopped brushing his teeth, hesitated, then gargled and retched a mouthful of toothpaste and phlegm. 'No, no,' he spluttered. 'Let's go and eat.'

Kondo thought Araki had suddenly become distracted. The journalist crushed the boiled egg languidly on to the toast and drew aimless pictures with his fork. The discovery should have rekindled the fire, but instead the whisky seemed to have nullified his inquisitiveness and he was distant as Kondo spoke again.

'From the way Tanimoto hid the list, it was obviously a sensitive document, and it links him, of course, with the Yanagida-gumi and their boys who operate from, or near, the Bali massage parlour. By simple conclusion, Tanimoto's

214

employers cannot be excluded from implication in the drug business. They're obviously making up for lost income from the corporate blackmail division.'

He sipped at his coffee, and then raised a finger. 'Didn't you say that Maki Takegawa told you that a few weeks before he died Tanimoto went into hiding, or at least was too scared to be seen around?'

'Yes, I did.' The two men exchanged a glance and though it was Araki who snapped his thumb and middle finger they both reached the same conclusion together.

'If he was scared and in hiding,' Araki asked rhetorically, 'what was he doing enjoying himself playing mahjong with a bunch of cheap chimpiras on the night he died?'

'Because he wasn't, was he?' Kondo said loudly.

'Well, he was there but he wasn't enjoying himself,' Araki suggested. 'There probably wasn't even a game, let alone a fight. That neighbour Chris and I talked to, Mrs Nozaki. She heard nothing at all from the Kawazus' on the Thursday night. The house normally rattled from the shouting and the rows when there was a game.' He chuckled, mocking himself for not seeing through the smokescreen. 'I should have realised how odd it was when she said the damned van with the same name as hers on the side had been outside the house since four o'clock that afternoon. I assumed it had taken the body to the Tama river when it was actually used to bring Tanimoto, either already dead or unconscious, to the Kawazus' house. They went on to use a car, a green one according to a witness, as a hearse.'

Kondo sipped his cup and frowned towards his colleague. 'A couple of points if I may. First, how did they get a body, or an uncooperative captive, into the house. Second, why even bother with the elaborate charade? Why not kill Tanimoto wherever and dump him straight into the river?'

Araki spread his paper and sketched a box. 'There's a metal stairway at the side of the building leading to the second-floor apartments. Here. You can back a utility van into the space under the stairs and manoeuvre a load with a degree of cover to the back door.' He crumpled the paper, pondering the second question. 'They created a complicated scenario to make it look unequivocally as though Tanimoto had died accidentally in a free-for-all scrap. They didn't want a murder. In view of the court's decision, they appear to have succeeded. Kawazu will be out of prison in five years.'

'But why bother?' Kondo persisted.

'Because it had to look perfect,' Araki said, a hint of irritation in his voice. 'The boisterous mahjong game, the money, plenty of booze, the pretended row and the fight, which nobody in the back-to-back houses heard. They must have rolled Tanimoto's body around a bit, banging his head on the corner of the table, finishing him off perhaps, and leaving his authentic blood and hair in the tatami mats. They would have spilt some whisky over his nice suit. The police have a simple case of manslaughter with a repentant killer. Casebook closed. If it had been a murder with no culprit, the police would have been required to conduct a full investigation. Whoever ordered Tanimoto's demise desperately wanted him out of circulation but did not want a police follow-up.'

'I think you're right,' Kondo said, his doubts erased, admiration returning. 'Tanimoto was murdered because he was after more than a delivery and collection job and he already held a ready-made list of clients for the evil powder.'

Araki shook his head. 'Don't forget there are probably a lot of lists,' he said. 'I only interrupted one of them.' He held the original code in his fingers. 'Tanimoto's problem was that the list couldn't give him enough information. It gave a full address and a hint of the district but he'd have to know the ward and the name of the contact or the client before it was any use.' He traced a circle around his plate with a fork. 'There must have been some sort of dual control over the customer names, and I would imagine Tanimoto tried to subvert someone who had the other side of the

216

notepad, someone more important in the organisation than himself, and he was disposed of because he was rejected and then seen as a threat.'

'It was a very clinical, very clever execcution, if you're right,' Kondo said, 'but they made a mistake.'

'They made several,' Araki said. 'The biggest was not creating a racket at the phoney mahjong session, but I suppose they didn't want to attract the police at the Kawazus'. They wanted to introduce the panic element to corroborate Kawazus' story. The next piece of stupidity was not clearing out Tanimoto's pockets properly. They left the matches which led me to Maki and the season ticket with the incriminating list. The little bit of yellow paper proves that Ogawa has branched into the drug trade. That's how they planned to keep their income up once the laws against the sokaiya's traditional work had been tightened up. I think I told you that when I met Ogawa his toughy was taking notes on the same size yellow paper. It ties up like this.'

Araki smoothed another napkin, touched the tip of his ballpen on his tongue, and drew more boxes with names alongside. 'Ogawa, the sokaiya, illegal but tolerated corporate extortionist, now, through his man Tanimoto's list of outlets, linked to stimulant drugs.'

He drew a line diagonally upwards to another box against which he had scribbled the dead man's kanji. 'Tanimoto's woman led us to the Yanagida-gumi,' he continued, tracing downwards to another box for Maki Takegawa and then to another below for the gang, completing three sides of a baseball diamond, 'who nearly killed me after I stumbled on to them delivering the drug.'

With a flourish, he drew the last line linking the country's 1,400-strong urban crime syndicate with the sokaiya. 'Tanimoto must have been the link between his boss and the gang. That would explain the season ticket from Ogawa's office in Akasaka-mitsuke to the Yanagida-gumi's Ikebukuro base, where they called themselves the Nozaki Transport Company, in the block behind the Bali massage parlour.'

He closed the sliding terrace door, poured a refill and wrote in frenzied bursts a new draft of the second of the salaryman profiles he had been basing on the subject Araki had pursued from the dead sokaiya to the salaryman's workplace in the Matsuhashi Corporation building, and from the bars where he entertained clients to those where he relaxed with his peers, and finally to the home his wife ran and where she raised their children. Between passages, he rang Maki's number with hardly a glance at the dial, passing the time by stirring his whisky with a finger and tracing patterns across each new sheath of condensation on the glass.

It was past midnight when he heard the click. He had the telephone cradled across his shoulder and was struggling in his mind with a basket of rhetorical questions to end his article. He bobbled the instrument comically as the voice grew impatient at the other end. Before he had finished his introduction and apologised for the lateness of the call, Maki had seized the initiative, chiding him in that same firm, uncompromising voice which was now tempered with a mild disarming compassion, even concern.

'You're not home much, are you? I called at least ten times in the last six weeks. I read about your accident and wanted to know how you were.'

Wanted to know whether I'd implicated her, Araki thought, remembering how he had portrayed her as the key connection on the base lines straight into the Yanagida-gumi.

'Thought you might think I was responsible,' she said speculatively.

Araki smiled wryly to himself, his pause eloquent in itself. The moment really required an immediate repudiation, but her gratuitous denial of blame seemed to trigger a spasm of pain in his still tender jaw.

In that instant, while Maki Takegawa prolonged her explanation with no hint of apology, he made up his mind to present the undisclosed facts of his misadventure to the police. But he wanted to have all the missing pieces. Even his friend Nishii might be strained to believe his story as it stood.

'Are you still working in Ikebukuro?' he asked, ignoring her and imagining the woman alone and relaxed in some carefully furnished and expensive mansion flat.

'No, I'm back in the Ginza. I've put the Tanimoto episode behind me and a good connection has found me a private club.' Araki listened in stunned disbelief. Was she so innocent as to believe the story of the accidental death or was she so callous she could ignore the strong probability that her lover had been murdered? Of course, if she had been a party to the killing, her composure would be fully understandable.

'I never did like the Turko,' she was saying in a voice which could have been describing a cake shop. 'It just seemed a good place to drop out of sight when things became a little difficult with Tanimoto.' He wanted to tell her about her unsavoury friends and their skills with a baseball bat, to have her confirm beyond doubt that she knew them and so connect her dead lover's employer, the sokaiya, to his assailants, the drug sellers; but he knew the telephone was not the medium.

'Have the police spoken to you again?' he probed, hoping she was wondering whether he had implicated her to the police with his knowledge of her gangland friends. He interpreted the pause as a positive sign.

'No, why should they?' she asked eventually.

Araki replied, suggesting much but revealing nothing. 'The Tanimoto case got a lot more publicity after the author of the story, namely me, was beaten up and nearly killed. This led the police to believe I knew more than they did. They became very insistent.' He could almost have scripted her reply and nodded comprehendingly at each recognisable nuance of her stilted response.

He remembered her face, her poise and the strange way her perfume, a delicate scent of lilies, had stayed with him

219

since their first meeting. There was no hesitation in his voice when she finished speaking.

'It must have been very painful, physically and emotionally, for you. It's difficult for me to express my sincere regret on the telephone. Perhaps, if you have time, it would be appropriate for us to meet again.'

'Of course,' he heard himself saying, almost gratefully.

# CHAPTER TWELVE

The bonnet of the black sedan rippled above the idling engine but the car was motionless against the pavement under a canopy of drooping willow tree branches. Smoke escaped through half-open windows and the voices of the four occupants were muffled by the car radio, deliberately tuned to a popular song show. Around the corner, in the shadow of the Olympic stadium, another black car waited, this one inconspicuously bearing the bridge-and-pine-tree logo of Matsuhashi Corporation below the keyhole on the driver's side. Fifty metres away in a lay-by close to Jingu baseball park, the driver of a loud mauve Cadillac leaned against his machine and read a comic book. While their drivers relaxed under a cloudless autumn sky, the three men in the car belonging to Teruaki Ogawa conferred in the plain and precise language of men who were colleagues in conspiracy but not friends.

Ikeuchi, in the back with Go Minagawa, had angled himself in a corner as if to distance himself symbolically from the man along the seat in the expensive light double-breasted suit who represented the interests of the syndicate and was in fact the patriarch Yanagida's son-in-law. Kaneda, behind the steering wheel, was also younger, which increased Ikeuchi's contempt for their familiarity and brashness. He blamed Ogawa and his team for the lapses of discipline which had tempted their now dead legman Tanimoto to see the chance to divert several batches of the product and use the proceeds to finance, no doubt, a disappearance to Hawaii or Manila.

'The teacher wants a meeting,' Ikeuchi said, his sharp

owlish eyes darting between the other men, and affirming the gravity of his toneless, staccato delivery.

Minagawa sucked in air, demanding the stage and asking for time. He held his hands out and collapsed each finger in sequence until only the thumb of his left hand remained upright.

'They met nine months ago,' he said, 'and agreed not to risk being seen together again.'

Ikeuchi would not be deterred, and continued in the same voice he would use to address a meeting at the company.

'Tell your principals that we are being threatened on several fronts. There are indications the police are being pressured to re-open the Tanimoto case and that the reporter has not yet been dissuaded from making any further enquiries. We must agree some emergency measures and a strategy for the future.'

Kaneda eased his cigarette butt through the gap in the window and produced a yellow notepad from the dashboard pocket.

'Details please,' he demanded curtly.

Ikeuchi eyed the book contemptuously, reflecting on the damage already caused by the careless listing of important data.

'Can't you keep it in your head?' he asked, his high forehead twitching with irritation. Kaneda made a show of closing the pad.

'There's a lodge called the Asama-so in Asakusabashi. The teacher will be there at seven on 3 November. That's one week from tomorrow. A woman will greet your principals. No one else will be present. Please urge caution and discretion.'

Minagawa and the Matsuhashi manager twisted their necks to check the broad, quiet road; Ikeuchi let a curious biker weave past before leaving with only a casual farewell.

He chose to meet Maki in the concourse at the west exit of Shinjuku Station, a place throbbing with Sunday shoppers and their families, excitable high-school girls and fashionably dressed office women and where, Araki reasoned, he would be secure from a second assault on his person. He saw her first circling slowly but staying out of vision until the same scent of freshly cut lilies was close enough to breathe. Standing alone, her head swinging methodically, her wide deep dark eyes scanning the underground plaza while people criss-crossed around her, Maki seemed more relaxed than at their first encounter. She wore close-fitting designer jeans with a white stripe down each leg held by a white belt with a square, embossed gold-coloured buckle. The off-white, almost grey, sleeveless blouse was taut and trim, with a border of frills around the row of buttons which reached her throat. A light mauve sweater was draped over her shoulders, its sleeves tied loosely at the front. She smiled when she saw him and returned his nod with a bow he took to be an apology.

They went to the large, ground-floor coffee shop run by the Odakyu department store in the station precinct. It was spacious, well-lit with at least three entrances which to Araki were emergency exits. Maki sensed the tension, following his eyes as he took more than casual notice of any groups of men entering the room.

'You still blame me for your accident, don't you?' she said stirring the ice-cream into her soda-float.

'What else can I think?' he replied, satisfied that the two youths in the nearest corner with heavily greased hair and sunglasses were too young to be more than street punks. 'I must have been fingered when I saw you at the Camelia, probably even before. Perhaps they thought I was getting too close to you, or they knew I had the list from Tanimoto-san's pocket. I don't know. After they failed to intimidate me by tearing up the contents of my apartment they went one step further and tried to kill me, or at least break my resolve by physical means.' As if to reinforce his innocence he said: 'All I wanted was a story with a strong line in sex and violence and your affair with Tanimoto had both.'

'And are you still feeling threatened?' she asked, not diverted by his hint of self-pity.

223

'The story is dead,' he said by way of reply. 'There's no reason for anyone to want me silent. But you've got to admit, the more I probed the more sinister it all became. You didn't help prove your blamelessness when you took the list from me in Shibuya.'

Maki cocked her head, emphasising the delicate mouth and the pout of her colourless lips. The tail of her hair, which was bound with a simple rubber band, brushed across her face with each twist of her head. She stifled an ironic scoff.

'You did say when you first got in touch through that message to my friend Shima at the Bali that you had something of Tanimoto's for me. I took the list to be that "something".'

'Fair enough,' he was forced to admit. 'Do you know what the numbers meant?'

The place was full. Restless children jostled behind them and crawled at their feet looking for a stray toy. Maki sensed the reporter's nervousness.

'Shall we take a walk?' she suggested, drawing her handbag to her lap in readiness and picking up the bill.

They strolled the pathways among the bamboo and birch groves of the west-exit park like other couples enjoying the October sunshine and the mild, unpolluted air. The broad, traffic-free roads and the multi-storey, empty office blocks shared the restful inner-city mood of an autumn Sunday in the capital.

Maki said, 'I suppose it was a code of some sort. I have no idea. Tanimoto was so busy towards the end I rarely saw him, only once in fact after I'd been to Shimoda for him. Did I tell you about Shimoda?'

'Yes you did,' Araki said, pausing to light a cigarette and observe her casual elegance a few paces ahead. 'You met him there and you delivered some messages for him.'

'More than messages,' Maki confessed. 'There was a package. It was soft, like a bag of flour, and about the same weight. I took it back on the train and got off at Atami to mail it. By then I knew exactly what it was,' she said, perhaps with genuine sadness.

'Do you remember the address?' Araki asked.

Maki shook her head and waved her hand dismissively.
'It didn't seem important, somewhere in Meguro-ku, I
think, Gotanda perhaps. I was only thinking about him and
what the future held for us both.'

'It was probably part of his plan to break away from the
organisation, that caused his death.'

Araki probed her defences, watching her eyes for some
movement which might betray her complicity in the drug
ring.

She accepted his suppositions stoically.

'The centre of operations was in an old office block behind
the Bali, where, as you know, Tanimoto commuted from his
office in Akasaka-mitsuke, carrying, I imagine instructions
from the top, and paying the troops. I don't know where
the powder comes from, maybe the route is one you've
come across in Izu, but by the time it has reached Ikebukuro it's hidden inside capsules, which are mixed in
with real medicinal pills and then distributed in innocent
looking first-aid boxes as sold in any chemists or department store. Does the name Nozaki mean anything to you?'
he asked.

Maki shook her head.

'They moved the boxes to customers in a van marked
Nozaki and it was the same van that carried Tanimoto-san
to the Kawazus' house on the night he was murdered.'

'Killed,' she corrected.

'Murdered,' he persisted. 'The brawl was a cover. The
van's crew would hand over a box,' he said, resuming his
narrative which was gathering in passion as he re-lived each
moment of discovery. 'They picked up something, the
money I expect, and moved on. They must have suspected
something, noticed me somewhere, and when we all reached
Roppongi there was contact with the rougher elements of
the team and it was me who was on the run.'

'What kind of places did they take the drugs to?' Maki
asked.

'Coffee shops, a hairdresser's, bars, places with a regular

clientele, where a small packet exchanged for cash would not be unusual.'

They had stopped at the edge of a murky pond where children were enticing some young orange-and-white carp to thrash and snap for popcorn. Maki stooped, picked up a lump of popcorn and tossed it into the deeper waters where an old brown mottled fish, almost half a metre long, rolled languidly to the surface and sucked in the morsel through its square ugly mouth before sliding below the surface. The three children were delighted and clapped their hands and offered Maki more popcorn to throw out where they could not reach. She obliged willingly while Araki slumped on to a bench, his hands in his pockets and legs outstretched, almost resenting the way she could so easily be distracted and puzzled by her swings of temperament. He had disclosed his most extravagant suspicions in a reckless attempt to draw a hint of a confession.

'Have you been back to any of those places?' she asked, joining him by sitting on the edge of the bench, her eyes wide and alert as she continued to display the caring side of her chameleon personality.

'No, I haven't.'

Maki moved to speak, but before she could Araki added: 'But the police will have.' He heard himself lying, remembering the information he had yet to pass to his policeman friend Nishii.

'In which case, they've probably closed them all down by now,' she said.

Listening to her impeccable logic, it occurred to Araki that he had never been back to find any of the places where the stimulants had been traded, let alone seen inside. Yet with this woman, whom he strongly suspected of closer involvement than she admitted, he somehow felt secure.

'What we could do,' he said casually, tapping another cigarette on its packet, 'is go down to Kyobashi and have a drink in the last place we stopped. That's if I can find it.'

Maki looked at him quizzically.

'And if it's open, of course,' he said by way of reasoning. 'On Sunday.'

'I suppose it's safe.'

'Don't worry. They won't try anything if you're with me.'

She let the barbed implication of her collusion pass, preferring to agree reluctantly but qualifying her connivance by reference to an engagement later that evening for which she must not be late.

The underground train was packed with shoppers and their bunches of coloured carrier bags. Masses of noisy young children jostled and blocked the passageway. Unable to reach a strap, Maki held the crook of Araki's arm as he hung from the ring for support.

'Do you have any children?' she asked, noticing his interest in the antics of some boys while the train paused in a station.

'Only one,' he said, 'about like that one.' He motioned to a child of eight or nine with a mop of hair cut uniformly straight round his head except for a three-sided rectangle around the eyes.

'You should be with him and your wife on Sundays,' Maki said, 'like these husbands.'

Araki leaned closer to her hair, luxuriating accidentally in the scent of lilies.

'Look at them carefully,' he ordered. 'They're almost embarrassed at being with their wives and children. There isn't a man in this carriage who wouldn't rather be at home sleeping or at the office.'

Maki giggled. It did seem that some of the men were reading the hanging advertisements a bit too self-consciously.

'By the way,' Araki added gratuitously, 'I'm not married any more.'

With the help of the clear evening light, Araki soon found his bearings. It was nearer to the Ginza than he had remembered from that awful night more than two months earlier and further east towards the kabuki theatre, where the buildings were older and shabbier and the shops less fashionable the closer they came to the expressway overpass

227

and the canals and waterways which fed into the docks around Tokyo Bay.

They shared a beer and ate spaghetti upstairs by the window of a café almost opposite the doorway Araki was certain led to a bar or restaurant where he had seen a box containing hidden drugs delivered. They had barely begun to eat when a man's head appeared at street level. He was climbing the stairs from the basement and seemed to be drunk, his emerging body swaying from one wall to the other, but was actually dragging a heavy, upright sign to the street to show it was five-thirty and therefore opening time. He plugged the cable into a socket somewhere in the doorway and the name of the bar, Orion, surrounded by stars which flashed on and off, shone reluctantly through the glass, awaiting the later, darker hours to display its glitter to full effect.

'Should we go over now?' Maki asked, curling the last strands of pasta in her spoon.

'No. Let's wait and see who goes in,' Araki replied, ordering another beer.

Maki shrugged. 'Did you actually see the box exchanged for money?'

'I was further down that way,' Araki replied, gesturing towards the Ginza, 'and it was raining hard by then, but the slimmer of the two, the one in the suit, was definitely carrying something under his coat when he came out. It had to be money.'

'They must have had millions of yen in that van by the end of the evening.' She sounded impressed by her own conclusion. 'And that was only one trip. What would they do with all that cash?'

Araki scribbled some circles on a napkin. 'The notes would be bundled up, packed in briefcases and passed from the first man to someone else and then another, like this, until it reached the final recipient who would have no idea how the money had been earned in the first place. It would then be washed over various accounts in small, local savings banks where large cash movements are not uncommon.

Some of it would appear again as cash, part of a big chain of payment to suppliers, processors, carriers, salesmen, strong-arm men and sometimes the police.'

'You're well informed,' Maki said, sipping her beer.

'The subject's always popular. We cover it a lot in the magazine. But that's not the end. The trickiest pay-off is to the financier. Someone has to fund the original shipments at their source, normally South Korea, Taiwan or the Philippines. The dead man's company . . .' He regretted his choice of words at once, withdrawing them before she could react and reaching involuntarily to touch her wrist. His hand fell short but the apology had been accepted.

'Tanimoto's firm would be the link through the well-known connections of his chief, Teruaki Ogawa with right-wing pressure groups and the syndicates that finance political factions from a treasure-boat of money from honest as well as illegal businesses. Ogawa could also call on his high-level contacts in the commercial and finance houses which pay him to keep the peace with their shareholders. I've even seen some of them in Ogawa's office.'

He had seen only one, a middle-level manager indiscreetly wearing the blood-red badge of the trading company Matsuhashi, but he knew he held her attention with his seemingly vast and fascinating knowledge of the characters she would know only from small talk in smoky clubs and steamy massage cubicles, and this somehow justified his exaggerations. Maki leaned forward, perhaps to challenge or just to consolidate her role as avid listener, but Araki had seen the first customers enter the bar opposite. Young, tanned teenage males with greasy brush-backed hair, probably assistants from the record and hi-fi shops closing down for the night in the backstreets of Ginza.

'Shall we join them?' Maki asked.

'No. Let's wait for one or two more to go in,' he said, his face at the window. I've told you what I know about the drug route, Araki thought. How are you going to react?

'You like this sort of thing, don't you?' Maki asked with a sudden open change of tone.

229

'What?' the reporter said, still watching the road and so confirming Maki's belief.

'You know,' she said, gesticulating aimlessly. 'Like this. Watching people from windows, photographing them and forcing your way into their confidence, following them about by faking compassion in return for intimacies which you buy with money and then expose to the ghoulish public like a dish of rotten fish and then justify with some supercilious comment on the evil just below the surface of our society.' Araki turned towards her. 'But what you're doing,' she continued, 'adds to that evil. You look for people's weaknesses and exploit them without conscience.'

The outburst was expected, even overdue, and consistent with the opinion he had formed of this woman who refused to be browbeaten. She defied any comparison with her scheming cohorts in the floating world or the horde of graduate office girls, timid and fearful of jeopardising their marriage prospects by appearing intelligent and assertive. And of course the housewife, the fallen cherry blossoms of Japanese society, prosperity's sacrificial goats.

Speaking slowly and deliberately, Araki returned to his vigil. 'I exploit no one who hasn't a good cause to be exploited, whether it's a politician off the rails, a baseball player who bets on his own game or . . .'

'Or a grieving bargirl,' Maki said, with only a trace of sarcasm.

'Everyone has a price in your world and mine,' Araki said. 'The only problem is finding the right amount.'

But his companion was not to be restrained.

'What about this man you're stalking?' she asked. 'The one you're writing about.' Maki brushed her hair aside, revealing cheeks flushed from the drink and subdued anger. 'You said he was an ordinary salaryman, one of the latter-day faithful samurai whose way of life should be praised not scorned. The one you chose at random. How did you choose him?'

A man two tables away shuffled his newspaper in admonition at the raised voices. Maki leaned forward, elbows spread across the table, her face creased. 'You chose someone you saw in the sokaiya's office, didn't you? Someone from a respectable company whom you would dearly love to implicate in this imaginative plot you've created.' She put on a playful voice, like a child begging to join a game. 'Can't you tell me who it is? Can't I take part? Can I play?'

Araki was stunned by her deduction, humiliated by her sarcasm and astounded by her thought process which had succeeded in concluding what he had not dared confess to himself, let alone to his English colleague Chris or his editor Kobayashi.

He had pursued the harried salaryman he discovered by chance in the office of the people he believed ordered a violent attack on his person and while genuinely writing an investigative article with the editor's authority had deliberately selected as his subject someone who, in his most perverse fantasy, might be an easy target for his own form of revenge. But had she deduced the connection with the man from Matsuhashi? Or did she know for sure?

'Sonna baka na,' he heard himself saying, 'what silly nonsense,' while in his head he screamed 'who are you' at its ugliest level of contempt and 'who are you working for? Ogawa? The thug Ezaki and his masters, the yakuza from the Yanagida-gumi, or someone else? Someone in control of all of them but much too important to be identified with the other riff-raff?'

'Shall we go in now,' she said, placidly, letting the baffled reporter off the hook and pointing out another pair of customers across the road.

Inside, the cellar bar was cramped and in spite of a pungent freshener the air was musty and still stale from the previous night's cigarette smoke and spilled drink. The people Araki had watched were already reddened from the opening rounds and were teasing the heavily made-up waitress who sidled provocatively between the tables. They sat at the bar and ordered beer. Araki's hands rested on the bar, his fingers tapping silently. He was only waiting for the barman to leave his post on some errand or other so that he could lean over and look for a white box.

Maki edged her stool nearer to his, bunching her knees, she leaned amorously across his shoulder so that the scent of lilies distracted him and her newly glossed lips brushed his ear.

'If you don't relax and stop acting like a bloody policeman, I'm going to walk out of the door,' she hissed through tight teeth. She pulled him even closer, stifling his surprise. 'Everyone else is having fun. You can make an effort too, even though you're not.'

She was right, Araki knew. The bar had clearly not been raided by the police: business, even on a Sunday evening, was brisk with young non-professional clientele drinking inexpensive whisky and who were obviously on close terms with the gregarious waitress and the barman who was quick to join in the banter at each of the three occupied tables. Another group arrived and more greetings were exchanged. Everyone friendly, Araki thought. Regular customers for booze and other good things.

'Tell me where you're from,' Maki said. 'There's a slight southern slur in your voice. I don't think you're from Tokyo.'

Araki detached himself to refill their glasses and find a cigarette which the barman hurried over to light and glance enviously at the attractive woman who must have some good reason for displaying such affection towards her scruffy companion. Araki played the part, finding himself tracing his rural upbringing in Shimane and the aspirations of his parents who decided their eldest son should be the first in the family to benefit from the generous rice subsidies by receiving an education which would end in one of the top private universities in Tokyo, leaving responsibility for the farm and their old age to the second son. He remembered their joy when he became one of only twenty graduates taken on by the newspaper and then the shame and anguish they must have suffered after his dishonourable dismissal a few years later.

Maki was nodding understandingly, contributing some low points in her own post-junior college life, when the lure of the television talent scene was too much for her parents who saw her as an office flower who would bloom and be picked by an aspiring section chief in the same company when she became twenty-five. Singing in clubs followed a short series of television appearances on male fantasy shows which process cute, mini-skirted dolls on an endless conveyor-belt of mediocrity, only to cast them off when they turn twenty or as soon as their bodies and behaviour begin to lose their unblemished innocence.

Araki motioned to speak but sensed his companion's body tense. Over his shoulder, he watched a tall, heavy-set man in a shabby dinner-suit survey the clientele and return the deferential greetings of the staff before manoeuvring his frame through the bar-flap. He produced small bags of change which he tipped noisily into the till. His voice was rough and he ignored Araki and other couples sharing the bar stools as he admonished his barman for not playing a music tape.

'Pay the bill quickly please and let's leave,' she whispered, gripping his arm so tightly it scared him. He was fumbling for his wallet when the manager followed one of the young drinkers who had left his table and made for the toilet. By the time Araki had finished his beer and elicited a bill from an annoyingly distracted barman, the two men re-emerged through the side door, exchanging a few words at parting. While he waited for his change, Maki was on her feet, head held low, already opening the door before he could follow her in retreat. He thought the manager, who had stopped in his tracks among the tables, was mouthing some words of farewell, which were inaudible amid the chatter and the loud pop music now droning through overhead speakers, but his eyes followed Maki and his words of recognition were directed at her.

Outside it was a warm, clear evening but Maki was

233

shivering in a doorway across the street, her arms crossed tightly around herself. She rushed to meet him, seizing his arm in that same fearful grip, and dragging him away.

'I have things to do,' she said, regaining her composure in the comfort of the crowd on the Ginza. 'I'll call you soon.' She managed a wave as she disappeared into the mouth of the underground.

# CHAPTER THIRTEEN

Helped by his son, Ichiro, the old man eased himself from
the car and stood motionless until his balance returned. His
son-in-law, Go Minagawa, waited nervously between the
vulnerable couple and the low wooden doorway which
opened on to a gravel yard and a short path of raised,
separated stones leading to the illuminated entrance of
the guesthouse.

A grove of bamboo, a clump of plum trees and a border
of cherry trees, its longest branches resting on the eaves of
the old wooden structure, stood as sentinels in the space
around the house. There were office and shop premises on
either side but the tall rich foliage rendered invisible what
was not protected by the high solid fence. The house had
belonged before the war to a buddhist priest and at the back
gave on to a temple precinct whose present comforter of
departed souls lived in a modern mansion block nearby.

Yanagida stooped his bald, mottled head painfully under
the slatted crown above the doorway and, motioning his
family away, walked carefully towards the lanterns. The
woman had been watching the arrival through a front
window and prised the sliding doors apart as the old man
reached them. He had to sit to remove his shoes while she
crouched in obedience, her rump in the air and her long
straight hair falling over the stiff kimono collar down on to
the discarded and properly arranged footwear. The heels of
his slippers clappered on the varnished floorboards as he
shuffled unsteadily along the corridor adorned only with a
fading caligraphic scroll on one of its sand-plastered walls.
The woman held his elbow lightly, guiding him into the guest

room whose doors were stiff and parted only reluctantly. The windows were closed and the opaque shoji drawn and were it not for the simple three-rock formation set into the tokonoma alcove the room could have been a temple cell. The walls were bare sand plaster above a skirt of wood panelling, and the tatami was old, with stained patches, cigarette burns and scuffed edges.

Teruaki Ogawa rose swiftly from the sunken floor and offered an arm to the old man. Twenty years younger than the arthritic syndicate chief and thirteen less than the sallow-featured man with the benevolent smile who propped himself awkwardly against the back rest, Ogawa was lean, with a head of thick, black carefully groomed hair which took a decade off his fifty years. They exchanged banter, while the woman came and went serving dishes of rice crackers and nuts, and the man whom the intermediaries had called 'teacher' reassured the others about security. The older two drank from glasses of malt whisky while Ogawa tipped sake from a flagon on to ice-cubes and sipped. The host motioned the woman away.

'It's a shame we don't meet more often,' he said. 'It would be a lot easier to solve problems. Our boys don't really get on, do they?'

The others nodded sympathetically.

'Anyway,' he continued, 'you know why we're here. Our three-year-old project has used your organisational skills, your resources, your many contacts.' He raised his glass towards Ogaway. 'Used the power, the legs, the outlets, the influence of your syndicate.' Yanagida acknowledged with a nod. 'We did our part too: we made sure the product from your people in South Korea, the Philippines, or anywhere in south-east Asia where it was available could find its way into Japan with the minimum of fuss. We took some risks but not many. And let's not forget the profits! Our success in the last years was entirely because only we three, and one trusted aide each, knew the identities in all three corners of the triangle. It was a perfect conspiracy.'

A silhouette of leaves, scuffed by the breeze, flickered

236

across the paper window frames, distracting the old man and inflicting a sudden edge of fear. He hunched forward, his chest now resting against the table.

'Do you realise we have only met face to face four times?' His companions nodded. 'We never discussed our individual methods so we could never be compromised or incriminated. Above all,' he said, tapping the table with a forefinger, 'we never discussed our motives.'

They tried to calculate the money their scheme had netted, while the woman re-filled the glasses. She allowed only a dribble of whisky to drop on to the old man's stacked ice but he admonished her kindly and pressed his hand over hers and forced a gush of liquor to fill the glass. The drink relaxed him again but its passage pained him. The woman left reluctantly.

'It was you,' he said towards Ogawa, 'who came to me first.'

Ogawa motioned to speak, but the old man raised his hand.

'I'm not placing blame,' he stressed. 'You simply pursued your profession as you and your colleagues always have. You somehow found out that Matsuhashi's financial well-being, perhaps even our existence, was threatened by our Mexican exposure and you approached me, as then head of the General Affairs Department, to discuss co-operation. You offered your services to suppress any unfavourable shareholder reaction and deflect adverse market reaction when the facts came to light.' He felt Ogawa's embarrassment and flapped a limp wrist in his direction.

'Don't feel bad. I think we deserved it.'

They all laughed nervously, breaking the tension.

'We got on well after that, didn't we?' he said, raising his glass in confirmation. 'You ensured that our problems were never raised at our annual shareholders' meeting; in return we gave you a generous fee. And then you came up with the novel idea that we should finance a project that you had been considering with our friend Yanagida-san here. A plan that would increase our flagging cashflow.'

237

The syndicate boss bowed in recognition.

'It was wrong, of course, and terribly illegal. Imagine! One of Japan's big names financing a massive drug distribution racket! But the risk, or the lack of it, was irresistible. Of course, half of the hundreds of millions of yen that accrued to me went straight into the company. And when I leave' – the others reacted instinctively, their senses aroused – 'I will have the satisfaction of knowing that I helped my company's funding needs at a very vulnerable time. That, my friends, has been my motive.'

Yanagida scratched his scalp lightly. Ogawa shifted uneasily on his cushion. The room was clammy, and heavy with smoke.

'Oi!' the man from Matsuhashi said, with enough power to bring the woman who was kneeling outside the door. 'Open the window a little please, and help me off with this.'

She tugged the jacket off his shoulders and eased it from his arms before drawing aside the shoji and glass layers, leaving only the insect netting between the room and the stillness of the evening.

Kosaburo Iwamura, ailing managing director and soon to be the first sacrifice to the Mexican disaster, inhaled the refreshing air.

'I shall have to take responsibility,' he continued, 'for the training of certain personnel who are now being blamed for our current precarious financial condition.' Anticipating their question he said: 'There's absolutely nothing I can do about it. To protest would suggest I had some sort of collusion and that is inconceivable. I do have to do the honourable thing.'

He paused to drain the glass of whisky, and continued before their questions could form. 'There are other reasons why there must be a re-assessment of our whole reason for pursuing this venture. The death of that man Tanimoto,' he said, directing his words to Ogawa, 'was regrettable but the code of secrecy was so tight I never imagined he was your key link with our colleague over here. Not until that reporter—' His voice cracked as a gob of phlegm blocked its passage, and he convulsed violently, his face reddening. Ignoring formalities, the woman who served him closely rushed to his side and thumped his back between the shoulder blades, dislodging the blockage. From her sleeve, she drew a sheaf of tissues which the old man used to clear his throat. The emotion in his voice when he recovered was one of rising anger which manifested itself in an involuntary twitch in one cheek.

'That man. What was his name? Arakawa?'

'Araki,' Ogawa corrected.

'Of course. His stupid persistence has endangered our business and may threaten our freedom.'

'He was warned all along the way,' the syndicate head said, with a certain grim satisfaction. 'From the time we noticed him at the Camelia coffee shop until we had to be more persuasive.'

'I don't want to know the circumstances of his accident,' Iwamura said forcefully, 'but it hasn't deterred him. He's been seen near one of my staff quite often.'

Without emotion Ogawa said: 'Is this staff member of yours vulnerable?'

'Not consciously,' Iwamura replied. 'He deals with the savings banks mainly and it gives him a perfect reason to carry cash between accounts and do other errands. But he is not a party to the business behind the transactions. We settle many accounts in cash, like everybody else in this business stratum.'

'But is he a threat?' Ogawa persisted. 'Does the reporter know that your man is part of our operation?'

Iwamura grimaced, genuinely hurt by the directness, by the openness of the remarks and questions. He looked around, as if the corners hid some secret witness, before lifting a beige folder from his side and laying it on the table. He spoke slowly to Ogawa.

'Impetuously and against all the rules we had fixed, this man visited your offices when he became worried because he had read that his regular contact, Tanimoto, was dead and the briefcases he had got used to collecting over many

239

months would no longer appear. He panicked, and knowing your company to be Tanimoto's employer, sought you out to try and find an explanation before he had to come to me, or rather my junior colleagues, to explain the sudden halt to the cashflow. You assured him that the problem was only temporary, that the deliveries would commence again soon and you bundled him out of the office at the very moment that reporter chose to visit you in pursuit of a story on the life of the victim.'

'An unfortunate coincidence,' Ogawa said drily, 'but this reporter, Araki, could not have known who your man was, or what company he belonged to.'

The Matsuhashi executive sighed, his fatigue betrayed by deep lines around his purple eye sockets. He opened the folder and spread the single sheets out like a fan. Yanagida leaned forward; Ogawa sat impassively.

'These are articles written by Araki in the *Tokyo Weekly* in the last six months,' Iwamura said, tapping the papers. He slid the top one away from the others. 'This one is about the activities of sokaiya and it mentions our annual general meeting in June. He was there.' He pulled another from the fan. 'In September he wrote about Tanimoto and in mentioning his sokaiya employer he referred to some of the corporations who have used the services of these institutions. He refers, among others, to Matsuhashi. A month ago he began a series on,' and he read over his glasses, 'the average salaryman, his hopes, his fears, his fantasies.'

He brushed the photocopies aside disdainfully. 'He talks about pride in the corporation, lifelong loyalty to the corporate identity, ties that are closer than those to his own family and, in passing, he mentions three companies: Fuji Bank, Sumitomo Metal and Matsuhashi Corporation. I don't know,' the tired old man continued, 'whether Araki has been able to prove the link between the three of us, but consciously or not, he's made at least three references to my company in three stories. Make your own conclusions.'

They passed the papers from one to the other, reading

silently the passages Iwamura had marked before weighing up the nuances.

Yanagida snuffled. He was too old to look for complications. He drew breath noisily. 'I don't think he knows,' he concluded. 'And if he does he can't prove it conclusively. Otherwise he would have told the police by now and we would have been questioned. Ne?' He looked for allies, but found none.

'Do you then share Yanagida-san's opinion?' Iwamura asked Ogawa.

'No, absolutely not,' Ogawa replied, leaning forward, both palms pressed to the edges of the table. 'I believe the reporter knows, or is very close to knowing.'

Iwamura squeezed his temples with the tips of his fingers, moving on to rub his eyelids with the same circular motion, and spoke solemnly to his fellow conspirators.

'The consequences of his knowing or not knowing are very serious.' And then only to Ogawa he said, 'Why do you think he knows?'

Poised to speak, the sokaiya chief held back when the woman returned to refill the glasses. She carefully avoided eye contact with any of the three men but when she knelt and bent forward to pour the sake into Ogawa's rough ceramic cup she allowed a trail of hair to fall across his sleeve. With both hands busy cradling the warm tokkuri, her only recourse to atone for this rudeness was to lift her head as delicately as possible, guiding the offending strands away with a sideways flourish which exposed the rim of her kimono at the neck. Ogawa thought her nape was lightly powdered, or more likely the play of light reflecting off the shoji drew out a paleness he had not noticed before. The movement also released a scent, one he thought he should identify but could not. The silk fabric of the kimono scuffed the matting: otherwise her exit was silent.

'Because,' Ogawa continued, 'he seems to know what we represent. Don't you get that feeling? He knows us all too well and won't give up until he finds a way to link a respectable segment of society, represented by you at Matsuhashi, with the disreputable, namely Yanagida-san and myself. Exposing us in his articles as wrongdoers will only amuse and titillate and confirm what society thinks about us in any case. But to name you,' he said, motioning to Iwamura, 'would release all those forces of public outrage which have been growing since your competitors at Marubeni helped to channel the Lockheed millions to Tanaka, and have been thirsting for their next scapegoat. Araki can't exact revenge on us,' he said motioning to Yanagida, 'but he is looking for something to tear at and throw to the wolves. That would suggest Matsuhashi.'

'That decides it then,' a voice said. To the girl kneeling outside the door and listening, it was a voice unrecognisable amid the garbled sounds of people talking across each other's words.

'Can we leave it to you then?' another asked.

'Of course,' someone said, a younger voice she thought. Then the sounds were muffled and indistinct, and she opened the door as Ogawa was easing the old Iwamura on to his feet.

She cleared the glasses and dishes of titbits and wiped off the ring marks from the table. The envelope was moist where it had lain against a cold glass, but the 200,000 yen inside was in dry, sharp, new 10,000-yen notes.

His eyes were pinched and almost shut by the exertion. His voice cracked at the final flourish, but the applause drowned the quavering end to Ninomiya's second rendition of 'My Way' that evening. He was unusually relaxed: the chain was fully operational again and seemed to be moving even larger amounts of money through subsidiary company accounts at small savings and loan banks around the city. He had had to open two more accounts to handle the volume and had dined out well on the goodwill generated. It was also Friday and his only night for social drinking after a hectic week with two evenings of hospitality by grateful banks and a working session at headquarters which finished at midnight. Yesterday he had redressed the balance with his general manager by losing heavily at mahjong. And now the young woman whose company he had enjoyed in the few weeks since she started at the Flora had joined him at his table, leaving a boisterous group of red-faced salarymen to play alone. She nudged him deeper into the booth so that their knees touched and they were shielded from general view.

'Are your friends coming later?' she asked, pouring him a stiff whisky-water. He inclined his head and hissed.

'Saaaa.'

'I hope not,' she purred. 'It would be nice just to talk to you alone. And you can sing just for me.'

He blushed, having no idea why this woman with the style of a Ginza professional and the cute beauty of a television quiz-show hostess should favour him with her attention. Perhaps he had evolved a mature desirability at forty, something he certainly hadn't possessed before. No woman, in university or at work, had sought his company. Even his marriage had been arranged and it was twelve days before a form of sex had taken place. He rubbed his tired eyes beneath his glasses as 'Tammy' chatted on.

'I often wonder why you men never go anywhere alone. You're always in groups and never with girls. Aren't there any nice office ladies at Mitsui?'

'Matsuhashi,' he corrected, slightly offended.

'I'm sorry,' she said, squeezing his knee as if to reinforce her sincerity. 'But aren't you tempted now and then?' she was loosening his tie. 'It can be relaxing, help you forget all that work. You have been very busy this week, I know. You haven't been here since last Thursday.' He was flattered by her recollection.

'There's so much to do,' he said proudly. 'When you're in the Finance Department you have to be ready to serve everybody else.'

'Finance Department. Oh how interesting!' Yoko regretted her exaggerated enthusiasm as soon as she spoke but her companion was so besotted he accepted the remark as sincere and saw it as a prompt to continue.

243

'The month-end is always busy, even more than usual. We settle a lot of trade bills in cash and that's where I get involved. I spend most of my time with bankers.'

Yoko had decided that her debt to Araki for his help with awkward visitors to her apartment over the years was almost fully repaid. She found this thin, ordinary company clerk so utterly tiresome and boring that she almost regretted agreeing to the deception. But she had really wanted to show her gratitude and had chosen a tight pink Vietnamese chongsam, long discarded to the memory of an apprenticeship in a Ueno cabaret, with which to tempt this miserable weed away from his workmates and the karaoke microphone.

'Oh really,' she enthused, slowly crossing her legs and watching his eyes follow as the fissure of her dress widened and it displayed her outside thigh almost as high as her panty line. 'But isn't it dangerous to handle cash? You read about all these robberies.'

Ninomiya flapped a hand, and delayed a response in order to drink deeply from the glass the girl he knew as Tammy had just refilled. He was intrigued by her ingenuousness and thoroughly captivated by the roundish face, the page-boy hairstyle and the long smooth neck held by the stiff collars of her dress. He was about to continue but saw that his companions were distracted by the Mama-san.

'I'm sorry,' she whispered, so close he felt the warmth and stickiness of her lips, 'I have to serve at the other tables.'

'Of course, of course,' he said, nodding sadly at the table.

'Ne?' Yoko murmured, as sympathetically as possible, and hoping she was not over-acting. 'Can't we meet later. You know. Go somewhere and talk.' She moved even closer, unbuttoning his shirt and describing circles with her fingertips. She put his lack of immediate gratified response to the fact that she was stimulating an undershirt. She was then conscious of Ninomiya's impetuous search for an access to her thighs and his inability to find it. A tremulous hand finally found a knee.

'Let's play later,' she urged, placing a restraining hand

on his chest. 'There's a taxi-rank a minute's walk if you turn right outside the club. I'll meet you there at a quarter to twelve. Don't keep me waiting. Ne?'

Ninomiya was unable to obey the signals which urged him to refuse. He simply nodded and muttered something about telephoning home.

She straightened and sidled past her client. 'Now please make me happier by singing something for me. How about ''Feelings''? Oh look! Some of your friends have arrived.'

It was not the appearance of colleagues that jolted him, or his near discovery in what for him was a very unusual situation. It was seeing the unsmiling, owlish face of his manager Ikeuchi among his regular drinking friends. He had never been to the Flora before, knowing it was a haven for the juniors, a place where frustrations could be harmlessly vented on mental punchbags of himself and his senior managers. But he had turned up with Aida from General Affairs, another man who enjoyed Ikeuchi's confidence, and two junior colleagues from Finance.

Ninomiya passed them on the way to the karaoke stack and indicated his booth to them. He sang for the woman he knew as Tammy, but while the joy in his heart was real, as were the smiles he exchanged with her as she flitted between the tables, he weighed the presence of Ikeuchi. His chief was alone with Aida in Ninomiya's booth and when a hostess came over to chat Ikeuchi waved her away brusquely.

'Saa, drink, drink,' he said when Ninomiya joined them. It was an order rather than an invitation. Aida spilt whisky over his trousers when he tried to level the bottle over the glasses. They had obviously stopped elsewhere to drink, with Aida a casualty as usual. The rims around his eyes were red and his speech hesitant. Ikeuchi ignored him when he spoke to Ninomiya.

'How are you getting on with the new man? What's his name?'

'Doi,' Aida prompted.

'Very well,' Ninomiya replied, the drink freeing him and

245

releasing his suspicions. 'Is there something the matter?'

'No, not at all,' Ikeuchi said assuringly. 'I haven't had a chance to sit down and talk about the changed circumstances.'

No, Ninomiya thought, as he bought time with another long drag on his glass, we haven't talked and I haven't been able to explain the shame I feel when this so-called business contact grins and breathes garlic over me and talks to the coffee-shop girls with phoney television low-life words which make us noticed. Where only the thin moustache stood Tanimoto apart from him or any other salaryman, the new man Doi had worn a chalk-striped light blue suit with padded shoulders and a thick gold-plated chain around one wrist which complemented the two matching rings on the same hand. His mouth was large and drooped in a permanent arrogant scowl and his skin was coarse and naturally dark.

'I want to know,' Ikeuchi was saying intensely, 'if he arrives late or if he brings anyone with him. I want you to look for any change in his behaviour. We don't want a recurrence of what happened before.'

Ninomiya was emboldened enough by drink to say, 'I'm not sure I know what happened before,' when he really wanted to ask what had occurred to make his chief take an interest in such a mundane part of his work, namely the transporting of high, but not unusually so, volumes of cash from a client to a bank.

It was true that he had been suspicious at the start, particularly as he had no commercial promissory note to hand over in exchange for the cash, but Tanimoto was pleasant, well mannered and professional, although the moustache meant he was not a top company man. He would be standing smoking by a pillar on a station platform and would only reciprocate Ninomiya's bow with a curt nod. He had been very edgy in the last few encounters but his death was a shock, especially in the circumstances. Ninomiya had anguished over whether to question Ikeuchi as to the nature of the business and the origin of the money but then it was reported that his contact was a sokaiya. His chief had insisted that the job must continue. But what exactly was the job? He had collected the black leather briefcases, and accepted receipts at numerous savings banks in urban Tokyo over the last twelve months which must have totalled hundreds of millions of yen.

Ikeuchi was talking to Aida, neither noticing how Ninomiya traced invisible figures on the table top. A million yen in 10,000-yen notes would make a small pile about a centimetre thick. The weight of the cases he was used to carrying suggested thirty, forty or more bundles of money, say up to forty million yen. The deposit receipt was always sealed in an envelope and he had never watched studiously while the bank clerks counted the money but he made a mental note to do so at the collection next Tuesday. Forty million yen would pay off his borrowings from Matsuhashi for the five-room apartment he had bought in a company housing complex, but more interestingly, at current rates he calculated it would generate 200,000 dollars, a healthy downpayment on a condominium in Hawaii but nothing much left afterwards. Or you could go to Thailand and live for ten years in Chiang Mai with three country girls to pamper you. And three or four caseloads would tempt a buddha! But how many could be taken before discovery? How much would it take to tempt Tammy, who even now was beaming smiles at him as she passed the table? Could he divert four or five consignments and slip away with her forever? He shook his head with a sharp jerk, trying to clear his mind of these evil thoughts.

Ninomiya's private reverie was rudely broken by Aida's demand that he listen to a vulgar anecdote. Ikeuchi had lost interest. He seemed re-assured, by what he had heard from his courier. He accepted a refill from Tammy with what was close to a smile and fifteen minutes later tactfully left his juniors to play, with instructions to charge the bill to him. Aida was reluctant to leave: he was drunk to the point of being abusive about the man who had just saved him 10,000 yen and about the other seniors and their reluctance to recognise and exploit his own obvious potential. The few

247

customers left were slowly drifting away. The girls no longer poured drinks with their usual enthusiasm and two had already said goodbye to their regular guests. The drink which had emboldened Ninomiya also filled him with luxurious visions of strength, freedom and virility. He made his decision and went in search of a telephone.

Aida was overcome by a spasm of nausea and when he found the toilet locked he stumbled up the stairs into the broad, two-way street where the multi-coloured lines of the nightly rush-hour taxis merged into a sickly kaleidoscope. He propped himself against a telephone pole and drew deep, refreshing breaths. The cool, damp air revived him and his focus stabilised in time to follow the path of a taxi slowing down for a light and if he could have stood erect he might have reached out and touched it. The man in the back, looking uneasily towards the bar, and apparently not recognising the figure wrapped around the pole, was unmistakably Ninomiya, the kakari-cho from the domestic finance department who had said he had to catch a train, and the woman leaning forward over the back-rest talking to the driver looked to his confused mind like the hostess who had been serving them both thirty minutes earlier. He shook his head to correct what he assumed was impaired vision caused by too much alcohol but when he searched again for the taxi and its familiar occupants, the images had blurred and the urge to vomit now became uncontrollable. He wiped his mouth on a sleeve and remembered Ninomiya and hoped to score a corporate point or two if he could remember to call Ikeuchi at home and tell him what he had seen.

Ninomiya was too confused by drink to be embarrassed at visiting a love hotel for the first time, or surprised at the discreet and knowing way Tammy exchanged his money for a key through a hatch in the dimly lit empty lobby. It was a cold place: no comfortable chairs, potted plants or piles of luggage. It was a place where no one except furtive lovers should be seen. Ninomiya waited by the lift, his head nodding forward and then instinctively jerking backwards as he strained to regain composure.

'That was easy,' the woman he knew as Tammy said, tucking some change into his jacket. 'Third floor, and don't forget your bag.'

He would have left it outside, since he was already stooping low in the lift to count off the buttons on the controls, his face screwed in concentration, almost touching the panel.

She gave him a hug and squealed, 'I hope you're as excited as I am.'

Ninomiya assured her he was.

The room had a sterile, precise warmth from a smooth, conditioned airflow and it seemed to have a sobering influence on the salaryman. It was totally unlike any of the five rooms in his apartment: in fact it was almost as big as all of them together. There was no need here to shuffle cautiously between sleeping children or hurry in front of his wife who sat reading or knitting at the low table a metre or two from the television. He wouldn't have to avoid outsize furniture, including an upright piano, or the low fluorescent lamps, while making sure at the same time his fingers didn't penetrate any more of the already pock-holed shoji panels. He had only seen this kind of room in the weeklies, with its carpets, mirrored ceilings, huge television-video stack with a selection of porno films, and a low circular bed on which the object of his lust was now flopped face down, one leg bent back until the ankle caressed her buttocks.

'Oide,' Yoko commanded, wagging her finger from the bed. 'Come over here.'

Ninomiya was momentarily deadened by a warning spasm which he felt passing up his limbs in a wave, leaving weakness in its wake and finally settling in his head with a numbing jolt before subsiding. It was not nausea, only a reminder that his body was no longer responsible or in full control.

Yoko saw him stagger and sprang from the bed. While he leaned against the wall, she removed his shoes, leaving them by the door with his business bag. She then ducked and reeled to avoid his flaying, uncooperative arms while she tugged at his jacket, finally succeeding in stripping him of it and leaving it also by the door in a tidy heap. She activated the video and tuned it to a soft porn film. Soft love music flowed from unseen speakers as figures appeared in contrived sex scenes on the screen, their only dialogue being the mandatory moans of ecstasy. At least they were communicating something, even if it was phoney. Her own partner was dribbling silently on the bed, his eyes struggling to stay fixed on the several couples writhing about on even more screens. His face was deathly grey. Yoko hoped he was not going to be sick and scolded Araki in her mind for making her repay him by going through this ordeal. She considered any debt due to him now fully written off. Another few minutes, she guessed, rubbing her hands together in anticipation before slipping off her skirt, and it's all over. She lay down beside him. He was so thin her hands rippled over his rib-cage. Yoko moulded her body to his.

'Should I record us?' she whispered, easing his shirt loose. Ninomiya breathed noisily and tried to turn towards the warm body next to him. Yoko stiffened, sensing there was some danger he might respond to the action on the video. She had been using her knees to probe for signs of life between his legs and there was a moment of awful panic when his arm involuntarily fell on to her chest and a low, wailing sound came from his throat. She recognised it from experience. It was not the sound of pleasurable pain but the familiar prelude to deep, drunken sleep which began as a groan but turned gradually into a dull snore that would tremble his lower jaw.

Araki sat with Chris in the adjoining room, one listening at the wall whilst the other watched the video. He had given her twenty minutes to put Ninomiya to sleep and she still had five minutes to spare when he heard the tapping signal from next door. When he opened the door to Yoko's room she had returned to the bed. Ninomiya's head was nestling in her lap, his eyes heavy and unseeing, and the message in Yoko's expression was simply a plea for Araki to hurry before the man chewing on the hem of the sheet woke up. The journalist was beginning to feel the tension himself; his clothes felt damp and cold with sweat. He took the bag, and the wallet and pocket diary from Ninomiya's coat and returned to the room where Chris waited by the window, watching the crown of light above the buildings opposite. Their street was quiet enough although they were only a short walk from the Akasaka night spots with their neons and the buildings with bright outside lifts. Araki handed the bag to Chris.

'See what's in this,' he ordered. 'And stay by the window and keep an eye on the street.'

'What am I looking for?' the Englishman asked, propping himself against the window frame.

'I've no idea, but if it's big and carries a baseball bat, shout. It's a mutual friend.'

Chris grinned.

Araki sat on the bed and perused the diary. The slumbering salaryman was a meticulous noter of appointments and events and his script was precise and unhurried. He had little free time it seemed, and the annotations had to be carried into the margins and into the strips reserved for weekend meetings. The pages of the black book, now three-quarters used, had thickened and swollen from the packed jottings, corrections and the messy workings of fingers as they flicked through the pages. He looked for the day he had seen Ninomiya at the office of the sokaiya and the meeting had been entered in blue, though others for the same day were in black. He supposed that Ninomiya had arranged the hurried encounter without appointment but being diligent and for the sake of good order he had gone back to fill in his diary. Araki looked at Chris.

'Everything OK?'

'No problem,' Chris said. The Japanese script in the note-book was confusing him and the numbers which lay alongside them were hardly more enlightening. He was giving the street more attention than the compromising figures.

Araki said, 'I've found the entry for the meeting between Ninomiya and Ogawa on the day when I ended up in hospital. It must have upset them when I went straight in and tried to interview Ogawa. I wonder if they sent a message straight to the delivery team behind the Bali in Ikebukuro. It would explain—'

He had not time to finish: Chris was beckoning him across, pleading for silence. He gestured down the street, to the right of their window. A couple were emerging from the concealed entrance of an inn, their figures breaking the cone of light which came from the lantern over the doorway and spilled across the road. The two men watched them scurry away, heads down as if embarrassed by the circumstances, towards the lights of Akasaka. Araki was about to withdraw to more urgent work when Chris held his arm. There was a movement below them, on the short paved walkway which led to the gate. It was a woman. She seemed agitated and when she reached the road she hesitated and hurried back to the hotel.

The journalists resumed their search. Araki was looking for recurring entries and turned the pages of the diary as slowly as he thought time would allow, hoping the repeated appointments would find him. The writing was impeccable, even for the painfully complex construction of the honorific added to many of the names. Those without title or similar polite distinction Araki assumed to be colleagues or friends. There were also a few annotations in roman letters, always the name of a foreign banker or visitor he and Ikeuchi might have to meet as senior officials of the domestic finance department, but some gave only a capital letter followed by a place and time. Araki assumed that the briefest of abbreviations referred to someone the writer knew well.

There were at least two encounters with an M, and S appeared twice as he turned the pages. Then the letter T appeared, and as Araki flipped the pages backwards, his excitement barely under control, it recurred regularly from the second week of the year to the very week Akira Tanimoto met his death. The letter was followed only by the Chinese characters for an inner-city station, either underground or surface and always within the Yamate loop. Araki supposed that was their territory, their designated sphere of operation. He called Chris over, a smile of self-satisfaction saying he had been right all along, and showed him some simple entries.

'Why did he do that?' Chris asked, pointing at a letter T. 'Why didn't he use a Japanese letter?'

'It's common, especially in journalism, to use a roman letter to identify someone or some place when we don't want to name the person or location directly. It might help to keep a libel suit away. We can't use the Chinese ideograph because we can't abbreviate without giving the game away. Either of the two characters in Tanimoto's name would identify him to the suspicious mind. The phonetic scrips are not much safer. The writer wanting to abbreviate Tanimoto into katakana or hiragana would have to disclose the first syllable.'

Chris looked puzzled.

'Look,' Araki said, finding an expressway ticket to scribble on. 'You can't reproduce the simple English letter T in Japanese. The tee sounds are restricted to these five.' He wrote and pronounced, ' "Ta, chi, tsu, te and to." You can't say a man's name begins with a T as you can in English. Can you see what I'm trying to say?'

Chris was beginning to comprehend. He nodded.

Araki continued, 'So if Ninomiya had wanted to abbreviate Tanimoto in Japanese he'd have to write "ta", which would be a giveaway. Now do you get it?'

Chris was almost convinced. He said, 'So the T could be anything. How do you know it's for Tanimoto?'

'The last T entry is 23 August, three days before Tanimoto died. It doesn't appear again.'

Chris looked at the thin, incriminating book, fascinated by the correctly formed T among the unintelligible hieroglyphics, Araki leaned across, guiding the Englishman's attention to the following pages with his forefinger.

'Within three weeks of Tanimoto's death our friend from Matsuhashi is meeting with someone whose initial is D.'

'Are you sure it's not the writing?' Chris suggested. 'It could be a T.'

'No chance,' Araki said confidently. 'It reappears every ten days or so. There's another lined up next week.'

'Are you thinking of going?' Chris enquired.

'Not possible,' Araki said, his disappointment obvious. 'It doesn't say where it is. Only the character for station.' He turned the page. 'The next one just says coffee. At least he's got the brains not to say which station or what coffee shop he's meeting the new sokaiya D at.'

But as he read on, sometimes back-pedalling, his tone changed. 'Look at this, Chris,' Araki said forgetting his colleague was illiterate in his tongue. 'Our friend next door doesn't have the sense not to put down the name of the bank he's going to next after meeting with T or D.' He looked at his watch, suddenly concerned for his neighbour Yoko who had reluctantly agreed to incapacitate the man from Matsuhashi. 'What's in the book?'

Chris flipped the pages casually. 'I can't read any of it except for the word for yen and lots of numbers.'

Araki studied the notes and then weighed the diary in one hand against the notebook in the other. 'So that's what he does,' he said aloud.

'What?' Chris asked, bemused by Araki's conclusions.

'He picks up briefcases full of money from one of Ogawa's men, first Tanimoto and now someone whose name begins with D.' Araki crossed the room, his arm cutting the air like a karate chop at each deduction. 'He takes the money and deposits it in a web of bank accounts with insignificant local banks. It can then be moved around without arousing anyone's suspicion.'

Chris was not convinced. 'Surely someone in the banks gets suspicious when this chap turns up every week or so with a fresh case of banknotes.'

'Not at all,' Araki said, taking Ninomiya's notepad from his colleague. 'In Japan we rarely use cheques. Cash is still the main form of paying bills. Either that or a straight bank transfer.'

Chris scoffed, 'It must be great being a mugger here. You can walk into the street and just wait for the bags of money to show.'

Araki had often been angered by his Western friends' belief that murder and street crime were the natural companions to economic prosperity.

'I can't remember the last time I read about a street robbery,' he said, his concentration on the contents of the book and the time on his watch which was crawling towards two in the morning.

'Why's that?' Chris was saying.

Araki dropped the notebook on the bed. He was tired, the complicated conspiracy to trap Ninomiya had left him emotionally drained and was beginning to play on his conscience. He felt unfit to debate the country's sociological attitude to crime.

'Because robbery's against the law,' he snapped.

'But the yakuza get away with it, don't they?' Chris countered.

Araki put an ear against the wall and, satisfied all was well next door, said, 'The Yakuza don't condone street crime and they don't rob banks. They only fight each other over territorial rights.'

Now there really was a noise in the adjoining room. Both men heard it at once and splayed themselves against the wall. Ninomiya was breathing deeply, emitting snores which surely were loud enough to shake him awake. There was a knock on their door and Yoko was there, her face wrinkled by fright. She was already dressed to leave.

'I'm sure he's going to wake up,' she stammered. 'Haven't you finished?'

'Sorry, Yo-chan,' Araki said, stuffing the notebook back into the briefcase while Chris tidied the room.

Next door, they could see, to their relief, that Ninomiya was still on the bed, a sheet crumpled and folded down to his waist, a pale, hairless leg dangling over the side. His eyes

255

were closed but there was some movement behind the lids. His abused body was agitated, tossed from side to side by the alcoholic devil he had been duped with. Araki replaced his quarry's belongings and took Yoko's arm.

'Make sure you don't leave anything, especially personal things like clothing or your address book,' he ordered, watching her move briskly and lightly, helped no doubt by her regular ballet training. She flitted on springy steps, one eye on Ninomiya who was still again, until she was satisfied the room was clear.

'Will he be all right?' Chris asked when they reached Araki's car.

'Of course he will,' Araki said, a little too casually for Chris's Western sensibilities. 'Missing the last train and staying in a hotel is part of the salaryman culture. He'll crawl home in the morning and as it's Saturday he'll lie on his futon all day drinking green tea.'

The English meant nothing to Yoko but intuitively, and helped by the scattering of Japanese words, she was able to comprehend the gist of the exchange and threw her support towards Araki with a nod and a smile.

On the short drive to the apartment block where Yoko and Araki were neighbours, the journalist wanted to clear up any uncertainties and cover any possible mistakes in the successful subterfuge now completed. Yoko was relaxing, the pressure having eased and her debt to Araki repaid. Chris was trying to communicate with her in his unstructured Japanese, an attempt, it seemed to Araki, to find out the price for short-time hotels of the kind they had all shared until moments earlier. Yoko giggled. She had heard what she thought was an invitation and accepted with a loud 'yes' in English, leaving Chris looking puzzled and even more convinced of the inscrutability of the orientals.

'You have left that club, haven't you?' Araki said, after they had dropped Chris at the taxi-rank under the pedestrian's bridge at Shibuya Station. He studied the mirror for other cars to pull over or stop. At this time of night any movement of cars other than taxis would be noticeable.

The November air had turned cold and when Chris opened the door Yoko held herself against the chill. Her skin had dried after the stress and clammy excitement of the evening. She drew her jacket around her, but it wasn't enough. She shuddered.

'I only had a month's contract. Last night was the finish. They asked me if I wanted to go back. Do you think I did a good job on that man?'

Araki leaned across and tapped the airflow outlet.

'It'll be warm in a second or two,' he promised. When he looked up, Yoko's smooth oval face held the question in the tired but still inquisitive, sensitive eyes and the pale, slightly opened lips. He brushed away a strand of hair which had strayed across her nose and which she had not the inclination to move.

Meiji-Dori was quiet. The figure in the doorway of a fast-food restaurant on the corner of Omote-sando turned into a uniformed policeman as the car slowed at the intersection. The only other vehicles were taxis, optimistically cruising between the clusters of neon lights in Harajuku.

'You were perfect,' Araki said, as he pulled into his place on the forecourt of their silent block. But he was still concerned. 'But you're sure they can't trace you? You didn't leave an address did you?'

Yoko pondered. 'I did when I signed the employment form, but it was a hotel I used to stay at sometimes in Ginza. I never go there now. Why? Is something the matter?' She was starting to sense her friend's unease.

'No, of course not,' he said with a conviction he didn't wholeheartedly believe.

'Are you planning to go out tomorrow?' he asked.

'Today you mean, Saturday.'

Araki smiled. 'Sorry. Today.' He looked at his watch. It was almost three o'clock.

Yoko yawned. 'No. I'll sleep all day and then go to the hairdresser's. Why? Are you inviting me out?'

'Not today, Yo-chan,' he said affectionately. 'I'm going over to Chris's when I get up to work on the final story.

257

After what tonight has revealed, I think the puzzle's solved. It just needs tidying up. How about Sunday? We can go down to Kanda and eat some broiled eel. Then see a film.'

Yoko squealed with delight and looped both her arms around him.

'Quiet!' he admonished with mock severity. 'I've had enough trouble from the neighbours lately.' He waited as she rummaged in her handbag for her doorkey.

'By the way,' she said, turning towards Araki, 'what do I say if he calls?' Araki was distracted with his own efforts on his door. He was so tired he had to lean against the heavy door to move it.

'Who?

'That man. What was his name? Ninomiya?'

'What?' Araki's attempt to contain his surprise to a contortion of his expression failed and the word echoed along the communal balcony. A kitchen light came on in one of the flats, its sallow reflection, broken by the security bars on the window, leaking on to the pathway.

'Come inside quickly,' he ordered urgently, taking her arm, this time more firmly.

'You didn't give him your address, did you?'

'Of course not. But I did give him my telephone number.'

Araki dropped on to a chair, his hands still in his pockets, his legs outstretched. He had been elated at the success of the operation, from the time when luck began to bless him by throwing the hapless salaryman from Matsuhashi in his path. Now he was deflated, and very tired.

'I had no choice,' Yoko was saying. 'I thought at one point he wasn't showing enough interest, he might slip away, so I gave him my number to entice him. He never called though. He didn't have to because from then on he was in my palm.'

Araki was silent. Yoko circled him slowly, then stopped behind him and rested her hands on his shoulders.

'Ara-chan,' she said, using an affectionate short form of his family name as she had heard no one use his first. 'I never asked you why you wanted me to lure that awful man into that silly trap. I've known you since you moved here after your divorce and I've trusted you more than any other man I've known.' They both smiled remembering the parade of frustrated salarymen, some of whom Araki had helped evict from her flat. 'I don't think you were working on a story tonight, although that's what you told me. You were scared. Normally you're mischievous, but after this caper you're worried about what I've disclosed. When I told you Ninomiya had my telephone number you nearly fainted.' She pressed her cheek to his. 'What should I know?' It was a plea more than a question.

Araki lifted his hand and held her face to his.

'I need another day,' he said quietly. 'I'm convinced Ninomiya is involved in some grand drugs conspiracy. The usual things. Stimulants.'

'And so?' she said, unimpressed by mention of something she was not unfamiliar with.

'And so I intend to expose the whole thing to Nishii. You know, my fellow countryman, the police inspector. Then I'm going to write the whole thing up in the magazine, maybe even a book. That's why I'm going to Chris's place tomorrow. We can talk through the whole thing logically. There are a couple of points to talk through.'

'But you are worried about me, aren't you?' Yoko said.

'Yes, I am,' he confessed. 'That's why I'm asking you one last favour.' He stood and faced his neighbour, his hands around her waist. 'Please stay here tonight and don't leave until I get back. It should be around seven or eight. Would you do that?' he asked.

Yoko smiled and rested her head against his chest.

'Of course I will. If you'll come next door with me and get some things.'

Araki relaxed.

'Thanks,' he said. 'Promise you won't let any man in except me, Chris or Kondo.'

She was still asleep when he left, but through the half-open door and the bedroom shoji he could see where she lay on

259

her side, her head turned away from him. He had moved his desk and chair aside and spread his spare futon on the living-room floor but Yoko had asked to lie next to him and within minutes she was deep in sleep. Closing the kitchen door, he finished his coffee and cigarette and left without waking her.

# CHAPTER FOURTEEN

Chris's apartment block overlooked a small dusty children's playground bordered by cherry and plum trees. Mothers sat in the sunshine while their young charges crawled and squealed in the sandpit or clung to the climbing-frame. Potted plants in the lobby and a low, soft sofa for visitors indicated a level of residence for expatriate foreigners or Japanese in the medical or entertainment professions. The rear of the lobby was entirely of glass and looked into the well of the building, a space barely large enough to hold two cars but which had been made into an ornamental garden of dwarf bamboo and clinging moss and rock plants. A length of mature bamboo was balanced on a pivot so that when dripping water filled its upturned mouth it tipped forward and fell with a hollow thump, spilling the water before springing back for a refill. There were only three flats on each floor, another sign of the exclusivity and privacy denied to all but a few Tokyo dwellers.

Carried upwards in a lift lined with imitation leather panelling pressed inwards at intervals with gold buttons, Araki wondered if Maki lived in a place like this. After five years on the Ginza, and probably with some patronage, this is what she could expect. It was what Yoko aspired to, but she was wont to spend as she earned, quitting a particular club and going on a long foreign trip. For the moment, she was content to live in the grey, faceless condominium with neighbours like Araki. The journalist would be surprised if the monthly rent for Chris's flat was under 300,000 yen, a third as much again as his own salary.

The first surprise, though, was to be greeted by a slim

Japanese girl, about twenty years old and looking very much at home.

'Is Bingham-san in?' Araki said, slightly off-guard.

The girl smiled and beckoned him inside. He made to take off his shoes.

'You can leave them on if you want.'

He looked up at once and then exchanged his shoes for slippers.

'He's only just got up,' she said. 'He didn't get home very early.'

Araki slipped off his jacket, taking a ballpen from the inside pocket. 'I know.'

She led him into a Western-style, carpeted room with high ceiling and net curtains on the windows. She wore a sky-blue happi coat, checked with pale, darkish squares, and wrapped tightly around her thin frame. It was held together by a black sash, tied over the hips in the traditional style, not much higher than the rim of the garment itself. Her face was round, well defined and carried no make-up. Her bright, long hair was cut simply and straight, in the manner of students everywhere. Chris appeared, a cup of coffee in his hand. His curly, blond hair was damp and his skin shone pink from a hot shower.

'Morning,' he said, studiously ignoring the girl. 'Coffee?'

Araki slumped on to the green sofa. 'It's lunchtime,' he quipped. 'Have you got anything more suitable?'

Chris looked at his bare wrist. 'Is it? God, what a night. Yea, sure,' he said, remembering the original question. 'Oh, this is a friend of mine, Ayako. Araki-san.'

The two Japanese exchanged perfunctory nods and polite mutterings of belated introduction.

'About third year university?' Araki asked politely.

'Still a sophomore,' the girl called Ayako answered with a smile. 'I'll be a junior next year. Tokyo Women's.'

'Fix him a mizuwari, Aya-chan please,' Chris requested in reasonable Japanese. 'Is that OK?'

'Sure, more whisky than water please,' Araki said, in Japanese.

262

'I knew you were living with someone,' Araki said glibly when Ayako had left the room. 'You didn't want to try the Turkish bath. Remember?'

'I remember,' Chris replied. He followed his girlfriend to the kitchen and came back with an ashtray, just in time to intercept Araki on his way to the balcony with the used part of his cigarette bending ominously.

'I might marry her,' he said.

Araki tapped the ash and went back to the sofa to find his notes. He sorted through the papers.

'I'm happy for you Chris,' he said, 'but if you love her take her to England.'

'Why? I could find something here. I'm sure Taneda's former newspaper would take me on.'

Araki rubbed his scalp. 'Chris,' he said, 'please don't be fooled by appearances. Don't copy foreign governments who are mesmerised by the reception they get from Japanese diplomats which they interpret as reciprocated expressions of sincere understanding. The parents of Ayako will forever hate you for taking away their daughter who they see as becoming the wife of a bureaucrat or a promising young lad from Matsuhashi or Fuji Bank or any of the élite corporations.'

'I think they can learn to accept me,' Chris said.

'I don't want to be cynical about it,' Araki said, lowering his voice, 'but you're a gaijin, and you always will be here, even if you stay for forty years. The more Japanese you speak, the more suspicious the locals become. You take a Japanese girl for your wife, thinking this will bring you closer to the people, and find you're both even more of outsiders. Have children, and they become the objects of derision and amusement at school and will have no possible chance to get a job here except as side-shows in the entertainment business, where they'll be known as halves.'

'You make it sound hopeless,' said Chris, his disillusionment evident.

Araki tried not to sound smug and didn't want Chris to

263

remind him he had failed to stay married to one of his own race in a country where divorce was still not as socially acceptable as in the West. Even worse, his former wife's parents could not possibly hold a foreigner in less esteem than they did their son-in-law.

'No it's not,' he said, throwing a well-meaning lifeline. 'Let her finish her studies and get a degree after you leave. A good cooling-off period. If you still feel the same about each other she can join you in London.'

Chris had composed a reasoned counter-argument but Ayako came back with Araki's drink. She sat dutifully next to her foreign boyfriend on the sofa, her legs folded beneath her. Chris put his arm protectively around her as if he expected another verbal assault on the problems of inter-racial liaisons. He opted to avoid it by moving straight to the topic they had met to discuss, but first he would implant a needle of his own.

'When we started working together on the Tanimoto story three months ago I asked you whether it was a journalist job or a pseudo-police investigation. I don't know what the exact boundaries of legal journalistic behaviour are but last night I think we came a little closer to crossing them. So where do we stand now?'

Araki sipped his drink. 'I suppose it was like a private eye's probe.'

'The editor still thinks it is,' Chris interrupted. 'In fact, he got very upset last week when he found out you were still stalking that man from Matsuhashi.'

'That man from Matsuhashi,' Araki sniffed, 'spends part of his day laundering money that has paid off stimulant drugs processed and sold by Yakuza under the general guidance of corporate extortionists who have branched out into more lucrative fields.'

'What are you going to do with all this?' Chris asked, placing a hand on the pile of notes. 'Kobayashi doesn't want any more Tanimoto stories or salaryman special surveys. You've withheld vital evidence from the police, conspired with suspects, almost died for your efforts, and worst of all put your job in jeopardy. What's it all for?'

What does Chris know, Araki thought, about the Japanese distaste for reality, cut open and laid bare? To pretend something doesn't exist was the essence of zen, and a feature of the Japanese mentality and something like a Christian's relationship with his conscience, except in the case of the Japanese there was no conflict or struggle with some inner confessor, sometimes torturer. We have the conscience of nothingness.

'Ten years ago,' Araki explained, 'I compiled evidence on the greatest case of sporting corruption since the war. You won't have heard about it. It was the fixing of baseball games by bribing players, mostly pitchers, to make dumb plays at crucial times. The yakuza paid them and bet heavily on the results. God, I spent months watching the statistics, following players around, bribing a few people myself.' He paused to drain his glass and held it towards Ayako.

'And what happened?' Chris asked.

'A week before my story was due to go to press,' Araki said, his voice controlled and low, 'the Lockheed scandal broke. It was similar to mine really. A painstakingly researched document showed exactly how a million dollars had been channelled through one of Matsuhashi's competitor companies to the prime minister.'

'Tanaka was convicted, wasn't he?' Chris commented.

'Yes he was, but clever lawyers, appeals, and a stroke followed by months in hospital meant he would never serve time in prison and he still pulls the strings in the Diet and controls the biggest political faction, which includes the current prime minister among its members.'

'Fascinating,' Chris said, in a voice which told the Japanese he was already fully conversant with the feudal elements in the political system. 'What happened to your dramatic disclosures?'

'They were published all right,' Araki said, with only slightly disguised disappointment. 'But the only thing the country wanted was Lockheed. It was like trying to arouse interest in anything other than Watergate in America ten years ago.'

'Was any action taken against the players you named?' Chris asked.

'One was banned from playing baseball for life. I felt a bit sorry for him afterwards. Some of the others were fined or suspended for the rest of the season. They only prosecuted a couple of the lower ranking yakuza, the designated scapegoats for the ones who actually compromised the baseball players by beating them at hana-fuda or mahjong and then forcing them to throw games. They must have earned billions from betting on the fiddled results.'

'I don't know much about baseball,' Chris said. 'I saw a few games in the summer. Is it that easy for a pitcher or any other player to cheat?'

'It's not easy,' Araki explained, 'unless you're in collusion with a few others. If you're the pitcher you need the catcher. The catcher calls for the right pitch. If the batter is good the catcher'll call for something low and inside or outside the swing range, depending on whether he's left- or right-handed. If you want to give up a game-losing blow you throw a fast ball down the middle to a good batter and he'll hit out of the ground. A fielder has to be a bit more subtle. He has to fumble a crucial ground ball and make it look like an error of judgement.'

Araki unpacked a thick wad of notes and assorted papers on to the table.

'This time,' Chris said, reaching across for a document he recognised, 'there's nothing in the way of your scoop. What do you expect from all this?'

Araki was suddenly on the defensive and cautious. The girl across the table, sipping fruit juice and looking distracted when Chris was speaking seemed to be trying to follow Araki's explanations in English and two or three times asked for a summary in Japanese. He could see why Chris was mesmerised by her. She had deep, almost black

266

eyes that shone from tear-shaped crevices when she was excited or involved in the conversation and possessed the attentiveness and consideration that Western men craved in women. There was nothing subservient in her behaviour; it was natural, honest and completely overwhelming for a young, unattached Briton. He thought about telephoning Yoko. He looked at his watch. She'd probably still be asleep.

'Sorry Chris,' he said sharply. 'I was just thinking.' He took a folder in his hands. 'On Monday, I'm sending this lot to Inspector Nishii. I'm demanding the police re-open the Tanimoto case and look at it as a deliberate murder to silence a man who was involved in the sale of drugs but who had decided to branch out on his own. The papers here will show that there was – *is* – I suppose – a conspiracy between an organised criminal group, a well-known sokaiya and, more significantly, a renowned multi-national company whose reputation around the world is of the highest. I've written up the whole tale as a feature-length story which will be published. What I want to do with you now is clear up some of the grey areas.'

Chris stood up, smoothing his trousers and moved across to the window. It had begun to drizzle after a carpet of low, heavy clouds had spread quickly from Tokyo Bay. The playground opposite was now empty, save for a figure, probably a man, on one of the benches with an umbrella whose inside ribs must have been resting on his head. Chris opened the window.

'The *Tokyo Weekly* won't publish your findings,' he said. 'They want short-lived yarns, high on conjecture and sensationalism. They don't want libel actions from the business world or bricks through the windows from the Yanagida-gumi.'

'I know that, Chris,' Araki said, watching Ayako rise and smooth out her wrap before collecting the empty glasses.

'Let's order some food in,' Chris said. 'We're obviously not going out for lunch.' And obviously Ayako's not going to cook, Araki thought.

267

'What's good around here?' he asked.

Ayako found a collection of menus. She looked at the restaurant names and summarised the choices. 'Sushi, tonkatsu. They also do katsudon and tendon,' she said, reading down the list.

'Katsudon sounds good,' Araki said, 'and some miso soup please.'

Ayako took Chris's order and went off to telephone. Araki explained how he had contacted some of the semi-intellectual monthly publications which were often used as forums for the presentation of controversial ideas or esoteric theses from the academic or literary world.

'Writers often publish short stories or even complete novels in them before they're printed for the masses,' Araki continued. 'It used to be the normal way for a writer to introduce his work in the West as well.'

Chris was not convinced. 'How do they protect themselves against libel action?'

'We use the same method as Ninomiya used to protect the identity of Tanimoto and now someone whose name begins with a D. I've used the time-proven deception. Initial M for the trading company, N for Ninomiya, Y for the Yanagida syndicate and so on.'

From the other side of the room Ayako shouted, 'Do you both want pickles?'

It was six o'clock when Araki put his pencil down for the last time. Ayako had tired of her maid's role, even for the Englishman, and especially for the Japanese with the unkempt appearance and arrogance of manner even more objectionable than the average Japanese male. The bottle of Cutty Sark was almost empty on the table, though she had cleared each bottle of Kirin beer as it was consumed by her lover. There were pools of water on the glass table-top from the ice Araki had fumbled during the afternoon.

He had used Chris to bounce off arguments, theories and downright shots in the dark, knowing that the Western mind was more likely to apply a logical deductive approach and not just hiss and lick the hand that fed it. Sometimes Chris had been a bit too argumentative but they were both agreed that Tanimoto was not killed in a drunken brawl but was deliberately murdered and disposed of in a thorough and credible way, probably by the same people who had wrecked Araki's apartment, beaten him up and left him for dead. People who had somehow known about the journalist's enquiries from a very early stage.

'Who singled you out for special attention?' Chris had asked when the lacquered bowls and the wooden chopsticks, stained with soya sauce and adorned with grains of rice, had been removed by Ayako.

Araki dabbed his lips with his wrist.

'My first contact with any of the three protagonist groupings was at the Camelia, the coffee shop whose book of matches his killers overlooked when they cleaned his body of evidence. And the list, of course. Maki had been sitting there too but she got a telephone call and dashed off before I could make her an offer for her story.'

'So it could have been her?' Chris said. His voice suggested that Maki was the culprit.

'I didn't think she looked at me for more than an instant,' Araki said, checking a sequence in his notes. 'But she could easily have overheard me talking to the waitress. I mentioned the magazine because there was one on the rack of the café. And of course I gave the girl my card. If Maki's sharp, which I know she is, she could have picked up all the information she needed.'

Chris raised a hand and said, 'She might not have noticed anything if she was in mourning. You know, and very upset. Was she crying?'

'I didn't see her face clearly,' Araki confessed. 'Mostly a view from the back. She had long, straight black hair and a light, sleeveless black dress. You could almost see through it when she dashed out of the place.'

'She must have loved him a lot,' Chris concluded.

'Why do you say that?' Araki said, surprised. He looked up from his notes.

269

Chris stood up and walked to the window. It was still drizzling but the sky was lighter and people were walking without stooping.

'You said she seemed distressed, and she was wearing black. She must have been in the middle of her mourning period.'

Araki jumped to his feet, causing Chris to recoil, spilling a dribble of beer.

'I assumed in my article she was,' he said. He joined Chris at the window. 'Do you know what colour people wear when they're in mourning?'

Chris looked baffled. 'Obviously not black.'

'You can take your choice,' the excited Japanese was saying. 'Traditionally, white was the colour for funerals and black for weddings and other happy events.'

Chris looked puzzled. 'Nowadays, the Buddhist tradition is interpreted ambiguously,' his colleague said. 'You go to a funeral in Japan and you'll see that the bunting and the garlands around the mourning areas are in black and white stripes.'

'So you're saying that Maki was possibly not in mourning for her dead lover.'

'She didn't have to be,' Araki said. 'For all we know she was the happiest person in Tokyo.'

'They must have identified you by the time you went to that place in Ikebukuro,' Chris said. Perhaps, Araki thought, noting his friend's reticence in actually naming the type of establishment, Chris had not told his girlfriend about their visit to the massage parlour and she did not look the type who would believe he had not enjoyed its pleasures.

Chris was saying, 'They reacted quickly when they knew you were trapped inside, as if they were expecting you.'

Araki nodded in agreement. 'Either the man on the desk or the girl' – he looked at his notes for the name – 'Shima. A signal or call from one of them could have summoned Ezaki and the thin one. Don't forget they were literally round the corner in that Nozaki Transport office.'

270

'What was the Bali then?' asked Chris.

'A front,' Araki said confidently. 'A place where lower forms of street life as well as well-dressed clientele can move in and out without attracting much attention. They might even be managed by the Yanagida syndicate through some nominee or covert member. They could simply have been customers for the pills and powders.'

'Didn't you tell the police about the Bali?'

Araki peered into the greyness through the broad, French windows, frosted by broken rivulets of rain.

'No,' he said casually, 'but it's all in my notes. I told the policeman when I was in hospital about the Nozaki office. Of course, when they raided it there was no one there and there were no traces of stimulants or any papers which might give the police some clue. The rent had been paid in advance in cash.'

'It must've been Maki,' Chris concluded after Ayako had left to do some shopping. 'She might not have put the mark on you at the Camelia, but she could have been in the Bali working on another happy client in the next room. Your girl gave her the name-card you conveniently left. All she had to do was make a quick call to her heavy friends around the back and your flat is in ruins.' Chris rubbed more salt into the wound. 'They probably hoped to find you in it too and you would have been in hospital sooner than you really were.'

Araki shook his head. 'I gave her my card at the end of the session. According to you, Ezaki and his friend were already on their way to my apartment half an hour before I finished. They knew I was there because I had traced Maki.'

Chris paced the room, wishing he was shopping with Ayako instead of getting slowly drunk.

'Every time Maki Takegawa appears in your conspiracy you make an excuse for her behaviour or look for some reason not to implicate her. You have to admit she turns up everywhere.' Chris poured himself a refill of beer before attempting to substantiate his argument by

271

counting off the relevant incidents on his fingers.

'First,' he said, trying to sound coherent and convincing, 'the Camelia. Then in Bali. Only indirectly, but her presence was there somewhere, otherwise she wouldn't have got the message from your massage girl. She then appears on request to meet you, claiming other priorities and appointments, but having the time to steal the list you'd taken from her dead lover Tanimoto. But do you know,' he asked, in the slow, emphatic, broken way a person uses when he wants to convince, 'the moment when I realised she was involved more deeply than we had thought?'

Araki shook his head, fearing an awful fact he had missed.

'When you took Maki to that bar just off the Ginza. One of the places on the drug distribution list. Remember? And she was recognised.'

Araki could only nod.

'She wasn't recognised because she drinks in there with her friends. That guy knew her because she'd been there with Tanimoto or somebody selling the goods or finalising the business arrangements.' Chris's voice rose as he became more impassioned and convincing. 'Once you had taken such immense trouble to trace her, it was as if she then locked on to you to watch over you. She found out what you knew and then kept in touch to see how far you were prepared to go. Maki is the link.'

'Is she linked to Matsuhashi too?' Araki asked.

Chris stood up in exasperation. 'If she is, you'll soon find out. Our antics last night with Ninomiya are bound to get back to the sokaiya or the yakuza, or whoever's pulling his strings.'

Araki rushed to the telephone, suddenly frightened for his innocent neighbour. He waited for a minute, his heart pounding, his stomach churned with fear. There was no answer. He slammed the receiver down and hurried around gathering his pen and cigarettes.

'I'll come with you,' Chris said, joining the clean up.

'No, stay here,' the Japanese said. 'Keep the papers and

if you don't hear from me in the next two days, deliver them to Inspector Nishii. His number's in there somewhere. I'm going to contact Maki and confront her once and for all. I'll try and get her to go down to Shimoda where the drugs trail seems to start. If I can tie in that last link I've got the whole picture.'

When he reached the door he turned.

'Be careful yourself, Chris,' he warned. 'You've been seen with me a lot lately. Keep your head down please.'

# CHAPTER FIFTEEN

He was lightheaded when he reached the apartment after driving carefully from Chris's place in Mita, conscious that the alcohol was slowing his reaction times, but he urged each red light to change and cursed any driver slow to move. The walkway was dark and quiet, any sound carrying easily and swiftly to the furthest staircase. If she had slept all day, he calculated, she should be awake. He looked at his watch. Ten o'clock. He had told her to fasten the chain and so rapped lightly on the door. There was no sound from inside, and no reassuring light in the kitchen or bathroom which both fronted on to the passageway. He pressed the bell. It gave out a friendly intermittent chime and would not be hurried in its cadence even though Araki held his thumb against it. Had she got bored and gone out in spite of his warning? She surely wouldn't still be asleep. He moved the few yards to Yoko's door, which was at right-angles to the other flats and formed the end of the balcony. He pressed the bell optimistically, hoping that the muffled sound of music he could hear came from inside. He lifted the flap to the letter box and put his mouth to the gap.

'Yoko, Yoko!'

There was no response. He repeated the plea at his own door before twisting his key into the lock. Opening the door, he felt for the chain. It hung down from its hook.

'Don't go out, don't let anyone in,' he had implored, now angry at Yoko for disobeying him and at himself for leaving her alone.

There was no light in any of his rooms except for a pale

glow from the stereo stack which had been left on. He rushed to the telephone, deducing that she would leave only to see Kondo.

Mrs Kondo answered.

'Is Yoko Mochizuki with you please?' Araki asked urgently. 'This is Araki from the *Tokyo Weekly*.'

At the other end of the line, a middle-aged voice began polite phrases of recognition and greeting. Araki interrupted.

'Is she there please? It's very urgent.' The voice went silent and then chose the appropriate words, apologising for having to give him a negative answer. Araki hung up abruptly and looked round for signs of intruders or damage. There was nothing unusual, except for the stereo. He checked the cupboard. His futons had been aired and properly folded away. Nothing was out of place.

Then he sniffed the air. Although the terrace doors were barely ajar, the thin net drape billowed out along the gap and there was a scent of something fresh and flowery, but at the same time slightly unpleasant. He drew the windows together and inhaled through his nose. As the air stilled, the sweeter smell was replaced by an odour which was bitter and foul.

'The bathroom, the fucking bathroom!'

Had he crossed the kitchen more slowly when he came in he might have noticed it then, but his pace and the draught served to clear the air around him. He clawed at the bathroom door with both hands and slid it so violently on its track that it shook the upright with a loud reverberating crack and bounced back towards him. He screwed his face as the stench was released and fumbled for the light switch. Pieces of Yoko's clothing hung over the high-sided bathtub and others floated in a finger-depth of water on to which the tap dripped lazily above. At first his brain could not comprehend and it told him that the transparent pinkness must be from the blouse whose colour had washed out into the water. Then, shaking his head in disbelief, he saw the reddish-brown trails and smears on the sides of the bath and on the tiled floor and some was now on his trousers where he had leaned against the tub. He held his hand tightly across his mouth, not only against the smell but to hold back the emotion building in his stomach and chest and which threatened to overwhelm him at any moment. He had to stay calm, he told himself. He struggled to control the muscles in his abdomen.

Yoko's legs protruded from the alcove housing the toilet and they were streaked with blood and excrement, the result no doubt of fouling herself during whatever abomination she had been subjected to. Araki was no longer conscious of the smell or the mess, only the utter helplessness of the situation for which he held himself totally to blame and the oncoming of what must shock: a numbness in his limbs and a feeling that what was happening was really an illusion, a nightmare from which he would soon awake.

Yoko lay on her side, her head between the wall and the base of the lavatory where it had fallen, an arm stretching over the bowl as if she had tried to embrace it. She was naked except for the skirt that had bunched, clinging wet and filthy around her waist. Araki was determined to touch her, perhaps to probe for some sign of life or more probably to transmit some tactile message of apology and regret. But first he had to retch again and again into the toilet, cleansing himself of the bitterness released inside. Then he knelt down in the narrow space and with two hands turned Yoko's ashen face towards him, unable to wipe away the tears that flowed freely and stung his eyes. The patterned scarf Yoko had worn the night before had been used as a gag and was soaked a dark scarlet. She had choked in her own blood and vomit as they stabbed her in the chest. Matted hair stuck to her cheeks and partly hid the lifeless eyes that stared transfixed at the ceiling.

At some point the shock and numbness faded, to be followed by panicked indecision interspersed with moments of lucidity. Why did Yoko let them in? They couldn't have known she was alone in his flat. They were coming for him! He was the target: it was so obvious. What panicked them?

Did someone tell them about last night? They would have got a description of Yoko from Ninomiya who must have rushed to confess his indiscretion. And they had her telephone number. When they were sure who she was, they tortured her in the bath, hence the record player to drown the worst of the noise and the gag which they could tie and release at will. Where was Araki? they'd ask, inflicting more pain. She must have lied, Araki reasoned, as they weren't waiting for him, or perhaps they'd crossed paths. Him on the way home, them going to Chris's flat. Then they had left her for dead, or to die.

She had managed to climb out of the bath but had fallen backwards, smearing the tiles with blood as she fell against the wall. Araki noticed the stains as he made to leave. There was a certain symmetry in the thin streaks and an almost deliberate precision in the markings. He forced himself to look closer, to ignore the ruined body of his neighbour an arm's length away. There were two lines clearly joined in one movement. They could have made the roman letter L, or a V on its side. With pain in his heart and a new spasm of sickness growing inside, he lifted Yoko's hand. The forefingers of her right hand had clearly been bloodstained but they were now only lightly discoloured, as if she had cleaned them or rubbed them on the wall.

He stared at the wall again, macabrely fascinated by the possibility that she had the composure to attempt a final message in blood. The thought horrified him, but here were certainly two lines and, as he looked closer, a third. A barely perceptible thread had been drawn through the other two, the whole thing resembling the arabic number four.

The telephone broke his trance and he backed away, his eyes fixed on the meaningless message. It was one more puzzle, he told himself, like the rest of the things that were unclear from the start. Codes; a murder disguised as an accident; another killing which went out of its way to look like a murder; a woman who was beautiful, enigmatic, a liar and a thief; and some yakuza scum who

277

appeared and disappeared at will to destroy and spread death. And now he needed the police before Ezaki and his killers found him again.

The harassed journalist gripped the receiver, but before he could speak there was a click on the line. They're here, he screamed inside, dropping the telephone and racing to rummage through his trunk for the cash he kept in reserve. Then he stuffed a pair of jeans and T-shirt into a sports bag and hurried for the door with his jacket, stopping short to take a last glance at the place of Yoko's death.

He had never imagined he was capable of such hatred. He wanted to know who her murderers were and he wanted them arrested, or preferably dead. After the Tanimoto whitewash and the police failure to arrest anyone for his own beating, the law could not be trusted. At least, not until he could show them proof they could not ignore. He dashed along the dimly lit balcony, the distant whine of a police siren the only sound apart from his heavy footsteps, and jumped three steps a time down the staircase.

The call had frightened him and he realised from it that they were checking if he was back. They could even be waiting for him to panic, watching his car from the dark streets around the building. When he reached the ground floor, he backed around the wall of the empty lobby, out of scope of the light which would make a moving figure visible from the outside. Calm, calm yourself, he told himself.

Gingerly, one eye on the main entrance, he eased the rear lobby door open. The jolt almost tore his arm from its socket. The janitor, on his final round of inspection, tugged the door from the other side. He was almost as surprised as Araki. The old man started to bow obsequiously but when he saw the unusual stains on his tenant's hands and clothes his face tensed and he recoiled in a state of revulsion and fear and, without a word, let Araki pass through the rear entrance into a small courtyard.

The siren was getting closer as Araki scrambled over the

low wall at the back of the block in the narrow, unlit passage which would take him by way of a footpath to Yoyogi Station. The cover of night was his only help as he walk-ran to the station, pausing only to look back when the siren stopped, and to acknowledge that the police car was at his apartment. He let a new, perverted conspiracy throb through his already confused mind; one in which the murderer waited until the friend of their victim, their real target, found the body and then called the police. It would take more than the mind of the thug Ezaki or his Yanagida yakuza to plot that one.

Did the killers know he had escaped, he wondered, as he washed the blood off his hands in the station washroom and rubbed water in the darkest of the stains on his trousers? He thought of taking a taxi but an observant driver would remember him. Instead, he caught a late Chuo-line train, but even as it rolled west he found it hard to look inconspicuous among the sparse Sunday-night travellers, most of whom were couples absorbed in themselves or Sunday shop-workers too drunk or tired to notice him anyway. It was only a few stops to Okubo, where he rented a four-and-a-half-mat tatami room in a back alley of cheap hotels and snackbars.

The old woman, her hair bunched and stiffened like the wig of the entertainer she probably was once, wore a faded grey kimono which matched the bedraggled surroundings. She counted the money carefully, her sight, Araki noted gladly, of limited power, and her attention on nothing but the notes. He paid extra to use a shower, which smelled of urine and mould, and fell on to an old, but well-aired futon in the cell-like second-floor room. The stillness and privacy as he lay stirred another bout of sobbing until it in turn gave way to cold planning and, as sleep approached, to imagined revenge and finally, a night of light sleep broken by fierce dreams of death and mayhem.

It was a cloudless, chilly day and Araki shivered as he left the rooming house with only a light baseball jacket over his

279

clean trousers and shirt. He dropped the bag with the bloodstained clothes among a pile of boxes and plastic sacks of rubbish awaiting the Monday collection. Waiting on the platform, he skimmed through the main morning newspapers but the murder of his friend was not reported in the early editions. A light, sparse growth of beard and a golfing cap he bought at Shinjuku Station would make recognition by the unconcerned passerby improbable. He found a bank of telephones which gave him a good all-round view and a degree of privacy as each red box was separated from the next by a plexi-glass partition. He stacked some ten-yen coins and opened his pocket diary.

'Could I speak to Ninomiya-san of the Domestic Finance Department, please?'

There was the usual childish voice requesting him to wait and then a click. No more subterfuge, he told himself, scanning the late commuters passing through the West Exit, looking for the eyes that met his own or a gesture of recognition or warning between two of them. He would tell Ninomiya he knew the salaryman had woken up alone in the love hotel and reported the events to whoever controlled him and had given them Yoko's telephone number. Did Ninomiya know, Araki was poised to ask, that his friends had traced the number to Araki's apartment house, paid a visit there and found Yoko in Araki's flat and proceeded to butcher her? Did he know that? All within twenty hours of Ninomiya's frustrated romp.

'Moshi, moshi,' he called into the mouthpiece.

There was another half minute of silence and then a male voice said, 'Who do you want, please?'

'Ninomiya-san. Domestic Finance. Is he there please?'

The voice sounded almost apologetic. 'Ninomiya has been transferred to the Kansai,' it said. 'Would you like to speak to his successor? Or his superior?'

'Who is his superior?' Araki asked.

'Ikeuchi-san. Should I connect you?'

Araki hung up. Ikeuchi, Ikeuchi. Araki programmed the name into his memory bank. He dialled another number.

'Inspector Nishii is on an assignment. He will be away from the office until Friday,' the efficient voice said on the next call.

The crowds had thinned, the salarymen and women safely in their offices. Araki looked for faces that wavered and pretended to be interested in newspapers on the bookstalls which spilled across the walkway, or in the ties on the rack in the corner shop.

'Christ, where are you?' Chris asked when Araki got through to the magazine. 'What happened? The police are here now. They've just interviewed me. Kobayashi's hopping around like one of those live prawns on a hotplate.'

'You've heard then?' the Japanese said.

'It was on the news. Ayako nearly fell out of bed. Poor Yoko, but nobody here thinks you did it. I told the police you were with me until eight or nine. Anyway—'

Araki broke in. 'Wait, wait,' he said. 'Can you talk?'

'Yes, I'm at your desk. No one's near. Go ahead.'

Araki fed another ten yen into the slot. 'Why should anyone think I killed Yoko? We were close friends. Everybody knows that.'

Chris said, 'Someone claiming to be a neighbour rang the police to say he could hear you and Yoko arguing and threatening each other.'

'That's a lie,' Araki hissed, his anger barely controlled. He turned away from a schoolgirl who had taken the booth next to his. 'The killers waited until I was in the flat. Then they called the police. They tried to set me up.'

'The witness doesn't help your case,' Chris offered apologetically.

'What witness?' Araki asked startled.

'You were seen running out the back covered in blood.'

'That was the senile old janitor, and I wasn't covered in blood.'

'Anyway,' Chris said, 'why aren't you with the police? You're not helping your case.'

Araki cupped the mouthpiece. 'I have to know for sure, as I told you yesterday, whether Maki Takegawa is anything

281

more than the girl innocently involved with the victim. If she isn't, she'll lead me to the killers of her boyfriend and Yoko and help me turn them in to the police – or lead me into a trap.'

'Don't be stupid,' Chris said through gritted teeth. 'They'll kill you, and Maki too . . . Come and talk to the police. They'll believe you.'

'At the moment, they seem to think I killed Yoko,' Araki said, his anger rising. 'Do you have my papers with you?' he asked, his eyes riveted on two policeman chatting to the ticket collector at the wicket.

'No, they're in my flat.'

'When you have the chance, go and get them and deliver them to Nishii,' Araki ordered.

Chris asked, 'Where will you be?'

'I'd incriminate you if I told you,' Araki said and hung up.

The palms of his hands were wet and his shirt stuck to his back. One more call he thought, relieved to see the policemen move away.

She was at home and awake and picked up the telephone promptly, as if she was expecting a call. Or perhaps Araki was on edge. Her voice was, as usual, reassured and free of feminine self-effacement.

'Moshi, moshi,' she said firmly.

'It's Araki here. *Tokyo Weekly*,' Araki said formally and unnecessarily. 'Am I disturbing you?'

'Araki-san! Where are you? They're looking for you everywhere. They say you killed your neighbour.'

For someone claiming to be no more than a casual screw, she was a brilliant actress. From the smooth, confident telephone manner her voice had changed to one of surprise and genuine concern.

'I need your help,' the journalist said, inwardly invoking a variety of deities.

'That's very difficult,' Maki said, preceded by a sharp sucking noise but without proffering a firm negative. 'You really should talk to the police. The longer you hide, the more guilty you'll appear.'

That was obvious. Chris had said the same thing minutes earlier. Surprising how close East and West were sometimes.

'In order to clear myself, I have to check one more detail. It could clear you too.'

Maki reacted scornfully.

'The police haven't spoken to me since Tanimoto-san's death. I'm under no suspicion for anything.'

'But I'm fighting for my life. Literally,' Araki said quietly but firmly. 'Unless I'm persuaded otherwise, I'll have to implicate you, Tanimoto and his employer Teruaki Ogawa, and Yanagida yakuza and certain top officials in Matsuhashi Corporation in a massive stimulant drug racket.'

The silence unnerved him. Was it the mention of the Yanagida syndicate or the trading company?

'Are you still there?'

'Yes.'

'There's one point to clarify. You mentioned a visit you made with Tanimoto to Shimoda where you collected some bags of powder. I want you to take me to Shimoda and show me the place where you picked up the goods. If you do this, I promise your name will not be mentioned in any information I give to the police.'

'Ah, blackmail,' she said. 'You've learned a lot.'

'It's called survival,' Araki hissed, trying not to raise his voice. 'I want you to help save me, clear my name.' After a pause he said, 'It may save you too.'

'What do you want me to do?' Maki asked.

'Meet me in Shimoda, in the station concourse, around five this afternoon. We'll take separate trains.'

'It would make more sense if we drove,' Maki suggested. 'They'll be looking for you at the stations.'

He couldn't argue with the logic. A murder in Tokyo was rare. One or two a month for a city of twelve million people made them the focus of public and media attention. And now he was that focus. All murders were investigated with utmost thoroughness. That's why Tanimoto's killers had gone to such unusual and complicated lengths to feign an accidental killing, he had concluded.

283

'What do you suggest?' Araki asked.

'I'll meet you somewhere on the way. Odawara, Ito, anywhere you suggest. We can't take your car, obviously.'

Araki tried to assess the problem. The threats were all around. The police, the yakuza and possibly the woman who now waited for his reply, the one person he wanted to absolve of any crime other than innocent infatuation with one of the players in the big conspiracy. If she helped him to finger the culprits at the source, he would protect her in a way he had not been able to do for his poor neighbour. He owed Yoko that much. Maki was worth protecting.

'Let's meet in the plaza in front of Atami Station. Say, around three?'

'Atami. Fine,' the woman's voice was saying. 'Look for a white Honda and please be careful, ne?'

'Sure. See you there.'

He took local trains, changing in Yokohama and Odawara, instead of risking the faster service and giving a sharp-eyed citizen an hour to make up his mind whether the nervous, unshaven man across from him was really the murder suspect whose photograph stared up from the newspaper in his lap.

As the train began its descent into Atami, the journalist made for the door. Steam from the hot-spring hotels crammed around the harbour and on the slopes around it spiralled below him and quivered briefly before the cool air vaporised it. He promised himself a weekend in the sulphur-rich waters of the resort when this was over, with walks along the dark beaches and a climb among the mikan groves above the town and a mind free from the fear of violence and thoughts of drugs and Matsuhashi. Before the train levelled and slowed he had a passing view of the weather-beaten hotel where he had stayed with Yoko when they had been neighbours less than a year. It jutted precariously from the hillside, defying the gradient with the rest of them.

The white Honda stood outside a shop crammed with cheap colourful souvenirs, mostly good-luck charms, key-rings and the local seafood produce in jars and packets. The

Tokyo weekend tourists had gone, leaving the town to busloads of pensioners and farmers from the surrounding prefectures.

Araki looked for exceptions among the stooped women in their kimonos or drab grey and brown clothes and the ruddy farmers in their suits. A heavy-set man in garish golfing trousers browsed at a magazine stand and a younger man loitered at a crossing repeatedly ignoring the green signal. Taxis moved around Maki's hatchback, their drivers throwing a disapproving look as they crawled in line to the station rank.

'Sorry to keep you waiting,' Araki said when she leaned over to open the door for him.

She smiled and said, 'I've only just arrived, I stopped for lunch outside Odawara. Have you eaten?'

It hadn't occurred to him and he realised he was hungry.

'I didn't think you had,' she smiled and reached to the back seat for a box and a can. 'There's some onigiri and a beer.'

'You know the road well,' Araki commented as the woman anticipated the curves and sharp bends in the road climbing out of Atami. He flicked some sticky grains of rice from his trousers. A boat scuttled among the seaweed beds to their left, cutting shell-edge trails through the calm, deep-green sea. The sheer hillsides to the right had been cut away to let the road and single-track railway through and where the danger of slippage was greatest the exposed face had been reinforced with steel and concrete, giving it a rough, grey lumpy appearance, like a badly built wall.

'We came this way a lot. It was safer than the train,' Maki said, guiding the car round another tight corner which left Araki with a straight view down to the waves breaking over rocks fifty metres below.

She was wearing the same loose, mauve, long-sleeved sweater she had carried across her shoulders the last time they had met. But now her denim jeans were greyer and had sharp creases. Her long fingers were tipped in coral red and rested easily against the wheel. The breeze forced through the gap at the top of the window on Maki's side, blew her hair across her shoulders towards Araki and stirred a familiar scent of lilies.

How could she be a drug pedlar and accessory to murder, he asked himself, his eyes straying to admire her profile and the way she brushed at an offending strand of hair.

'When we first met, you said you travelled from Shimoda to Atami by train. You didn't say you made regular trips to Shimoda to pick up the drugs.'

Maki shrugged. 'I don't recall you asking, but yes, the Shimoda trip was not infrequent and yes, Tanimoto was diverting some of the shipments for his own profit. All he had to do was visit the packaging house in Shimoda and claim to be there on behalf of his boss and they gave him a package.'

'But it didn't take them long to find out he was cheating, did it?' Araki said, toying with a cigarette.

'He was stupid,' Maki replied flatly. 'I tried to warn him.'

Araki turned his head abruptly towards her. 'Warn him from what?'

She changed down behind a petrol tanker struggling up an incline.

'From the people who wanted to protect the business,' she answered.

'But he didn't listen, did he? And so they killed him.' Araki looked at her. 'Who did it? Was it the big one, Ezaki?'

Maki crashed the gear into second and took the cumbersome tanker on the next bend, causing Araki to lean back and press an imaginary brake.

When the car was cruising comfortably, Maki said, 'They killed him in Shimoda. I'll show you the spot. One of the gang held him down and Ezaki hit him with a bat. He was rushed to Tokyo and the accident scene was quickly arranged at Kawazu's house in Koto Ward.'

'Why did they take him to the Tama River?'

'Because it was on the way back to Shimoda,' she said, as if the answer was obvious. 'There was a shipment to be processed and they had to get back to the base.'

286

'They could have just dumped Tanimoto off a cliff. Nobody would have cared.'

'You know the reason for that,' Maki said emphatically. 'You said in your second article that you suspected a cover-up. The police would have investigated a murder until they found the motive and the culprit. An accidental killing could be cleared up in hours.'

Maki took her eyes off the road and pierced him with a flashing glance. It was over too quickly for Araki to tell whether there was any compassion or revulsion in those smooth features.

'But you'll have to wait to find out, won't you?'

He changed the theme and asked, 'Did you know Tanimoto's chief, Teruaki Ogawa?'

Maki pondered her reply. 'I knew who he was because Tanimoto-san was the link between Ogawas people and the Yanagida-gumi who ran things from Shimoda.'

'So what was your role?' Araki probed. 'What were you doing at the Bali? You're not a cheap massage girl.'

They were approaching Ito, another sprawling resort and fishing port. The road was congested where the Hakone skyline disgorged the tourist traffic which had chosen the longer, scenic route across the highlands, hoping for a glimpse of Mount Fuji between the periods of dense low cloud and mist.

Finally, Maki said, 'The Bali was one of the syndicate's bases in Tokyo. They also had a short-term office in the building behind, but your little adventure spoiled that. I kept a contact point there myself, no more than that.' She risked a quick glance across at him. 'You took your investigation seriously,' she said, smiling wryly.

'So you arranged for my flat to be wrecked,' Araki said without malice.

'It was only a warning. You were in no danger yourself.' Her voice rose. 'I did my best to distract you after that but you insisted on pursuing your silly vendetta.'

'So you work for the yakuza? The Yanagida-gumi.'

'At least that's something you're not sure of,' she said

teasingly. 'But you're wrong. I don't belong to the syndicate or to Tanimoto-san's sokaiya. I was just a link.'

Araki persisted, each time more insistent. 'And your affair with Tanimoto. Was that just to keep informed of what he was doing?'

'Yes,' she said, candidly. 'Let's have coffee.'

Araki looked at his watch, but before he could protest she had pulled on to the forecourt of a garish chalet-styled restaurant, the back of which afforded a view over the ocean. The place was empty save for a family of four eating ice-cream.

'You can see Oshima Island,' Maki said, pointing out to sea, but Araki was not enthusiastic and she returned to the topic.

'I liked him a lot and we had fun.' Her fingers played sadly with the coffee cup. 'But he came to see the possibilities for a bigger share for himself. He had access to the material and he had the contacts for the sales. Well, at least he had part of the information he'd need to find the outlets.'

She was referring to the list, Araki assumed, while Maki spoke in a monotone, slightly apologetic way. 'And, of course, he handled the cash.'

'He was getting greedy,' Araki offered.

Maki nodded.

'The list Tanimoto had, the one you took from me, only gave the address and the amount to be collected. Somebody must have had a list with the names of the people to contact.'

Maki nodded again. 'There were always two lists, a simple piece of security. One would be meaningless without the other. It wasn't Tanimoto's function to hold either of them. He was the man who carried the cash collected when deliveries were made and took it to the next stage. I suppose he found the list in Ogawa's office.'

'Did you expose him?' Araki asked bluntly.

Maki looked out to sea: she didn't have to answer.

'Who are *you* loyal to?' he said.

Now she looked towards him and leaned on the table,

288

supporting her chin with a fist. The gesture asked him to continue.

'I think you're too intelligent to work for Ogawa and his blackmailers. You're obviously far beyond Tanimoto's league.' Araki pondered and then nodded. 'Yes,' he said, in a low, suspicious voice. 'I'm sure you used Tanimoto to keep in touch with what Ogawa was doing. And I'm sure you don't belong to the yakuza Yanagida and I suppose you hung around the Bali and the Nozaki office just to pick up information and keep in touch.' Araki's voice began to betray his bitterness. 'So it must be the money side, where the brains are. It has to be Matsuhashi.'

He looked for a change in the pale, fine features of her face, some passing flush of inadvertent admission. 'Tanimoto met regularly with a junior manager from Matsuhashi's finance department, a man so forgettable, so conspicuously the average salaryman that unlike your friends at the sokaiya and the tattooed freaks from the syndicate he attracted absolutely no attention at all as he laundered your dirty money through the small banks. He was the face of respectable, corporate Japan and he was used by someone in Matsuhashi because he could move money without bother.'

'Did he tell you this?' Maki asked calmly.

'Who? The Matsuhashi man. Ninomiya?'

'Yes.'

'Of course not,' he said, letting her recognition of the salaryman lie among the mounting evidence he was stacking against her. 'He never knew where the money was coming from or where it went after he put it in the bank. If he did know, he played the loyal employee to perfection. I tried to call him this morning, to tell him what had happened to my friend whom he'd been with the night before, but he's already been put out rapidly of circulation. He'll spend a few years in some branch office in the countryside. Whoever the top man is in Matsuhashi, he's high enough up to move staff around with no advance notice.' And then he said, 'Do you know who he is?'

Araki had played his final tile, his hand was exposed, and

289

he waited for his opponent's move. Would she now give up the game, play for safety and receive his forgiveness in return for a promise to confess all to the police, or would she risk him pricking among the last few hidden clues and thereby condemn herself as a cold-blooded accessory to drug peddling and two murders?

The family made to leave, the young children boisterous and impatient as the mother assembled their bags. Maki looked on concerned.

'We should follow them. If we're left completely alone, the staff will have time to study you,' Maki said, easing her chair backwards. She paid while Araki moved out of sight of the cashier and the loitering waiter.

'I have to go to the toilet,' she said, holding out the keys. 'I'll see you in the car.'

He watched the door swing shut behind her and had to side-step against it to let a quartet of wind-tanned golfers pass through the inner passage into the café.

He stared at the door. It wasn't the distinguishing caricature of a woman which froze him rigid, leaving his limbs cold and immobile. It was the letter. The Japanese word for woman had been written in a box, the size of a small hand, so that country visitors would not be left confused by the gender of the picture. He twisted his head sideways, running his fingers over the kanji, tracing what could be a roman letter V on its side with the shape of a bending cross drawn through it. Three simple cuts from the print setter's knife, three motions of pen in hand to produce the easiest of Chinese characters, one of the first learned by children struggling for literacy in a language where thousands of constructions had to be memorised.

'It can't be. It can't be,' he said aloud, his mind racing back to the terror of the previous night and the dried, brown smears on the bathroom wall. Mentally, he erased the horizontal line in front of him and transported it to the streaks on the tiles. Without this last stroke the shape would be little more than the arabic letter four. With it, the unmistakable character for woman screamed at him in Yoko's blood.

They drove in silence.

' "Don't let any man in unless it's someone you know from the magazine," ' he had said.

He stared blankly ahead at the broken centre lines, tears welling in the corners of his eyes. An attractive, polite woman had rung the bell and the trusting almost relieved Yoko found someone with a name Araki had often mentioned in passing. When she released the chain, the killer or killers pounced from the darkness and forced their way in. Yoko had trusted another woman. He squeezed the bridge of his nose and then the rims of his eyes, hoping the driver would not look across to see the dampness on his fingertips or witness his agony. And lying close to death in appalling pain, Yoko found the strength to write in her own blood most of the character for woman, a word needing only three flourishes of the finger but for which she could only manage two before passing out.

Could this woman have caused such hideous suffering, deliberately and in frustration at not finding him there instead, or as well, and was she now driving him into the arms of the killers, in a last effort to remove the irritant once and for all?

Deep in his own thoughts, he had been staring at the wing mirror on the side without particular interest until a car with a broad silvery grille which reflected bursts of light centred itself about a kilometer behind. He turned round, wondering how long it had been there. What with the dips and bends in the last fifty kilometres, it could have followed them from Atami.

He was surprised at his own nonchalance, caused, he realised, by an inability to be shocked or frightened any more and by thrill of discovery at last of the truths he had suspected. He now wanted only to confront and expose the last principal agent and this desire seemed to minimise the concern he felt for his own safety.

Araki breathed deeply before lighting a calming cigarette and returning to the conversation Maki had broken at the restaurant.

'It can only be someone high up in Matsuhashi,' he heard himself saying as he looked out on the hillsides packed tightly with cedar, birch and pine, and crowned in flaming reds and purples by the last rays of a tired sun setting on the other side of the peninsula. 'Who is it?'

Maki's grip on the wheel tightened. 'You wouldn't know,' she answered.

'Try me. In the last six weeks I've memorised the names of every general manager in the company and all the directors. The board members have their photographs in the brochure which gives the annual accounts. They gave me one at the shareholders' general meeting in June, the time I first came across Tanimoto. Is it Kanematsu?' he probed. 'He's the one in charge of overseas projects and he's spent a decade on the Asian continent. He'd know the safe routes and which shipments to hide the processed powder in.'

For the first time, Maki misjudged a rising bend and the tyres screeched in protest when she pressed hard and late on the brake.

'It can't be Ebihara. He's never left Tokyo, knows nothing about finance and he's only there out of seniority. No. There must be a line,' he went on, 'from Ninomiya through to the top.' He ventured a glance out of the car's rear window. 'It is not conceivable he could meet unauthorised people without his immediate manager Ikeuchi knowing what he was doing. Above them there's Hatano, the general manager of the department and he's also a director on the board. Is it him? Is Hatano the Matsuhashi link?'

Maki was driving faster, and her chest heaved heavily as she fought to contain the tension. Araki was close to the ultimate truth and his skin prickled with excitement.

'I suppose it could be Denda, the international finance director, and I thought at one time it might be the President himself, Ryoji Moriguchi, but it's obvious he lives and breathes Matsuhashi. He's honest, and so is his probable successor, the banker Watanabe, who'd have too much to lose by cheating. The one I don't know about is Kosaburo Iwamura. I remember him from the shareholders' meeting

292

in June. The other directors sat like statues as Tanimoto and the other sokaiya put down any dissent and pushed the motions through but Iwamura was wriggling about as if he was in pain. He was in finance in his early career but mostly it has been general affairs and personnel, a job which would let him know which staff would co-operate and which were vulnerable.'

He paused to let the names settle in her consciousness and then went through the rest of the illustrious board roll. She still said nothing, and this tried his patience. A wave of anger engulfed him, fuelled by a recurring vision of Yoko's body and a rising need to smash the porcelain façade.

With clenched teeth Araki said, 'I want to know who it is. I have to know.'

'I can't talk like this,' she said calmly, looking, Araki was convinced, longer than necessary at the mirror. She braked at the top of a rise.

They were ten kilometres from Shimoda when she drove off the road on to a gravel lay-by carved into the bush-topped cliff which overlooked the Shirahama beach. The souvenir shops and food stalls along the front were closed down for the winter and the broad, brown wedge of sand, with its tide-line of plastic rubbish, flotsam and stranded marine life, was deserted save for some distant surfers who, lying near the shore on their coloured boards in black wet-suits, looked like basking seals. She led him down a twisting overgrown path towards a cove of black pebbles surrounded by hardy trees whose roots pushed through the smooth rock face below them.

So this is where they're going to do it, Araki thought, holding back as his companion dropped deftly on to the loose stones. She stood looking out to sea, her legs apart, hands on hips and her head tilted upwards in submission to the clean breeze with its hidden scent of brine and forest. He looked around in the undergrowth for a weapon, something to hurt her with, something to inflict pain, even if only a fraction of the suffering she had caused Yoko. The bits of wood he found were rotten. He looked around and pulled at a length of solid branch until it snapped and then broke it again under his foot to make a club.

Maki turned when she heard the crack. Araki stared in the fading light, disbelieving. He saw that her eyes were swollen as tears welled and fell across her cheeks and nose. Dropping to her knees, she clutched the inside of her thighs and rocked to and fro, her sobbing growing louder as her distress mounted. Araki was confused. He stood petrified by the uncharacteristic behaviour of the woman, his stick half raised. He looked at the piece of branch as if it were a snake and threw it away, but then he remembered the bathroom of his apartment and the blood on the wall. He rushed to the kneeling woman and lifted her roughly by the sweater, shaking her wildly.

'I know you killed Yoko,' he screamed. 'And now, and now . . .'

It was like shaking a puppet. She offered no opposition to his rough handling, her arms bouncing loosely at her side, making Araki feel foolish.

'And now I can't kill you. I can't even hurt you like you hurt her.'

In frustration, he pushed her unresisting body backwards and she fell on to the thin stretch of sand where the shingle ended. A shallow wave broke behind her, the foam hissing across her body.

'Why, why did you kill her?' he said in desperation, standing over her.

Maki held up a hand defensively and shaking her head and trying to articulate between convulsions of sobbing she said, 'I thought they wanted to make you a final offer to stop meddling. I didn't know they were going to kill you.' She wiped an arm across her nose but the fabric was soaked and gritty.

'They knew you'd only speak to me so I went to your apartment with Yanagida's son. Yana—'

'I know who Yanagida is,' Araki broke in.

Maki looked down and sniffed. 'He's not a violent man.' She was stopped by another fit of sobbing.

Mention of the yakuza reminded Araki of the car behind them and revived memories of his last encounter with them. His fear returned and he looked anxiously back towards the beach before kneeling beside the hapless woman, now stripped of the self-confident spirit she had shown him so far.

'But you killed her,' he said, gripping her shoulders.

She shook her head. 'When Yoko recognised my name she let me in.' She paused for breath continuing in a broken staccato voice. 'Then Ezaki and the other one came from no-where and pushed me out of the way to get in. Yanagida sent me home in a taxi. I made some calls. I tried to save her.'

'But you've brought me into this trap,' Araki pronounced, waving dismissively at the patch of territory around him.

The words reminded her of her mission for she snapped alert. The sea was silent and the breeze momentarily calm. They both heard the noise. The metallic click of a door, and then another, high above them where Maki had parked. They stood up together and the hands she had used to restrain him now clutched at the collar of his jacket.

'Let's go,' she said urgently. Araki was speechless. He looked at the woman and then at the spot the killers would come from after following the path downwards.

'Baka! Fool,' she barked. 'Let's move,' and she pulled him off balance.

A headland capped with sharp teeth like a dinosaur's back, jutted from the bluff into the sea and separated their cove from the long Shirahama beach. It was too steep and rough to climb. On the other side of their prison was a lower bridge of rock but it led only to a deep inlet of the sea. There was no escape that way.

'Let's try and get round this way to the beach,' Araki said seizing her hand and leading her towards the headland.

Holding hands they waded into the dark, unfriendly surf, shuddering from the sudden shock of the cold when the sea reached their knees. Araki palmed the rock for support with his free hand and flinched as the shells and fossils encrusted on it cut into his flesh. When they were waist deep, a wave broke over the spine of rock, throwing a fine, salty spray into their faces. Maki lost her footing to the undertow and almost dragged Araki with her as she fought for balance. Her clothes were heavy when he lifted her from the waist. She hung to his neck, almost stifling him. The spine of the rock had fallen away and was slipping below the surface. Araki glanced back at the cove. It was empty and in shadow. He hoisted Maki over the rock and then mounted it himself as if it was a horse and let the swell of the Pacific carry him across.

'Keep your head down,' he ordered as they inched their way back, along the ridge which had before imprisoned them but was now rising to protect them. The promontory of rock now concealed them completely from the cove and its bed spread painfully under their feet.

They were a few metres from the shore when Maki, her shoes lost when they had entered the water, cried with pain, her legs buckling under her. Again, Araki picked her up forcibly and lifted her on to the shore, where they tumbled exhausted on to the rough sand.

Her bare feet had been lacerated by the sharp, hidden rocks and stones but Araki urged her on and half-dragged, half-carried her up the beach towards the sea-wall and the road beyond. The last crest of light was shrinking on the trees on the hills above the town.

'We have to move,' Araki said, surprised at his own physical strength, as they rested on a flight of cracked concrete steps which led to the road. Maki shivered violently against him.

'Where do we go now?' she stammered. 'I can't stop shaking.'

'They'll be in the cove,' Araki said, his own shivering eased by the body hugging him for warmth. 'They'll look for us around the paths for a while. Let's see if your car's being watched.'

They ran-walked up the hill they had passed so easily by car only thirty minutes earlier, Maki keeping to the softer grass verge for comfort, both flinching at the headlights from the oncoming traffic. Her car was not guarded, though a four-door silver Nissan saloon was parked among the trees opposite.

'The keys,' Araki whispered, as they cowered in the cover of the bushes.

They exchanged a look which said they both saw the likelihood that the contents of Maki's pockets, however tight the jeans were cut, had spilled out as she thrashed about in the sea. But they were there, kept in place by a soaked handerchief. They moved towards her car but retreated when Araki claimed he could hear voices. Imagination, he thought, a trick, of the wind in the bracken and branches.

'Now!'

They spurted towards the car, their hearts pounding. The doors were open, as she had left them.

'Lock your side. Lock it now,' he ordered, revving the engine which started at the first turn. They were on their way. The view in the mirrow showed a clear road behind as they rounded the bend on the road which led to Shimoda.

The Irozaki road was, as usual, congested where it narrowed after passing Shimoda Station, but Araki bore left after the tunnel into the side-streets in search of a discreet inn he knew would welcome their custom on a Monday night in November. The name and grade were of no interest and he chose the Daien-so not for its view over the harbour but for the covered parking-lot out of view of the street. They smacked the dried sand off their clothes and Maki changed her wet sweater for another from the weekend case in the boot. With relief, she replaced her missing shoes with a casual pair. Combing out their matted hair gave them just the right dishevelled look of two people who had spent the day by the sea in a stiff breeze.

From the shoes lined neatly in the genkan there were only two other guests, a couple rather, and the inn was too small to have more than a desk in a reception area decorated with scenic pictures of the area and a railway timetable. The obsequious hostess accepted them with unnecessary

297

gratitude. Araki looked for signs of recognition, for eyes which would look blank while the woman sought to remember where she had seen the face. But there was no second embarrassed gaze of rising suspicion and she gave them large rooms, with their own family ofuro bath, in a corner of the house which gave them a view, if they were interested, over the tiled roofs of the tightly stacked houses to the harbour, where the lights of the fishing-boats flickered.

They could have been mistaken for a married couple rather than illicit lovers. They had little to say. Maki ran the bath and emptied her toilet bag methodically. Araki sneezed and risked exposure by going to the front to buy cigarettes. When he returned, a maid was laying out a meal on the low table over a sunken well which contained a welcome electric heater. She arranged individual portions of tuna, yellowtail, squid sashimi and small dishes of tempura shrimps, aubergines, carrots and shiso nettles. There was a bowl of jellyfish appetiser and a shallow dish of root vegetable pickles. Later, when her guests had bathed, she would return to serve hot miso soup with clams and steamed sticky rice and pots of heated sake.

'Dozo,' Maki said demurely, motioning towards the bath which she had topped up until it brimmed over on to the tiles. She wore a calf-length grey and blue checked yukata, the same kind that awaited Araki after his soak. She had washed and combed her hair forward so that it fell in shiny, black trails around her cheekbones, almost down to the obi of her kimono. A strand or two strayed across her mouth. She leaned against the bathroom door, slightly off-balance to take the weight off her torn feet.

'Let me see them,' Araki said, remembering the scream and the way she had gripped him.

'It's nothing, I've got some cream I can use. What about you? Let me see your hands.' He held out a palm and she probed and stroked around the grazes which the sea-water had cleaned and bleached. 'I'll rub some cream in when you've taken your bath.' She had rubbed some colour into

298

her lips and added a touch of blue to her eyelids. And, of course, the fresh scent of lilies.

Araki felt filthy, cold and frighteningly tired. It had been only twenty-four hours since he had found Yoko and the woman who had unwittingly, so he wanted to believe, caused her death was now his ally. He washed the dirt away, luxuriating in the ladles of hot water he poured over his head. He almost fell asleep in the bath as the water lapped his neck and shoulders soothing his mental and physical pain. He was dreaming, but a sharp crack of the door sliding against the rut shook him alert. He wafted the steam and looked helplessly for a weapon.

'What's the matter?' Maki asked and then realised. 'I'm sorry if I frightened you. Dozo.' She held out a glass of cold beer which he took gratefully. 'We're safe here,' she said with confidence.

They ate greedily and filled each other's tiny cups with warming sake and ordered more. When they had eaten, leaving the room filled with the smell of mandarin orange, the maid cleared the table before laying out the futons in the next room. She drew the shoji together, leaving the room lit by the two electric lanterns in the corners. She brought two more pots of sake before dismissing herself.

They stayed seated on their cushions at the table, relaxed and enjoying the warmth from below them. Their feet touched, tingling from the bars of the heater.

'At last I'm warm,' the beautiful woman said finally, smiling for the first time today.

Araki ventured a smile in return, offering the flask to a willing cup, but the smile died quickly when he saw her face harden.

'It's Iwamura-san,' she said, staring down into her sake.

'The old man? The one that's ill?'

She nodded. 'He's not very old. It's just that he's very ill.'

'He's also a murderer.'

'He's also my father.'

The subdued light from the lamps threw their weak beams

299

across the table leaving the tears that welled and flowed down the dark side of her face unseen by Araki.

The journalist stubbed his cigarette in the ashtray and flattened the tiny mounds of ash already there. He could only repeat her last word.

'Father?' And then, 'But he's in his sixties.'

Maki drank the mellow sake in one swallow and held out the cup for more. She seemed to use the pause to find a place to start. Then she began.

'He used to go to the Kyoto geisha houses, or what was left of them, when he worked in Osaka. His wife and children had stayed in Tokyo of course. The children's education.' Araki nodded understandingly. 'He met a woman, not really a geisha, but she sang and entertained at one of those places. He was already over forty at the time, but I'm the result of their affection. I was brought up by my mother's family and I only saw him occasionally. He was more like a grandfather.' She spoke without a trace of emotion after the tears had dried.

'There was no question of him recognising me as his daughter. He was rising quickly in Matsuhashi; it wouldn't have looked good for him to have been seen to have spent so much time frivolously at a time when the company was fighting for survival. But he was kind and determined to be responsible for me and my mother and her relatives. He gave us a regular income and paid all my school and college tuition.'

That accounted for the educated manner, Araki noted.

'After I graduated, I drifted into entertainment with the talent shows and modelling. I suppose because I had no real parents to pressure me into office life and an inevitable marriage to someone like, well, like someone from Matsuhashi. But we spoke often on the phone and met from time to time. His family knew nothing of me.' She spoke without sadness and the depth of her affection for her father flowed with every word.

'Two years ago, my father asked me to work for him and it was then he told me about the financial problems he was

300

facing in supporting two families, college tuition for his own children and his own huge medical bills. He wasn't complaining; there was no self-pity or even the hint of a suggestion that he wanted to stop helping my mother's relatives in Osaka.'

'He's very ill, isn't he?' Araki asked sympathetically.

Maki sipped on the tea, which was still warm. 'He may live for another year, perhaps eighteen months. His heart is very weak and he has a tumour on the spine.'

'How did he get involved in drugs?'

He regretted the bluntness, and saw a slight reaction in her expression.

'My father has been the Head of the General Affairs department for many years and, as you probably know, this is the heart of any company. It was my father who had to deal directly with the sokaiya every year and make sure they received their money and performed for Matsuhashi at the shareholders' meetings.'

'And then he met the chief, Ogawa,' Araki suggested.

'Yes. Before that it was very discreet, but then Ogawa made a big move. He had raked up a lot on the company's problems in Mexico and knew about the real-estate transactions that went awfully wrong, but in the usual way, Matsuhashi co-operated with the sokaiya.' Maki shook her head and seemed to be on the verge of tears again. 'Then Ogawa found out my father's own financial problems and suggested they work together somehow in a complicated three-way deal with the Yanagida syndicate.'

Araki tried to sound helpful in finding an excuse for the old man's approaching criminal life. 'Could Ogawa have found out about you? Could he have blackmailed your father into helping him?'

'I've often thought that's what happened,' Maki said, 'but Father's never told me. Anyway, Ogawa's offer was too tempting for him. He knew he didn't have much longer to live and here was a way of providing for me and my family.'

'But there are others in Matsuhashi,' Araki said gently.

Maki nodded. 'My father confided in some of the people whose careers he had nurtured.'

He didn't have to prompt her.

'Hatano. He's also a director. Younger and more junior than my father, of course, and very aggressive. He brought Ikeuchi, who runs the yen finance section. He was also enthusiastic. They both saw it as a profitable side-line, for themselves and for Matsuhashi. There are two others, juniors, who run errands, but they know nothing.'

'Ninomiya was one of them?' Araki asked, already knowing the answer.

'Ignore Ninomiya,' Maki said with sudden viciousness. 'He was suspicious but knew nothing.'

She must have remembered, Araki thought, that it was his suspicion after Tanimoto's death that took him to the sokaiya's office and a fateful observation by the reporter. And Araki knew that somehow Ninomiya's date with Yoko was discovered and he, the impassioned salaryman, had had a hand in pointing to his neighbour's flat. Probably someone in the Flora overheard them make the arrangements to meet afterwards.

'Did your father decide that I had to die?'

Maki forced a cyncial smile. 'I never believed they wanted to kill you. But I was so naive.'

'Was it because I'd seen the list with the drug customers on it?'

Maki shrugged. 'Ezaki turned your flat over as a warning. I told him, or I told his superiors that someone, you of course, was asking the waitress at the Camelia questions about me and Tanimoto. When Ezaki went straight round and leaned on her, she was very forthcoming.' An understanding smile creased the journalist's face.

'What would have happened to me if I'd been in my apartment?' he asked.

'If you were prepared to interrogate the waitress like you did, they knew you would look for the Bali. Although you didn't ask for me when you came, the man at the desk was

302

on the look-out for strangers. I'd given him a rough description of you.'

Araki drew breath and let it out slowly and noisily. 'What was their intention when they caught me in the shrine,' he asked ruefully.

Maki toyed with the tea-cup. 'Another warning,' she said, 'more persuasive they hoped. The last message.'

'But they came close to killing me,' Araki complained.

'That was Ezaki. He gets too excited.'

'And what about tonight? Was I supposed to die, or was it to be another warning?'

She paused to pull the robe together at her throat. 'Three weeks ago, my father met secretly with Yanagida and Ogawa and I served them at the table. They'd only seen each other face to face three times before, that's how secret the operation was kept, but they talked as intimately as if they were brothers. Father was certain you knew what was going on and when I was outside the room I heard them discussing your fate.'

She stared across the table at the man who should be dead.

'And I was assigned to ensnare you,' she said, a wry smile on her lips. 'When the meeting broke up Ogawa gave me an envelope with 200,000 yen in it. I knew then that he was the driving force.'

And then she said casually: 'Are the police as convinced of a conspiracy as you are?'

'They soon will be. I've left the facts for them to read in case something happened to me in Shimoda.' Maki's face was as lifeless as a mask. 'And if you help me to tie up the loose pieces the police will have to start making arrests. By the way, is that why you are talking to me now?'

'What do you mean?' Maki looked startled.

'I'm hardly pressuring you and you're talking to me like an old schoolfriend.'

'You asked for my help, didn't you? In return you gave me my freedom.'

Araki lit his cigarette, an interval he needed to contemplate

303

a more terrifying possibility. He tried not to show his fear.

'Have you changed your mind about leading me into a trap, or is there another one coming?' Araki asked cruelly.

Maki seemed to be looking over his shoulder, her wide dark eyes forming her mind's private images against the sliding door. After a while she said softly: 'You might – when you've found where the yakuza prepare their drugs, and knowing the truth about Ogawa, the man who manipulated my father and the yakuza boss, Yanagida-san, two sick old men – you might just feel some compassion for my father and give him enough time to die free.'

Araki looked for a tear but the eyes before him stayed dry.

They yawned together, and smiled at the coincidence.

'We should rest,' she said softly, looking for a watch that wasn't there.

'Tomorrow could be tiring.'

Araki's own limbs were stiff from the exertion but he helped her to her feet, which were swollen and painful.

'I'll sleep next door,' he said, when he had led her to the mattresses laid side-by-side by the adjoining room and started to fold one of them.

'Don't bother. It might be safer if we're together.'

Araki slumped to his knees and slid beneath the cover, watching Maki as she limped back from the bathroom, a brush buried deep in the hair she held taut with her free hand. Their bodies moulded into the thick, comfortable futons and they were quickly asleep.

It sounded like the crunch of a car tyre on the gravel of the courtyard, but it was enough to wake Araki, leaving him alert, expecting the next disturbance. Maki was lying on her side, her hair spilled over the cover which was drawn up to her shoulders.

Araki rolled off the futon and eased the opaque window-screen aside. There was already enough light to distinguish the shapes of two cars through the plastic sun-cover in the yard. Then there was a movement below and he flinched instinctively and moved sideways, his nose against the rim of the window. Again the crunch on gravel, out of sight at the rear door. Araki looked out and saw a youth mounting a bicycle at the gate, its two paniers heavy with the morning newspapers.

Araki sighed. He looked at Maki, admiring her calm as he watched her eyes pop open like those of a mechanical doll suddenly shaken.

'Is something wrong?' she murmured.

Araki shook his head and closed the window-screen. He said, 'We ought to go. It'll soon be light.'

'Let's wait until there are more people about. It's safer for you.'

Araki rubbed his scalp, unable or unwilling to argue with the logic.

'Come and lie down!' she said.

Maki shifted slightly while lifting the corner of her own cover. Araki knelt down between the two futons, as if undecided which to choose, but in the end the decision was made for him. Maki leaned across and with two hands unravelled the knot of Araki's waistband. He looked at his own bedding and then at the crumpled green gown on the tatami near Maki before slipping into the futon beside her, where the warmth of her body released the hidden scent of lilies, exploding buds of fragrance in her hair that threatened to drown him.

# CHAPTER THIRTEEN

He woke to Maki's voice and gentle shaking. She had been kneeling in front of the television turning through the channels until a photograph of the man she was with appeared on the screen.

'. . . journalist with the *Tokyo Weekly*,' a man's voice was droning when Araki joined her. 'Police efforts last night moved to the Izu Peninsula, Shizuoka Prefecture, after reports from the public that the man they believe can help them solve the brutal murder of a cabaret hostess Yoko Mochizuki had been seen in the area. He is believed to be accompanied by a female.'

In the next room, the maid was laying out the breakfast.

Araki turned the television off, as if the woman hearing the muffled sounds would immediately associate her guests with the fugitives. If the others are watching the news downstairs they certainly would, Araki thought, if they had any sense.

'Don't rush,' he cautioned, as Maki drank greedily from the soup bowl.

'They know where we are,' she said, abandoning the seaweed soup for the broiled fish.

Araki went out of the way to be recognised when he paid the bill, asking about local places of interest and the outlook for the weather. However much the woman bowed, refusing to meet his eyes, her trade required powers of observation and she wouldn't have missed the shabby jeans with greyish water-marks or the creased water-stained shirt and jacket. What would she do, Araki mused, wanting only enough time to pinpoint the drug traders' warehouse.

He offered to drive and was uneasy when Maki insisted and steered the white Honda into the street. The morning was clear and sunny, with a light, cool breeze. The car worked its way up the narrow streets and around the hill which had been tunnelled to give access to a small bay on which a floating aquarium had been built. The road dropped sharply to another wider bay with distant clear promontries bending inwards like claws. Above them the Tokyu Hotel was visible on the crest of a bush-and-plant covered cliff. An old tunnel, dripping water through mossy cracks, led to a sandy beach behind which was a hillside of cedar, pine and poplars and thick undergrowth. Among the trees, and largely hidded by the lush woodland, land had been cleared for dozens of wooden chalets connected to the bay by a central curling road and its web of tarmac feeder drives.

'They're mostly company chalets,' Maki said, pointing to a signboard listing the owners or tenants of the properties. Managed by resident caretakers, the houses were used all year round by company employees on cheap overnight trips or longer stays. Nothing unusual, Araki thought, in a constant procession of different, anonymous people and visits by vans bringing food, drink, lots of drink, and everything else needed to support the holiday makers. Substitute packets of stimulant drug powder and encapsuling equipment and you have the perfect, secure base.

'Does Matsuhashi have a chalet here?' Araki asked hopefully.

'Not directly,' Maki replied, steering round and returning to the tunnel where she brought the car to stop beneath the overhang of the cliff.

'A small subsidiary of theirs rents a place and two more close by are leased to paper companies controlled by Ogawa's sokaiya.'

Araki went to lock the car and stopped abruptly to drag Maki into a recess of crumbled boulders. A vehicle had entered the tunnel, its headlights blazing and moving at high speed. Araki picked up a rock as the menace seemed to be slowing when the Honda was in sight. They both smiled with relief as a utility van with a young, grinning driver went by. The fugitives made their way back to the access road to the chalets.

'Who staffs the buildings?' Araki wanted to know, his mind sharp and determined.

Maki sucked in air. 'They're almost all from the Yanagida syndicate. The material is landed at various places on Izu and the Shizuoka coastline and brought here for processing and despatch to the markets in Tokyo, Yokohama and their suburbs where they have customer circuits like the one you broke into.'

They had climbed past several sliproads when Maki drew her companion by the arm off the road on to a footpath trodden through the undergrowth where they were quickly swallowed by the trees. The road had been steep and they were both breathing heavily.

Maki continued: 'Ogawa arranges for money from Matsuhashi to finance the operation and then collects the income which he feeds back to be washed through Matsuhashi-connected bank accounts. Ogawa also personally ensured that customer lists were in two parts so that loss of half would not constitute a great threat. At least, not until you cracked the Ikebukuro base,' she added a touch sardonically.

'We should also be able to get above the main house through here,' she said, as the branches and bushes threatened to engulf them. They left the path and side-stepped on the grassy slope where Maki beckoned him to stoop low until they reached an outcrop of rock which overlooked a clearing in front of a Swiss-style two-storey chalet with a swooping roof that hung low over a verandah.

'Have you seen enough?' Maki whispered, settling back behind the rock. 'I'm frightened.'

'If this is where you say the Shimoda drugs base is, the answer's yes.' His voice was dispassionate and cold. 'My story's finished. All I want now is for them to pay for Yoko.'

308

'Do I pay for Yoko too?'

Araki turned to her. The question had stayed fixed in the moist, sad eyes, her fear showing the way she bit lightly on her lower lip. Araki scratched his scalp and sat beside her against the stone. Everybody's going to pay, Araki had vowed when he saw Yoko dead in her own blood, but hours earlier, as he lay unspeaking in the arms of a woman he now wanted to believe was innocent, he struggled for a response to the question he knew would come.

'Your father's a conspirator to murder and other crimes,' he said dryly. 'You knew Tanimoto had been murdered but you denied it all along.' He shook his head, a list of her sins arranging themselves in his mind, but before he could speak a man's excited voice broke the quiet.

'Move, move,' the voice was shouting from the clearing. 'It's too late. Leave everything.'

Araki fell to the ground and crawled forward to the edge of the ridge, joined quickly by Maki. More voices were raised, excited and panicky. Then a man ran from the house wearing only trousers and shoes and struggling on the move with a shirt. He was joined by two others carrying between them a large laundry bag half-filled with cartons the size of cigarette packets but when they heard the desperate order from inside and then picked up, as Araki did, a distant, shrill burst from a whistle, they dropped the basket, letting the packets spill down the steps and under the verandah. There were more shouts from the direction of the trees around the clearing and men came running down a path.

'From the other chalets,' Maki said, 'but what are they doing?'

'That was a police whistle,' Araki said, his voice full of excitement and relief. His arm shot forward, pointing towards one of the men.

'That's the one who held me down when Ezaki worked on me with the bat.'

A car engine started out of sight behind the house. Then Maki gripped the journalist's arm in instinctive reaction to

309

the appearance of two well-built men in suits and behind them the figure of Teruaki Ogawa himself.

He was no longer, it looked to Araki, the imperturbable ice-man he had met before. He was waving an arm, trying to bring some order to the rising panic around him. Araki's cheek was so close to Maki's he felt the warmth of her breath.

'Who are the other two?' he asked.

'The one in the light suit is Yanagida's son. He's the one who pushed me out of the way when Yoko answered the door. He let Ezaki in.'

Araki nodded ruefully.

'The other man's the old Yanagida's son-in-law. He's a lot brighter than the son.'

'Muscle and brains,' Araki suggested.

A low, stretched saloon car swerved uncertainly into the circular drive and Araki drew breath as Ezaki, the double killer, who probably regretted not having increased his tally by two at the beach, shifted awkwardly out of the car. He seemed smaller to Araki now, as he stood by the door, his shapeless bull-like neck twisting from side to side, looking for the unseen threat.

A new arrival ran to the group, emitting disjointed, staccato words from a high-pitched voice and warning that police with rifles were on the approach roads. Araki saw a hand-gun flash at young Yanagida's side while Ogawa paced around the car, talking to the implacable son, trying to control, to bring order to the general public. There were some whistles, this time louder and closer.

Ogawa suddenly pointed to the place where Araki and the girl were hiding. Had their over-confidence exposed them, Araki thought, a heavy pain raking his chest as he tried to roll out of view. They hadn't been seen but the men in the clearing were looking to the hillsides for their escape. At least, some of them were.

The gangster's son ordered four of his followers and his brother-in-law into the car giving one of them the gun before they drove off in a noisy, dusty screech. Ogawa waved the last clutch of men away, telling them to separate. He joined Ezaki, who clutched a wooden baseball bat, and the Yanagida son and these three ran towards the ledge where Araki and Maki lay exposed. Araki reacted first, pulling Maki to her feet and taking her into the dense ferns and bushes, slithering in the undergrowth, searching for cover in the crevices and among the trees. They dropped into a hollow surrounded by the thick, tentacle-like roots of an old cedar. They could hear Ogawa, urging the others forward, and then arguing whether escape was easier on the beach road or by staying on the higher mountain paths.

Maki was panting noisily. Araki could feel she was on the point of panic, knowing that the men so close to them now knew of her betrayal. She gripped Araki's arm until it scared him.

'The beach. Let's got for the beach,' a voice within earshot said. They were so close some pebbles and dirt the three fugitives disturbed fell into their hide-out. Maki wriggled, as if trying to free herself. Araki leaned across, urging her to stay calm, his body straddling hers.

The voices melted away and when Araki dared reluctantly to stand up, and peer through the overhanging grass above him he realised why. Five policemen, two of them wearing blue flak-jackets and carrying rifles with sights, were coming up the paths through the trees. Araki thought of calling out to them, warning them that their quarries were hidden somewhere close, waiting for them to pass, but if they were suspicious and inexperienced, never having been in this situation before, they'd hold the two of them until they could prove their identities, and Ogawa and the killers would slip away. Araki withdrew to the roots gain, drawing Maki with him.

The police officers passed by and when he looked out again, Araki saw that Ogawa and the other two were moving down the hillside again. They would not escape punishment,

311

he told himself as he dragged Maki with him, slithering together on the loose ground, stooping when he thought the figures ahead were too close.

'They'll come out at the beach,' Maki guessed. 'Behind the police, near my car.'

She sensed his worry. 'I've got the key.'

It was an easy trail to follow. Ezaki, heavy and clumsy, had fallen behind the other two and was too busy trying to keep his footing to look behind. Even had he looked, the trees were close together and their lower branches low and tangled, giving cover to the pursuers.

There was a muffled explosion in the distance, then another. Ezaki turned towards the noise, not towards Araki and his companion, who might have been caught between cover.

Out of sight, the car with the five gangsters had driven down the twisting access road towards a makeshift barrier of cones the police had built where it met the local road to the town centre. A man and his delivery van were being searched by a uniformed policeman while special squad members looked on wistfully. When they heard the tyres screaming on the tarmac above as the Yanagida-gumi car braked on a corner they waved the van through and drew their pistols. They were reinforced by colleagues who came running from a string of black-and-white cars when they realised the danger.

The saloon ploughed into the cones, spinning some of them into the air, and hit the rear of the slow-moving van, cracking the back open and spilling empty beer bottles like a crystal shower on to the road. A policeman fired at the tyres of the erratic car, whose driver was already struggling to control it. It turned awkwardly into the town road, a crushed cone trapped in the wheel arch, but – it may have been broken glass, the bullets or the driver's panic – the car ran out of control.

Two metal strips along the side of the road deflected the car's course initially but failed to stop it breaking through and rolling down a rough, weedy slope where it turned on its side on the bed of the stream which flowed into the bay a few hundred metres away. The engine was still engaged, and palls of steam and traces of smoke spilled from beneath the bonnet. A policeman sprawled on the bank, his pistol, held with two hands, pointed at the stranded car. One of his colleagues screamed for restraint as the passenger door opened and a figure struggled to gain enough leverage to push it open.

'Throw the guns out. Throw them out now!' a voice bellowed.

The arm went back inside and after what seemed like uncompromising minutes a limp wrist hung out of the wreck and dropped the only pistol they had into the stream.

On the other side of the hill, Ogawa and the Yanagida killers had reached the beach road, crawling into the course of a wispy, mountain stream until it disappeared into the drainage system which would lead into the sea. They hugged the hillside, the bullhorn exhortations of the police audible behind and above them, and made for the straight dark tunnel which cut through a stubborn outcrop of rock which expended itself as a rough promontory in the ocean.

Araki cursed the police for not spreading their cordon wider, for leaving the road and moving up the mountainside. The three criminals were making for the tunnel, at the other side of which they would no doubt split, one of them taking the path round to the aquarium, the others losing themselves in the streets and narrow lanes which spread out from the beach and led to the town. Only Ezaki paused at the white car parked by the cliff. His brain was slow and his instincts were on escape rather than revenge for the betrayal the owner of the Honda had perpetrated the day before, when she should have delivered the reporter who wouldn't quit into his hands which held a smooth, rounded baseball bat. He tapped the weapon against the car and soon lumbered after the other two, who had already reached the tunnel's mouth.

'Let's go back and get the police,' Maki urged, tugging at Araki's sleeve.

She couldn't get his attention.

'They're dangerous, I'll get the police,' she insisted.

'Do that, please,' Araki said, his face stained with dust and sweat. He left her standing and went to the Honda.

'You'll do this,' Maki said, tossing the tiny bunch of keys over to him.

He paused only for an instant, and quickly had the Honda pointed towards the tunnel, its engine gunned and throbbing, where the outlines of three figures bobbed in the arch of light from the other end. He drove towards the opening, his mind oblivious to the danger or the legal consequences of his impetuosity. His urge was uncontrollable.

Turning his headlights on to beam, he drove the snub-nosed car into the dark void and picked out the figures of Ogawa, Yanagida and Ezaki. They seemed surprised, looking round, shielding their eyes from the beam and then looking for shelter and escape as the car drove at them at high speed.

The Honda hit the tunnel wall first, then bounced into two of the men, one of whom, Ogawa, was flattened against the wall, his legs broken and ribs crushed. Like an insect trapped by the light, Yanagida ran before the car and was somehow lifted on to the bonnet, his arms swinging wildly, finally smashing into the windscreen with frightening force, fragmenting it into crystals. The car hit the tunnel again and careering across to the other side, threw the gangster to the ground, his neck broken in the whiplash, his face smashed to a bloody pulp against the wall.

Araki punched a hole in the windscreen caring not where his victims lay or what their condition was, and saw Ezaki, winded and slumped on one knee, close to the rim of light at the end of the tunnel. He was exhausted from the flight and raised a palm defensively, although he still held on to the bat he had used to batter Araki close to death.

The reporter gunned the battered Honda through the gears and aimed it at the fat, lumbering figure who had now raised the baseball bat in a final desperate attempt to survive.

The car hit Ezaki's thigh as the big man turned to escape, rolling him against the rocky rim of the tunnel. Araki's brakes screamed and he cursed at the miss. He crashed the gear into reverse and threw the car again at the limping figure of the yakuza who had murdered Tanimoto and Yoko and all but killed him twice. Ezaki had staggered to a crash barrier and was attempting to climb it when Araki drove blindly and deliberately at the man struggling by the railing. Araki heard a contact, a solid thud of pliant material sandwiched between metal. The yakuza buckled and a scream, which rivalled the engine's own whine, and the din of breaking glass reached Araki, whose body recoiled from the impact.

He tried, unsuccessfully, to control the car as the wheel spun out of his hands, cracking his knuckles. He couldn't hold it, and clutched his head in his hands protectively as the car found a weak point in the barrier and nose-dived on to the pebble beach a metre below. Araki smelt a metallic dust and tasted blood, but he could move his fingers and had sensations in his arms and legs, and then passed out.

When Chris Bingham was allowed to visit Araki in hospital, the reporter had already been interviewed by a succession of policemen. Alerted by the notes Chris had passed to his friend Inspector Nishii, the police had moved on Shimoda, spurred on by Araki's observations in the papers and by the sightings of Araki and the girl the previous day. The police had swarmed over Shimoda and when they found the white Honda, mentioned in reports, they concentrated on the hillside which held the holiday chalets. When the police moved around the area, armed and in force, they were noticed by look-outs who started to panic. A man was stopped who was obviously trying to run away and that was when the police decided to move in.

Their one mistake, and Nishii had apologised officially, was when the officer on the beach road by the tunnel decided to move up the hillside to trap the escapers and in doing so had let Ogawa and his friends slip by. Nishii had coughed in embarrassment, not wishing to scold his friend for the mayhem he had wreaked in the tunnel. They could only be thankful, all had agreed, that none of the fugitives had been killed, although Ezaki's back was broken and he would never walk again.

Kosaburo Iwamura died within a week of the announcement that several senior officers of Matsuhashi Corporation were being investigated for alleged conspiracy to murder, dealing in prohibited substances and illegal movement of money. His many infirmities finally overwhelmed him, the obituaries said generously, though Araki wondered whether he had killed himself. He did not tell the police about Iwamura though he supposed Hatano and the others would no doubt expose him at their trial. He hoped they wouldn't. The president of Matsuhashi resigned quickly, taking responsibility for the dreadful events. Thirty-two members of the Yanagida syndicate, including the patriarch himself, and two members of his close family, were arrested for murder, grievous bodily harm, drug trafficking, illegal disposal of a body and a handful of less serious offences. Ogawa and six of his sokaiya faced a battery of similar charges, of which resisting arrest was the lightest.

In June 1983, at the quiet shareholders' meeting, newly-elected President Watanabe, the former banker, announced sharply improving earnings and apologised for the unforgivable behaviour of his former employees.

Araki watched from the street as family and close friends said farewell at the house of Kosabura Iwamura, and he stood in the rain two weeks later outside the official company-sponsored memorial service in Aoyama. Maki Takegawa appeared at neither ceremony; and Araki never saw her again.

THE END

**BALEFIRE**
By Kenneth Goddard

Nothing is more frightening than a terrorist who is not afraid to die . . .

A small city on the southern California coast is the scene of a series of brutal, unexplained killings which have angered and frightened local citizens and stymied the police. Stunned and confused by what seemed to be senseless murders, the cops are almost helpless to defend the city, their families, or themselves against these meticulously planned 'random' attacks by an unseen predator. Until – with dawning realization that the havoc might be a cover-up to something even more shocking – a select team of investigators and crime lab specialists begin to fight back.

'Compulsive reading! Riveting descriptions of terrifying violence . . . sheer explosive energy'
*Eric Van Lustbader*, author of THE NINJA

'Comes at you like a firestorm . . . the action starts fast then accelerates straight through to the last page'
*John Saul*, author of SUFFER THE CHILDREN

'I was hooked . . . intriguing and gripping . . . and what a terrific ending!'
*Clive Cussler*, author of RAISE THE TITANIC!

0 552 12393 5

**ECHOES IN THE DARKNESS**
By Joseph Wambaugh

'A stark and engrossing tale of crime and punishment'
LOS ANGELES TIMES BOOK REVIEW

'Riveting'
COSMOPOLITAN

'Don't start it late at night'
GEORGE V. HIGGINS, CHICAGO TRIBUNE

'Highly atmospheric'
NEW YORK TIMES

'A bizarre, wonderfully sordid story'
USA TODAY

'The words leap off the page'
MORDECAI RICHLER

'A superior book . . . absolutely compelling'
CHICAGO SUN-TIMES

0 553 17555 6

**THE SICILIAN**
By Mario Puzo

Sixteen years ago THE GODFATHER opened a new chapter in publishing history, selling over twenty million copies world-wide and being adapted into two Oscar-winning films.

Now, with THE SICILIAN, Mario Puzo has surpassed himself. Drawing on the real-life adventure of the bandit Salvatore Guiliano, and his struggle to feed the poor in post-war Sicily in defiance of the corrupt government in Rome and the local Mafia, Puzo has forged out of history and myth a novel of explosive suspense, heroic action, and corrosive evil.

'Mr Puzo tells a good story and tells it well'
THE DAILY MAIL

'Compelling storytelling'
NEWSWEEK

'Plain and punchy'
THE FINANCIAL TIMES

'A fine, fast-paced thriller'
THE NEW YORK TIMES, BOOK REVIEW

'A cracking good read'
THE IRISH INDEPENDENT

'An entertaining read'
TIME OUT

'Superbly and vividly told'
BOOK BUYER'S CHOICE

'Even more alluring than the characters who made THE GODFATHER a modern day myth'
NEW YORK DAILY NEWS

'Breathlessly paced, an operatically grandiose tale of treachery and vengeance'
PEOPLE MAGAZINE

0 553 17204 2

# A SELECTED LIST OF FINE NOVELS AVAILABLE FROM BANTAM BOOKS

THE PRICES SHOWN BELOW WERE CORRECT AT THE TIME OF GOING TO PRESS. HOWEVER TRANSWORLD PUBLISHERS RESERVE THE RIGHT TO SHOW NEW RETAIL PRICES ON COVERS WHICH MAY DIFFER FROM THOSE PREVIOUSLY ADVERTISED IN THE TEXT OR ELSEWHERE.

| | | | | |
|---|---|---|---|---|
| ☐ | 17279 4 | **THE PRINCE OF TIDES** | *Pat Conroy* | £3.95 |
| ☐ | 17489 4 | **THE GREAT SANTINI** | *Pat Conroy* | £3.99 |
| ☐ | 17490 8 | **THE WATER IS WIDE** | *Pat Conroy* | £2.99 |
| ☐ | 17557 2 | **THE LORDS OF DISCIPLINE** | *Pat Conroy* | £3.95 |
| ☐ | 17240 9 | **THE ALCHEMIST** | *Kenneth Goddard* | £2.95 |
| ☐ | 17354 5 | **BALEFIRE** | *Kenneth Goddard* | £2.50 |
| ☐ | 17194 1 | **THE WALKING DRUM** | *Louis L'Amour* | £2.95 |
| ☐ | 17386 3 | **LAST OF THE BREED** | *Louis L'Amour* | £2.95 |
| ☐ | 17293 X | **THE EMBASSY HOUSE** | *Nicholas Profitt* | £3.99 |
| ☐ | 17204 2 | **THE SICILIAN** | *Mario Puzo* | £3.95 |
| ☐ | 17555 6 | **ECHOES IN THE DARKNESS** | *Joseph Wambaugh* | £3.50 |

*All Corgi/Bantam Books are available at your bookshop or newsagent, or can be ordered from the following address:*

Corgi/Bantam Books,
Cash Sales Department, P.O. Box 11, Falmouth, Cornwall TR10 9EN

Please send a cheque or postal order (no currency) and allow 60p for postage and packing for the first book plus 25p for the second book and 15p for each additional book ordered up to a maximum charge of £1.90 in UK.

B.F.P.O. customers please allow 60p for the first book, 25p for the second book plus 15p per copy for the next 7 books, thereafter 9p per book.

Overseas customers, including Eire, please allow £1.25 for postage and packing for the first book, 75p for the second book, and 28p for each subsequent title ordered.